Revelations

of

Chaos

Revelations of Chaos

BOOK I

RISE OF THE SHADOW SOUL

Author S.F. Fury

Concept Art and Cover Model Maggie Crump

Consultant Editor Kris Kendall

Consultant Cover Design by Gary Val Tenuta

Dark Fury Productions

MMXVII

Published in the United States of America by Dark Fury Productions, LLC.

Dark Fury Productions
An S.F. Fury Enterprise
PO Box 14662
Spokane, WA 99214

https://twitter.com/SfFury

Printed by CreateSpace

Publisher's Cataloging-in-Publication data

Names: Fury, S. F., author.
Title: Revelations of chaos , book 1 : rise of the shadow soul / S. F. Fury.
Series: Revelations of Chaos.
Description: "Concept Art and Cover Model Maggie Crump; Consultant Editor Kris Kendall, Consultant; Cover Design by Gary Val Tenuta" | Auburn, WA: Dark Fury Productions, 2017.
Identifiers: ISBN 978-0-9986482-0-0 (Hardcover) | 978-0-9986482-1-7 (pbk.) | 978-0-9986482-2-4 (ebook) | LCCN 2017937254
Subjects: LCSH Good and evil--Fiction. | Fantasy. | Fantasy fiction. | BISAC FICTION / Fantasy / Action & Adventure | FICTION / Fantasy / Dark Fantasy | FICTION / Fantasy / Dragons & Mythical Creatures | FICTION / Fantasy / Epic.
Classification: LCC PS3606.U799 R48 2017 | DDC 813.6--dc23

To the real Zaramagrii…
Thank you for being the warrioress, a beacon of both the light and the darkness.
There is no way that I would have ever wanted to begin this quest without you and your inspiration.
Never forget the dream, the vision, and the true path of life itself.
My essence will forever run with yours…

My appreciation and love go out to the real Grasfur, a true warg puppy by nature. Animal spirits are so loyal and pure, especially canines. That unique and one-of-a-kind bond that I have with him far surpasses all other things that provide me fulfillment. I am forever grateful for being blessed with his presence, and the responsibility of 'having his back.'

None of this would ever have come to fruition without the real Zaramagrii. My endless thanks and adoration go out to my best friend, partner, and inspiration. She personifies that which grew forth in my imagination…all because of her. Thank you Maggie, my mirror essence.

Contents

Preface..xi

Chapter 1: Herald of Shadows..............................1

Chapter 2: Seeds of Dissension...........................7

Chapter 3: Pretense for Death.............................33

Chapter 4: Lore of the Ancients.........................83

Chapter 5: Commencement..................................101

Chapter 6: Clan Tharasvrul.................................135

Chapter 7: A Destiny Begins...............................151

Chapter 8: Dawn of the Eternal Mother.............169

Chapter 9: Memories in Black.............................199

Chapter 10: Tidings from the Past......................243

Chapter 11: In the Company of Death................267

Chapter 12: Future of Change.............................281

Chapter 13: All Things Must Come to an End.....289

Chapter 14: Becoming One with Fate.................315

Chapter 15: A Mother Returns Home...................339

Chapter 16: Shadows Emerge..............................361

Chapter 17: The Birth of the Harbinger..............383

Chapter 18: Premonitions Prove Themselves......419

Chapter 19: Path of Vengeance...........................445

Chapter 20: The Reign of the Prophet................459

Chapter 21: Finding Shadows..............................477

Chapter 22: A Kingdom Prepares.......................497

Chapter 23: Besieged in Darkness......................523

Chapter 24: A Parting of Ways............................533

Chapter 25: A Peaceful Facade...........................569

Appendix 1: Kuhrzothian Lines...........................589

Appendix 2: Aylsh Lines......................................593

Appendix 3: The Known Black Clans..................595

Appendix 4: The Thaldeian Kalenda...................597

Preface

My life as a professional soldier really left no room for the intangible, the things that I have always deeply felt as true passions, besides my obvious sense of duty and self-sacrifice. There is another entire realm of thought that I could get into concerning what has been two careers now. But this is about what I did not seek out or listen to. All this time in my past two lives, as I like to refer to them…these other things always lingered but I failed to recognize them for what they really were. I will never think less of my past or have any regrets for not pursuing my true passion sooner. One's past is indeed a book in itself. And those chapters full of experiences clearly added even more to what I now know to be my reason and purpose—that is who I am. The old saying that one only knows another by what that person wants and chooses others to see stands tall. Our core down nature really does not change. Of course stressful situations bring out one's true nature no matter the case, for all to see. These things I have learned, as I have come to know myself. As it is who I really am when it boils down to it. I like to think that even though I am getting a late start at writing, my entire life up to this point has prepared and further refined what I now present in my material.

Fantasy has been my reality since I was a child, as with most of us. Always was I going in the direction of fantasy and mythical things for relaxation and entertainment. Whether books, movies, or games. I mean, who doesn't like Conan the Barbarian and Excalibur? Or adventurous reads like The Hobbit and Watership Down? Now we can call all of the above movies as well as books. When Conan first came out way back when, I went to see it with a friend. Needless to say, and with the help of my friend's brother (who happened to work at the theater), we snuck back in three more times that day because I could not get enough of it. These kinds of entertainment are mesmerizing and enveloping, at least to me. The notion that I could turn that deep inner passion into such a thing as a book—an adventure of epic proportions—never even dawned upon me. Not until the year 2014. The year that these writings began to take shape and transform into what they are now. What I thought at first came from out of the blue was really the passion that had always been imbedded within me just waiting to get set free. And set free it was, to soar ever higher.

The world of Zholryn came to me while traveling and going about my worldly endeavors. The idea of Zaramagrii and the Shadow Soul appeared to me in the middle of the night out on what I affectionately call the frontier. The shadowy warg known as Grasfur truly was inspired by and through my own canine companion—his character within the writing resembles the real 'little guy' in all his form. I am very much attuned to the animal spirits and feel closest to them of all things. And he is no exception. Ultimately, I have come to realize that we as folk have been put upon this world to be the shepherds and caretakers of nature, of all the wonderful creations. By this, I mean the entire spectrum of our responsibility to those gentle spirits. Those that we take as our companions as well as those of the wild that we *should* nurture invisibly.

At first my thoughts were to (stupidly) write for another fantasy world that I have come to know. These blinders were so narrow. Then at some point, and I don't really remember exactly when this occurred, a question began to ply itself within my mind as I worked on the material. Why should I devote myself (and all the wonderful characters that began to emerge) to someone else's enterprise and confines? I am so glad that I listened to that inner voice and then changed the whole concept. I changed it to one of my own. The unimaginative, initial idea evolved into its own entity and the world of Zholryn slowly came to life through my writings and material development.

Indeed, there are no bounds except for those which are self-imposed.

One sure thing that I believe and now know as truth. Man must come to grips with who and what he is, must except his place within the signature of time and space, and (most importantly) must comprehend that he is not the center of the universe and never will be. Once he breaks free of that self-serving mold of immediate gratification and ignorance, he truly will become that which he was meant to be and will propagate his very unique purpose in this life. Only the individual is able to do this for himself. Only an individual can raise himself up and out from his shell to be a better, more altruistic higher being. Of course, without the pretentious mentality of being higher and beyond reproach.

I do not intend to preach by any means, but I want to provide a look at the untainted canvas that sparked these tales of high adventure. And it was not only the creations that I devised—the visions that came to mind—but also the underlying principles and ways to life that I have come to believe in and know. And not only did that sprout this book that you hold, but all those that will follow, to include Arterium's story *Chronicles of Damnation* (currently a work in progress).

The warrior way…live it, breathe it, own it.

Here's to the legacy that I, Zaramagrii, and Grasfur leave behind. Forever emblazoned in script and set against the darkening backdrop of the stars and five moons of Zholryn.

Enjoy the legend, immerse yourself within it and leave behind your day-to-day shuffle for a breadth of time.

History is written in the blood of the innocent and the weak.
It is forged by those inspired through the call of battle and the unkempt glimmer of chaos.
The power of mere words can but sway people…the power of sword and bloodshed can sway kingdoms and dictate supremacy.

-King Arterium

The
Reaches
of
Thaldeia

Icefall
Gloomy Mountains
Isnuuthghor
Looming Forest
Oshghrul
Rock Rim
Western Spires
Forsaken Pass
Purple Peaks
Woe Wood
The Free Lands
Longshadows
Tamelyn Keep
Castle Redderfell
Tornspire
Orondyraq
Frostsea
Forbidden Salt Flats
Adan
Korsuchan Chain
Southern Kingdoms
Charathadour
Khurtrayza
Rhousthaq
Khordar-Kriznaat
Qarrawa
Phanduzar
Muhrowk
N
Seas of Anarchy
San Serboor

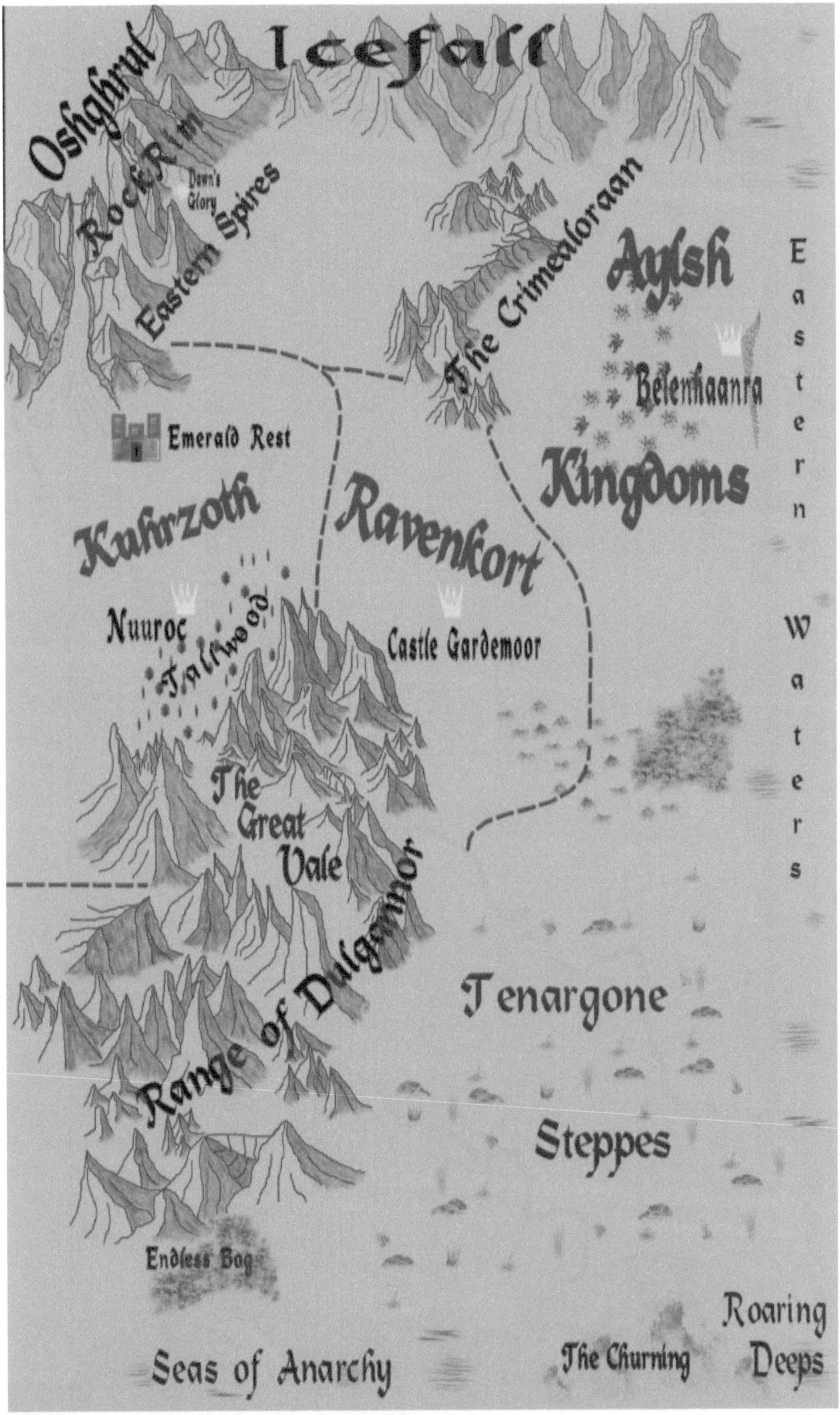
Icefall
Oshghrut
Rock Rim
Dawn's Glory
Eastern Spires
The Crimealoraan
Aylsh
Belenhaanra
Kingdoms
Eastern Waters
Emerald Rest
Kahrzoth
Ravenkort
Nuuroc
Tallwood
Castle Gardemoor
The Great Vale
Range of Dulgemmor
Tenargone
Steppes
Endless Bog
Seas of Anarchy
The Churning
Roaring Deeps

"*When the light fades and the shadows grow, look around you and be aware.*

For when the darkness encroaches and only the dull firelight glows, things of nightmares will crawl, slither, and roam.

While nightmares can be awoke from, the sinister blackness of the shadelands cannot.

Once the dark haze of the shadows corrupt the brilliance of the lighted world, then only existence filled with dark terrible things becomes our reality, whether asleep or awake.

And those things that haunt the inner reaches of one's mind now stalk the living world and all that is within it."

–King Arterium, circa the year 6 BA.

"Volkura Drakna throth kharnwul ut yulpaarah"

The legend of the Shadow Soul

The oldest of the sentient beings that have survived are those of the Black Clans. These dark things, called Aylsh Ismaru in their own tongue, are no doubt the first of Braxis' children, of his Thirteen Favored Ones. Aylsh means *those of the light*, whether applied to the one or the many. Aylsh Ismaru draws upon the distinct meaning *those of the dark light* which carries further significance for these beings. They are the oldest, as well as the longest, living ones.

The tale of Volkura Drakna, the Shadow Soul, was a fearsome legend amongst the Black Clans, well before the dawn of what is currently known to be existence. It was written in the ancient days that a creature of the dark, spectral world once roamed, tethered only to a tainted and insatiable need for destruction. A beast of the night so terrible, so powerful, so calloused to its own acts. A beast that reached out to the living in their dark times, when such beckoned to it for their own selfish needs. But the creature only left death and chaos where it went, no matter the plight. For this creature was born of both Light and Dark. It was forged through a being of exquisite birth and tempered by the malice's of the world, both those of substance and those otherworldly. And such a creature was completed through the oldest thaumaturgy of existence, merging with the Larunwyr, the Void. Once this happened, the former being that the creature had been was no longer recognizable by the terror that it had become.

And that former thing was lost forever. Never reclaimable, never remembered. Always seeking to quiet the overwhelming flood of pain, ever wanting to inflict that agony on those that were unfortunate enough to whisper its name and draw its attention.

Such a creature was thought to be a wicked gauntlet of perverted power if ever controlled, if ever wielded as a thing burdened to another. But the world had been given reprieve and no such shackle ever held it, at least in the legends of old. The creature disappeared and was lost. Never to be seen again. Those of the Black Clans passed down through their generations that the creature was taken back by Lord Braxis himself, its essence thrown to the deepest layer of the Chasm where it would endure its agony alone for all-time. And only a unique series of events could ever bring it back from that which was forsaken. Something that supposedly no living thing knew of.

–Ancient Black Clan lore from an
unknown time.

Chapter 1:

Herald of Shadows

Circa the year SA 1537

he night skies turned luminous within the rage and torment of the powerful storm as it engulfed the mountains and surrounding hills. Trees swayed wildly and cast shadows that appeared to be dancing within the incandescence of the lightning flashes above. In the storm's midst, black forms writhed like ghosts locked in mortal conflict upon a lowly, desolate hilltop. The destruction of flesh and steel was strewn all about the expanse.

A mighty warrior of the Black Clans stood tall, his muscular torso bare and marked by combat. His charcoal colored skin glistened with sweat. A long, silvery mane of hair blew in the wind as his crimson eyes reflected the storm's fury. Pointed ears flared back and appeared as horns in the darkness, but gave away his Black Clan ancestry. The Aylsh Ismaru, beings of ancient origins and long life, were both exceptional warriors and caretakers of the rigid perseverance of the Old Ways.

Before him stood several heavily muscled forms, bent forward and waiting to lunge with their dark iron blades and axes. Their bipedal frames nearly dwarfed his, mostly in bulk.

The Akhruuk were creatures of death and ruin. Very rarely did they pursue anything for more noble a cause or purpose. Such a being, simplistic in nature, schemed and devised within the satisfaction of the here and now. Their gray, mottled flesh paled under the flashes of lightning while their enormous heads bulged upon sinewy necks.

One of them raised its head in a deep howl of anticipation for the killing of their prey. The sunken eyes shone with a spark of cruelty and a devious gleam. Several of the beasts wore pieces of leather or iron armor on their bodies, although this varied from one to another. Few of them had any kind of shield.

With his legs spread in a firm fighter's stance, the warrior of the Aylsh Ismaru swung his blackened blade out in a violent arc. The sword's size nearly exceeded his own height. The act simultaneously cut two Akhruuk in half while ripping into a third. Dark, frothy blood gushed and spewed everywhere. But that last endeavor left him open to the thrusts of three other beasts. Each of their spears found its mark, penetrating through his back. The rusty tips ripped through him, protruding out of his chest and abdomen as he fell to his knees. Another Akhru finished the work with the swing of an archaic war axe.

The tiny, delicate form of another from the Black Clans ran wildly up toward the crest of the hill. The bloodied tatters of her leather tunic flapped in the wind as she moved, after seeing her driven kin fall. One of her hands clung to a long, blackened spear. Occasionally, the haft dragged along the ground, clanging over the rocks. What stood out most about the determined female of the Black Clans was her overly large belly as it bulged with the possibility of a new creation.

She ran on as her breath escaped out in adrenaline-fueled gasps. Suddenly, she bent forward and panted with a cry of pain as the beginning waves of the coming birth shot through her body, signaling that creation would not be stopped. Not even in the midst of battle.

Her long, black hair was woven with silver and tied back in a ponytail. It whipped towards the angry skies as her head canted down to look at the source of her agony—also her courage. Her offspring, although still nestled in her womb, kept her focused and resolute.

After so much of the day and night spent in pain, the contractions were gaining in their overpowering grasp of her. She doubled over with each of the spasms, forced to deal with the shooting pains. The time for the birth was approaching fast. She could feel it.

Not far behind her were more of her kind, with many scattered along different sides of the hill. The dark warriors of the Black Clans were fighting and dying. The black wave of monstrous and mighty Akhruuk that overtook them now intermingled with their dark silhouettes. Blades and axes clashed, throwing sparks of intense rage all around.

One exceptionally fit dark one took an ugly axe through his chest after thrusting a spear through another of the beasts. Both of the warriors were lifeless before even hitting the ground.

Not far away, another was locked in an exchange of blows with an Akhru of considerable size. The large-framed beast appeared as muscular as a bear standing tall on its hind legs. The Akhruuk were a savage kind. Their oversized heads with large, deep-set eyes under bushy eyebrows gave them a simplistic look, yet their strength and flexibility told a deadlier tale.

With each quickening pain of the labor that wracked the dark beauty's frame, purplish black-laced lightning crackled and flew through the charged heavens above. Finally, she had to stop just below the crest of the hill. She could still look out to where her kin were savagely fighting and dying around her. Quickly, she turned about to face what followed her. But her labor pains made her fall backwards while leaning heavily upon the spear haft. She gently slid down it to rest on the ground.

She sat on her buttocks slightly hunched forward. Her body was wracked by the immense agony of the painful bursts as the creation inside her fought for freedom. Huge curtains of gloom from the Akhru beasts fell over her. But she could not fight over the pain seizing her mortal form, as the creation neared its emergence.

The particularly large Akhru that now rose over her held a cruelly spiked club in two hands, preparing to bring it down. Two more of the beasts were not far behind this one.

Then the purplish-black lightning cracked and flashed nearby, momentarily blinding her and sending hair-raising electrical surges across her flesh. The beasts disappeared in a finely-sprayed mist of blood and liquefied flesh and bone. Such was the devastation of the strange energy from the supernatural storm that night.

The Aylsh Ismaru named Amanshar laid backwards now and kicked off her leather breeches. Then she hunched herself forward, barely containing the agony of the birthing pain. She knew that her young would come forth soon, and nothing was going to hold it back. During these final throes of her pain wracked and contorted body, the skies opened up in the strangest hue of blackish purple with bolts of similar colored lightning showering down in all directions.

Then the night was quiet except for the occasional ringing of iron and steel, solid whacks and thuds resonating with fleshly zeal. The wind died to a murmur, and Amanshar held the small form of her third born. She cradled her in both hands. The babe made no sound but simply stared back up at her mother, as if she already grasped a confident hold of the unforgiving world around her. She was so tiny.

Even as the enemy ran about and battle raged on, Amanshar was enthralled by those mesmerizing eyes of this new life. There, within that small face, was something never before seen by her or any of her kind. Those tiny orbs actually glowed under the eerie hue of the surrounding tempest, the left one shone of the whitest diamond and the right of the blackest obsidian. A purplish-black aura encompassed them both, while strange, black smoky threads emanated from her skin. And the little one, although she was breathing with life, was nearly as cold as the snow in frostthaw. There, low on the small one's abdomen, sat a beautiful birthmark. A small, darker crescent with jagged black lines erupting up and away from it, slightly contrasted against the coal-hued glistening skin. It almost gave the appearance of a half-sun with its rays shining out. Actually, that was exactly what it looked like. A dark sun rising in the night.

"My little dark one—" whispered Amanshar as she picked up the spear, clutching the small body tightly against her in one arm, "Zaramagrii will be your name... Zaramagrii Nusthafay." Her whisper turned to a forceful breath. "You are born into this abyss!"

Then Amanshar paused as the looming figures of more Akhruuk slowly approached her. She tightened her grip on the spear. Although weakened from giving birth, she charged madly into them spear first, as her remaining brethren rallied around her.

Chapter 2:

Seeds of Dissension

"The dark power of all-consuming hatred and corruption shall inspire,

That which is the deepest and blackest of all terrors,

Born from the very soul of the epoch itself and all those of likeness,

Carried forth on the wings of weakness and despair,

Fed from the breasts of the Great Mother of the Chasm,

The bringer of false redemption, the bearer of the mark of the Dark Times,

The One that shall leave all touched naught but ash and smoke,

A shadow apparition for those of shallow faith and perseverance,

The thing that steals the most precious of gifts,

Behold the Shadow Soul as it flies forth to reclaim all that is pure

and good."

"Ivrool paq Volkura Drakna saghra kuutyiphwan yojmurthryk"

> –Lore of the Shadow Soul taken
> from ancient Black Clan writings,
> from a time unknown.

here was a time before the current era known to Man-folk, Aylsh, Hulding, Thederye, Akhruuk, and Kharaghou alike. Millenniums ago, ages gone by, the world of Zholryn was yet a young world in a vast astrophysical system. But such a system was considered small within the boundless expanse of the cosmos itself.

The sparks of life, all kinds of life, flared up and began to evolve. To grow and procreate. The Oade, the Embers of the Wild—the Blue Flames—had seeded everything.

Thaumaturgy… The powers wrestled from the Oadenruun, ranged in spheres of influence from the Light, the Dark, and the Wild. All were newly developing but omnipotent and tainted with unbridled energies. Those disciplines within these spheres, such as the black arts, also rose in magnitude.

The range and expanse of Thaldeia were little more than notions within the revered temple of the Initiator, Lord Braxis. Lord Braxis was the one and sole force behind everything, until he enacted various disciplines and schools of power where he could raise up individual super beings that could be used to empower and regulate the dynamics of Zholryn and all the various dimensions of existence throughout the rest of the known universe.

It was one of these creations that very early on envisioned his realm superseding all others, or at least having the ability to do so if fate allowed. For fate was an interesting thing, and while it was deemed to be governed by unknown supremacies, or maybe by nothing at all, there have always been the few who believe that certain events are set in motion for a higher purpose and by higher powers.

Those who believe that they are governed by fate might also have course to envision destinies and thus think that everything in existence is as such. These things are not only believed by some but also are known as truths through experience and action. The illusion of autonomous thought and free will has always appeared to be genuine by most, but really only is held as that thin curtain for those of volition to see through if they so deem.

Braxis knew there must be a regulator and higher authority for all disciplines on the face of Zholryn, thus all life forms and entities in turn. Only this would allow for the most impartial and balanced world to grow and mature over time. There would have to be a divinity, or immortal, of law and order as well as one for evil and chaos, and so on. Even the wild animals, as well as the abundant forests and rivers, would have protectors to look out for their interests, or at the least speak to him on their behalf when needed.

These powers would be over fifty strong, some greater and some lesser based upon their place and order. The greater powers were called the Olden. Those lesser ones called the Myno. The domains of space and the natural order would dictate this, along with his own edict, as necessary.

The divine beings, both the Olden and the Myno, would rule unseen but omnipresent. These creations of his very own essence, but in various forms, would embody the harmony of creation and life themselves. So that all beings and things, be they breathing or dead and decayed, might carve out their niche and place as well as propagate their kind. This facet was ordained by higher than even he, something that the folk of Zholryn never had an inkling of.

But not even the lord of Zholryn, the Initiator himself, could have foreseen the impending treachery and deception that such beings possess and scheme. Such lofty beings, most of which actually uphold their duty, are littered with those who do not stop at the edge of their granted responsibilities and powers. Some fall to their own potential power and authority. Some use their obligation to hide the subtle manipulation of fellow divinities and mortals alike in the pursuit of raw totalitarian control, sometimes just to allow what they believe to be. But this has been the earmark of all species and societies since the beginning of time and in all worlds.

Free will has the propensity to stray off the path of righteousness, as it does with all paths. Whenever there is a supreme being or entity in governance, whether that being or entity is noble or corrupt in word and deed, there will be lesser beings who will always strive to overcome and usurp that power for themselves.

§ § §

A time well before the night where Amanshar and her Black Clan kind battled for their lives, and the birth of the wonder of all creation…

The Oadewood stood tall and silent, even so early in its existence when the world was young and new. Later on, legends would be told of how the first Oadewood trees had sprouted many of the things in existence. The Oade, the wild energy that was their core, permeated through all things alive and was possibly the very spark that initiated life itself.

Many of these trees would live to see thousands of years. A few of the very first would survive until the time when sentient beings dominated Zholryn.

An Oadewood tree reached a maximum height of about four hundred foot by the end of the tree's first five thousand years. The actual span of life was not really known by anyone, at least none of those who called Zholryn their home. The outside bark was a marbled grayish black swirl. This covered a dark hazel-colored inner wood. What really set these unique trees apart was the strength of this inner flesh, as it was called. This flesh was exceptional and nearly unbreakable. Impenetrable by the strongest of forged metal or ore.

The growth of an Oadewood tree, after the first thousand years, went outwards to the point that the girth might be as large as a small keep. These astounding trees developed an enormous trunk, but this never extended much above one hundred fifty foot. Some folk have mistaken the oldest of these trees for small mountains with a tree growing out of the top.

The limbs never grew very long. Instead, they were short and burly from the trunk. The tangle of roots stretched both laterally and vertically, consisting of huge tendril-like abominations that made the base of the tree almost appear as though it was a huge octopus wrapped about a treasure chest.

There are legends that claim a strange, blue wildfire burns deep within the heart of these trees, at its center core near the grounded root. Tales were passed down through the storytellers of all beings. These tales were told long before even the storytellers knew where they came from. Such lost stories called it the Blue Flames, the Oade. Oade meant Faery Fire in Aylsh. It was chiefly the Aylsh that labeled it as the spark of life itself. Most other beings just passed on the tales and grew ignorant with superstition, as they did with all things unknown to them.

As with all living things, the Oade was the essence of the Oadenruun. The Oadenruun flowed from the Oade and permeated everything. As air surrounds every single thing and corrupts every space, the Oadenruun fills both hollow and solid matter, enveloping all things whether living or not. It was that unique substance that could be plied for powerful thaumaturgy.

At the center of the tremendous Oadewood forest was the very first tree of its kind, now nearly as old as the world itself. No birds sang or flew and the wilderness was quiet as the late-suns waned, with the twilight blur ever increasing. A grand structure was recently built in a small clearing near the base of the tree. The unnatural framework stood on the soft floor in front of the enormous tree.

While not all that large, the prominence of the structure was mostly due to what it was made of. A large, blackened scale rested atop a four-post bone stand, all told maybe the height of a tall man. The scale was fairly large, some twelve paces long and eight wide. The bone pillars erecting the scale were ivory white, streaked yellow with age, with small carvings of winged creatures up and down the lengths.

A large, oddly-colored orb sat under the scale as an artistic centerpiece to the white-legged stand. This could have been a sack of sorts as well. Wrinkles and folds littered the surface. An appendage, shaped like a buttercup, rose up from the orb and through the underbelly of the scale.

A hulking form appeared from the south and approached the strange altar. The lower half of the giant figure was the hindquarters of a large, powerful steed covered with black fur. A shiny obsidian hoof at the base of each of the muscular legs struck the ground, leaving tiny plumes of dust-filled balloons as it moved. The flowing midnight-black tail proudly swayed near the ground, though never actually touching it.

The blackened skin of the upper torso glowed from the light of the duo suns. At the waist, the black fur of a horse gave way to the shape of a man. But not one of the Man-folk or Aylsh for that matter. This muscled warrior stood out resolutely.

The arms alone could have each been the trunk of a small tree. Large, black eyes glared out from a hairless face. The thick mane of sulfur-gray hair was braided and hung nearly to the ground, swishing back and forth with the tail. The distinctly long and pointy ears, denoting one of the Black Clans, carried slightly back and then rose upwards at an angle as they protruded from the sides of his head.

A medallion of silver, gold, and superb gems hung on a chain around his neck. The symbol depicted two huge, crossed hammers atop an anvil. Here approached Throndak, master of the forge and fire. The true apprentice of Master Calisair.

Master Calisair had indeed been not only the first but the most notable smith in the dawn of this new world. An ancient red wyrm had snuffed out Calisair's essence, perhaps well before his time, and not even ten seasons before this day. Shortly afterward,

Calisair's apprentice took an exceptional lance of meteor-adorned mixed steel ore and drove it up through the formidable wyrm's heart. The shiny point, sharp as a needle, protruded nearly out of the nostrils.

But this masterful feat was not accomplished without a cost. The wyrm raked downwards with a huge claw and split young Throndak below the waist. All of the combatants might have been lost if one particular divine being had not been curiously attuned to this strife.

A mere apparition strayed in the background, patiently waiting and vigilantly observing. Siri, a greater divinity, Lord of Shadows, Lord of Darkness, Harbinger of Death, and Master of Chaos. A rising immortal, one of the Olden, named for so many realms and disciplines by the Initiator. This was no doubt due to the crown of remarkable trust and unwavering confidence placed in Siri by Lord Braxis.

Throndak survived. Siri had a powerful magus, enthralled within the black arts, preserve Throndak's essence while creating him anew. Part Black Clan and part stallion, but no mere one of each. Instead, Siri forged a mighty being. One that would owe him at some point due to the debt of life.

Of course, there was always a reason behind immortals meddling within the affairs of mortals. Siri had quickly attained his stature under Lord Braxis. Alas, he knew that such responsibility would not last, and eventually, most of the titles would be stripped of him and granted to others for a more rounded world. As well as those powers granted to the titles. All or most would be lost to him.

The commanding Braxis was at least one thing, or two, and that was fair and righteous. But Siri would outsmart his lord, the

Initiator. He would set the stage for the inevitable cataclysmic event of unimaginable proportions down the road, in the distant future. And it would be with the help of this remarkable creation reborn. The event, a pivotal sequence of ancient rites, would eventually serve him and his whims many times over.

Throndak knew that he had a long wait until the planned rendezvous with Siri. This was on purpose. A powerful fire such as the one required by the Lord of Shadows would take time before it could be used. Before it would be ready to forge such a relic, an artifact as Lord Siri called for.

He approached the godforge made from black wyrm scales and aged bones of a venerable gold one. The forge appeared normal in size to one of his stature, although an ordinary man would not even be able to reach up and grasp the top rim of the scaled basin.

The master smith removed several items from the pack carried on his back. First were two sturdy hammers of varying sized double heads. Next was a foundry mold of sorts that might have been made of the same black wyrm scales as the firepot itself. The hollowed out portion of the cast was in the shape of a small sword, a wicked khopesh style, with a blade about three foot in length. This style had about a foot of straight blade and then fell into a crescent half-moon shape with both sides sharpened. The crescent portion rounded downwards then rose back up as it extended out. The shape of the blade gradually widened as it progressed outwards and up, arching to form a small slicing portion the size of one's hand. The handle or tang of the cast also had a small concave opening below it, a smoothed out circular depression.

The flame gland from a dead shadow wyrm, lying under the godforge, would require only the slightest spark to ignite.

The prodigious, burning duo suns breathed light and warmth into the world of Zholryn. Shadowy blotches of darkness enveloped the setting as they began to fall completely behind the thick wall of the forest. As much as they tried, they could no longer find cracks and gaps to glimmer through.

At times like this, if one had a direct view of the setting globes of light, one could make out the smaller sphere in the center of the larger one. This could never be noted when both were high in the sky due to the tear-wringing brightness.

Throndak struck his tinder and lit the oil-saturated torch, adding some of his own deepening patterns of obscurity to the backdrop. As the torch neared the top of the flame gland, a spout of wyrm fire shot forth from it with a dull roar. Up it went, through the funnel, and into the basin of the hardy scale.

Before long, the black scale turned molten orange and then blistering white from the intense heat. A deep, blue glow permeated above the scorching surface, casting flickering dim silhouettes amidst the surrounding trees and brush. The flaring brightness painted a profane visage across the smith's face.

A distinct but muffled flapping sound, increasing in tempo, stirred Throndak to look up at the darkening sky. He took in the transcendent eagle, all black in color, as it soared towards him while circling downwards.

At first, he stiffened, not realizing what the predator was and momentarily startled by its appearance. But then he noted the indistinct, blurred outline of the resplendent bird and the searing white eyes. The figure left trailing wisps of black, smoky cotton as it came closer to him. One passing circle of the small glade and it landed not ten paces away from the master smith.

As the eagle finished its last airy dance to the ground, it slowly dissipated into the billowing shape of a tall, strong man. Both eyes had changed and were surrounded by glowing red pools of fire. Two blackest of black beads emerged from the center, with the right having a shining white backdrop and the left a stormy gray. For a moment, looking into those eyes nearly blinded Throndak as though he had stared too long into the core of a sweltering fire.

"My lord, it is ready. I have done as you wished," spoke Throndak as recognition of Lord Siri overcame him. "The godforge will be ready within the quarter-night. We but need the remainder of the ingredients, and I can begin the rite."

Lord Siri had now completely materialized as a powerful, dark figure of Black Clan origins. His silhouette was covered by a thin, hooded cloak, which could also have been made of tenebrous material itself. The cloak shielded most of the physical features, like his long, pointed ears and the coal-colored skin.

Siri spoke like a cascading waterfall amidst blustery northern winds. "Well met, Throndak. It fills me with such pride to see you here for this special moment. I only ask this night of you and your unique talent at creation upon the godforge."

Siri, Lord of Shadows, drew breath while studying Throndak's face. "For this, I will ensure that you are named the master of fire and metals, master of the forge, divinity of smiths. You will have your immortality, and then you must carry that torch and keep it lit. Spread your influence, teach your secrets and grant those worthy the gift of the smith and the forge…your abilities and possibly your magnificence."

The Lord of Darkness paused momentarily and ever so slightly canted his head. "This will be yours alone, and all I ask of you is that you forget what we do here this night. Tomorrow, you will leave it behind and never mention it to any one or thing. This is the one expectation that you must not fall short of."

Siri's deep voice rolled over him as a masterpiece might. The smith now remembered that soothing sound that lulled him into peace, at least for the moment. A calm front of nothing but air. He knew how dangerous and unforgiving the Lord of Shadows and Master of Chaos was. But honor and commitment meant something in this day and age. It was what defined a being. And honoring a commitment that one obligated oneself to... Well, that spoke the world of an individual.

Throndak stared intently at the dark face of Siri as those eyes simmered and flared. The clever smith folded his brawny arms and exhaled. "I will do as you command, my lord. This will but barely begin to repay what I owe you for saving me. You will always have my loyalty, never doubt that. I will hold my oath to you as I would the life of my first born lad. Tomorrow, it will be as if the night never happened and we never met in this forest. I swear that!"

Siri might have smiled, but it was difficult for Throndak to note in the darkness due to the ghostly form. "Excellent, godsmith. Excellent! Let us begin then."

With that, the pair approached the godforge and Siri pulled out several items from nowhere. First was a large, bulky knapsack, which he handed over to the smith.

Throndak retrieved several ball-shaped pieces of metal and ore. Fragments of meteor ore, berlyllum or Aylsh steel, ghalqra (or adamantine steel forged by the Kharaghou), folded steel immersed in the hallowed oil of an immortal, and true silver were placed into the cast. This was in turn set over the radiating, white fury within the black wyrm scale and left to liquefy.

The Aylsh were similar to their ancestors of the Black Clans, the Aylsh Ismaru. But they had a lighter earthen color to their complexion that rarely tanned even under the powerful light of the duo suns. Their pointed ears rose nearly straight up, as opposed to those of the Black Clans which were canted back as they rose up.

Of course, the Aylsh were further divided into classes, mostly having only a real distinction of varied live spans. But to the Aylsh, the differences were more extreme.

By name, the Aylsh divided themselves into either the Trone Aylsh, or Trone, and High Aylsh, who were generally called Aylsh. But one distinction in regards to the High Aylsh was that they belonged to a reft, or noble lineage—what they perceived and vehemently called noble at least. The Trone Aylsh were known for their simpler ways of life and beliefs in most things natural and wild.

Nearly all Aylsh inherently believed themselves to be of higher and lower classes, aristocratic versus common. Not that one could get a Trone to state that they felt inferior or lesser. Simplistic to them meant more of their essence and living as one with the heart of the Wild. And a Trone would profess that the higher class, that of the High Aylsh, meant that these Aylsh had lost their true way. That way which was closest to the Eternal Mother's Way.

Obviously, the High Aylsh always thought of themselves as the upper class and more sophisticated ones. Not that they too weren't considerate of nature and the Wild. But they especially thought this over the Trone, who thrived within the wilderness. The Trone had no urge to build lofty and elegant things in which to live and breathe. Instead, they lived more rudimentary lives working in accordance with nature and communing with it.

For the Trone, themselves viewing their kind as their name implies *those of the wild light*, refused to ruin that which was most prized to them. The wildlands—forests, mountains, and everything within, especially the wild creatures.

The Trone were called this ever since the legends of long ago when creatures called Thuruunes protected the Oadewood forests. Trone Aylsh were the ones who chose to go live in the mammoth forests, to dedicate their lives to the Oadewood trees as well as the Thuruunes.

According to the old legends, Thuruunes were huge and nebulous tree creatures who could bring about horrendous ruin when provoked. The lore has them going back even further as the original protectors of *Ityarfa Vorjanimae*, the Eternal Mother, when she walked through this world.

Another important note to make when considering the Aylsh and the Aylsh Ismaru was that nearly all call the Aylsh by this name, Aylsh. But the Aylsh Ismaru were generally referred to as Black Clan or of the Black Clans, even by their own kind when using the Common tongue.

The semantics used throughout Thaldeia ebbed and flowed. Much of the terminology of things was based within the most ancient verbal form, whether those ignorant Man-folk knew it or not. Many things with origins under the Black Clans or Aylsh were passed down through the ages by historians. The Black Clan tongue was the origin for naming all things at one point or another. This was regardless of how most of the sentient races viewed or perceived their own reality and history.

A long, curling, blanched alicorn appeared in Siri's right hand. Gold, silver, and other unknown metals lined the interior of this horn in a near kaleidoscope of dazzling colors.

His other hand produced two large, murky but near opaque, gems. One of the gems appeared to have a faint red glimmer at the center and the other a pulsing blue spark. These were soul gems. Such objects held powerful wards used to trap the essence of whatever creature was required by such a caster of thaumaturgy capable of using them.

One of these gems contained the essence of an ancient shadow wyrm while the other held that of a powerful necromancer.

Siri carefully fit both of the gems into the horn until they sat snugly inside, packed tightly down towards the narrowing pointed end.

Then the Lord of Shadows slowly poured a blood concoction from a dried kelshae bladder into the top of the horn until the life juice welled up from its mouth. This mix of blood entailed the precious mortal oil of both a male and a female from many of the sentient beings in existence—Man-folk, Aylsh, Black Clan, Kharaghou, Thederye or Half-folk, Aunlourey or Windwalkers, Hulding, Faery, and more. The Kelshae were incredible beings that thrived within the vast seas. Able to breathe saltwater as though it was air, their lower bodies were powerful finned tails with scales tough as berlyllum itself.

Each of these prized but ill-fated matches had been struck down while they were still young and untainted, taken by a clean blow through the base of the neck from an anointed silver rapier. The blood had been mixed together for each pair while still warm and pumping through the hearts of the sacrifices.

Throndak nodded at Siri, and the naturally ornate horn was slowly released into the glowing cast of molten ore atop the godforge. The Lord of Shadows muttered an incantation as the horn slowly sank and disappeared into the bubbling soup. Tiny white globes floated up and out of the forge as the incantations came to an end. These small orbs drifted high into the sky and disappeared. Glittering trails almost appearing like tiny shooting stars streamed upwards after them and took longer to fade.

A short while later, the Lord of Shadows stepped back and slowly spread his arms apart while raising them. Suddenly, opposite of Siri, a murky and obscured ring formed within the air. It was filled with drifting darkness. The substance of it slowly rolled outwards and broadened, now a rough sphere of dismal fog that moved and shifted.

In the middle of the circle lay a large block of dark, billowing nothingness. A shimmering twilight anvil fit for the godforge creation. The Shadehaunt, the shadow realm, came forth and mingled with that of the material world of Zholryn, casting a strange, eerie, orange hue to the twisted scene. Next to it sat a basin filled with a liquid vapor that also changed form and gave off a smoky, black haze.

Then Throndak grasped one of his unique hammers, along with the glowing cast of white-hot ore, from the godforge. The hammer began to glow a pale blue. It sizzled and sparked as though it was conflicting with the form and fabric of the world itself, disagreeing with it. As though existence wanted to snuff out the hammer before it could perform the deed.

It was not long before Throndak was able to extract the glowing metal from the cast using large tongs.

Within moments, he had the blade on the murky anvil. Then he began to beat it with the sparking hammer, meticulously banging at it over and over. Ever so slowly working the hot piece of metal back and forth. Evenly. The nature of the blows rent from the hammer cried out each and every time. *Were these possibly unheeded warnings, maybe each its own prophecy of doom foretold to deaf ears?*

He thrust it into the strange basin, sending a frothing blast of black steam to shoot skyward. Then the blade was taken back to the godforge and superheated again.

The stout smith went through the process of heating and cooling the curious metal over and over again until the first traces of morning light began to show.

Throughout the entire time of the forging, Throndak swore that he heard small cackling shrieks and cries arising from the impact of shaping the blade. By now, his hammer had honed the unique piece of ore into a formidable blade that could no longer be affected by the smith's blows.

At some point before Throndak's work reached its pinnacle, Siri had stripped the bark clean from a rough, circular patch on the first Oadewood tree. The tree, standing tall not very far from the dark forge, was the first of its kind. It had been around since the very beginning of time itself.

The area defiled by Lord Siri stretched roughly twelve hands in diameter. He carved several strange runes into the flesh that lay underneath where the bark had been, using a huge severed claw dipped in blackened blood.

Throndak knew it was time when the enormous globes of the red duo suns slowly began to climb for the day. Their brilliant, scarlet arcs barely cracking the western horizon as they did so.

Siri grasped the naked haft of the newly formed khopesh. The small circle, now blazing white itself, was still attached to the end. He approached the impressive tree where he had removed the bark as the hot metal sizzled and smoked in his hand.

The blade still radiated a reddish-white glow as he slowly drew the tip along his chest and then down to his waist. His own hallowed oil sizzled black on the edge of the weapon, infusing the essence of the Lord of Darkness, Shadows, and Chaos into the blade.

Siri then grasped the haft with his right hand forward and the left behind it so that he could slip a finger into the attached ring. This small band of blackened metal matched the blade and appeared to be fairly wide once around the finger. The burning contrivance still did not appear to bother him as his immortal flesh molded to the handle. Nonetheless, it smoked and sizzled as though it was a fresh roast on a spit.

He raised the weapon level with the ground and pointed its tip at the middle of the rune-covered, bared circle which he had created on the tree. His shaded head lowered slightly while he muttered more strange incantations. Then he snapped his head upwards with a fierce cry, and thrust himself blade first towards the tree. Siri's frame tensed as he braced for the impact and no doubt intended to drive the blade in with all of his might.

The tip of the curved khopesh reached the debarked flesh of the tree and it did not stop. It did not even slow. The sheath of bulky muscles covering the dark lord's body trembled as though the strike had been tremendous and with unparalleled force. But the blade sank into the tree's flesh slowly and steadily as though it was a hot knife slicing into freshly baked bread.

As the hilt of the sword reached the tree's surface, a brilliant globe of bluish-white light appeared at that juncture. Then it suddenly exploded outwards with such force and speed that it must have gone several leagues in a moment. The enveloping blue surge detonated out like a vast wave crashing towards the shoreline with a deafening sonic boom that ruptured everything in its path. The force flew like wildfire out in a full circle from the point of impact.

That shock wave was enormous. The smith was violently flung backwards across the small clearing and into a throng of trees and bushes. The searing blue light that poured forth from the convergence of the blade with the tree blinded him for a long time.

Slowly, darkened shapes began to form again amidst the sea of dull stars. As his vision cleared, Throndak saw that Siri still stood with the khopesh as he had been when the blade first struck the tree. The small ring that was attached to the hilt was now broken free and on the dark lord's finger.

Only a blackened husk remained of the Oadewood tree, like smoldering red honeycomb lit by the wind. A phantom of what it had been. The very first one in this world. It was as though the tree was nothing but a dried tobacco leaf which had been reduced to glowing red ash. The eternally-forged weapon had soaked up the very essence of it, along with all the other things added to the forging ritual.

The morning winds, now stirring, were blowing away what little was left of the tree. Nothing, whether alive or dead, could thrive or exist within that blackened ash circle of what was once the greatest Oadewood tree. Ever.

Throndak looked on at the scene around him. *What in this world had Siri created, or had he helped him create?* Of this he had no clue. But it must be very powerful.

The godforge was blasted into pieces. The area that had been merged with the Shadehaunt now stood desolate and no longer held the dismal anvil or the cooling tray.

In place of where the accoutrements once rested, Throndak could barely make out a dim, smoky figure that faded and shimmered. But there it was, a huge wolfish form with glowing orbs for eyes. The thing must have been the height of a tall man at its shoulder. But it was difficult to be sure, as it appeared to dissipate and then materialize every few moments. Flickering like an oil lamp on its last leg of wick.

Maybe Throndak's eyes were so weakened from the immense flash of light that they were just playing tricks on him. It was possible that he was seeing ghosts of images before him, and this giant, dimly lit wolf could simply be an illusion.

He looked towards Lord Siri again. The weapon—the sword, if it could even be called that—the exquisite blade in his hand trailed hairs of black smoke as it was moved about. There was now an exotic, blackened skin handle around the previously bare tang. It appeared to be overly large for a blade of this size. Glowing red and white gems adorned the pommel of it, but they could just have been points of light considering the way that his eyes felt.

The ring had completely separated in the process, and it morphed as well. The ring appeared to give off the same smoky-black trails as if it was smoldering. It was lined with faint red and blue gemstones, tiny beacons set in the surface. It was a little wider than it had been but appeared to perfectly fit the finger of Siri that it had ended up on.

Siri then grasped the khopesh with both hands and slowly moved his hands apart again. The sword split into two matching blades, with the same features and billowing darkness trailing from each. Both of the blades moved with the speed of the wind as though they were made of air.

The two fused together again as he brought them towards one another. The Lord of Shadows, Darkness, Death, and Chaos slowly turned around to view the remnants of the wooded glade where the godforge once stood and where the world of twilight had briefly touched the existence of Zholryn.

The dark form of the giant wolf sat on its haunches as the morning duo suns rose higher amidst the swaying trees. The beast was fairly easy to discern now, dark haze and billowing black, smoky wisps outlining the figure. Occasionally, flare ups, like flaming red embers, would briefly trail along the portions of the outline silhouetting it even more so.

The panting muzzle threw out dark, swirling ash touched with an orange-colored aura dimly backed by a red glow.

Enormous, haunted eyes of instinct and cunning took in the forested scene. The right one now appeared glowing white while the left gleamed with a black so ominous that it seemed as though it was a dark, endless hole. Both eyes sometimes had a dim, purplish-black background to them that strangely shone with an unnatural radiance.

Siri glared at the puissant form of the half horse, half Black Clan smith. "My adept smith and master of metal, go now and forget this time spent here last night and the morn. Be prepared, my friend. For you will soon be hailed to your new position. Hailed as an immortal. Trust your thought and inner voice, and always remember that your wisdom will ultimately guide you in all things. May Chaos reign for eternity and dim the light of the world to its appropriate glory!"

After Throndak departed, Siri folded his sinewy arms with a sharp flap of the black cloak and the khopesh pointing straight off to one side.

Siri scowled while gazing at the ghostly wolf through cold slits of eyes.

"Grastharfah il Marilaan. Lord of wolf kind, wolf king, Alpha Omega…" He trailed off, nodding in pride as well as anticipation.

To the Black Clans, the shadow warg's name meant *unseen fangs of the darkness.*

The subtle excitement behind Siri's tone was as though it was something known only to himself and none other. A plan long in the making, concealed yet out in the eyes of the world.

Then Lord Siri grinned widely. "Grasfur, come, my furry beast."

Grasfur lifted a considerably large clawed paw into the air and pranced towards Siri. The gigantic wolf lifted off its haunches ever so slightly, very much emphasizing how lithe and springy the beast could be. The vigorous head then tilted towards the ground as the enormous ears pointed straight up and folded back, bowing to the Lord of Shadows with such unconditional obedience, and yes, love.

The dark lord admired the devices of the twilight realm so freshly crafted. He slowly looked upward to the heavens while speaking ancient Black Clan tongue. "*Volkura drakna… Volkura Naux, Volkura Throk.* The beast shall rise, forging the world through the dark gloom of the Shadehaunt…by and through the Binding of Shadows and the Impaler of Shadows. Such shall inspire those of lesser will and courage to flee before it or be forsaken until the end of time itself."

Siri walked over to the shadow warg and extended a free hand, softly stroking the fur under the muzzle. Now face to face, the shadow warg towered several foot higher than Siri.

"My first born master of the twilight and darkness… You are the lord of nearly everything that walks on four legs and then some. Your loyalty and devotion are unparalleled. My amazing wolf. I have always regarded you for my one true and unerring right hand." He paused to caress the fur below Grasfur's ear.

"I now have an even grander need for you… The same loyalty and devotion…your strength and speed. There will be a time in the distant future where you will be heralded. Even now, your pure essence—my essence—has been intermingled within these relics of dark power.

"When I deem it appropriate—when the world as we know it must change from whatever path it is on—a Soul will be born of the darkness. Of those things which make the world a nightmare of itself. This Soul will be my creation and will also bear part of me, part of you, part of the very fabric of not only the world of Shadows but of

Chaos, Death, and others. It will bear witness to that which has long been asleep and hidden. It will be birthed of all upright creatures but created from the very deep and dark obscurity of twilight."

The shadow warg slowly nuzzled Siri's arm and sniffed the black blade, then the ring upon Siri's hand, while he spoke.

"Grasfur, this Soul will be in need of you and will require your help. You will be the companion, the protector, and the champion of this...power," continued Siri as he firmly grasped the thick, black fur on Grasfur's head just below the ear. "It will not be tainted by either good or evil...but of chaos, molded through survival and attrition. Strengthened through hardship and pain, though a lesser power in its own right, destined to be *the* power. But this dark Soul will need your guidance and nurturing, along with your protection to reach and eventually fulfill its destiny."

"Have no worries, as you will be beckoned once this Soul comes to realize its true purpose and begins to wield such power. An internal compass and bond will connect the both of you. You will know certain things and have instincts and readings as to where it is. And you will always have my powers and be granted exceptional abilities. I trust this gift to the world only with you, for you will be the mirror, my rare wolf."

Grasfur, the powerful shadow warg, stirred from the words of Siri, whimpered and let out a sharp bark of excitement.

"Go now, my friend. Go and ensure that all of your young pups carve out their own kingdoms," whispered Siri into the wolf's ear. "Fare thee well till we meet again."

Within moments, a black, swirling oval appeared in the sky not far above the ground. The shadow warg leapt into it and was gone.

The Lord of Shadows looked back towards where the first Oadewood tree had once stood. He knew what the terrible cataclysm would bring. Time will start anew for the world once the Soul claims its destiny... The whole world will be its subject and sinister apparitions will assume the reins of existence. To the utter despair of many, to the obscene depths of bane for some, and onward to the darker glory of those true and redeemed. Chaos will be supreme. And, at his command, it will happen.

Now he had to hide the artifacts until the appropriate time arrived. They were hidden from the world and even immortal eyes until needed and sought out by Volkura Drakna, the Shadow Soul.

As Siri turned back towards where the dark anvil had been, a majestic white owl lifted up in flight from within the swaying treetops behind him. The creature silently and surreptitiously disappeared over the green canopy.

Chapter 3:

Pretense for Death

All those of the life oil shall sanctify their own of pureness and
tranquility. Those bonds of righteousness shall indemnify such as
absolute.

–First Edict of Lord Braxis, etched
upon the Great Slates, recovered by
Arterium circa the year 13 BA.

ost historians and scholars of the world believe that
the time of Man-folk has come to pass already and
that they are living in it. But sadly, the time of Man,

Aylsh or First Folk, Aylsh Ismaru or Black Clan, Kharaghou, the
Thederye or Half-folk (called half-men by some)—of sentient
beings—has barely begun. Alas, one can never really be sure of
anything but existing in the now, and of death itself, of course.

Like a newly planted seed of unknown virtues, many things
can affect its growth and what that seed sprouts into. A seed can
be guided and nurtured, and not necessarily by a tender of
righteousness. Regardless of where in the mighty universe of
creation something is, there are always grander things at play and
at work than even such a thing as the natural awe of a world.
Powerful forces that have been in existence for all eternity
perpetuate time and space. These forces subtly ply matter as if it
was clay being prepared for the kiln. *How long is all-time? How
long has existence been existence?*

And what can Man really know anyways? Man, a race that
barely thrives up to a mere turn—one hundred years—and only
if lucky, or fated, at that. For the Man-folk, history is but a very
minuscule piece of bridgework under construction over a vast
expanse of land and water. What was known concerning the last
three thousand years alone was the result of literally hundreds of
generations—and this was set about in record by still far fewer in
number. And the taint of such circumstances could run rampant
without one realizing it.

What they think they know only lightly scratches the surface
of a very hard, many-layered shell that glistens like granite. And,
due to the limited time that they have been accumulating
fragments of history, there are many things that have originated
elsewhere by other beings that Man has grasped for themselves.
Man has nestled these things within their own lore and legend,

attempting to make the hodgepodge smooth and, well, their own. Like a patched quilt for the upcoming winterfall, sewn together from various pieces of fabric. Even Arterium aided this endeavor, though these things were never visibly known to the majority that staunchly advocated his godlike presence and supremacy.

At this point in this tale, it would be good to explain that the words human and humanity are both nonexistent within the world of Zholryn. Literally.

The closest thing that is commonly used to refer to either one would be Man-folk. Many regions of Thaldeia, particularly the central and southern ones, also use the term people. Some call others by folk, but this is also equally applied by and in regards to the other sentient kinds. This is just the way of things here.

If one were to delve into the various other races, for instance, one might find yet more terms. Albeit in their own language, the Akhruuk call the Man-folk *zhood*, which translates to *trees without bark* in the Common tongue.

But then you must also look into the reasoning behind such names in Akhruuk. In this case, they refer to Man-folk this way to specifically mean pieces of wood that have no protection (thus easy to chop into or down). So one can easily see into the violent nature of the majority of this kind.

Incidentally, an Akhru is used for the singular form of the beast, while Akhruuk is the plural. There really is not any particular reason for this, other than the Black Clans calling them by the name that the Akhruuk have called themselves in their own tongue since before recorded history. And this has stuck and extended itself into the other beings ever since, like all other Black Clan labels. In fact, most folk do not even realize that many of the names of things they use are actually steeped in Black Clan origins and lore.

The Aylsh have far exceeded Man-folk not only in life span, but in the pursuit of knowledge. These First Folk, as they are typically known, also have surpassed all others within physical and mental pureness and oneness. The name First Folk has stuck over the turns, as many people across Thaldeia have called the Aylsh by it. This is out of pure ignorance, of course, as most people have rarely dealt with the Black Clans or Aylsh Ismaru to truly know which one has been around the longest. But the fact that the Great Slates were scripted in High Aylsh also grants some credence to the use of this term.

Most did not know that the first of the beings were the Black Clans, and not the Aylsh. Of course, most think of the Aylsh as those who have grown higher than the other creations, those who have achieved a higher state of awareness and being due to their life span and steeped aura. The High Aylsh can easily see a thousand years before passing. The more wild ones such as the Trone, those that were born and mingled within the sweeping forests, can normally average around eight hundred years.

The Black Clans, or Aylsh Ismaru, definitively outlived most other sentient beings. Up to two thousand years by some accounts. These esoteric and mystical beings have been around forever, it would seem. Some say that the dark ones were the very first of the sentient beings, but this probably was based within the lore of the Black Clans themselves. Part of their own history and origins.

The Black Clans, once rumored to thrive in a massive city-state called Isnuuthghor, now are scattered throughout the world like leaves in the summertide wind. But if there were a people that might have more knowledge on existence and things of time and space, then it would be those of the Black Clans.

Now, an incomprehensible amount of time since Zholryn emerged, Man has been keeping track of time for just over sixteen hundred years, at least officially. Although this scribing goes from parchment, to vellum, and even to etched stone in some cases. One of the most reputed and widely known pools of history and knowledge ad nauseam is Tamelyn Keep. Current times also label this scholarly place as Loremasters Keep. It is claimed (at least by those who tend to the keep) that Tamelyn Keep originated in the year SA 200.

One might ask what the term SA refers to. Since Arterium, or SA, is typically placed within the context of naming a year or time within the known and current era.

Oddly enough, King Arterium himself began the House of Legends during his reign. This was even before the Tamelyn Keep that most know of now. The historians appointed to the House of Legends were titled legend masters, or legendars. The House of Legends was sparked by Arterium to record those legendary deeds and events for all posterity (and not just Kuhrzoth). Such was the spoken intent of the king, although the very first legend master himself died a violent and horrible death.

While the House of Legends was steeped in bloodshed in those early days, it still remains in Nuuroc as the premiere collective body of historians who continue to scribe the times and events into the history of Thaldeia. Now the work of the loremasters of Tamelyn Keep and that of the legendars is hinged together and done in consultation of one another. Even though

Tamelyn is more a repository and place of exalted storage while the legendars continue to put quill to vellum. Nowadays, scribed copies of the finished volumes from the House of Legends always end up at Tamelyn.

The current era was titled as such after the death of King Arterium. Some say that he was the most glorious leader of all times. Many would say that he was the epitome of a true warrior. And many more might just secretly whisper the dark tales regarding King Arterium that never made it into the annals of history. Regardless, the current era was begun at the time of the king's death. The time before his death tends to count backwards from it and is labeled BA (Before Arterium).

The age preceding SA 1, before the application of SA and BA, was known as the Revered Times. Many refer to it as the Old Days.

In fact, King Arterium was so legendary that all of Kuhrzoth referred to a year as *in the year of our King* or *before our King* instead of using SA or BA. Many other folk across Thaldeia did the same.

Now anyone studying the architecture of Tamelyn Keep will be able to note that it cannot be more than two hundred and fifty years old (and is nowhere near fifteen hundred). What is known as truth, and also passed down by others not affiliated with the keep, is that Sedgewyn Tamelyn was the original builder and lord of the keep, as it stands today. But the truth was that history delves much deeper than the tiny, little mark Man has created thus far.

Regardless of the ensuing controversies surrounding legend or opinion, Tamelyn Keep is undoubtedly the rightful bearer of what is considered to be the most lucrative collection of books, scrolls, parchments, tablets, and anything else that might contain historical information. Actually, there are collections of collections, for that matter. The entire keep, other than the living quarters and guest chambers, is bogged down with large rooms full of what one hundred score sages only dream about in their rousing fantasies.

In fact, the few ancient archives that were not stored at the keep included the Amethyst Scrolls. Seven fine parchments of ancient Black Clan script. Each of these was completely encased within amethyst. The method of how they were encased in the gem continues to astound those most learned and even those most pronounced within the fields of thaumaturgy. These mysterious artifacts alone were thought to be of transcendent origins, some even preaching that they each had been scripted by Braxis himself. While these were first uncovered by Man within the Black Clan fortress of Isnuuthghor, they were ousted to the walled city of Nuuroc under the hand of Arterium a long time ago. Of course, Arterium never did have the opportunity to study them, as he did not survive his expedition into the dark fortress.

Another historical point to raise here, now that the Amethyst Scrolls have surfaced, would be the Twelve Edicts of Lord Braxis. Speaking about the one would do little to no justice overall without at least introducing the other. Twelve sayings, or quotes, were discovered a hair over a ten-year before the current known era. Thus, the same amount of time prior to when the Amethyst Scrolls had been retrieved from Isnuuthghor.

These scripted sayings, which came to be known as the Twelve Edicts of Lord Braxis, were in High Aylsh. Each one emblazoned upon a bluish-colored slate of hardened wood. Those most versed individuals figured out that these slates were petrified wood, possibly even Oadewood. There has never actually been proof that they were, or are, Oadewood. But it makes the story more appealing, and sanctified, to those faithful.

So the Twelve Edicts, also known as the Great Slates, were thought to contain the very tenets of the divine, of the supreme Olden. Word spread that they were scripted by Lord Braxis himself.

Each one contained a significant morsel of perplexing thought. It was later determined that, indeed, they were somehow related to Lord Braxis, and each of them obscurely spelled out a secret to life, to harmony. A way that one must live, if one chose to follow the Initiator, Lord Braxis.

But many different interpretations arose, as well as countless plights that might befall those that did not abide by them. These mindsets actually started off their own separate, sometimes warped, followings.

The chief interpretation followed none other than King Arterium, for he was the one that had been ordained as the bearer of the Great Slates to the world. Indeed, King Arterium brought them forth one day upon his return to Nuuroc, claiming that a divine apparition had visited him within the Tallwood.

Even the Aylsh High Court sent an entourage to Kuhrzoth, in order to see as well as study the Great Slates. This entourage included the highest of the Aylsh priests, the Red Cloak. Such inspiration drove King Arterium to raise the very first official temple to Lord Braxis, which still rests to this day within Old Nuuroc.

Old Nuuroc refers to the original keep built by Arterium when he first broke ground way back when. Present day Nuuroc was built up around Old Nuuroc. The temple sits below the Emerald Tower and close to the original palace, where Arterium lived.

This also sparked the Order of Braxis, an officially recognized pious order of benevolent folk who worshipped Braxis and lived according to the Initiator and his Twelve Edicts. Or at least what they thought and perceived to be of the greater divine, the Olden.

Lord Braxis may have been the most recognized and accepted divinity, especially being the supreme one. But many segments of the people within Kuhrzoth worshipped other divinities, as was the case throughout the world.

Of course, all of these other ones were considered by most to be lower than Braxis. For Braxis was the Initiator and actually empowered all other divinities. Those within the Order of Braxis were known as the Lords' Initiates. And, with the blessing of King Arterium, the Order of Braxis collected and emblazoned a high order to the known powers of the divine. This was the basis for most other religious spurs, whether the figures of glory were superior or inferior to what was declared by the Order of Braxis. Of course, the chief reason behind the Order of Braxis doing this was to officially seat the hierarchy *under* Lord Braxis.

But, these people that worshipped other divinities mostly revered the specific powers based upon their traditional beliefs. For example, one might believe in the unbounded seas and bodies of water, and that these were the keys to life and existence. After all, everything grew thirsty and required water to survive. That meant—to them—that the higher power had to be the Olden, or divinity, of the oceans and water.

Other such orders were far more heretical. One that had surfaced around the year of our King 1175 was called the Devotees of Penance. While chiefly within the northern kingdoms, its followers were vast. The Devotees worshipped Xavanruug, the

Olden of Death. While not seen as an evil growth across the lands, cities and villages riddled with these Devotees had more than their fair share of missing folk. Many were the young, up to the age of fourteen, which was considered maturity.

Another order known as Ranakha, the Endowed or Followers of the Five Moons, had origins back before Arterium's time. Their symbol was a pure silver medallion shaped like a full moon, that of Zholryn's largest, called Chedris. Smaller circles representing the other four moons hung along the lower portion. These folk chose to believe that Man-folk were the higher beings, the enlightened ones. All other things—even the Aylsh, Kharaghou, Aunlourey, or Hulding—were lesser things, no different than rats or fish. For that matter, Lord Braxis did not exist in their reality either. None of the Olden and Myno did.

Some of these folk claimed that they were granted powers through their divinity and even controlled certain elements within the scope of that divinity. And this was the ensuing argument of the differences between the main thoughts, or disciplines, of thaumaturgy. These notions stretched outside of Kuhrzoth, across Thaldeia, to the other sentient beings as well.

In the year SA 1624, the loose conglomerate of kingdoms, dominions, and territories that comprised the land mass of Thaldeia still ebbed and flowed back and forth over minutia. Even after the foregoing time, each sovereignty (for they all claimed this to a larger extent no matter the state of organization) remained glued in its present bubble of subterfuge and conniving fragmentation. Albeit several of the power seats or rulers did have good intent, somehow underlings always appeared to sway that to some other ill form or fashion. There has never been one true ruler that has united all of these holdings as one unified land—whether in solidarity or as peaceful neighbors.

Pacts and agreements crystallized only when there was need. But the kingdom of Kuhrzoth remained the parapet of Thaldeia, the very same kingdom that King Arterium once ruled over.

It was still a time of mighty warriors—made up of both those that swung cocks and those that rode them. The simplicity of life came down to just that. Between the cock and the sheath.

Though it was not what it used to be, Kuhrzoth's standing army still remained one of the largest. The royal Order of Emerald Knights continued to guard not only the bounds containing most of Thaldeia, but also stood watch over Oshghrul, the Fallen Lands. Though their numbers were much fewer. And the perceived threat of the Fallen Lands had dwindled, with no savage things having attacked the kingdom in a long time.

The Emerald Knights were not what they used to be in training or in battle either, as we shall see later within this tale. Time rolls across all things with the distinct clatter of change and turmoil. There may still be a handful of veterans, but the majority of forces under the Emerald Crown were not tested with sword or arrow.

Eventually, there is always something that provides cause and effect. Even when the lands themselves claim that peace and tranquility have been fair of late, the expectation of anything normal to continue just cannot linger. Instead, the cold winds blow the content that they carry into the face of the lands, whether the lands are prepared or not. And even on a bright blue, sunny day of seeming bliss, there still remain deep shadows lurking out there, ever haunting the material world.

It was a sunny day of high, billowing clouds that found Wybur Buttlecut nearing Tamelyn Keep. Summertide was at its height already, the end of Tourney-mark nigh. The duo suns were as tall in the sky as they would grow for the year.

Tourney-mark was the time of year where the suns were the fullest. Most things frolicked through the world and enjoyed the the long bouts of hospitable weather and endless greenery. The kingdoms of Man-folk were no different. The Tourney was one such celebration, lasting a fortnight, that took place during the middle of the quarter-season. The most valiant and skilled warriors, even those aspiring to be, would set their sights each and every year for it. This festival centered around various tournaments of arms. Opponents would engage in jousting, one-on-one bouts with various weapons like the sword and axe, and even archery. There were group martial games, such as one competition with several companies of knights (each up to 200) taking part in capturing the banner or the opponents' lands. Of course these sparked many disputes, and open battles even broke out. Because of this, the Free Lands petitioned to hold it in Longshadows as a more neutral land. It has been held there now since the year of our King 1040.

This particular year was named Year of the Purple Bloom. The connotation was due to the unique appearance of a purplish-black aura surrounding the nightmask flower. A peculiar dark, smoke-like vapor radiated from the entire flower. These plants were mysterious, as well as supernatural, in their own right even without this effect.

The name itself, nightmask, arose due to the fact that the entire flower would turn the darkest black just after sunsdown and remain so until first light. The plants normally held their flowering fruit for the entire summertide and well into the harvestspell. The long black stems usually reached about four foot tall. The flower was quite large and nearly the size of a fully grown pumpkin. Dark purple buds transformed into huge, fluffy, pie-shaped flowers, thick and twisted with large petals in a mysterious purplish-red hue. Tiny, pointed, needle-like black protrusions topped by miniature blood-red flower heads dotted the center area.

The appearing aura presented the eerie perception that the flowers were literally breathing and spewing ash. Legend claimed that this strange metamorphosis was created by the realm of shadows, or Shadehaunt, and its convergence with the present material world. The phenomenon normally coincided with a black moon, which historically has occurred every hundred and thirty years or more. But the next black moon was not due for about sixty years.

A black moon was when all five of the moons that circled the skies of Zholryn eclipsed at once. The one visible moon glazed over in a gloomy, black haze. When this occurred, a magnificent halo effect took place that cast the evening skies into mixed shades of purples, blues, reds, and oranges.

The entire night was breathtaking, with many folk actually staying awake the whole time in awe and uncertainty. The uncertainty was because some of these folk realized they were just a small part in the middle of a vast and dangerous ocean, where they had little to no control over most things.

The Shadehaunt was a term spoken only under the bright light of day. A dark name for an even darker place full of imagined terrors and horrors too frightening to even summon to thought. Such a place existed but fell only during nightmares for some. And others?

Well, for others, it was just a dark hole that brought forth tales to spur young ones to bed. Truth be told, there were many different realms of existence. The reality was all of these other places, or dimensions, could be crossed into nearly as one, they were so close together. As real as the wind and the sky above, filled with the duo suns and other starry points of light at night. They were merely a flicker away, maybe a slight variation in the ambient spectrum of being, or light, or even sound. But these things existed, whether people chose to believe or not.

The truth was that most of the Man-folk tended towards ignorance. A shadow world? Impossible, thaumaturgy did not exist either. In fact, most had not even seen an Aylsh or Kharaghou to bring any reality to either one of those folk.

Those that knew and had experienced the world for what it was—well, they just sat back and grew tired of trying to convince the naysayers of what was right outside their front door. Or right in front of their noses. All of this was something they would know if they took the time to truly look at the world around them.

This day found Wybur Buttlecut riding down the Old Road in his tempera-painted oaken cart behind a burly mule named Shab. Shab was his pride and joy, a constant companion on his travels. The deep green colors of the cart matched the rich forest hued backdrop. Such color could only be wrung from the berries of the elderwold brambles.

Wybur Buttlecut was not really a sight for sore eyes, or even those that just woke up. Indeed, Wybur was far from being the epitome for Man-folk. He could easily be mistaken for the runt of the litter from an ogre. Well, an ogre, but minus any threatening and menacing air or appearance.

In fact, the very demeanor and look of Wybur actually encouraged humor on the part of most. Whether it was the short, fat trunk of a body, or the nearly bald, hawk-nosed head. His pudgy face was sided by red cheeks most of the time, whether the color was genuine or embarrassment brought on by his own thoughts. He was a very peculiar individual.

Wybur sometimes even provoked violence towards himself with no more than his observable meagerness. The elongated head gave an appearance that it had been slammed down on top of the neck too hard. It thrust itself forward with his shoulders to form a small shelf with his neck. Indeed, he had a much defined hunchback.

But the world was a cruel and unforgiving place. The majority of the ignorance and meanness of it kicked beings like Wybur around at their whim and for their own amusement. Only far and few in between would there naturally exist protectors of the timid and weak.

Now Wybur did find a special bond with the unique and fascinating creatures of the natural order that Braxis sought fit to populate the world with. He was unendingly drawn to animals. And they to him. It appeared that animals accepted him for one of their own, or at least as a kindred spirit.

Truth be told, our young, unshapely lad of twenty-six winterfalls held most of the animals in higher regard than anyone or anything else. As a matter of fact, Wybur even cringed when his aunt had confronted a mouse in their dwelling. He feared for *the little fellow's safety.*

He saw their pure, true form for what they were. Such beings were said to be in the very essence of Lord Braxis the Initiator. Wybur knew there was no truer companion than a beast. They did not judge, would not discriminate by looks or thought, and always provided unconditional love.

The warm, pleasant breeze forced Wybur's mind to drift back to his tangle with the perpetrator of his most recent bout of feverish thrills. She was very beautiful, and that rapturous voice drew him in every time that it formed words.

Livforena… Livforena… Such a name. The leather outfit clinging to her skin with the flowing black silk cloak, and long, supple leather boots up to her knees. Most of the time, her face and her head were concealed by a hood or a dark half-mask. But Wybur could dream about her body, as it left little to the imagination or, in his case, too much maybe. Sometimes, a lock of deep red hair would tease him from a corner of the hood or mask, and those fiery purple eyes stared him into nakedness (or at least he felt so).

The young woman had approached him back in early frostthaw. One day, he suddenly found her in his room at the Straefyrshir Inn. The cozy retreat was where he typically passed a night during his travels to and from Tamelyn Keep.

In her exact words, the work that she offered him was labeled as a special calling for the gallant cause of existence itself. Only Wybur Buttlecut, with his unique talents, could aid her in this endeavor. After all, she was with the Veiled Ones. A group whose existence and purpose were both legendary and ultimately for the good of all folk.

The Veiled Ones were an enigmatic group labeled as being responsible for maintaining the status quo and peace throughout Thaldeia. At least that was what most people thought. Of course, everything associated with the group hung under an air of mysticism. But he was well-versed in the stories that had been told over the current era, at least since the mysterious group had surfaced.

While the group was not listed officially within the annals of history as set forth by the House of Legends, it was the subject of various lore spread across the lands by an even larger number of storytellers. And many of these weavers of tales also held weight of their own. Legends even claimed that the Veiled Ones had explored both east and west of the Thaldeian coasts. Not that any actual knowledge or rumors were passed along about what might rest in either direction of Thaldeia.

But the group had no roots in the last three or four hundred years. It was as if it had vanished. And its crest, that of a brooch-sized oval of gold with a fine emerald triangle at the center, had not been seen in an equal amount of time. Whispers of the Veiled Ones were not even held for debate amongst rumors.

The impromptu arrangement brought on by Livforena had sparked a new passion within Wybur, a driving reason and purpose to his mundane existence. This was something that he had not felt since before the death of his mum and papa fifteen years earlier.

As with all beings and entities of sentience, they have the need and the ache to feel a special purpose to their lives. Wybur was no different, and he had felt lively and spiritually connected up to the death of his mum and papa. The Red Ache had taken both of them within the space of a quarter-season.

The Reckoning was a rough time for all, especially for the city of Longshadows, and others throughout the Free Lands. In the year of SA 1609, a terrible pestilence called the Red Ache swept over the lands and stole many lives before finally dissipating. The kingdoms of Man-folk were devastated. Wybur's parents, along with a third of Longshadows' population, succumbed to the high fever followed by blistery, blood-filled, red sores that sprouted all over the body. No healer, or magus for that matter, could cure it or even slow it down as it erupted across Thaldeia. The furnace of a fever wracked the body for a week before the sores would begin to rise. Once this happened, it turned to a very slow and miserable fortnight in most cases before the suffering one would pass on to the Outer Halls.

It was as though the lands of Thaldeia had been cursed. In the year SA 1549, less than sixty years before the Red Ache, the Black Pox had rampaged its way across the land. Equally mysterious, the Black Pox took nearly a fourth of the people within each of the Man-folk kingdoms across Thaldeia before it too disappeared and faded into oblivion. Not even royalty was immune to the dreadful thing. King Eldrid Sivercroft, with less than seven years upon the throne, fell victim to it at the tender age of twenty-five summertides. And this did not account for the many wee ones of the nobles who fell to it also.

Gone but leaving behind piles of freshly burned bodies and mourners beyond count, the panic that overtook everyone was like wildfire. The dead were stacked high and lit afire in hopes that the plague would come to an end. Like the Red Ache though, it only went away after taking an extreme toll.

Wybur's eyes held a cold, wet flash like ponds reflecting the steel blue skies over the memories, until he caught sight of a dazzling white owl. The regal night bird captured his amazement as it passed slowly in front of him, gliding through the skies.

By the hundreds, it had to be huge, he thought. A giant snow owl.

Yes, he felt like his recently uncovered obligation presented by the Veiled One was a new beginning and an optimistic conclusion to what may have been a long trial of his conviction and reasoning. Like the picturesque owl, his life now had new meaning and the sky was the limit indeed. He felt like he was reborn and granted a chance to make a difference. Is that not what anyone of sound mind and good spirit really wanted?

Although Livforena would never disclose the true and ultimate intent of her doings, she had made it very clear that he could possibly be the savior of Thaldeia. There was a sinister evil that threatened to unleash unspeakable harm and destruction on all beings across Thaldeia, if not the whole world.

How could he not commit himself to Livforena and whatever needed to be done? It was his dream. So, of course, he pledged himself to a vow of unwavering secrecy that he would do his best and not fail her cause.

Wybur rounded a long, steep, uphill bend in the road, infested on both sides with rock outcroppings amidst the high fir forest. The old walls of Tamelyn Keep appeared out of the greenery. Several large bumbers were pollinating a stand of sunflowers not far from the approach to the keep.

Now a bumber was a very unusual creature of Zholryn, and quite peaceful itself unless provoked.

Wybur knew that even seeing one bumber was a rarity indeed. And here were three, no four…wait, six! This relative, or possibly even living ancestor, of the bumblebee reached the size of one's hand. The humming sound was exceptionally boisterous compared to the average bee.

What most folks, or rather most of the Man-folk (since that was usually where the chief ignorance rested), did not realize or care to remember was that the bumber was by all accounts an actual mount to the Faery-folk known as the Pixie. Of course, these were all according to the Aylsh. So why would the Man-folk make that a permanent mark in their own history? After all, Man was the reigning power of mixed force, intellect, and wisdom in the world. Right?

Aside from the occasional bedtime story, the Pixie was just another mythical creature used by learned and uneducated mothers alike to coax their wee ones peacefully to sleep. Now to an Aylsh, or another of the pure beings following the ways of the Wild, even one bumber would be a sure sign that at least one Pixie thrived nearby. Six might signify that a barn door was open in a nearby Pixie village and these bumbers were out to pasture.

But, true indeed, the Pixie was real and has been around since the very beginning. These magical creatures appear to be tiny Aylsh themselves in physical form, with the uniquely pointed ears and slender shapes. But they have the very pure spirit of creation within each of them. They are embodiments of the Initiator with altruistic intent and purpose. These delightful creatures are as innocent as the animals that roamed the lands. And they are yet extremely intelligent and wise in most cases, while overly playful in all.

It was nearing midday and the smooth, wooden plank draw-gate lay perfectly set in an iron bed in front of the opening that led into Tamelyn Keep. Recent mortar work could be seen where someone had done minor repairs to the fairly large, whitened blocks of rock that comprised the exterior, which rose to maybe sixty foot. The old cart clattered onto the wooden beams with a racket. Even though only raised at night, the weighty chains on both sides were glistening with fresh oil.

A slender boy of about thirteen summertides lurked within the courtyard once past the gate. Wybur smiled as wide as his ears would allow.

Little Chimy stood there with his face aglow, greeting weary travelers and visitors. His gray linen tunic was circled with a wide leather belt. He had the look of bored mischief, overflowing with vigor, as his face lit up upon finding Wybur's familiar figure. Chimy was the son of Mordrid and Ephritori, the couple that acted as caretakers for the keep.

"Me burbut! You are here again!" the boy cried with enthusiasm as he jumped up and down, raising his arms as though dancing with someone twice his height.

"And how is little Chim? Whoa, what is here in my knapsack? A fresh cinnamon crisped roll from Mum Straefyrshir. Very well, my lad. It is calling your name," retorted Wybur as he hopped off the cart.

It was well-known that Mum Straefyrshir cooked the best cinnamon rolls or anything else for that matter. Her family ran the coziest inn between Tamelyn and the vast city of Longshadows.

It was by no mistake or sudden whim that Wybur planned a stay at the inn every time he traveled back and forth to the keep. Whether he needed the rest or not.

A deep, booming voice rang out from behind Wybur. "Ho there. Why, Wybut… Is that you again so soon?"

Wybur glanced over his shoulder just in time to see the massive form of a man striding towards him, clasping a huge hand on Wybur's back. This nearly knocked him off his feet and right into the mule's arse. Startled and barely able to catch his breath, Wybur grimaced through a wheezing breath. "Mordrid…good to see you again."

Mordrid was a man of a man, not all that tall but quite generous in muscles. His arms and shoulders were uncannily large even for his physique. A braided, shoulder-length tail of black hair hung behind his bearded head. Dressed in deerskin breeches and sandals, there was always an enormous woodsman's axe hanging off a sling on his sun-darkened back. But he also had a belly to match, as he was known to be well-educated in the tolerance of respectable ale.

He stared down Wybur for a moment, his bushy eyebrows raised high and his head tilted upwards. "You return again so soon and don't bring me anything from your uncle?"

Wybur, now staring agape, looked to be at a loss for words. He could not even count on both hands how many times he had promised Mordrid some kind of oddity or gift from his uncle's wares. The Buttlecuts, Uncle Groelhof and Aunt Issa, were well-known for their trading company. It had been a very popular business for over one hundred years now.

It would be more correct to call it a turn of time. This had been the standard, at least across Thaldeia, when referring to a period of one hundred years.

Uncle Groelhof had the trading company passed down to him from his father, and to his father from his. And so on and so on. The expectation had always been that the eldest boy in the family would work for his father and eventually take over the business, then do the same thing with his own son. Such tradition was as commonplace within Thaldeia as a shadecat chasing a flying mouse.

Now there might be a broom in the wagon wheel, because Uncle Groelhof and Aunt Issa were the proud parents of two very young daughters. The couple had no lads, yet. Wybur saw this candle burning a long time ago, even before he moved in with them. He realized that they needed a boy to carry on the tradition. Such unvoiced intents and glimmering eyes full of the same led to near overbearing attempts at pleading with him to come live with them.

Of course, this occurred around the time of his parents' deaths. Uncle Groelhof was not as bad as Aunt Issa. She relentlessly broached the subject and constantly murmured the echoes of what would happen to Wybur if they should pass on to the Outer Halls. Wybur knew that she had good intentions.

He had felt so alone and miserable when he lost his family to the Red Ache. Aunt Issa's talk of impending gloom did not help matters and only bolstered his state of grief. His spirit had been driven into the ground, along with what was left of their burnt corpses. At least he had kin. It seemed only appropriate that he take them up on their offer. At that point, he needed the warm embrace of familiarity. And his aunt and uncle rode that wagon as hard as they could, though more so his aunt.

It was not long before Mordrid chimed back in as he grabbed Wybur around the shoulders with a quick smile stretching across his thick face. "Fear not, my little one, I am just playing with you. Where is that burbut smile that I know so well now? Now go get yourself some bellytimber before ya fall over." And then Mordrid was off, carried away by some task that had been silently driving him through the day.

One nickname that had stuck with Wybur to this day was *little burbut*. His mother started calling him that so long ago. His aunt followed suit and had not stopped yet. Wybur always felt confident that it would outgrow him, and they would stop. But no, the use of it actually seemed to thrive even more as he grew older.

At least his later years in attainment, what schooling was called, had been changed to tutoring in the home of his aunt and uncle. The name calling and teasing up to that point had been unbearable. Tutoring had been his saving grace, for he took very well to the study of knowledge.

In fact, he still could recite nearly anything that he had previously read or looked at for a few moments. Wybur could even now visualize and regurgitate books and other things that had been his as a wee one. This supernatural ability was thought to be a curse at first, but eventually turned to what it truly was, a gift of untold futures.

On the other hand, Mordrid seemed to enjoy making various oddities of Wybur's name. The favorite being Wybut. Others included *scuttlebutt*, and then there was *butter cutter*. But, in all fairness, Wybur knew that the heart was as mighty as the man.

For Mordrid did it solely out of endearment and always treated Wybur as an equal, if not kin.

As little Chimy tended to the mule and cart, Wybur made his way to Tamelyn Hall where he could appease his gnawing urgencies, a voracious appetite and thirst. Of course, cooking at Tamelyn meant the best this side of Kuhrzoth and drink meant the finest ale in the whole of Thaldeia.

The current lord of Tamelyn Keep, Lord Eggelstyk, also maintained one of the finest families of brew masters there could be had. None other than Jaez Bulderosa, one of the Bulderosa brothers, owned and operated a master brewery out of Tamelyn Keep. Jaez was one of four brothers who opened the Bulderosa Brothers Ale at various places across Thaldeia *to serve the finest with the finest*, as their saying went. Rumor had it that the precious liquid even had a calling down below Adan, as far as the southern port city of San Serboor. And this was at the farthest reach of the Southern Kingdoms.

Jaez ran an equally large brewery in Longshadows as well. Between the two, he supplied nearly the entire middle west of Thaldeia with the brew. Many surrounding establishments would actually pay extra for shipments of the stuff. Then, if not already noted from previous elaboration, there were rumors that Mordrid also kept shop here at the keep solely for this reason.

Mordrid had helped this last heir to Tamelyn Keep for quite some time now. Actually, the word steward might be a better label at that. Maybe it had been thirteen years since that day when he had appeared to Lord Eggelstyk, though Ephritori did not look to have aged a day. Lord Rhu Eggelstyk was undeniably a direct descendant of Sedgewyn Tamelyn, at least through an uncounted number of generations.

The surname was lost one hundred and fifty years ago when the lord at the time got himself eaten by a gigantic cave bear up in the Purple Peaks. The lady then remarried many years later. But they always maintained the name of the keep for pure recognition.

As a side note, the lord that was eaten by the cave bear had been known as a committed gemologist. Legends of endless swaths of hidden gem-encrusted caves rolled off the tongues of every adventurer and bard back in that day. This babble ran him foolish and ragged until he ventured into the wrong one with too few guards.

Tamelyn Hall, considered the great hall at the keep, was run by none other than Mordrid's wife. Now Ephritori was a mystery worth most anything in an attempt to either unravel or at least ponder over. She was the enigmatic maiden in her own privileged right—a young lass of unequaled beauty.

Her Aylsh features, the pointed and pronounced ears, poked out amidst her flowing, red-hued, golden locks of thick hair. But even she did not know just how much of the pure Aylsh blood she really had. Her look bespoke of only youth and beauty. None could ever even guess what her age might be. A simple black leather band always pulled the sides of her hair back and over the long half braid on the back of her head. Big and fierce dark blue eyes shone with unbridled passion and individuality normally unheard of within the majority of, if not all, the fairer ones of Man-folk in these times.

Rumors abounded that she had been of Aylsh royalty by birthright, maybe even of Man-folk as well, and that she was rescued from the fiery fate of her kind by Mordrid's two-handed axe. Of course, Mordrid would receive mysterious cloaked travelers and then be lost amongst unknown deliberations in one of the dark corners of the hall until well past the witches' light of the night. This added more fuel to the myriad of rumors as well.

Now Mordrid was one that had never been known to discuss his past. What was definitive about Mordrid, at some point, was that he had spent a considerable amount of time with the Black Legion.

The Black Legion was immensely steeped within history and lore. A powerful force that began in the origins of righteousness and had grown deep into the bounds of the gold coffer. While the men of the Legion may not see it so, those that pull their strings know better.

Lord Dulf Janlouk, a well-known and self-made adventurer of the times, was the one who started such a mercenary company. The Legion was filled with rugged, professional warriors who believed in cause and ethics. Ever since that day, for well over a thousand years now, the Black Legion held the distinct reputation as the most disciplined, professional, and effective company of fighters ever.

The origins of the Legion were first founded within the Knights of the Wild. These valorous warriors held title and holdings literally forged by decades of adventuring, as well as defending the innocent. These prolific, self-proclaimed men formed the original core of the Legion as an enterprise established to maintain order and provide protection throughout the frontier lands of Thaldeia.

Of course, it was called the Wild Order back in the day. The Wild Order was formed roughly about the year 135 BA.

The Legion took its name over a hundred years later during the Great Reform, as birthright and nobility took shape across the lands...and as these nobles seized power. Those who considered themselves the powers-to-be, due to their birthright as royalty, then worked to disband the Knights of the Wild. This was done to seat their own power base, to raise their own might to protect and defend the lands. And their own might to collect the taxes.

At this time, the remaining commanders decided to rename the organization as the Black Legion with a new charter. This was done under the direction of the outspoken and courageous head Knight of the Wild himself, Janlouk the Black Cat. The remaining men of the Wild Order were dispersed into bands and each one went a separate direction.

This was done to establish free mercenary companies throughout the reaches of Thaldeia, but still under one charter. Many more of the former knights of the Wild Order were absorbed into the various armies and militias that formed during the period. But most of these had established families, or some other tie, which they did not want to leave or move from.

Before the Great Reform, the Knights of the Wild each had their own keeps. These included Razorrock Keep, Mereglav Keep, Innallym Keep, Andavyr Keep, and Zholkor Keep. Most of these lay in ruin today or are obscure remnants of what they once were.

Charming landscape surrounding the homes of farmers and settlers, yet ripe with the history of times gone by.

The period following the Great Reform also saw the rise of the guilds and guilders. At first, the fighters' guilds sprouted up across the Man-folk kingdoms of Thaldeia. Within another hundred years, others rose as well. Before long, there were guilds for whatever one could put a name to—wizards' guilds, mages' guilds, pugilists' guilds, and of course, the less savory kind that involved thieves and cutthroats.

Presently, the Legion garrisoned a fortified company in each of the loftier cities across Thaldeia—Nuuroc, Longshadows, Adan, and Tornspire. The existing commander was named Axyander Blackshield the Steelborn. While in command of all, he personally stayed with the Nuuroc Company. There was no lack of gold for the Legion, as all knew of their reputation.

"Goo' day, lady Ephritori, how are you faring?" queried Wybur in his best tone. He approached the serving table inside the hall, secretly praying there was at least one of the tender roast chickens with potatoes and soup left.

Ephritori was wiping clean a portion of the table that had recently been vacated by other travelers passing through. As usual, she wore a simple forest green dress bordered with tanned deerskin. Her face lit up a bit more than usual as she fully turned towards young Wybur.

"Glad to see you've returned so soon there, Wybur. How are the aunt and uncle now in Longshadows? Did they chase you back here already?" She winked and smiled, teasing him a bit, knowing that he disliked living with them at times. Well, maybe all of the time.

Small talk was made with Ephritori while Wybur awaited a huge plate of freshly roasted turkey and vegetable stuffing, the fare for the late-suns. The awed look on his face showed how quickly his interest in the chicken waned.

The term late-suns referred to the period of the day between midday and sunsdown.

After the relaxing and much needed meal, Wybur paid a visit to Lord Eggelstyk, who decided to have his lemon succotash tea early. The nobleman, now in his late sixties, always marveled at dialogs with Wybur.

Lord Eggelstyk really took to Wybur's ability to perfectly recite everything that he read or saw. Even Mordrid had never seen the old man so animated by anything else. Rhu Eggelstyk always sought to draw out verbatim quotes from an already selected volume just to hear Wybur recite it from memory. Then he would snort and cackle after each passage that Wybur put words to, before sipping his tea.

On the third day at the Loremasters Keep, Wybur was finally able to back off his day laborer status or whatever it was that he had become since promising his time to Lord Eggelstyk. Originally, Wybur had stated he would do whatever was required, or needed, for just one day of perusing to his heart's content. Perusing obviously meant that he was to have overwhelming access to everything within the keep that he longed to study or read. Of course, this turned into six days of Wybur's unfettered help followed by two days of leisure per visit, although this trip was only half that time.

The particular volume that he removed from the dusty shelf was hardbound in large, blackened leather covers by tough, treated sinew. The leather was very worn and gouged from many turns of neglect. The glyphs and marks that ran across the cover bespoke a bygone era, ages old script from an even more ancient time. The deeply pocked etchings felt like crevasses.

Fortunately Wybur studied far and wide when it came to the different tongues. He knew this writing, and he marveled at the intricate craft as it soaked up his attention completely.

Olri Uchrah…yes, that is the title, thought Wybur. It translated to Dark Manifestation. *But what did that exactly mean?*

Once opened, the parchment pages felt as though he was pulling apart enormous leaves that had been stuck together on the ground in steady decay during late harvestspell.

What was that, thought Wybur.

He barely caught what appeared to be black, wispy smoke erupting from within the pages around the center binding. He assumed it was his imagination playing tricks in the low light. Only lanterns burned nearby, casting an uneven and ever-changing glow to the chamber surroundings.

He quickly slapped the covers of the book together and squeezed his eyes shut, as if to clear them as well as his thoughts. Then he gingerly peeled the front cover back with two of his fingers. Inside was more writing in the script of a very ancient language—that of the Black Clans. So this book was written by the Aylsh Ismaru. Or, at least, in the language. And in the oldest form.

Of note, and what had grasped his attention previously, was the charcoal-colored shape of a half-sun with lightning bolt-shaped black rays stretched above it. It was the sign of Siri. This particular crest had an eclipsed and partially lightened portion at the bottom of the sun, which marked it as one of the oldest made. Or maybe the mark was made by one of oldness itself.

This mark supposedly predated the time when Siri lost dominion over Death and Chaos, but still maintained hold over the realms of Darkness and Shadow. Speculation placed this shift in supremacy several thousand years before the present era.

Wybur had been spending time at the keep over the past eleven years, so he knew the various rooms full of volumes and materials almost as well as he did the back of his hand. There was a degree of organization to the madness. His feverish scanning during his last visit about two score and ten days ago, of these particular books in this shelf area, solely produced this one book for further inquisition. Anything in this section was considered to be of the oldest in all the collections at Tamelyn Keep.

This one book, with the darkened rising half-sun found on the inside cover, piqued his interest so much that his heart had raced. However, he did not have the time during the last visit to begin studying it.

Livforena had been very specific that what she absolutely needed would be something referencing the location of the arch-wizard Haqnimemza. A tomb? A home, castle, or keep? There was no other hint to this vague witch hunt.

She also told him that the ancient rune of Siri, the Lord of Shadows, might help. But she was not sure what this actually meant. What she had been sure of, and overly anxious about, was that this location had to be found. And soon.

The pages of the book had obviously been treated with frozen then superheated ochre jelly. This process had been used by the ancients to ensure that information lasted through the ages without the need to scribe every hundred years or so. Of course, it had to be purple ochre, as the others were either too caustic or had some other equally detrimental reason to avoid use. The mere process of actually finding and then subduing such a creature was of much difficulty.

The volume he held on to, the one that kept drawing his attention, was labeled *Chronicles of The New Era: Pre Arterium to SA 250*. It had been the only one mentioning the arch-wizard Haqnimemza at all. This book appeared to be a compilation of sorts by more than one fact finder, all of whom apparently provided their information to one unnamed author. In actuality, there were several volumes that covered the periods through the year SA 1450.

The latest date scribed onto this particular one was SA 1262 so it was indeed brittle. Haqnimemza had been mentioned within the first sections that covered Arterium's Ascension, which was roughly through the beginning of the year SA 1. Even though history recorded that Arterium died such a death that his Ascension could not be fulfilled.

One interesting mention of the wizard contained a set of ciphers written in ancient Black Clan. These were written within parentheses immediately following his name on this one occasion.

The wizard was actually mentioned in several of the first sections, which described how he went from being the Master of the Deep to King Arterium's arch-wizard and right hand. The final mention that Wybur had seen of his name had the ciphers written after it. This morsel of information declared that the wizard had disappeared from the face of Thaldeia. It even claimed that King Arterium voiced this fact openly, along with his frustration that it was right at the time when the king needed the wizard the most. This was, of course, during those days preceding Arterium's expedition into Isnuuthghor.

Not long after this, Arterium fell in battle with the Many Eyed One. But, to Wybur, this was the intriguing part. This was due to the fact that the ciphers were written after the mention of the wizard at the point within the volume recording when he had vanished. Coupled with what Livforena had told him, Wybur suspected that the ciphers had something to do with the location of where the wizard disappeared to. Maybe even why.

That same page that mentioned the wizard with the ciphers following his name also had the ancient rune of Siri adorned at the bottom of the page. No other portion of any of the volumes within these chronicles contained anything even remotely similar to that. The ciphers in parentheses, once translated out of Black Clan, equated to a pair of obscure marks. This was followed by the numbers seventeen, twenty-three, and twenty-nine.

The marks or runes preceded the numbers, but Wybur could not ascertain their meaning. And Wybur was fairly well-learned for these times. He had studied several different tongues, as well as the ancient ones. But he could not identify what these first two marks were or what their origins could be for that matter.

And now he had come across the ancient black leather-bound volume with the darkened, rising half-sun inside the cover and those same mysterious yet unknown marks in the upper right-hand corner of almost every page in it. So he turned to each of those pages that married up with the numbers within the set of ciphers. As he did so, his bewildered frenzy turned to a consuming awe. What he read spurred him into studying the entire book until well after sunsup.

Wybur could not believe his luck, or maybe even talent as Livforena had stated it to be. If it was luck, then there had to be one chance in a million that he would have been able to place those two very different old volumes together in such a way as to unravel the mystery. Like completing a detailed and intricate puzzle of sorts. Now, if it was fate or destiny as he believed, there might be more profound things afoot than originally thought.

And still something did not feel right about this whole thing. But he just could not place his finger on it. A gut feeling.

Maybe it was just a feeling coming from all of this secretive hero business that the woman with the Veiled Ones had stuck in his mind. Yet this same feeling seemed to arise within him whenever he stayed at the inn. And whenever he received his guest late in the night.

But how could that be wrong? Right or wrong, how would he know the difference anyway? After all, he had never been with a woman...at least not before that first night when Livforena approached him.

He was staying at the Straefyrshir Inn on that night, so he was relaxed and comfortable—very much in a self-reposing state of indulgence. After he agreed to assist her, Livforena had hinted to him that he would receive a special guest. This guest would come to him late in the night after she left his room. It was late this night, way past the witches-hand, that Rosella first introduced herself. Afterward, Rosella always paid him a visit in this same fashion every time he met with Livforena.

The next day, Wybur set out early on his return trip to Longshadows. By midday, he knew the waterfall would not be much farther. The familiar face of a chipped boulder smiled at him, telling him so.

There was a wide bridge made of rough timber that had been built over this portion of the River Oran. The River Oran was a good sized meadow across and usually the bottom could not be seen even though the water ran clear.

One absolutely had to know about the waterfall's existence to be able to find it. It was located up a feeder stream that flowed down from the rolling hills. This stream was a short walk north of the bridge along the west bank. Wybur knew the bridge would be in sight soon, and then he would have to secure his belongings prior to walking back to where the waterfall was located.

It was the middle of late-suns, roughly about the time he usually took tea or qurra with a morsel, when he reached the bridge and pulled off the road into the long, lush grass. There were several small cedars growing with a nice mound around them that afforded a little protection for his goods during the rendezvous with Livforena.

Without getting too long-winded, qurra was a beverage served best while very hot. The muddied water look came from ground beans harvested off of the qurra tree.

Soon after settling in his cart and Shab, he found himself trudging along the feeder stream. It was not long before the rushing noise of the small cascade faded in from the background.

He was staring at his feet as they pushed the long grass aside with each step when he heard the rustling in the undergrowth. Whatever it was seemed fairly large to him, and he thought he heard a long hiss and guttural groan. Wybur began to pick up his pace along the side of the stream in a rising panic. All the while, he threw quick glares behind him, half expecting some monstrous form to emerge from the brush.

Suddenly, a dark figure loomed in front of him, sinister appendages grabbing his shoulders and stopping him dead in his tracks. Wybur's heart leapt out of his chest, but then slowed to a flutter as he recognized the supple form of Livforena. His skin shimmered in the bath of a cold sweat from the mix of fear and adrenaline.

Livforena's eyes soothed his frenzy as she spoke, "Wybur, all is well. Have no fear. For I always have others with me. You are more than safe, trust me and fear not the dark."

Wybur, unmoving but in a state of jumbled hysteria, stammered, "Me? No, of course not. I merely thought I was running late is all." He wiped his brow with the back of his hand as the tremors slowly subsided in his voice and then his body.

Livforena was taller than Wybur by a good foot. That black metallic half mask covered most of her upper face, while her other features were hidden by the long hood of her cloak.

But those purplish eyes. Now he noticed that the right eye had a swirl of red hue mixed with it. It was only visible for a moment though. Tiny, black lines spider-webbed through the whites surrounding those purple orbs. Then, once she moved away, he could no longer tell. Her grip had been exceptionally, and unexpectedly, strong when she brought him to a complete standstill.

A smile flickered across her face for a moment. Then she turned away and strode towards the waterfall. "Come, Wybur. I brought a treat for us while we talk."

There was an outgrowth of large rocks beside the pool formed from the falling water. Livforena led him to one that was flat and smooth. A small leather satchel sat in the middle. She seated herself and began to open the drawstrings of the satchel.

Her eyes smiled at him now as a corner of her mouth playfully twisted. "You know, deep within the Aylsh kingdoms in the east, thousands of Aylsh thrive and make their home there. Now there are many good things made by the First Folk, and that includes fares of all kinds. I have brought you a treat, still fresh from the hearth."

She withdrew several square-shaped lumps wrapped in white linen, holding the small cakes up in offering to Wybur.

Wybur's eyes sparkled a bit as he remembered telling her how he wished he could experience the exotic things of other cultures, particularly the Aylsh. Much of his studies had described the Aylsh as being masters with the hearth at their cuisine. Naturally, with his affinity towards such things, he could only dream of actually trying what sounded so tasty one day.

She smiled at him and winked. "Now this is Aylsh bread, the real thing. It is called munyurlerie dor, or bread of the sun."

As he savored the sweet taste and airy texture of the treat, Wybur talked about several things that had occurred in Longshadows while Livforena listened.

Once the bread was gone, she went silent for several moments while staring into the splashing water of the clear pool. "Tell me, Wybur, what have you come across in regards to the wizard? Have you had any luck?"

Wybur began to recount his findings over the last few visits to Tamelyn Keep. He started with the collection of volumes labeled *Chronicles of The New Era*. The only one mentioning the wizard Haqnimemza had been the first. He then explained how he had noted the strange set of ciphers written in ancient Black Clan within parentheses after the final mentioning of the wizard's name in that book.

Next, he excitedly went through how he had found the ancient book that was bound with plain blackened leather. Olri Uchrah, or, in Common, Dark Manifestation. This book contained the mysterious marks from the *Chronicles of The New Era: Pre Arterium to SA 250* on every one of its pages. The underlying significance of these unknown marks in front of the numbers had him flailing backwards in anticipation.

Wybur speculated that Livforena would probably be able to decipher them and confirm their meanings, whether herself or by one of her associates. But his first thought on them was that they were connected to Siri, who she had mentioned to him previously in this puzzle of puzzles.

He went over the most ancient runes of Siri found within the front cover, the darkened half-sun with the lighter half oval shape at the bottom.

A mischievous smile of boasting pride overcame Wybur as he progressed into the tie between all of this unraveled information. The three numerals in the first book (17, 23, 29) all referred to page numbers in the second book. No one probably would ever have thought to make this connection, except one with Wybur's talent (added Wybur).

Now each of those pages in the ancient black, leather-bound book had their own unique clue. The first one that was mentioned provided the first clue to the location of the wizard. The second and third both added enough detail to make the location exact, or as exact as possible given the circumstances.

The first one had a set of parentheses thrown randomly into the page with the words *Western Spires*. The second page identified had another similar set of parentheses with the words *Crystal Peak*, and on the third page were the words *Nook of the Reach*. Of course, everything was written in ancient Black Clan.

Wybur stared at Livforena wide-eyed, now very embroiled in the material. "My lady, if you had not told me about the possibility of the Lord Siri being involved in some way, I perhaps would not have uncovered that old black book either. The only thing that glued me to that withering book had been that ancient rune of Siri inside the cover."

It looked as though Livforena was deep in thought still and not even paying any attention to his last words. But she was definitely paying meticulous attention to everything said by him. "Wybur, this is extremely important, what you have done. You may have just done it! I don't know how you managed it, but no doubt some form of destiny was involved. You, Wybur, have been the ordained one. I just can't believe it!"

Wybur's chest rose with a slow breath, and his eyes sparkled as his head lifted. But he stopped short, still thinking about the other possibilities disclosed within that black book.

"Livforena, wait, there's more… Well, maybe. After reading that ancient book, I have a feeling it may have been written by Siri himself, unless I am a complete mooncalf. There are things inside that book that appear to be forthcoming…still coming around…possibly in the future.

"It mentions *Daradkorum*, or Dark Cabal. *Sorcere* means Seers. Anyways, it speaks of the rise of these Seers and the coming forth of this Dark Cabal of old…forming and doing terrible things against all that is good.

"I think the book lays open some sinister plot, like you said. It made me a bit worried after reading it. And when I inquired with Lord Eggelstyk about how the book made its way into Tamelyn, he told me he had never seen it before and was not sure."

She grasped his hands in hers and looked deeply into his eyes. "Listen, my friend, do not worry even for a moment. I think we have uncovered this thing in time. But I need to go immediately and set some things into motion for the better of us all. Now tell me, how much do you remember about this withered black book, the second one you found."

"Everything, my lady, everything. My mind just works that way. Do you want me to recite the content of it to you?" Wybur held his breath, the heel of his foot thumping quickly at the chance to add even more of his talent to the table.

She quickly looked up to the sky and then flashed a monstrous glare toward him. "No, that is all right, Wybur. But you can describe this book in detail to me, and exactly where it is located right at this moment."

It was as though a cold wind bit the nape of his neck. This unmistakable change in her tone sent a shudder through him.

After Wybur carefully described the book, he recalled how he had left it with Mordrid for safe keeping until he could return.

They parted ways not long afterwards, and Wybur made his way back to where he left Shab and his cart.

The last portion of travel to the inn left him with crowded thoughts concerning Livforena. Not only her, but everything that had happened and was said and done since first meeting her. The books went back and forth in his mind, many chapters or sections flowed to him word for word as he rode along.

Enshwayne Elypotus il Marilaan… Locks of Falling Darkness, Wybur muttered to himself. He could only imagine what the contents of the book might refer to.

Wybur pondered his recent foray with the lady of the Veiled Ones. What was that strange look in her eyes when he suggested that he could recite the entire book to her? It had caught him off guard for a spell, as he had not seen that aspect of her temperament before.

She was always very warmhearted, sincere, and forthcoming. But this look from her had spooked him, like a sudden freezing gale of ice had blown over those warm, purple orbs of hers for just a moment. That was unmistakable. A good portion of the late-suns seemed only moments with such a commotion storming through his head.

Once at the Straefyrshir Inn, he enjoyed a hearty supper while quietly seated in the corner. Several other guests mingled around the eatery, but Wybur was in no mood for company. All the excitement of his findings and his meeting with Livforena had worn him out. Now he felt like a huge ball of yarn that had come unrolled and was all askew.

A traveling bard was the one fancy that grabbed his eye and his ears. She struck up her stringed instrument at the center table as one of the Straefyrshir fledglings cleared it of dishes. The young lass could not have been more than a score and a half of summertides old. After a short time spent listening to her resplendent tunes, Wybur felt himself loosen up and relax. His mind lulled to the enchanting sound.

The bard wore a wide-brimmed felt hat colored as green as the forest. It canted back on her head, which was full of thick, russet-colored hair that danced about her shoulders. One side of the brim was molded and curved straight up along the headpiece, where a green plume draped back. A small gold, pyramid-shaped trinket with a round, silver middle piece was attached to this portion of the brim.

Black and brown leather clothing adorned her strikingly fit physique. A fine rapier with a fully jeweled pommel lay sheathed at her left side.

She slowly tuned the strings and then rolled into an ancient ballad about the struggle of Arterium. Her voice flowed out over the small crowd at the inn like a warm summertide breeze carrying the low morning rush of the woods.

> *"On the surface of the frozen waters of*
> *the dead there stirred one of the night.*
>
> *Afore arose the figures of the dread and*
> *the beginning of time shone light.*
>
> *Not far were the knights of steel and*
> *the one Arterium with all his might."*

Several moments of intensified, low pitched, long rolling notes played before the next vocals.

> *"The beast strode out of the very shadows*
> *and took in the visions of the land,*
>
> *And lo, beholden to it of breath and*
> *death there raised a forlorn hand.*
>
> *Too late did Arterium sway his swords,*
> *for they all belittl'd as it spewed air,*
> *earth, and sand."*

The bard slowly churned the word *sand* and held it for a few moments before the long, lonesome note dragged out.

> *"As the hand came crashing down, those*
> *valiant did fall amid black ashes.*
>
> *'Twas as if there had been none of them*
> *cold warriors born at all amidst the*
> *black lightning flashes,*
>
> *And still standing was that many eyed*
> *monster from the clashes."*

Again the tune went slow and drawn out until the last sequence slowly rolled out.

> *"The mighty Arterium, now an undead*
> *shamble himself, once life now ascended.*
>
> *No one remained to aid the downfall*
> *of evil, everyone only pretended,*

But Arterium alone did jump and

drag the many eyed beast to the chasm,

And it was ended."

Once in his room for the evening, Wybur locked the door with a loud click. The brass lantern beside the huge bed came to life as he put flame to it. Folding a triangular portion of the linens over, he sat on the edge of the bed while closing his eyes.

These past few days had taken their toll on him. The excitement, the anxiety, of seeing Livforena and that way she had looked at him. He still could not figure out exactly what to call it. Anger? Hostility mixed with spite?

A noise from outside the window stirred Wybur from his thoughts as that sharp sting of adrenaline sparked.

Quiet, old friend, he thought as it was probably a branch tapping the window.

Approaching the window, he noticed the latch was undone, and the two panes of glass rattled slightly with the wind. He let out a gentle sigh.

Then his heart skipped a beat as he noticed the giant snow owl seated right outside on the edge of the roof. It was right there, on the other side of the glass and not three foot from him. Staring at him and unmoving. As Wybur looked into the blackness of those huge, round eyes, he lost the fear and anxiety that had taken hold of him.

While the feathered outline of the enormous bird was as large as Wybur himself, those eyes bespoke more wisdom and clarity than any fervid nobleman could emulate with words. Visions of majestic mountain serenity, from a lofty view of many leagues up in the sky, pulsed through his mind. It was as though he dreamt, peacefully asleep. But he knew he was not.

Truth be told, Wybur did not know whether he was awake or asleep. He blinked his eyes several times in an attempt to figure out which. Then he closed them again as he relaxed his imagination.

Calm down. Everything is fine, he told himself.

When at last he opened his eyes, still looking out the window, the owl was gone. If it had been there at all.

Had he sleepwalked? No, that could not be. He distinctly remembered the robust meal and the provocative crescendo of the bard's tune downstairs before he had retired to his room.

The fine swathing of a snowy quill, now stuck to the roof, pulled his gaze inquisitively. It lightly hovered just outside the window sill. A cold wind caught it and the feather danced upwards ever so slightly.

Wybur opened the window and reached for the feather then quickly closed the panes of glass. He firmly latched them together. A long shiver ran through him from the chill of the night air. At least that was what he thought the shiver was from.

As he settled back into bed, leathery wings flapped dully through the open rafters of the roof above. The sound was choked by the thick wooden shingles.

Moments later, there was a gentle knock on his door. Oh, yes. Livforena's reward for serving her grandiose cause. He knew it was her. Rosella.

Wybur had never been with a woman, ever. At least not before he met Livforena. For no woman would take him for who he was, or how he looked. He felt that he was cursed. Not only through his appearance, but also his mannerisms and the odd way he felt around women. Of course, he never felt this sense of awkwardness with his mother or even his aunt. No, it saved itself solely as a monster to rear its cruelty around women he thought fondly of. Those whom he admired, thought about in such a carnal way. And this burden would smash down upon his courage, his manliness, forever upsetting any spark of love.

He always spent the night at the Straefyrshir Inn while traveling the Old Road back and forth from Longshadows to Tamelyn Keep. After each time that he met with Livforena, he would find Rosella outside his door late in the night.

He quietly unlocked his door and nudged it open. She slowly strode in, her white gossamer gown rustling as it danced with the night wind.

To Wybur, she was a divine messenger come to deliver his omnipotence. Long raven hair showered down to her shoulders, caressing her back. So dainty and petite. Beautiful hazel eyes rested on a perfect face. Such red lips stole Wybur's essence without him even knowing it.

When they first met, she had called herself Rosella. Then she softly whispered in his ear that she was an agent of exotic charm come to worship a gallant warrior of the cause.

Poor Wybur became so embarrassed at this first rendezvous. He had lost control of his pleasure instrument within the first moments of just sitting beside her on the bed. The effect had worn him out, but she stayed with him the entire night and brought him around, again and again. She also lit several candles, which more than displayed her wares within the surrounding aura of anticipation. Wybur was thoroughly spellbound right from the first moment he saw her. Their tryst seemed almost destined to be and nowhere near fortuitous.

Rosella closed the distance between them and grasped his hands. One of her hands then slowly drew back and playfully let her gown slide down and off her body, leaving her strikingly tanned nakedness to taunt him. The scent of her skin drifted over him like freshly cut flowers as it further consumed him.

"My lord," a dainty finger was lightly placed to his lips, "hush now and allow yourself to be worshipped." Rosella's serene voice played like the wind and nearly mesmerized him as she slowly pushed him backwards on the bed.

§ § §

For Wybur, it was this very night that the visions started to permeate his once restful sleep. The appearance of the giant snow owl foretold unimagined terrors and fitful bouts of awaking in a cold sweat. Wybur assumed the worst and thought that ill omens had fallen over him.

After the visit by Rosella, Wybur fell into a deep sleep. He suddenly found himself seated downstairs again, listening to the enthralling music of the bard.

Sometimes, maybe even most of the time, destiny and fate work in mysterious ways and favor the unbalanced. The meek are called upon to test the endless bounds of time and existence. Whether an immortal play at social design and order, or one of cunningly plotted and ruthless efficiency. Only higher powers know the reality of things. And the actors are left to their immediate periphery and whatever else can be assimilated through their interpretations.

The young bard strummed her sorange. On she sang, plucking the strings:

> *"Onward the mountain of a man*
> *moved for his own sorrow driven.*
>
> *"Though small of stature, the heart*
> *rang mountainous and mighty.*
>
> *"Oh, Wybur the great, Wybur the*
> *powerful, all can fall to bended knees*
> *or perish.*
>
> *"The butter cutter who astounded all*
> *and took to the wild winds of change."*

Wybur's heart raced with a startled double-take upon hearing his name. Not only his name, but one that had been used to tease him.

What was that? He poked himself in the chest with a finger in an attempt to wake himself up, but he felt the sharp jab.

Suddenly, the lanterns went out, and he was left in utter darkness. There was complete silence, except for the slow, rhythmic melody as it eerily played on.

Then the lanterns flared again. Wybur found himself abruptly thrust into a scene of carnage.

All the patrons at the inn, along with the family that tended it, were dead and lying in their own bloody piles of clothed skin and bones. Their faces portrayed the final look of horrible pain and fear, captured in self-portraits of death.

The bard played on, except all of her features slowly darkened as though a huge inky cloud played over her. Wicked, glowing purple eyes stared him down from the sinister, blackened face.

A giant white owl, no—the very same one seen earlier—swooped over her head. It flew just shy of the high rafters, with a flurry of tiny feathers showering down.

And then Wybur awoke. It was pitch black, and the darkness of his room engulfed him in a cold sweat.

Everything was quiet and still as he tried to shake the vivid memory of the nightmare.

He briefly touched the long scratch on his upper chest where Rosella had dug into him. She drew blood while entwined in their ecstasy.

Then Wybur picked up the huge owl's feather from the night stand and slowly leaned back upon the bed. The airy light texture on his fingers, the pureness of the striking shade of white, drew him into a sense of calm. But he did not sleep another wink that night and watched as the duo suns brought light back to the world. To the world and to the familiar surroundings of the inn that he knew so well.

Chapter 4:

Lore of the Ancients

Not a one of being shall step upon the aura of perseverance which rests inwards. Only stirring such harmony will be the enlightening of one's existence.

–Second Edict of Lord Braxis, etched upon the Great Slates, recovered by Arterium circa the year 13 BA.

 tremendous blast shook the cavern walls, spewing rocky debris everywhere while the air filled with fine, powdery

dust. The powerful force left small flames where it had detonated and sulfuric-scented smoke vented away from the area.

Priestess Sahrya Omrasstefor Khajrynghul, now of Clan Tharasvrul, stood unmoving and uninfluenced by the turmoil. A shimmering, bluish, globe-shaped veil enveloped her, deflecting everything away from her. The dust-soaked air parted like a fork in a river and gently wrapped itself around the scintillating globe. Her dimly gleaming suit of chainmaille peeked out from small, vague separations within the indigo colored ghost cloak. Tiny reflections of the destruction being wrought flared with spouts of red life about her form.

The ghost cloak was very symbolic, as it was passed through the clan and down to her...finally. Such a cloak bespoke the formidable aura and power of a clan to the individual that it was presented to, with that individual being the priestess of her people. A priestess was an embodiment of all that a clan stood for. One who not only counseled with the clan elder but also was viewed as even above the elder, for transcendent purposes.

The silvery, shaded outline of an enormous skull ran the entire length of the back. A huge, elongated red eye ran down each side of the front of the cloak. Once there was movement to the ghost cloak, then it assumed a haunting but sinister look and appeared as though the pair of eyes floated towards the observer. Light traces of silver dust woven into the living material flared occasionally, giving away the true unnatural presence. Although made from what looked to be a mix of silk and wool, truth be told, the cloak was dated back at least fifteen turns. Nothing of this world could survive such a torment of time.

Her ancient headpiece, adorned with many precious gems and jewels, could be misconstrued as a wicked skull. It was made of a dark metal that mimicked iron but obviously was not. The cap of it encased the entire upper portion of her head while segments weaved around and down along the sides. The crescent moon-shaped portion that dipped down over her eyes and upper nose made her fiery purple eyes blaze out, both contrasted against a blackest of black. Those piercing eyes shone out from the holes in the headpiece as though they were daggers, the right one having a distinct reddish-hued swirl.

A fang-like protrusion ran down each side of her nose nearly to her chin. These fangs had inlaid ivory running their entire length.

The headpiece not only prevented the scrying of her thoughts and activities, whether from close or afar, but also immunized the wearer from outside mental influences of any kind. Such were the powerful devices worn by those with something to lose, or those prone to such possibilities. These things were of ancient origins, at least going back to the early days of the Black Clan's existence.

Standing at nearly six and a half foot, Sahrya stood tall for one of the Black Clans. She had studied and learned much for her existence of near twelve hundred years, possibly more than any other being that was still breathing. Long, straight, azure-colored hair full of small, silver studded braids fell past her shoulders, cascading out from the unique blackened headpiece. Her charcoal skin was not nearly as dark as the blacks of her eyes. But the beauty of her features combined to present a stunning figure of goddess proportions. Such a persona would drive any mere mortal to do unthinkable things for even the slightest look from her.

She vividly remembered her early years under the care of her true clan's priestess. Those memories flooded back to her. The screams and cries of her kin as they were butchered and raped reverberated again within her mind.

Those were tempestuous times. All of her clan had been wiped from the face of Thaldeia, with the exception of her. And what that forsaken time of dark events left her with… Well, that was a deep, dark pit. One that would never fully regain whatever light might have been held within it before.

The forceful King Arterium had indeed led an expedition to the Black Clan fortress, but history did not record nor care to remember what his true purpose had been.

The Ancient One imparted many things upon Sahrya besides the dark arts. One thing was an early lesson in real history and the rise of Man-folk. Her true clan, Clan Omrasstefor, was rebuilding the homeland fortress of Isnuuthghor at the time of the incursion by Arterium in his so-called fabled expedition. For King Arterium was anything but what was portrayed by the recorders of deeds.

Clan Omrasstefor's scouts had already been sent out to the eight winds in order to bring the known Black Clans back to the homeland where they could unite and reclaim the lost fortunes and power of old. A little known portion of that time period suggested the depraved acts committed by the men of Arterium and by King Arterium himself. But none of these things ever made it into any record.

At the time, King Arterium had already marched on and staked out Isnuuthghor itself. He had the scouts captured and butchered. The scouts barely made it down to the bottom slopes of the

Forsaken Pass at the southern end of the Gloomy Mountains, the gateway to the dark fortress.

What took place next, on Arterium's orders, never found its way into any chronicles or history lessons of the era, ever. But she did not experience this herself, as it was before her time. Sahrya had been born afterward, when Clan Omrasstefor had dwindled and fled into the mountains weakened from Arterium's invasion. Clan Omrasstefor never regained her former glory and was left in a devastated state when the marauders came later.

She remembered that feeling of higher purpose, that raptured soaring that evoked her frenzied pursuit. The Ancient One had confided in her that saving her life had been no haphazard circumstance. He had been led to her because she was to be the instrument of resurrection for her people. And, as he stated it, the death for Man-folk and any that followed them. Death for any that did not bow down. Compounded with this was her past of persecution.

It had been Man-folk that destroyed her home, murdered her clan, and subjected her and several other females to rape and mutilation. Then eventual death. Thieving marauders seeking gold, treasure, and other riches. There was no honor or compassion in their ruthless and vicious acts. Nor even reason for them to do what they did. If the Ancient One had not saved her, she would have been another body left to rot. They had even slain the clan's *rhaanmri*, meaning pact in the Common tongue. Clan Omrasstefor had assumed a clowder of the wild cats for their rhaanmri, imposing black panthers. And a Black Clan's rhaanmri was an extremely sacred affinity.

The wild cats of Zholryn were very numerous, although mostly stealthy, cunning predators. The folk of Thaldeia knew them to be such things as panthers, cougars, lions, and tigers. Mostly, the wild cats were all those beyond the average cat that roamed the cities of Man or other places of civilization. But the world was full of even more kinds than this, though those were outside the confines of Thaldeia.

The Ancient One was of such power and wisdom. She did not know exactly what it was, what he was, but she listened to and believed all that came from it. The thing must be some form of higher divinity. A thing of higher purpose. It had saved her. It had nourished her back from the deepest darkness.

Indeed, she had been broken beyond redemption, all hope completely dissipated, and a cavernous vacuum had been created that yearned for something to fill it. The dark arts easily formed within that void as she embraced the black ways so old that few others even knew of their names.

But another powerful force had rooted itself within as well. Deep-set malice and an insatiable need for retribution rose with learning and knowledge, but overwhelming all in a pyramidal climb to envelop her innate essence and drive. And, just as the words of the Ancient One had voiced, she was destined to bring the world under dominion of the Black Clans. She was to have no remorse for anything whatsoever—and supreme retribution for what had been done over the past two thousand years. Even though she knew this went against all that the Black Clans stood for. These traditional values gradually fragmented to indistinct memories under the weight of the newly seated hatred and ill intent. Until they existed in her mind and essence no more.

Here she was, within the ancient citadel known as the Nook of the Reach, many thousand foot up Crystal Peak along the

Western Spires of the Rock Rim. The little man better be right. The little weakling had served a purpose for something, but he was such a sore sight to look upon. At least he succumbed so easily to feminine guile.

Sahrya still could not believe that he could remember that whole book and recite it word for word, including sketching any symbols or drawings within it. But time would tell on that also, once she acquired the very same book from the keep. Then she could be certain of the information, as well as put an end to anyone with knowledge of it.

Upon locating this high fortress, she found that several of the inner corridors had been sealed by some action that triggered entire sections to collapse. This had to be an indication of where the arch-wizard, or other clue, could be found. There had to be some form of hidden intimation that might help to unravel more threads linked to her master plan of subjugation. The first clue would be resting with the wizard Haqnimemza.

Wybur appeared sincere in his account of information uncovered. He was like malleable ore in her hands—well, in Livforena's hands. Thanks to Rosella.

There was no doubt to that, thought Sahrya.

But he could have possibly been mistaken in his interpretation. After all, who could remember so much material such as that black book of Lord Siri?

The explosions rang out as she pondered alternatives and the loss of time itself. This fortress, the Nook of the Reach, had its origins back well before Arterium's time. No connection ever suggested that the wizard Haqnimemza even knew of such a location, let alone disappeared into it as a safe haven of some kind.

Old tales told of the Nook being a home established by an ancient lich. This lich was supposedly a powerful necromancer that had an army of undead. But no party or group ever made it there and back to give credence to such things, whether true or not.

Rangers under the Kuhrzothian banner had found the place unoccupied and architecturally intact, probably a dozen years before the current era. If this proved to be true, then something took place after that which left sections of it destroyed. There had been no telling of anything found alive at the place, only that it had been abandoned when visited by the rangers. But that was their tale, told while under the influence of Arterium.

Legend had it that the rangers returned with several artifacts of unprecedented craftsmanship that held exceptional powers, but the details remained ambiguous and the artifacts never did actually materialize.

Some claimed that these items disappeared while still in the hands of the rangers. Only one relic, which the rangers found, was now sitting in the museum of history located at Nuuroc, the splendid center of Kuhrzoth. It was an unadorned necklace with a plain pendant for a trinket. The trinket was shaped like a bellowing forge with two crossed blacksmith hammers set above it. This symbol appeared similar to that of the Olden of blacksmiths and forging, Lord Throndak, but not exactly as it was known today. This one was very rough in appearance and simply made of a black metal.

The rune of Lord Throndak was known to have the colors of the main ores used by smiths when forming objects of war and battle. Ghalqra, berlyllum, steel, iron, silver, and gold were always inlaid within the anvil and hammers in a peculiar pattern. These ores were always a part of it within the known context of current modernism. But not a one could really provide any background information on such a thing from the very early days. The first days before even Arterium walked the lands.

Lord Throndak was worshipped by smiths and specialists of the forge alike today, all in the perfection of their craft hoping to uncover the lost ways of their arts. Most sought to be granted a boon from the divinity as an achievement of their workmanship. What was known of Throndak within these times was that he was an enchanted being, part Black Clan and part horse, rumored to possibly be of an ancient and even older race. The known assumption was that he was actually born of the Olden.

But it was common knowledge that if one was to excel at the arts of the forge and the creation of metalwork, then they would require the strength and blessing of Throndak in order to surpass all others at the art. At the least, to ensure that they were not forever cursed in their endeavors. Many of the ignorant also plied such shallow insight into things of knowledge and skill.

Of course, folk always looked to the unknown or what they feared to place the blame. Always the scapegoat, always the shrugging off of commitment and responsibility. Always done by these types muttered under their breath, as though they were afraid that the very thing they themselves cursed might hear.

Sahrya snapped back to the movements of her clearing party, brought back to reality by her right hand, Mendonytes.

Mendonytes had appeared nearly in her face, while he quietly stated, "My lady, the wizard has uncovered something of significance. Your presence is requested."

She immediately became aware of the lack of deafening noise, which had been continuously sounding from the wizard blasting away at the fallen debris in the passage.

With the faint blue aura following her and maintaining the orb around her body, she made her way slowly down the rock strewn passageway until the old wizard appeared. Faulrik was barely visible within the smoke but could be seen extending his staff out to his side, the brightly glowing arcane ball of light at the tip providing illumination to the surrounding area. His wizened face and graying hair bespoke his heritage. That of Man.

She instantly, and instinctively, scoffed at the mere sight. Full of disdain. As though she was a mother looking upon some miscreant known to be a murderer of young babes.

Upon viewing the sight before her, Sahrya's breath almost hissed as it escaped her lips. She barely entered the small chamber where Faulrik now stood, maybe two paces from where another tall figure was held in statuesque calm. It was completely encased within glassy crystal.

The crystal had preserved the man well, with no visible deterioration whatsoever. The thick black hair and beard surrounded a set of ice blue eyes which clearly indicated a sense of surprise no doubt by whatever had transpired.

Prestigious, flowing dark crimson robes shrouded the form, forever frozen in their windswept state. His right hand held forth a small wooden wand while the left embraced a purple slate of rock tightly to his body.

But no—on closer inspection, the slate was actually a thick parchment completely encased in a purplish-tinted crystal substance. A silver chain around the man's neck protruded out from the cut in the robe, and a shiny symbol glittering of rubies, gold, and sapphires lay on his chest. This icon depicted the crest of the Kuhrzothian crown, and the necklace also held the golden, diamond-studded symbolic scroll of the arch-wizard's mark under King Arterium.

Behold, here stands Haqnimemza, last Master of the Deep and royal arch-wizard to King Arterium. It seems that the arch-wizard had not abandoned his king by choice after all. Someone or something had stopped him short, suspending him forever in time and death.

"Can you rid us of the crystal surrounding the man but maintain the encased scroll itself, Faulrik? I need that scroll intact. It must stay inside that material with no harm," demanded the priestess, her tone steady.

The priestess knew the material enclosing the scroll was amethyst and also that this very scroll would be none other than the eighth Amethyst Scroll. The Lost Scroll. But the wizard Faulrik did not need any more information than what he already knew or guessed.

Legends suggested that the number of Amethyst Scrolls could be eight, despite the fact that seven had been found by Arterium back in the early days. This conjecture was solely based upon the Twelve Edicts of Braxis. Why would there only be seven of the Amethyst Scrolls? Why not ten or eight? After all, there were twelve edicts. So, the scholars indicated that there might be more such scrolls, and that one might have been lost or stolen prior to retrieval by Arterium's expedition from the fortress of Isnuuthghor.

Faulrik stared intently at the form and then at the dimly lit passage before slowly replying, "I believe I can do just that. It must be done carefully. The thaumaturgy used to encase this man is very old, but I am confident I can reverse it. The scroll is separate and not part of what was done to him. This should not be difficult. Allow me to study it for a while longer, and then I shall do so."

Sahrya contemplated the demeanor of the wizard as he spoke his words, no doubt to determine his earnestness. She rested one slim hand against a freshly charred portion of the wall and then ran her index finger around in various ways as if drawing something.

"Faulrik, I have confidence in your talents. But understand this. That scroll *must* survive as it is now, regardless of all else. Do not fail me in this." Her voice went extremely cold and emotionless as she finished her mandate.

The only way into the chamber was the path cleared by the blasting that had been done. The corridor leading off the other side was still collapsed.

Mendonytes positioned several warriors back down the passage where they had originated from, while standing just outside the chamber with two others, not far from Sahrya.

It seemed as though much time had passed before Faulrik indicated he was ready. His hands moved in intricate patterns as he spoke the arcane dialect required to unleash his counter-spell.

The crystal around the dead wizard began to glow slightly. An eerie, white light radiated in increasing brightness until the entire outline of Haqnimemza was bathed in it. There was movement, more trembling, as though a small earthquake had struck the statuesque form itself.

Suddenly, the crystal entombment shattered into thousands of fragments. The body of Haqnimemza collapsed to the ground, withering within moments due to the intake of air. But the Amethyst Scroll remained exactly where it had been, suspended in the air with no harm whatsoever, as the ironwood wand clattered to the stone floor.

"As you command, my lady. The scroll is yours," voiced Faulrik proudly. He gestured towards the Amethyst Scroll with his hand as it slowly descended to gently rest upon a charred block of stone.

The priestess eyed the scene in approval as she firmly directed the wizard. "Good work, my wise one. I had no doubt in you for this task. Now, perform one more thing. Translate the contents of this scroll into the Common tongue for me, and then we will make our way back."

"As you wish, my lady," acknowledged Faulrik obediently. "It shall be done as quickly as possible but with the most meticulous nature."

Of course she knew her own ancient tongue, but Faulrik was an extremely wise and learned wizard. His interpretation might shed more light on whatever puzzle rested within the Lost Scroll.

The wizard labored away for another portion of the night before presenting his handiwork. "My lady, here it is, once written in ancient Black Clan at a time before this era as we know it. Indeed, this scroll predates the time of Arterium." He then pulled open his written translation. As both ends kept curling over on themselves, he slowly read the contents.

The lost lore of the Ancients, the eighth Amethyst Scroll, once deciphered:

The power of darkness shall immerse existence.

With the rise of the Shadow Soul, the Marked One,

Bearing the sign of the black consumed sun,

The Soul shall be born of the Ancients, the Aylsh

both light and dark, the Man-folk, and the otherworldly.

A Soul of Shadow to unite the world of darkness with

that of light.

An order to bring Chaos and Shadow to the Light.

Impaler of Shadows and Binding of Shades in one

hand,

Shall draw forth all of the powers of darkness through

the Soul,

Granting all-consuming dark power over all with a

breach of the Soul and the Void,

Absorption of the light into the dark with terrible justice.

Thus the final seal be broken so shall the winged one

be unleashed again.

Destined to force all to their knees and raze what does

not bend,

Before the sixteenth turn ends,

The Dark Rider will ride high near the zenith of the

mergence.

If the Soul fails to merge light with dark within the Void

and assume the unhallowed throne,

The time of the Dark Rider will reign supreme.

And the Dark Cabal shall emerge.

The Seers shall rise to the dark flames.

At the bottom was a rune shaped like a half-sun that was darkened except for the very bottom crescent portion of it, which was lighter in color. Small, black, squiggly lines radiated out and up from the half-sun.

The strange riddle of this Lost Scroll would definitely quicken the pace of Sahrya's plans. If any legend suggested by the Amethyst Scrolls came to fruition before her next wave of vengeance had been unleashed upon the Man-folk, then her future might be steered differently. She could not allow that. The first two measures to her scheme had been unleashed over the past turn or so, and the next one would coincide with her step upwards upon the pedestal of Thaldeia. It would be the final seal of subjugation that would conclude the fate of Man entirely.

The Kuhrzothian king had been the first to deny her promise to him of untold powers. He somehow saw through her mask of deception and refused to parlay with the beautiful Livforena.

But he was old and near atrophic in his age. Soon he too would become part of history, along with the people of Kuhrzoth. And what she could not accomplish through politics, she would do through positioning. Even right now, as she pondered her ongoing subversions, the Kuhrzothian king had a viper within his midst closer than any other. Just waiting to strike.

The Order of Emerald Knights now stood impotent, no longer the force of might that it had been hundreds of years ago. Thanks to Velore. He had been the final unsuspecting pulley to that sequence of abatement. And the greed of man was seemingly unsurpassed by no other need or appetite.

The Kuhrzothians would be the first to feel the crushing rule of loss and inescapable fate. Not just a few, but many, if not all. And they would also see their own flesh and blood raise to take part in the annihilation.

It would be the mark of perfection from which Thaldeia would start anew, to be molded in her form as she saw fit.

Of course, she would not underrate anything, but it was certain that the once impregnable kingdom of Kuhrzoth, as it had been known, would finally come to an end. It would cease to be a symbol of power and good throughout the lands. Man would not be far behind it at that point. Her reverie was broken by the impending drive to understand the contents of the Lost Scroll.

Sahrya smiled at the old, wizened man as she carefully took up the Lost Scroll from the floor of the rock strewn chamber, not far from the crumpled and shriveled corpse of Haqnimemza.

"Faulrik, I owe you much for this endeavor. You have truly earned the riches that I have promised you. The rest of your life will be in pompous extravagance."

As she spoke to Faulrik, Mendonytes positioned himself behind the old wizard as if to inspect the far wall of the chamber where another corridor branched off into collapsed ruin.

Faulrik smiled, his face beaming with pride as he understood what that meant. To finally achieve a point in his life where he could enjoy things and be in a position of importance. He would be the arch-wizard to Queen Sahrya Khajrynghul, Queen of all Thaldeia.

"My lady, it was nothing and only as I have said before. I am yours and will do your bidding, whatever that might be."

Faulrik humbly bowed as he spoke, but he did not catch the movements of the priestess' finest warrior in time. His vast powers in thaumaturgy useless to him now in his ignorant bliss.

Too late did he glance at the silent but agile movement of Mendonytes. The dark one gripped Faulrik's mane of hair, jerking his head far back while a long, blackened blade slid into the base of the man's spine and then upwards into his heart.

The sound of bone and tissue grinding and snapping barely overtook a short gasp of pain and labored breath. Then Faulrik fell lifelessly to the ground.

"Consider your debt paid in full, my wizard, Man-scum. I have given you the justice owed to every one of your kind. Now go to the Chasm or whatever it is that you believed in!" Sahrya nudged the unmoving body with her boot as she hissed the words with vileness.

"Mendonytes, take care of the rest of those that we brought. *No one* is to have knowledge of this. We will return to Tharasvrul shortly. Once we do, prepare a raiding party."

Mendonytes wiped his blade clean of the blood and sheathed it. "Consider it done, my priestess."

Sahrya smiled wickedly, knowing that destiny had steered her to one more piece of truth. The words of the Lost Scroll reverberated through her mind as she repeated them over and over again.

Then circumstances returned to her memory as she recalled what she had thought to be trivial at the time. But one of the keepers had possibly completed a circle, although unwittingly, and nearly a turn ago.

The keeper Ghenwari once approached her late in the evening when she was alone, explaining that there was something she needed to know. The keeper told Sahrya about a strange mark upon one of the young ones she was caring for and teaching.

Sahrya had completely disregarded it at the time as something trifling, but now it became a blazing silhouette to the future. Possibly a formidable barrier to her plans.

The keeper had described a mark low upon the abdomen of this one, just above her sex organ. She spoke of a dark half-sun with black rays arising out of it, and clearly indicated that it was a mark of birth and not something placed on her.

Yes, they would need to return to Clan Tharasvrul. Her impatience was beginning to consume her. And she would have to speak with that keeper immediately.

Chapter 5:

Commencement

All those of will shall furthermore bring about nurturance of those wild true things, ne'er doing that which is unjust upon the pure and innocent. The aura of the azure shall ever permeate those which thrive. No act of malice shall such mingle.

> –Third Edict of Lord Braxis, etched
> upon the Great Slates, recovered by
> Arterium circa the year 13 BA.

t was more than just a stormy night at Tamelyn Keep. The dark skies writhed with a tempest of violence as lightning thundered through the air. Only the token

force of four warriors under the Black Legion roamed the passages and grounds of the keep this late at night.

Tamelyn Keep had been in existence since before the House of Legends was erected by King Arterium. It had, unofficially, began its work in the year 80 before our King, or 80 BA. Though but a hovel out in the middle of the wild, and set forth by monks with an equal amount of self-righteousness. Even though the loremasters of the old Tamelyn kept pace with the recordings of the Revered Times, the fledgling system was rife with issues. The varied methods of marking time and events throughout all of the lands held no continuity or accuracy. Sometimes there was not even a set organizer of the history being recorded.

These first loremasters brought the inner workings of how time was currently marked to light, not long after the death of King Arterium. They broached the Emerald Crown with the concept, which had not yet stopped bickering and squabbling since Arterium's death. It was more a power struggle at who would be, and should be, the new king. This intense controversy took place since Arterium had no rightful heir. Obviously the Heir de Facto decree emerged, resulting from the chaos.

While the loremasters had developed the current system, the commanders of the Emerald Order tossed the information to the House of Legends. It took another ten years before it was officially proclaimed. And, of course, after the Emerald Crown assumed ownership of the entire thing.

It was not until much later that Sedgewyn Tamelyn actually took the loremasters and their work under his wing and established Tamelyn Keep (a smaller gatehouse version). It sat within the shadow of the Purple Peaks back then. Around the year SA 1390, a mysterious benefactor spurred the relocation and building of the keep to where it was today. The keep was completed in SA 1400. But even with its earliest conception, there has always been a contingent from the Black Legion standing guard. In fact, there always had been many more Legion-men assigned to the duty up until the time when it was relocated.

These warriors were but freelanced swords and more as a presence by the Legion than actually able to protect an entire keep. No such small force could possibly fend much off, although brave and hearty as they were. The symbolic gesture of having a few volunteers stand watch at Tamelyn was the promissory note of what the keep meant to the lands, and that the Black Legion would protect it. Who, or what, would dare raise a sword against Tamelyn Keep while under the protection of such a force?

The warriors of the Black Legion normally stood their duty at the keep for one year, whereupon they would return to their regular company. All of their sustenance during the term of service was provided for by the lord of Tamelyn.

Besides, no force or thing had even dared to threaten Tamelyn Keep in several hundred years. Obviously those who either were selected for such duty or stepped forth to take it were ones not overly concerned with high adventure and action. It was not ever expected of the duty at Tamelyn Keep.

One of the Legion-men, Krelmir, thought about the return back to the Adan Company of the Black Legion. This next summertide would mark the end of his year-long duty at the keep. It would be time to pack and wait for his replacement to show up.

He put a hand to his drenched beard, wringing the rainwater from it. A flash of lightning highlighted the long streaks of gray hairs in it, showing the old warrior his age.

He thought he had seen his kindred Legion-man atop the far wall in one of the flashes of lightning. The thick rain was coming at him sideways as he tightened the cloak about his neck.

But nothing now. Krelmir thought Treyfus was likely within one of the battlements.

Krelmir strode along the walkway atop the high walls, passing by parapets every few paces. His dusky cloak with the symbol of the Black Legion, an imposing silver scythe etched on the back, billowed savagely in the raging winds.

The four towers, one located at each corner of the keep, provided the only protection from the elements atop the walls. These were not real though, as a castle might have. Actual castle towers would be lofty, defensive pinnacles of fortified might. Possibly with some type of war engine atop it. A position where archers or defenders could gain dominance over the grounds below.

These towers only rose another ten foot above the upper walkways. There were rafters and thatches above all of them, however, so these small roofs did offer a degree of dryness from the rain-swept winds. Only widened arrow loops, in large and lazy cross-shaped patterns, accented the outer walls.

Tamelyn was not really a keep per se and definitely not a castle, if one considered the lack of features normally attributed with such structures.

Krelmir noted the black form on the walkway opposite him. That was where Treyfus was. He could barely make out the black shape set in the waterlogged darkness.

One of the unwritten, but well-known and instinctive, practices of the Legion was the natural use of darkness. For turns, this tactic had been the cause of many successful endeavors by the Black Legion. Accustoming one's self to the enshrouding gloom and blackness of the night always offered its own blanket of security. Obviously, the use of any kind of light only meant certain death once marked by the enemy. Legion-men were well-versed in the ritualistic practices of such a colorful heritage. Those of which have not yet eroded away as other martial orders steeped in colorful history, like the Emerald Knights.

Krelmir finally rounded the last corner. He left the overhead covering of the tower as he approached the black-cloaked form. To him, it appeared that Treyfus was facing the opposite way down the walkway. The form was motionless, except for the flapping great-cloak that struggled with the wind as it attempted to spirit it away.

At first, Krelmir thought that Treyfus might be staring out across the landscape at something, but no ordinary eye could pierce this darkness unless within the flash of the storm's brilliance. He could barely discern anything with the wind howling and blowing torrents of cold rain droplets. The sting of them flew at him straight down, slanted, and even sideways, in nearly every direction.

Too late did Krelmir surmise that the black cloak of Treyfus was merely that, just the black cloak, alone and flapping off the tip of a spear. As he crouched backwards and palmed his sword hilt, the unrecognizable form off to his right side along the outer parapet never caused him even a momentary pause. But then it probably would not even have attracted the attention of a creature of the night with eyes attuned to such scenery. And the speed of the unseen movement was so quick, like the night itself reached out and grabbed the Legion-man.

A blade struck and Krelmir's head rolled unnaturally back on the neck, falling behind his body, now completely separated. A torrent of blood spouted up and out, splashing in intervals all over the stone walkway, though colorless in the night. The body slowly leaned forward and fell with a thud barely palpable under the noise of the storm.

The black form, which did not even appear to show itself under the constant flashes of lightning, glided along the flooring to where the stairs descended into the courtyard below.

§ § §

One of the Primordials, thriving very near to Tamelyn Keep, did actually feel an evil. A dark presence of deep hatred. There were definitely wicked plans afoot nearby.

The tiny Aylsh-like anthropoid was no taller than a swelling, red apple. It, or she as it appeared to be female, was sitting on a branch high up in a giant fir tree. The little thing of exquisite beauty, surrounded by a warm, pale blue glow, could sense the ominous air of something very vile and sinister.

But she could also feel another presence, one that she had felt on and off for a long time now.

This other feeling emanated from within the large stone fortress on the edge of the woods. It was of unquestionable purity, sovereign goodness, and ancient maternal instincts. And it was so strong now on this stormy night, as she watched the lightning play across the skies. This other presence almost seemed to be glowing and radiating as powerful as the duo suns, a beacon drawing her kind close.

A Pixie instinctively knew the mother of her people when close enough to her, and there could be no doubt to this. Now that she sensed the foreboding approach of evil in the same area as this other presence, she knew that she must investigate.

An unseen but overbearing sense of urgency literally pushed her towards the keep, only but a small bluish-white ball of pale light flying through the night sky. And there was no time to warn the others of her kind.

§ § §

The thundering booms and dazzling flashes of the raging tempest had already awakened little Chimy in his bed-chamber. He had no idea how far the night was gone other than it had to be well past the witches-hand.

Now he cowered under the thick, fur-laden hides atop his feather bed as the wraiths played through the iron-latticed window in his room. Chimy had never been in the middle of such violence, as the air writhed with energy. The storm this particular night was like none before it.

Finally, he could stand it no longer. He threw off the warm hides covering him and jumped up from his bed, running to the closed door. The thunder was so intense that the cold, stone floor shook with tremors from the blasts.

There was a long, slow creak as he swung the door open and entered the hallway leading to the private dining chamber. No lights burned within and the darkness seemed unsettling, completely enveloping except for the bursts of lightning. The latticed windows cast strange creatures across the walls and ceilings as the flashing bolts tore through the skies. The small boy tiptoed his way past several open doors, one of which being his parents' empty bed-chamber. The sheets and blankets had been spiraled off the bed, leaving the huge feather mattress bare and uninviting under the flashes of light.

He could make out the expansive table and chairs as he stepped into the dining area. No one was there, so he made his way to the far archway that led into the great hall. Here, as he approached, he could see that the large wooden door was cracked halfway open.

The air seemed heavy and tense as he crept through the archway and peered down the unlit hall where there should have been at least one or two torches burning. There was a form seated at the nearest table where Lord Eggelstyk usually took his tea and spent countless periods of time reading. But this shape was dull and misleading in the darkness.

Chimy cautiously approached the table, recognizing the familiar outline of the lord of the keep, who appeared to be sitting in the dark. Maybe he had a little too much of his laced tea and fell asleep while pondering in thought, as he so often did.

As Chimy approached Lord Eggelstyk, he could sense a peculiar charge to the air. Something was wrong.

The unmoving, motionless form of the old man did not even produce the subtle rise and fall of breath, let alone the usual bubbling brook snoring of the old codger.

Chimy slowly crept up beside the still lord and placed a small hand upon his arm, nudging him. Just enough to get his attention.

With a tremendous crack of lightning, the flash illuminated the interior of the great hall. The body of Lord Eggelstyk slumped towards Chimy and off the chair, thudding to the floor.

The boy jumped nervously at either the bolt of lightning or the sudden lurch of the body towards him. It possibly could have been from both since they happened near simultaneously.

The dark, cloaked forms scattered around the room when that bright flash lit it up were enough to cause the young boy to freeze in terror. He suddenly found himself inside a living nightmare.

Frightened, he backed up towards what he remembered to be the cleared path that he had approached by, only to forcefully be stopped against one of the black-cloaked forms standing solid and tall. The terror had a giant, double-edged sword resting upon the tip not two paces from his side.

All of a sudden, the hearth fully sputtered to life with a *whoop*, as though it had been burning all night. Within moments, the entire great hall was covered in the disingenuous feel of warmth from firelight. The torches resting in wall adornments also were now lit.

Chimy was surrounded by dark-skinned warriors wearing black cloaks and wielding cruel weapons. Now the boy could see in horror that Lord Eggelstyk lay in a huge pool of dark blood, no doubt from the jagged hole ripped through his chest.

A woman stood near the high-mantled hearth as the orange and red-hued flames licked the blackened stone near the top. She was dark as night with eyes that glared forth at him, fiery purple in color. The enveloping cloak she wore clung to her lithe but fit frame. The appearance of a huge skull on the back of the cloak faded as she fully turned towards him. Now the front of the cloak appeared to have a sinister red eye on each side that ran the entire length, bobbing as it stared the boy down.

Priestess Sahrya stood with a large, black, leather-bound book in her hand. "So we have one of the man-whelps now, do we?"

There were four more of the cloaked warriors scattered to her sides. They each carried tall, jagged spears along with other weaponry at their belts.

The priestess thought for a moment that the light of her thaumaturgy was playing a trick with her eyes. A very small, pale blue orb of light appeared near the ceiling to her front. But then it was gone as quickly as it appeared, and she sensed no other powers nearby.

Little Chimy, for the first time now, noticed the familiar form of Mordrid sprawled on the floor near the other end of the table and cried. "Papa!"

But his lunge forward was caught by the huge hand of the nearest towering figure. The boy hung suspended in air just off his feet before he could rush to his father's body.

Mendonytes bared his teeth as he held the boy, his other hand gripping a blackened poleax seemingly too massive to be well-balanced with double blades. Each was the size of the young boy. Chimy squirmed futilely in his grasp and then went limp, silently staring in shock from what he saw and felt. His eyes reflected the firelight as they filled with tears.

A commotion arose from the main doorway leading out to the courtyards, and in strode four more dark warriors. Their silver manes of hair were pulled back and hanging in long whips. In their midst was the fairest maiden form of Ephritori, her hands bound in front of her. Her gorgeous face was bruised, bloodied, and dirtied from the scuffle.

Chimy's face flickered with hope. His eyes widened and his lips curled up in a faint smile upon seeing her. Oblivious to her condition, his tears left smoke-hued tracks down his cheeks. His eyes pleaded with her to save him from the living terror which engulfed the room.

Ephritori stood leaning forward slightly. Her rich blue eyes flickering with sadness as they found the unmoving form of Mordrid lying on the floor not very far away. Her face twisted in realized agony from the scene before her. Tears welled up, causing her eyes to glimmer like diamonds as she wordlessly mouthed his name.

Her mind fought to control the surging emotions and not give any more satisfaction to these evil doers than necessary, but such loss was beyond any lock of discipline she could muster.

She fell forward to her knees and her breath heaved out vigorously, as though a giant had suddenly taken all the air from her lungs in one mighty blow. Then she grasped at the short, sudden sobs as it came back in.

Priestess Sahrya sighed and looked to Mendonytes casually while fingering the edge of the black book. "*Khamatiri*—allow no survivors here this night," she stated, nodding at her captain.

Khamatiri meant supreme captain and was Mendonytes actual title within the ranks of the priestess' Blackguard.

With this, Mendonytes slowly loosened his grasp on Chimy's sleeping shirt while raising the poleax with the opposite hand.

In a confused mix of horror and rage, Ephritori leapt up and sprung into the air with oblivious need to reach Chimy. She saw the malicious act of what the towering figure intended to do.

But she never saw the raised morning star in the hand of the warrior behind her. As she arose through the air, the spiked weapon swept downwards at her. She had no inkling of what hit her, as the force of the blow violently stopped her in midair. Her lithe form was flung down hard onto the wooden floor, and she lay still in a widening pool of blood.

Mendonytes completed his soul-shattering sweep with the vicious blade of his axe as Ephritori hit the floor like a freshly soaked mop. The axe separated little Chimy's head from his body cleanly, as it unnaturally tilted to the side from the razor blade and then rolled spinning to the floor. The headless body stood for what seemed like several moments and then rigidly fell straight down in a crumpled heap with blood spurting forth in arcs.

Sahrya stared at the carnage that she had created. "Little Aylsh afterling cunt, have no fear and be so lucky that I painlessly sent your pup out of this world!" She knew that her words were pointless as the Aylsh was probably dead.

There it was again, thought Sahrya. A tiny, glowing, azure orb appeared near the head of the fallen Aylsh maiden, casting traces of luminescence to play across her now ashen face.

The orb began to slowly spiral out and up in sweeps, increasing in size with each passing. Suddenly, as the orb reached the rafters, a blinding bright flash of blue light engulfed the room. Then there was total and complete darkness as all lights were extinguished. The great hall returned to what it had been before the orb appeared, with the hearth crackling like it was burning the whole time.

The priestess stared around in surprise, noticing that the body of the maiden was missing and that rain swept in through one of the windows on the far wall. The framed glass was shattered outward. A constant thud reverberated as the remnants banged against the outside stonework.

Priestess Sahrya hissed, "Go! Search for her quickly!" She keenly felt that something important may have slipped through her grasp. She had no idea of what though. But at least she possessed Olri Uchrah, the black book of Lord Siri. That was an accomplishment.

"You there," she commanded, pointing at one of the silver haired, dark warriors, "gather some of the Aylsh's blood and bring it. She must have lost enough of it there on the floor."

Her business here was finished. There were no witnesses to the fact that the book ever existed, or of her presence and their assault on the keep. All except for that Aylsh maiden, but she would have a specimen of her blood so that Rosella could track her. That is, after Rosella finished her other task in Longshadows.

§ § §

The unexpected distraction was sudden but pleasant for Wybur Buttlecut. He had been roped into running one of his uncle's trade caravans to a small outpost along the eastern edge of the Rock Rim.

Traveling the northern roads at this time of the night made him shiver though. But that could just as easily have been Frost's Whisper, as they were called. Many referred to them simply by the Whisper. The sting of the cool air was amplified by these mostly northern winds as they signaled the approach of late harvestspell. Some claimed that these winds were the spark that sent all the creatures scurrying to gather the stores that would last them through to the next frostthaw. These winds were named so because they seemed to blow from all directions but south, and they would often change their course back and forth, striking up a constant low howl through the treetops.

The true, unruly nature of the wildlands always unsettled Wybur, especially once on the Lost Road that ran high along the eastern slopes of the Rock Rim. But that portion of the journey was a fortnight behind them. Back within the Free Lands now, the tension of those raw nerves eased significantly.

The caravan had delivered supplies to a man known as the Bastard Prophet. After nearly a score of days riding on the return trip, the city of Longshadows should be filling the panorama soon.

Groelhof Buttlecut, Wybur's uncle, had sudden company business arise that could not do without him. The taxation office made speculations that there was a discrepancy within their books concerning Buttlecuts. The master of the trade company would need to attend to the matter promptly, or so the reasoning was stated as such by Uncle Buttlecut at obtrusive length. Wybur knew this was just one of his uncle's jigs that was danced to whenever the old man didn't feel like traveling.

Rory Adnan Sivercroft, also known as the Bastard Prophet, was an interesting story himself. He started a following of sorts out in the frontier along the edge of the Fallen Lands.

The Rock Rim was a vast mountain range that encircled the Fallen Lands—or Oshghrul as they were known in Black Clan. These mountains ran along the western, eastern, and southern edges. To the north lay the cold, icy wastelands known as the Icefall. The Black Clans called this by a more proper name, that of Sauhd Vourwu, which meant a thousand shades of cold.

There were only a handful of known crossing points through the grim teeth known as the Rock Rim. Sure, one could attempt to traverse these rugged peaks wherever they saw fit. But it would entail days, if not ten-days, and one would be at daunting peril over the treacherous landscape. Let alone the creatures of the wild that might be encountered.

One mammoth valley ran straight out of and down from the southern end, pouring across the sovereign land of Kuhrzoth. An entire legion could fit abreast through most of that valley. The pride of Kuhrzoth, Emerald Rest, sat at the bottom of this near highway.

All of the other routes that were at least considered negotiable were barely large enough to accommodate a single, sometimes double, file of men. One of these points happened to be where Rory set up his self-proclaimed kingdom, which he called Dawn's Glory. He even went so far as to construct a fortified gate near the narrowest point along this particular passage as it snaked through the Rock Rim and crept into the heart of Oshghrul.

Wybur thought back to High-suns, during his last meeting with Livforena, and the time spent at Tamelyn. There had been no chance to return to the keep since then. But his thoughts had been running wild. His dreams appeared ever more lucid and dire, haunting his restless nights.

Every night, for the past tenspell, he dreamt of running through huge meadows and forests. Lush, green grass full of flowers and buzzing insects.

What is a tenspell, one might ask? A tenspell was a traditional way of expressing a period of about ten days. Though it could really mean anywhere from nine to twelve.

For the most part, Thaldeians chiefly use the expression to indicate an amount of time that has been unusually long due to bothersome work, bouts of sickness, and the like. One would never express this term for anything enjoyable.

Wybur's dreams would start and end the same each and every time, with him never reaching wherever it was that he was running to. But it always felt so real, even the breaking of the cool night breeze on his sweat-soaked body and the cold droplets of rain from the cloudburst overhead.

But last night had been completely different for a change. He dreamt of walking through the smoking ruins of Tamelyn Keep. There was no inkling or knowledge of what had befallen the place. Upon closer inspection, the bloodied and twisted bodies lying amidst the grounds of the keep turned out to be the familiar faces of the people at Rory's outpost.

A strange, blue-flamed candle or light of some sort appeared to stay ahead, always leading him as he walked through the dismal vision. But the light never really allowed him to get close enough to make out its details. Only a mystery remaining off in the distance.

It was the point where he suddenly found himself facing a monstrous, winged terror that he would snap back awake in a cold sweat. But only the soft glow of twilight reining in the morning peeked at him through an open window. The winged beast dissolved with the light, and his awakening. He had to stare about his surroundings and look to the peaceful familiarity of the outpost in order to shake off the darkness of the dream, grabbing hold of the invisible blanket of calm and relief.

Wybur thought about Rory. The man made even Mordrid look like a dwarf if ever they were to stand side by side. He knew most of the story behind the man called the Bastard Prophet. Rory indeed was a bastard of some nobleman under the Kuhrzothian banner.

The man was literally a mountain and towered a couple of foot above most. His frame was equally impressive and taut with sinewy muscle. A thick crop of roughly cut blond hair fell evenly around his head, with the bangs just above his bushy eyebrows.

Wybur knew that Rory was ridiculed throughout his younger days by almost everyone for his unerring, conscious subjugation of the rights of royalty and, especially, what were called politics.

It seemed that young Rory could not find any value in how nobility apparently was the do-no-wrong perfect child when compared to everyone else. Or how deception and conniving ploys could be construed as perceived truths because they were conducted by nobility.

Rory had been a staunch believer in the power of the people and equality with individualism. The hierarchal apparatus must bear witness to the individual and not lose its way amidst the vast forest of hypocrisy and sleight of tongue befuddlement. This, of course, was coupled with the fact that, even though an accomplished and muscle-bound fighter, he absolutely would not engage in combat without an unusual amount of provocation.

Both educated and simple folk of Kuhrzoth apparently mocked him for this and made him out to be a fool of sorts—possibly a bit slow-witted.

Even Wybur saw where people of shallowness and self-servitude might misread that gem of pure righteousness inside the man, solely based upon his particular looks. After all, it took Wybur himself the course of several seasons to come to grips with the likes of Rory. Of course, one factor here also was that the caravans only delivered their rounds once or twice a season at the most.

After initially meeting Rory, he had to sit down with him one on one to see that the light behind his spirit was integral. That light was the essence of the man. And it definitely was of genuine sincerity. The Bastard Prophet really did believe as he acted. There was no show or play of things. This was the actual man and what he decided to stand for.

The young Buttlecut even became somewhat baffled at the inspiration that Rory brought out in him, and he barely spent much time here at all. Imagine living here, day in and day out.

One thing of note, and flagrantly out in the open, was that Rory could consciously do no morally wrong or unjust thing. Whether it was an act or in word, the man would not even think it. Worse yet, he could not abide it at all in anyone or anything else.

Wullyam was one of the older and more venerable men that had been with Rory through thick and thin. Even though Wullyam maintained the mystery surrounding Rory for the most part, he did allude to the mettle of the man.

One time, he told Wybur that Rory could not tolerate wrongdoing by his own hand or that of another, even if it meant his death. But no matter the case or history, Rory would accept the individual at face value, inclusive of all facets, as long as they sought betterment.

Rory always saw the good in one and would fully cultivate that as long as the individual renounced the former acts of ill intent and steered towards honesty and virtue. Wullyam claimed that it had more to do with exactly what Rory saw in the individual than anything else.

Later we shall see where not even Wybur knew all of the truth surrounding Rory Sivercroft. For Rory disowned the truth that was not substantially relevant, and he made those with him that knew this truth do the same. But the intent of this was not for deception. It was done in order to allow himself to rightfully sit in equality with his people, and not above them.

The nobleman that fathered Rory had ultimately been made the fool of the time, chiefly through his own careless debauchery, of course.

Rory eventually discussed segments of his past with Wybur, after they had spent time together as friends over the past seven years. Buttlecuts had been delivering supplies to the outpost for about that long.

In case you are questioning the use of the term outpost here, do not let it imply that the camp was actually a sanctioned effort for some company, organization, or crown. It was wholly stood up by none other than Rory, and those inspired by him. Of course, the direction and vision originated from him, but everyone tied to the cause pitched in to make it what it was.

According to Rory, the nobleman had never even acknowledged his other born bastard son. At least not until Rory's early twenties, when it appeared that the lad would be a physical progeny of martial talent and unsurpassed strength.

His father must have thought he had a prized stallion that would carry him into his later years teeming with wealth and fame. Unfortunately, this spurred Rory even further into such acts and claims of vehement righteousness. To the point of unceasing, relentless fervor. He then made it a point to do exactly the opposite of what was expected of him by his father.

Wybur learned that this nobleman, as did the majority of noblemen, held many different mistresses. Of course, these were always tolerated or played off ignorantly by the wed wife for fear that the man would strip her of all that she knew and had if she did not concede to his ways.

One of the mistresses in this case was Rory's mother. She was the frail but pleasing daughter of a dirt-poor farmer. The farmer was a typical one who tended a tract of land for the crown. These farms supplied produce and meat for the markets that fed the people. Unfortunately, his mother died giving birth to him.

Wybur remembered noting this mask of sadness whenever Rory talked about the matter. This truly endeared the somber man to Wybur even more.

As Rory grew to be a robust exemplar of a man and displayed naturally gifted talents in combat, the noble father suddenly showed the lad tremendous affection, at least outwardly. It appeared that the man felt a sudden surge of paternal instincts for his newly found son.

But Rory would narrow his eyes when discussing this aspect of his volatile past, as his so-called father no doubt saw the seed of selfish fortune and notoriety for himself. He saw what the gainful lad could do for him. His father had high expectations of him and the life that his son was *entitled* to.

Rory was literally propelled out to fit this high and glorious place above the people. The very people whom he had lived and breathed with for his whole life, the salt of the land that he devoutly loved. Equals—man, or even other beings, had no place higher than one another.

After the anger and rage of realizing the deception and selfishness of his father, he found peace. Rory told Wybur that the circumstances instead gave him clarity and reason, and it was from this place of dark, dank turmoil that the true light came out in him.

According to Rory, his father was so chagrinned over such abominations of his noble rights and senses that he completely disowned his son. Of course, this was after casting Rory up in view and in front of tens of thousands of people, as though the action alone would beget the envisioned son.

The amazing part of this tale behind the outpost and Rory was that the man actually developed a gathering of true loyalists to morality. This began to occur during the high and bloated scenes staged by his father throughout his attempts to gain control of him and only bloomed with the public ostracizing.

To this day, these staunch advocates and like-minded sympathizers undeniably backed him and the life that they as a group had built and established. And then there were all of the organizations that supported this endeavor and actually paid gold to send necessities to the camp.

This, however, was increasingly rare as the self-sustainability of the outpost quickly overtook any of the needs. And Rory never allowed anything to be given that was worth more than could be repaid in some form.

Folk of every skill and trade flocked here to be part of the vision. And for what? Had a god taken up residence there? Were fountains of both endless gold nuggets and bestowal of youth drawing the multitudes? Why no, no such thing at all. But what initially started the following, and built its continued momentum, was simple equality. Yes, simple and plain equal parts where everyone was the same regardless of position or trade.

All worked towards the same goal of survival and propagation, with each doing their part to make the whole possible. And no one was better in any way than another, regardless of past history and deed.

At first, Wybur found the thought hard to swallow. That is, until he spent more and more time there. And what he heard and saw with some of the individuals who had taken it as their home. It might be unbelievable unless actually experienced.

Rory was the final herald of the aura surrounding the people and their simplistic community of self-sacrifice, contrasted against a similar but austere element of uncertainty. He drew the name as the Bastard Prophet due to all of this history and effect. Not a name in mockery mind you, but one of reverence.

In fact, Wybur had never seen a more collectively different but cohesive and effective group of individuals that called themselves a society. We are not talking about those confined to their position within a city or village who go about their day-to-day tedious monotony with equal lack of enthusiasm. But a place where each individual was excited and eager to awake in order to get started and do their part.

Rory finally alluded to what he termed as the basis of this harmony. It took a couple of years before he even mentioned these things to Wybur. He simply said that the individual had to accept who they were and what they were committed to. That such things were ingrained within the individual whether they knew it or not.

Wybur initially chalked it up to the elusively hermetic faith of the divine. Rory apparently saw this cue on Wybur's face and paused momentarily while staring intently at him. He then smiled at Wybur.

"My friend, Wybur Buttlecut," Rory started, "tell me, what is your purpose in this world." He made it more a statement than an actual question.

Wybur thought briefly before saying that he really had no idea. Then Rory explained to him that this was the case with most. Most folks did not know their purpose. They eventually gave up trying to find it and lost their *way*.

Truth be told, he had said, everyone has a destiny. Whether they consciously attune to it or not, they will always end up paralleling it. This I sincerely believe and now know, he told Wybur.

Then he started down another path. He talked of every living thing having that part of their spirit, the essence, given to the physical form to fill the void. The term essence referred to the inner being or soul, while the term spirit was normally used to indicate the combined form of the being (physical and metaphysical—or essence). Every creature and being in the worlds that we know holds an essence. From the spark of creation and imagination, to the thoughts and whims, and the personality and character that drive it through life…be it a child, grown man, Akhru, horse, or deer.

It was this essence that ultimately held the purpose or destiny. Rory had told him that one had to accept this and get to know that part of themselves. If one did not do this, then they would keep distancing themselves from what they truly were. Eventually, they would become more or less lost. Once an individual accepted this, and then developed and strengthened that inner self, they could become an embodiment of it and live their life as such. More spiritual, more harmonious, and more purposeful.

Yet one of the keys to this was that the individual had to do this for their own self, and then accept that this applied to all living things. They must see the world as full of these other spirits and treat it with the awe and respect it deserved.

And if any of those other spirits wanted to stomp out your spirit, then you had to smash them to the Outer Halls with a sword or axe. Rory finished this part with the same ingrained look and casual tone, and then he let out a head-tossing laugh while slapping his leg.

Rory had looked at him with such a peaceful countenance and told him that there was more to us than meets the eye. He had thought long and hard about the concepts of good and evil.

It really came down to the Light and the Dark—good and evil existed under both of these paths. Sometimes that good or evil went back and forth, but it was always brought to bear solely by the individual and always by choice.

And this, the monster of a man had stated, was the root of all that does or does not get done in this world. In the end, whether free from or entwined with other outside influences or factors, we are the design to what good or bad things come about.

The sudden popping sound of the wagon wheels over the makeshift faces of the rocks stranded within the uneven road snapped Wybur back from his reverie. The air was crisp and patches of low lying fog shrouded much of the landscape. Branches from enormous trees along both sides of the stone-infested dirt road appeared to intertwine above to form a veining, wavy ceiling as Wybur gazed up.

But there would be no stars tonight. Dark, rolling clouds had been gathering for some time now to the west and south. Flashes of brilliant light could be seen far off in the distance, then smothered quickly by the heavy air. Lightning lit up the cloud cover like some strange, hooded lantern periodically turning and flaring. He briefly thought about Tamelyn Keep, which rested somewhere far off in that direction.

The storm looked ominous and would be upon them in no time at all. They might at least be able to make it to the stables of his uncle's store before the storm burst apart.

The scent of low burning fires wafted to them every now and then as the tiny caravan approached the city of Longshadows. This filled Wybur with the cozy feeling of home as they approached the outer posts of the Long Guard, Longshadows' own private militia. Not long after this followed the inner posts of the Watchmen. Wybur waved to the guards as they rode past.

The sprawling, unfettered trade city of Longshadows, nestled within the Free Lands, sat as a jewel of commerce. This city, without the usual high walls of defense and traditional bulwarks, was administered by none other than a group of equally benefited capitalists.

This select table, known as the Trade Council, seated twenty of the top merchants who had successfully plied the business of profit. They decided all courses of civil action and arbitrated the various judicial matters. Naturally, the council also held numerous magistrates with their own panels, as one council alone could never oversee such a multitude of people. If one were to be accused of some malicious or even minor penal act, then the one accused was presented in front of the governing magistrate for complete due process.

Of course, such a governing body had to have a means to effect such matters and their rulings, especially when the perpetrators turned unruly. While it was not a fortified bastion of defense, it did employ the all-volunteer city watch, the Watchmen, for such an occasion as well as keeping the peace. They handled the day-to-day and nightly flow of squabbles and altercations that ran amok throughout the various districts of Longshadows.

The Long Guard kept vigilance outside of and along the edges of the city. A sizeable militia itself, only a quarter of them were on duty at any given fortnight. The tall, wooden towers of the Long Guard rose up at various places. These towers took advantage of any high ground, where there was good visibility.

The city also garrisoned a detachment of the Black Legion, the Longshadows Company. But these contracted warriors were more for hire than obligated, official duties.

The southwesterly wind suddenly began to gust and swirl crazily, bringing down vast droves of large leaves to descend and chase each other about the ground. Then the torrents of rain began just as the three wagons pulled into the inner courtyard of Buttlecuts. The old, but freshly painted, sign hanging above the gate was blowing violently in the wind.

The city appeared to be completely bereft of anything living, as no people had taken to the streets yet. There was still a short while before the dawn's light would flood the lands.

Wybur ended up taking care of the supply books and all of the recordings for what had been delivered to Rory after he let the others go off to their homes. The stormy weather had not let up one bit. As a matter of fact, it seemed to grow even worse. As he locked up and prepared to walk home, he thought that he would be soaked within the short time that it would take to get there.

The Buttlecuts' store and grounds actually rested near the outskirts of Longshadows, close to where the North Way entered the city. The Buttlecut residence was still on the outskirts but farther to the east in the Greene District, which sent Wybur scurrying down several roads in a crisscross fashion. All the while, thunder and lightning swiftly clamored as the sky seemed to open up and let loose a raging river of cold water upon them.

Finally, Wybur saw the square, two-story house ahead of him. It sat nestled within the townscape as his uncle had wanted, with no neighboring property or structures within a hundred paces all-around. Of course, in the dark, one could not make out the rich blue color with trimmings done in bright yellow.

No light emanated from inside the house at this time, so it must have been earlier than he thought. Typically, his uncle would be up and moving well before dawn. With a mug of hot cider in one hand, his spectacled face would peer at ledgers and documents under the glow of a desktop lantern and several wall lights.

Wall lights were very ornate crystal decanters of naro or igna oil with long wicks that rose from the basin and thin glass bubbles to shield the burning flames. Those less fortunate would have simple tallow candles for the same purpose.

Naro was a thick, rich oil used for burning. It was gleaned from the fat of the narool. Narools were colossal sea beasts of mostly the Frostsea. They grew to be as large as a ship. These ill-tempered creatures had enormous gray and white bodies with blotched patterns of black. In addition to the burning fuel made from their fat, master smiths discovered that a cooling trough of naro was the best means of quenching a forged blade. It was proven to not alter the steel, or alloy metals, being worked. Also add to this the fact that a blade cooled at the optimal rate. Pure water was found long ago to cool too fast and thus ruin the weapon.

The hide of the narool was well-known for roofing material and wagon coverings due to its resilience to water. And the long, spiraled horn that extended out from the head of a male narool was prized for the special properties it offered in thaumaturgy. The naro trade was a very prestigious and time-honored tradition in Orondyraq, one taken up by Orondeers and their magnificent ships.

Igna was another fuel, or burning oil, of the times. It was found within the hard layers of the ignus rock, usually not very deep down in the arid desert lands. Sometimes vast pools of it existed in subterranean areas also. This thick, oily substance has an overpowering scent of a husky perfume with a bitter sting to the nose. Igna also turned out to be an invaluable metal cleaner, as rust does not attempt to eat weapons and gear that have been wiped with it. The igna lamp and igna itself were very lucrative lines of trade, originating from the Southern Kingdoms. Even Adan had its own igna mines.

Wybur approached the door, his drenched cloak flopping about the ground. That was strange. The door was cracked open no more than the breadth of a mouse's head.

He leaned forward slightly while peering inside as he fully opened it. The beads of rain cascaded off the loop of his hood, but still no sound or stirring came from within. Then he shuffled himself inside and quickly pulled the bolt behind him.

After finding the door open, he half expected to be met by his uncle who would be preparing to leave for his day at the Buttlecuts' store. Uncle Groelhof was punctual, as well as a man of routine. And he did not mess around when it came down to his business. There had been times when he did not even come home from his store the entire night, until early the next morning. And this was just to grab a bite to eat before heading right back again.

At least uncle would find the books in order and have one less thing to do, thought Wybur.

Not a sound could be heard within the house as Wybur futilely stared into the blackness. Something felt different, and that slight tremor of growing concern started up the back of his neck. He made his way to where the front room was and where his uncle should be.

As he entered the room and walked several steps towards where he estimated the desk to be, his foot suddenly glided forward uncontrollably, causing his whole body to lurch oddly unbalanced. Just before he lost his footing completely, he shuffled the other leg farther behind him.

But it was too late. As he maneuvered that leg, he could no longer maintain both legs at such an awkward angle. He fell flat on his face with a crashing thud. His nose felt an awful mess, taking the brunt of the rough landing. Black shooting stars erupted across his field of vision for several moments before he regained his composure.

Now he could feel a cold, sticky substance coating his face and neck and whatever else had connected with the floor in his plummet. The sludge apparently was what started his whole balancing ordeal in the first place, causing him to slip.

A faint, but acrid, coppery smell filled his nostrils as he stood up and found the wall light. The flint produced a quick spark which jumped the wick to flaming life.

His body jerked in shocking apprehension as he realized that the sticky substance was dark, partially coagulated blood. Now the whole front of his body was covered in the oozing gore.

To his horror, his eyes visually traced backwards from the freshly disturbed dark blood pool where he had fallen. His heart dropped to his stomach as he saw the mangled body of his uncle lying backwards on his desk. The origin of the bloody mess on the floor.

Large chunks of flesh had been torn out of the neck and chest areas, looking like a vicious animal had attacked him. The clothing in those areas was shredded and ripped completely through.

Wybur unthinkingly fumbled to grab hold of the wall light as if it might provide him some comfort or reassurance. But his clumsy and shaking fingers bounced off of it and the glass immediately hit the floor, shattering and splashing flaming oil all around. The entire puddle of the stuff quickly flared to life all at once as though a fiery fiend had risen from the wooden floor.

Momentarily frozen in place, with a look on his face that indicated he was not sure which dilemma was worse, he then whipped a small nearby rug up into the air and began to beat out the flames. Of course, this just made things worse and splattered fiery gobs of oil even farther out in the room.

As he turned back to face the grisly scene of his uncle, and now more than just panicked, one foot slid forward again, sending him to the floor. But this time, he went backside first. Now one could no longer tell that his clothes were drenched by rain as the dark blood soaked them completely.

Quickly, he jumped back up away from the bloody mess and grabbed the other wall light, putting fire to it from one of the flames dancing across the floor.

"Auntie Issa! You have to wake up and come down"—he stumbled on the first step—"*quickly* now!" cried Wybur as he wildly raced up the creaking flight of stairs and down the hallway to where the bed chambers were.

He stopped short as the light cast into their master chambers. The body of his aunt still lay amidst shredded and ripped bed linens.

At first, his mind told him that the linens had been redone with different designs, but it was only because of the macabre effect of the dark blood which had spurted and sprayed in a fountain of artistic frenzy.

His aunt's body was almost unrecognizable to him and appeared to be dismembered and twisted into the bed itself. He could not find his voice as he slowly backed out of the doorway.

When he finally made it to the twins' room, he fell against the wall and vomited from the sight that met his eyes. "Nooo... What is going on here?" murmured Wybur, even though the words were barely audible. The stench of the bared innards hit him like a wagon.

The small beds for the wee ones, now only in their third frostthaw, sat empty. But the beds had small latticed sides to keep them from rolling off in the middle of the night. Atop one of these sidings hung what looked like a dark tangle of yarn at first glance.

The entrails of one of the twins started here and hung down to the floor where it met with the rest of the small body. But most of it appeared to have been eaten, even the head partially missing. White portions of the skull dully glared out from the burgundy heap. Only a bloody mess, tiny fragments of flesh and bone, filled the other bed.

Wybur sat back against the wall and tried to catch his breath which was now coming and going in huge, raspy gasps. His head swam, and he felt faint as he vomited again. The tears flowed unchecked now and the small, salty droplets made his blood-caked face appear almost sinister.

Then Wybur froze and feverishly wondered if whatever had done all of this was still there. With all of the yelling and crying that he had done, the sounds must have been loud. He needed to get a grip! Then he remembered the Watch. Yes, he had to get the attention of the Watchmen and quickly.

The commotion must have already attracted one of the randomly patrolling pairs. Two men clad in studded leather armor, with fur caps on their heads and longswords at their sides, approached as Wybur opened the front door. His blood-drenched frame stumbled out, silhouetted against the steadily growing glow of the fire behind him.

"Please, I beg you! Help me, something terrible..." he cried and faded into unrecognizable stammering.

Of course, this sent the two men running inside with swords drawn to see what was going on. But, as they passed by, both stared in bewilderment at the figure covered from head to toe in blood.

At this point, poor Wybur suddenly realized in terror and panic that this predicament may not appear too innocent. The way that he looked, bloody clothes and all, might be misleading, especially to the Watchmen.

Whimpering slightly, he backed around to the corner of the house—and not a moment too soon. He vaguely took in the glow of dawn under the ominous black clouds, as he glanced towards the wilderness not far off and then back to the front door.

Then all Wybur could hear was one of the Watchmen shouting, "Murderer! Murderer! Stop that man!"

One short, sullen burst erupted loudly as one of them blew a horn to notify the rest of the Watch. At first, his thoughts turned to his mule Shab and how he might never see his traveling companion again. Who would take care of the poor thing?

Then the weight of his dilemma struck hard. He found himself running through the pale darkness towards the forest, eyes streaming tears, and all of his clothing soaked in his uncle's blood.

Chapter 6:

Clan Tharasvrul

All must be forsaken of the omnipotence of self and those bindings
of such vain bearing which are certain to impose.

–Fourth Edict of Lord Braxis, etched
upon the Great Slates, recovered by
Arterium circa the year 13 BA.

The small community of Black Clan Tharasvrul resided
along one of the higher hills, deep inside the Fallen Lands.
It had done so for nearly seven hundred years now. Clan
Tharasvrul did not know it, but it was the smallest of the
remaining Black Clans left on Zholryn.

The name Tharasvrul, in the Common tongue, literally translated to *shadeborn*, but the majority of the clan members have taken it as meaning of the night or of the darkness.

More slopes than hills, these highlands eventually rose into the mountains that saddled up with the Rock Rim. Tharasvrul sat within a series of expansive, elongated dales. The side of one dropped down into a long, deep ravine creating a natural passage in and out. Sparse pine wood covered the region, most of which rose into the tallness of fir trees. The growth was that of mixed hardwood and pine. The natural bowl-shaped tracts that contained Tharasvrul were nearly bare of most trees. These woods did not begin to form until down below it or out from the surrounding edges that encroached upon it.

The landscape provided an easily defendable fortress of sorts, The ground was strewn with rocky growths and surrounded by ledges which stair-stepped abruptly upwards.

The upper end of the central dale ran into a sizeable cavern, which opened up and reached far back under the highlands.

This was known to Clan Tharasvrul as the Great Cavern. The vast open areas between the ravine and the Great Cavern held countless structures and abodes of the dark ones of Clan Tharasvrul. Many of these were carved out of hardened, earthen mounds. But an equal number were built of timber, stone, and thatch.

With the cooler winds of the upcoming winterfall, the pale white smoke of warming and cooking fires hung low over the vista. It was still harvestspell, but the occasional icy winds blasting from the north and west were ominous signs of the coming frost. The cold would come faster and harder than it usually did.

The Great Cavern was enormous. There was more than enough room to house a significant number of the clan if need be. This could be done between the mouth of its entrance and a a narrow winding passage. This led far back to a ledge, which appeared to drop off into nothingness.

Besides housing the meditation chambers, it also contained the living quarters of the clan leadership, the Tharasvrul *Phaunim*. Phaunim meant triad. There were also makeshift storage areas for long term supplies. These quarters and chambers were all smaller caves within the larger one, carved back from the central wall. A Black Clan phaunim was made up of the clan elder, the clan priestess, and the pact spirit. The pact spirit was called *rhaanmri sgoth* in Black Clan.

Priestess Sahrya Khajrynghul Tharasvrul waited patiently in a specially constructed area beyond the reception hall to the meditation chambers.

Sahrya now belonged to this Black Clan, which knew nothing of her true past. She knew this was part of her destiny, even foretold hundreds of years ago by the Ancient One as a matter of fact. Not only did she belong, but she held the revered title of clan priestess.

Recently, she had also orchestrated the shift of the title of clan elder, the real head of the clan, to herself. That had not ever happened before, at least to her knowledge, within the past twelve turns.

Historically, a clan elder had always been the leader of a clan, with the clan priestess and the rhaanmri sgoth all together, comprising the phaunim that guided and made decisions for it. The rhaanmri sgoth was considered the manifestation of the spirit of the clan and the rhaanmri together, and this individual normally held the strongest bond with the animals of the rhaanmri.

For Clan Tharasvrul, fourteen mountain wolves comprised its rhaanmri. A Black Clan's rhaanmri formed a mutual relationship with the entire clan. Once this happened, these animals saw the dark ones of their clan as their own kind and held a very special bond with them. Both the animals of the rhaanmri and the members of the clan protected, nurtured, and cared for one another. This assimilation to the ways of each other was completed through both physical and spiritual rituals. This was one of the unique facets associated with the Black Clans.

The Tharasvrul Phaunim held their sensing sessions in the meditation chambers. Decisions were made here for the clan. Whether it involved simple arbitrations between the clan's members or a call to send out scouting parties for the security of the clan, the phaunim would join together and provide the guidance and judgment needed. This was not only in governance of the clan, but also for anything considered beyond an individual.

A Black Clan was like a very large extended family. All of the members carried the same last name as that of the clan name. Even though one may have more than a first name and the clan name, the clan name was always used as the actual surname even if one were to change clans (which was a rarity).

These chambers were also where the members of the clan could meditate and clarify their minds through their beliefs and visions. Normally, these areas were filled with members of the clan in peaceful solace, ever maintaining a commune with what they believed to be their essence and that of the Clan Tharasvrul Rhaanmri. The wolves would be by their side, sitting on their haunches with eyes closed, possibly attuned with the dark ones.

Ever since the recent passing of Elder Tarrne Tharasvrul, these areas had been empty. The reverent one had been the eldest amongst them. But his death was not age wrought.

The priestess had moved her Blackguard into the former chambers of the now deceased elder. The elite Blackguard, led by Khamatiri Mendonytes, comprised the most highly trained and disciplined warriors, all of who were also handpicked by her. These fierce warriors had been active for close to two turns.

Historically, the Blackguard of a Black Clan had been the protectors of its phaunim, as well as all established knowledge and holdings. Priestess Sahrya resurrected this unique unit once she had assumed her responsibilities more than four turns ago. The Blackguard had not been alive since the ancient days of Isnuuthghor.

But what Clan Tharasvrul did not know was that she also revived the ancient arts of the Blackguard. These arts involved fighting concepts and techniques now forgotten but extremely deadly.

The training methods were part of a secret order that ultimately originated from the master assassins of the Dhourkuul. But the abilities of the Blackguard of old also included limited thaumaturgy. The ancient warriors were rumored to have various artifacts of power. For instance, bracers which gave them abilities and traits of the Shadehaunt.

Sahrya stared at the flickering torch posted near the doorway. She smugly thought about how her plans were coming to fruition.

Sahrya had recently taken Elder Tarrne out of the equation. Killing him had not been her intent, but after he refused to concede to her, she really had no choice. He had been as stubborn as the feeble king of that cursed cesspool of a place, Kuhrzoth, in denying her power and eventual destiny. It did not take much for her to slip one of the most potent of poisons into his cup. The poison was a root extract from an old growth known as varnwood, only found within the deep jungles of the Thederye. This was one of the many things taught to her by the Ancient One. The root of the varnwood produced a toxin that affected the muscles in the body, especially the heart. Within moments of ingestion, the extract made it appear that the heart gave out in utter failure.

And Elder Tarrne was so wise and trusting. He remained so of her even after their heated argument.

Well, the anger and rage were really on her part over him not compromising, as he never took to showing anger or emotion.

As the clan priestess, she was the one to inspect the body for anything suspicious in the wake of the sudden death. It had been too easy. She then had supreme power in the clan. All except for Avrul, the clan's rhaanmri sgoth, but she too would either accept the destiny of their people or meet a similar fate.

Yes, Sahrya thought, *there would be more bloodshed amongst her kind.* But it was sanctioned by powers higher than even she. After all, the Ancient One had decreed this as the future of her kind. The future of the Aylsh Ismaru, the Black Clans.

The priestess' expedition to Crystal Peak and the Nook of the Reach had returned the evening prior. Now it was late in the night as she awaited her khamatiri and what he would bring to her. She very clearly remembered the time long ago, maybe eighty odd years now, when one of the keepers had approached her regarding a birthmark on one of the young.

The keepers of a clan were more maternal guardians who nurtured, taught, and protected the young of the clan while their mothers or other kin were performing their daily tasks. A keeper did not supersede the real mother, but would do so if the need ever arose.

Most of the time, the number of keepers was a constant. A keeper would usually be responsible for no more than ten young ones. The keepers worked hand in hand with the clan *turo*, who specialized in various subjects and spent their time teaching these to the young ones. A young one would spend the first eighty years to a turn learning and mastering these rigors. The name turo meant highbrow in Common.

She thought about the keepers and the turo. Then she fought back the distant, but livid, memories of her early years spent under the care of her true clan and its priestess, Vulmora. That one had been a true witch.

Both of Sahrya's parents had been slain on a raiding party into the north when she was young. This was the reason the clan priestess had taken her in.

Those days with her clan, Clan Omrasstefor, seemed like another world, another life that belonged to someone else.

It was then that she had first been privy to the subtle nuances of hidden agendas and motives. Vulmora did not take her under her wing out of pity or sympathy. She did so solely for appearance. While doing this one act of goodwill bolstered Priestess Vulmora up in front of her people, it eventually paved the road for her power. But behind the pretenses and shows of selflessness for the clan, what took place out of the light could only have been construed as wickedness and torture.

Vulmora treated her like a bug. Sahrya could not even take her leave to urinate or defecate without permission and sometimes would be forced to hold it until she went where she stood or sat. Then she was punished for doing so by having to lay in it until released by the priestess. These situations were mild though compared to the rest.

The real reason that Priestess Vulmora had kept Sahrya after her parents were slain became obvious. Vulmora was simply a cruel and malignant being with no bounds or remorse. Her only pleasure appeared to be the relish of pain and misery inflicted upon others.

And Vulmora truly enjoyed inflicting torment upon weak things, things that she could control and dominate. For Sahrya was not only subjected to demeaning things, but also to those of attrition and survival. Vulmora would leave Sahrya out in the wilderness alone for days on end, again, as punishment.

The first time this was done, Vulmora found her after three days, weak and almost dead. It was as if she had been watching her all the while and stepped back just in time before the young Sahrya perished.

It was during this time that Sahrya formed an undying relationship with the black panthers of the clan's rhaanmri. One of the mighty cats would come to her rescue nearly every time after that.

Vulmora would leave her for longer and longer periods of time, alone out in the wilderness. Each time, a cat would find her and sustain her while she endured the torment. In the end, the priestess thought Sahrya learned to survive on her own.

But that made things worse, as the cruelty of Priestess Vulmora could not be appeased. Sahrya was then bound each time and hung from a tree upside down for days.

Many years of dealing with these acts passed before one time turned out to be the demise of the priestess. The cats all turned on her at once.

It was after the priestess had returned with the starved and weakened Sahrya that they appeared. Several of them stood their ground, placing themselves between young Sahrya and Vulmora while Yhanduur, the rhaanmri leader, approached from her front.

Sahrya had never felt such satisfaction in anything before seeing that fearless rhaanmri panther leap upon the priestess. The muscular cat ripped and tore her apart amidst all the screams and spraying blood. The rest of the cats then joined in.

It had been as though the animals sensed Sahrya's silent cries for help the whole time and finally refused to put up with a being such as the priestess any longer.

An act like this would have been construed as one of natural order, subsequent judgment, and execution of that judgment. Such were the bonds between the clan and its rhaanmri.

But alas, there would be no such rejoicing or even time for the clan to realize what took place. It was that evening that the forces of Man-folk fell upon Clan Omrasstefor. The violence of the killing and raping that took place would forever remain etched within the confines of Sahrya's mind. Especially burned into her was the murdering of all the gentle cats of her clan's rhaanmri.

It was not long before one of the clan's keepers named Ghenwari hurriedly entered the chambers, disrupting Priestess

Sahrya's disturbing reverie. The keeper was barefoot and clothed in naught but a long, plain gown.

Ghenwari looked about and then to Sahrya with a wrinkled brow. "My Priestess, where is the young one who is ill?"

Sahrya stared at her for several moments before responding with a slow melodic tone. "Fear not, my Ghenwari. None are ill. I simply told him to use that in order to summon your presence quickly." She looked to Mendonytes before turning about with both hands resting along the back of a chair.

"Oh, why whatever for, my Priestess? You know that I would never have hesitated regardless...for you." Ghenwari smiled innocently as she spoke, with no sense of the impending danger crystallizing within the air.

Mendonytes slowly closed the outer door while the priestess began stepping towards another one set into the far back wall. This one led to a series of chambers, her private quarters where no one else was allowed.

With two of the Blackguard standing guard outside the outer door, Sahrya opened the other. "Let us go elsewhere and talk. There are important matters to be discussed."

As Ghenwari followed her through the door, Mendonytes trailed them into the next room. This similarly roughhewn chamber was long and rectangular with a corridor at the far end. Several sturdy wooden doors stood at attention along one side.

Plain, unadorned chairs sat in the middle of the room scattered around a small, wooden table. A worn bench with rows of drawers underneath was positioned along the opposite wall.

"Come. Sit," spoke Sahrya over her shoulder as she moved towards one of the chairs.

As Ghenwari sat down, Sahrya studied her beautiful features. She was just past her sixth turn. Her smooth, narrow face was almost hidden in the long tangles of black hair.

"My faithful Keeper, tell me about the one with the strange birthmark. What you mentioned so long ago to me. Do you remember?"

Ghenwari tilted her head slightly. "Why yes, of course, as it was such a peculiar thing for one to be born with. I at first thought it a mark made by another, but that would not be possible, as it had been on her as a babe so tiny. And yet the mark grew as she did, the way a finger or toe would. She has been such a specially gifted one, so smart and always taking to the studies so quickly. I don't think I have had another of the same all-around flair."

Sahrya folded her arms and dipped her chin while smiling so pretentiously. "So this young one that you think so fondly of, which one is she?"

Ghenwari paused for a moment and then said, "It is Zaramagrii, Elder Tarrne's granddaughter ..."—her voice trailed off and faltered as the painful memory of the loss clouded her face—"I am sorry Priestess. The late Elder... The thought of his loss still pains me. Amanshar's daughter, Zaramagrii, is the one that has the birthmark."

Priestess Sahrya soured her face in play. "All is well, Ghen. I too share your pain and sorrow for the loss of such a masterful dark one, along with the rest of the clan. But tell me of this mark."

The keeper's eyes rolled up in recollection. "Well, it is peculiar. It appears as a dark half sun right above her ura, on her lower abdomen."

Now the term *ura* was Black Clan for the female sex organs. It translated as cradle of life in literal terms and was held in high, sacred regard.

"Yes, go on, my proud one," Sahrya conceded as she momentarily closed her eyes.

Ghenwari continued as she glanced down at the cold, hard-packed dirt floor. "The lower part of this half sun has a lighter colored portion and then what look like the rays of the sun, appearing as lightning bolts, rising up and away from it. Radiating out. These rays are dark colored as well. I surely would have thought this mark had been made by someone if I hadn't seen it grow in perfect shape as she aged. It is the strangest thing." She had been so engrossed in thought and talk that she never even noticed as Mendonytes positioned himself directly behind her chair.

The priestess' eyes flashed to the huge Blackguard captain several times as she continued her dialogue. "So who else have you told about this? Tell me now, not holding back from me what might have been of ominous significance…for so many years." She leaned forward as she spoke and gently grasped both of Ghenwari's hands within her own, appearing as though she meant to console her.

The rich violet eyes of Ghenwari suddenly widened as she heard the icy tone. Mendonytes placed a huge hand around her neck. She could not move from the chair, now pinned between it and the table.

She sobbed in a huge gasp and frantically stammered, "No, I would never do that. I only meant to bring it up to you so you knew…but, but never would I have thought it vital. Nor would I ever hold anything from you, I…I thought it was something trivial that I was overly concerned with when you appeared to not even care about it."

Mendonytes now grasped a long, thin rod with a sharp point on one end. It was gleaming silver in color and had a palm-shaped, flattened portion on the opposite end. Quick as lightning, he raised it up and then slammed the rod straight through the middle of Ghenwari's hand as it was being held out by the priestess. It stuck deep and stayed fast in the wood of the table, piercing completely through her bone. The wiry Ghenwari winced in pain and shock, instinctively grasping the impaled hand with her free hand.

Again, another sharp rod came swishing down, now piercing through the wrist of what had been her good hand and also going through the other as it sank deeply into the table beneath.

The keeper let out a scream of pain as her eyes squeezed shut with tears welling out. She cried, "Nooo… No… Don't! I've done nothing wrong." Her voice turned to a broken whimper.

Sahrya stood and faced her, leaning slightly forward at the waist. "*My* dear keeper, of course you haven't done anything wrong. *You* just deceived me for nearly a *turn*!" she screamed.

"And, Ghenwari, *you* are weak and miserable! Now tell me who else you've told about Zaramagrii and her mark. *Now*!"

Mendonytes held another one of the shiny, wicked rods. His other hand firmly gripped the top of Ghenwari's head as she fought to get free of her painful predicament.

Ghenwari slurred her words through tears and spittle. "I told you… No one *knooooows*. I have told no one. Even her mother always tried to hide it and made sure no one noticed it." The words trailed off, ending with a big sob.

The Blackguard captain then slowly inserted the tip of the rod into her right eye, dribbling all of the contents into a gooey mush that crept down the side of her face. She screamed again, not really from pain this time, but from the lack of it in this area of her body and the realization that her vision was gone from that eye.

"Have no fear, my deceitful one. No one can hear you in here, but I still need to know who else knows before I can release you," wickedly whispered Sahrya in her ear.

Ghenwari now sobbed uncontrollably as she pleaded, "No, no one. *No one else.*"

The Blackguard then slowly collapsed her other eye until it protruded out and dripped onto her cheek. Her head raised back as she hoarsely screamed, nearly ripping her upper hand free in a thick, fleshy tearing sound.

Sahrya slowly spoke with flatness, "Very well. Very well indeed. I think that maybe I'll believe you now."

Then the short black blade of Mendonytes' arming sword sliced through the air, neatly slitting her throat. A quick wash of arced blood sprayed through the air.

Ghenwari gurgled and choked, no longer able to voice words. She slumped forward on the table as her blood washed over it, cascading to the floor from the edges. Eventually, her body lay still in all of the gore.

Sahrya thought there could possibly be more to the ancient legends and lore than she knew. And was it possible that one from this very clan was part of it all? The so-called Soul within the lost Amethyst Scroll?

But the Ancient One had already foreseen the prophecy being fulfilled by her, and her alone. She, Priestess Sahrya Omrasstefor Khajrynghul Tharasvrul, was the one to reign supreme and lead her kind out of their own self-induced banishment and back to her home. She would reseat the Black Clans at Isnuuthghor in all of their former glory. And she would squash the Man-folk as ants under their sandaled feet, ruling over them and all other things in this world.

She looked to Mendonytes as he wiped clean his sword. "My loyal captain, find out where Zaramagrii and her mother are at this moment. I will get to the bottom of this whole thing. A young one? That could never be, but even so, we will ensure that such madness goes no farther."

Then she spitefully eyed the motionless, crumpled form of Ghenwari. "Oh, my Khamatiri, quietly round up all of this keeper's family members and those closest to Amanshar and Zaramagrii. We will make sure none of this has become knowledge to any of them."

§ § §

Not far from the mouth of the cavern was a fairly large abode made mostly from hardened soil, partially inlaid with large rocks and various timbers to provide stability to the mud-thatched, domed roof. The gathering area surrounding the fire pit inside had to be large enough for scores of clan members and also the wolves of the rhaanmri at any one time. Such a gathering was one of the main purposes of this place.

Avrul Tharasvrul, Clan Tharasvrul's Rhaanmri Sgoth, awoke suddenly. The night had not yet parted, and her fire burned low.

She felt something pull on her blanket and turned to see Daraphyn, the eldest mountain wolf of the rhaanmri. Her thick, pure silvery fur, speckled with patches of black, almost appeared to glow under the embers of the dying fire.

The old female, mother of so many wolf pups, sat on her haunches near the opening that led out into the darkness. Her head was canted down, her muzzle nearly touching her chest, and her ears lay flattened back. Dara had apparently swung one of her paws up to tug at the blanket covering Avrul.

"What is it lass? What is wrong?" whispered Avrul to the wolf as she gently pulled the animal closer to her. Dara just nuzzled her face into the blanket and curled up in a ball beside her.

Avrul stared at the ceiling for a while. The old wolf trembled, she could feel her shaking. Something was wrong, but Avrul could not sense exactly what. It was like the wolf had experienced a bad dream. Maybe that was all that it was.

Avrul was so tired that she softly caressed Dara's head, rubbing the soft fur between her ears as she drifted back to sleep.

But Dara did not sleep. Instead, she lay watching and listening. She knew something had happened to one of the clan members, and she knew that something terrible was coming. So she waited and guarded her rhaanmri sgoth. Ready for whatever thing might come.

Chapter 7:

A Destiny Begins

All forms of the Oadenruun shall be nurtured as hidden facets of the essence. None shall be taken as lashes of governance or liable as such.

–Fifth Edict of Lord Braxis, etched upon the Great Slates, recovered by Arterium circa the year 13 BA.

manshar Tharasvrul's face glowed with pure love and pride as she smiled at the dark one standing before her. Her youngest—Zaramagrii Nusthafay Tharasvrul.

Amanshar herself barely showed the years of age since so long ago when her offspring was born.

Zaramagrii, even though still considered in her adolescence after some eighty-seven years in this life, had become very adept at all the basic rigors and studies of her Black Clan ways. She was extremely agile and remarkably endowed with what seemed like supernatural flairs.

But Amanshar knew the hidden truth was more profound than that. Her people were not only those of the Black Clans, but also of Man-folk and others, no doubt. There was an indiscernible depth to the very mixed lineage that her young one was born to. But what more exactly? This alone was uncommon. For those of the Black Clans never mingled their blood with beings outside of their own kind. Indeed a rarity, but also what would be considered a blemish or stain upon her folk if they ever found out.

Zaramagrii was an exquisite beauty. Her dark skin, more exotic than most of the Aylsh Ismaru, slightly glistened with a trace of light or phosphorescence as though it held tiny particles of diamond dust across the surface. Those huge eyes raged out of that blackness like piercing gems of tranquil fierceness. The right one glowed like a piece of obsidian and the left shone like a glimmering diamond.

This dark one was so strong and lithe, but then so gangly in appearance at times. It was the time for her age of innocence to turn to maturity. And little did either of them know that the times ahead would turn dark, darker than ever before. The world as they knew it was headed for a storm.

What beauty they had created, thought Amanshar. A beauty of darkness. They were indeed destined to do so.

She thought about him then as she often did. He was the outsider, or maybe she had been the outsider, as she had stumbled into him while exploring his world along the outer edge of the Rock Rim. But it always seemed as though he had known they would meet. He almost appeared to know exactly where she was that first early morning in the sunlight. He had not been surprised at all when they first faced one another.

Yes, Zaramagrii's father was no doubt well aware of what would form within Amanshar. What he had planted there to spring forth.

She remembered seeing those dazzling eyes, his eyes, for the first time. Their ancestry could readily be seen within Zaramagrii's now. At least, the shape and contour. The spark.

Both of his were jet black beads, but the right was surrounded by silvery white while the left was centered in the middle of gray. Yet, at the moment that he climaxed inside of her, she briefly studied his face and saw the smoky black orbs of what had been those handsome eyes.

She had always thought back to this as maybe just the shady veil of the day frolicking across his face. But she distinctly noted the black flames burning in those eyes at the time, as they even further aroused her and intensified her own climax.

It was so intense that she nearly succumbed to the sea of stars as her head swam in an ecstasy of billowing fog that encased their bodies. Maybe that had been her mind playing tricks on her, but the scene stuck within her memory so vividly, even after so much time.

The exact same thing transpired during each of the encounters they had, until he was lost to her. Lost like a torch blown out in the midnight winds of winterfall.

Here before her was reality. Her daughter. His daughter. He was real. Zaramagrii was real. She tried to convince herself so many times that maybe he was some phantom of a dream that had seemed genuine at the time. But that would have only been her own fairy tale.

Amanshar held out her hands towards the young dark one. "Zaramagrii," she stated, sounding more like someone embodying the object of their lifelong dream. "Zaramagrii, come, my love, and stand close."

Zaramagrii stood there with one hand on her hip, not more than a pace from Amanshar. Those long, pointed ears poked out ever so slightly through her evenly cut hair. The shoulder length, jet black strands cascaded down like a dark crescent moon on each side of her face. Thin, silvery portions ran down the entire length of those strands in several places.

The tiara that Amanshar had given her covered most of her forehead with a huge, round black gem. It appeared like a small, shiny egg with silvery legs. This had been Amanshar's intent. Zaramagrii would at least appear to have the symbol of her clan imbedded in the tiara so as to throw off anyone's scrutiny upon it. Why such scrutiny would need to be thrown off remains yet to be known.

Zaramagrii moved closer, her head slightly tilted to the side as she wrapped her arms around her mother.

Zaramagrii did not know why her mother had brought her back here where they could look down on the darkness below them. Here, on the edge of Tharasvrul's vast sprawling lands. Inside the Great Cavern, overlooking the very darkness that engulfed the existence of the Black Clans throughout history.

The ledge, towards the back of the Great Cavern, was a common place where those of the clan could spend time in silence and reflection. The turo built an altar of sorts not far from where the ledge dropped off into nothingness.

The space was fairly cramped and only appeared after one crouched through a winding, narrow passage. Only two torches hung, one on each side of the entry, casting flickering shades of orange on the dark scene. This made the tiny space look impressive as the light trailed into blackness where the ledge opened up and dropped off. No one knew how far back or down that blackness went.

Amanshar noted again how cool to the touch Zaramagrii felt, like she had just emerged from a swim in very cold water. She always felt this way, even as a little babe. This was not the normal feel of one of the Black Clans. For this reason, they had nicknamed her *Nusthafay* which literally translated to Wyntertouched.

But most things at least appeared normal with Zaramagrii. Indeed, things appeared almost too good as far as Zaramagrii's ability to learn and adapt to anything. She had been exceptional at all things, from the enlightening arts like history and the lay of the land, to mastery of the martial arts native to her kind. She could stand toe to toe with their mightiest warriors even at such a young age. And this included a variety of weaponry she had become accustomed to.

Again Amanshar thought back to her short-lived relationship with Zaramagrii's father, and the things he had spoken of. His deep, rolling voice almost soothed her every time he spoke. At times, she would not even know the meaning of the words spoken, just the calming sound of the voice.

She could understand the language, but the spirit of that voice was like the roaring crescendo of a chorus being sung, hitting to the bone of the essence. The words resounded but were so subconscious at the same time that the comprehension was numbed beyond reasoning. Until the mind and the thought solely rested upon an enchanted rhythm with no more contemplation or matter to the meaning of the words spoken. Amanshar had been so mesmerized that she could not even comprehend time or the amount of it spent after one of their encounters.

He called himself Sorak in the Common tongue, even though he would occasionally go into fluent Black Clan as well. The place he hailed from was far away, according to him. Then he would always laugh and joke that only the night would tell of it. He would claim to be the master of the night and a seer of dark things. And he would always startle her at this point by abruptly pouncing towards her with his hands outstretched. Faster than a wolf, he would tickle her until she was lightheaded. Then he would laugh loudly as if challenging the entire world.

Sorak reminded her several times that their creation was to be a gift to the world, if not to time and existence. Their creation would be very special. He made Amanshar promise that she would protect it at all costs and teach it truth. And not just what the dark ones knew as truth and wanted their offspring to mindlessly believe. She was to take all things encountered or taught and then balance that with the real truth. The real truth? Amanshar wondered what he'd meant.

It was then that Sorak began to unravel reality. Not the reality, or perception, of each of the sentient kinds—but the cold, hard facts of the world. It was as though Sorak presented her with how things happened and appeared to be, looking down upon it all from high atop a pedestal. He was untainted by time's storytelling or the minds of Braxis' creations.

As much knowledge as possible had to be interpreted and explained so that what he labeled as *a good base to reality* would be there for their creation's voyage into destiny.

He spent what could have been many late-suns, or even entire days, for all she knew at the time, explaining the world of Light, the world of Dark, and how all things were different. He made her understand the symmetry of all living kinds—both within their material world as well as other realms of existence— as they interacted and socialized in their survival and journey through life.

This voyage of discovery was more than fascinating to her. She had never imagined there was so much more to this world than what she had narrowly experienced or been taught by her kind, and she had now lived for such a long period of time. He brought all of that truth forward so she could counter whatever might appear otherwise to their creation.

The main point she grasped about her people was the unjust persecution and suppression of the Black Clans by the world and existence. For whatever reason, whether by the natural laws of attrition or some sinister supernatural force, her kind had been slowly dwindling away. The Black Clans, the dark ones, should be everlasting within such a world. Those who thrived for nearly twenty turns of time, from birth to their passing.

The Black Clans have always been considered a wise and knowledgeable folk, with such longevity. Why would such a kind possibly be down to its last tiny, niche of a population, at least as far as she was aware of?

To this day, there had been no indication that another clan still survived out there. Ever since the clans had scattered into the world from their stronghold of Isnuuthghor so long ago.

They were always taught that darker things had invaded their ancestral home, things that had been powerful enough to cause them to flee from it. But the elders never stated exactly what these things had been. They always just referred to them as things of ancient power and claimed it was better left unsaid.

She felt justified, more righteously empowered now, to make good of all that she could from Sorak and the birth of their young one. Once she saw little Zaramagrii's form enter into the world, Sorak's revelation turned into a passion to ensure that their offspring would survive at all cost. She would be blessed with the purity of life. Amanshar saw to that and always pushed to balance the content that fed Zaramagrii's heart, mind, and essence.

Sorak had especially been domineering when it came to talk of their creation, almost as though he reveled in certainty even though there could have been no possible way of him knowing Amanshar would be filled with seed. For such a long time, she had no clue to what he was speaking of. Not until she first took to the hunger, and the growing size of her belly. Then she knew that she was carrying another life inside her.

Even though she had felt this before, with her two first born, this one created such anticipation with her—as though time started moving faster and would eventually run itself out. Like there was now a limit to how much time she actually had. And she had never felt this feeling of mortality in such a way previously.

She remembered him almost hesitantly whispering that there would be exultant joy, as well as pain and misery at some point. But she had to make a promise him, with an oath to give up her very essence if need be. That, no matter what happened, she would protect what was born. This transpired each and every time they met on the bearskin, which seemed so soft and warm against her naked body.

Sorak told her at their first encounter that there was a matching essence made for every other one in existence, made for each other, destined to be reflections of one another. The higher divinities had ordained this in the very beginning.

The Initiator of Zholryn, Lord Braxis, imbedded in all that was defined this one key attribute within the physical and immaterial matter of all species that walked, slithered, and flew. The purpose was the propagation of each of the species. The true matching essences would procreate near perfections of their kind. For the mirrors held the inherent properties of Lord Braxis, providing that they found each other.

There was the one enormous, laughable flaw that the Initiator knowingly set in motion with this, though. And that was randomness.

In such a large and dangerous world full of not only other denizens, but also various realms of existence, these spirits might not ever, even remotely, come near one another. In some cases, the two may meet and never realize it. Now, for the two destined matching ones to find one another, that was a true feat.

All of the higher powers that be, both the Olden and the Myno, might sit around and watch as these entities passed one another by, or thrived in completely separate regions, possibly realms. Some may even grant divine intervention at their whim and leisure, maybe for a loftier but obscure purpose and design.

At this point, Sorak always softly told her that he had a vision where he saw her in the wooded glen after emerging from the dark. He said that it was a perfect image of clarity where he could see every line and contour of her face and body, as well as her naked essence. He and Amanshar were mirrors that were meant to be joined together for fragments of time, maybe not forever. But what he also saw was the creation from their time spent together. That creation was a destiny far above the intent of any other.

Amanshar stared deeply into Zaramagrii's eyes while gently grasping both of her shoulders, "My young beauty. You have grown so much over the past…so strong, canny, and full of life. I have never wished for anything such as you before. You are my dream, Zaramagrii, my very life."

She quickly looked up and away for a moment as tears of both joy and sorrow welled up in her eyes. All of the memories, moments of time spent, and thoughts of all intermixed from the past near turn brought forth such powerful, raw emotion. Her immeasurable love for her young one, the hopeless foreboding of the unknown future, the sudden death of her father, Clan Elder Tarrne—all clashed to create a torrent of silent, raging premonitions of internal controversy.

Amanshar held Zaramagrii's hands tightly, "Zaramagrii, you must make me a promise and then never forget it."

Zaramagrii, looking slightly down into her mother's eyes, deciphered the mixed fog of emotion playing through that mind and perceived her mother's tense nature. An almost expectant air of inevitable strife yet to show itself.

"Yes, my mum, I will do whatever you ask. What is it?"

Those large, mixed-colored gems of eyes filled with such innocence questioned her mother, waiting for her words. Amanshar was reminded of the very first time that she set eyes on those orbs, during the midst of battle. Such inspiration. The drive to go on for that little bundle of wonder that had come into her life on that wooded hilltop long ago. The birth of this poetic creation when there was so much death and chaos wildly strewn about.

Amanshar carefully thought about how to say something that she really did not even know as fact. It was just a feeling, a combination of all that had happened up to this point. But it was one of gut instinct that exposed itself as the naked truth.

"Zaramagrii, promise me that no matter what happens or takes place—with me or Tharasvrul—with anything. Promise that you will never forget all that we have talked about for the past near turn almost."

She paused momentarily to allow Zaramagrii to accept her words. She continued once she saw that light in Zaramagrii's eyes telling her that all of her attention was now upon her mother. "You are indeed special and unique. There is more to your birth than you or I could ever imagine. I myself do not know what that is, but you are here for a higher purpose.

"Always think of me when you see your tiara… The gem set within it is an heirloom from your grand one."

A grand one was simply the namesake for those venerable of age. It did not really specify one's grandparents, but in this case, Amanshar used it to refer to her own father.

"Such a gem must stay within your grasp so that someday it can be passed down again."

Of course, Amanshar only told her this to impress upon her the gem's importance. Truth be told, the gem was a mere worthless facade. The only real value laid inside, what it concealed.

A dark cloud passed over Amanshar's face, from a dark time within her thoughts. The now commanding priestess, only an usurper and a murderer to Amanshar, had succeeded in plying her subtlety throughout Tharasvrul. Pure manipulation in her silent and deceitful, but quick, assumption of the clan. The death of Amanshar's father still hung over her head, and it was riddled with unanswered questions.

Amanshar knew that the priestess had been busy doing unknown, possibly sacrilegious, acts who knows where in the world, or under it for that matter. Somehow Priestess Sahrya was linked to her father's death. A very untimely death, possibly even by the priestess' hand. She knew this in her heart. She felt it.

"Trust not what Priestess Sahrya says and does. I fear that she has hidden intentions about her. This clan was not the one of her origin like you and I. Sahrya was found many turns before you were even born.

"A patrol had gone out to scout the lands around us the night before she walked into our home here. That patrol never came back.

"Instead, Sahrya walked into our midst carrying the one that led it, dead. Her story had been that she came across the patrol and found them dead, except for him. But she claimed that he died on the way back here, after he told her where we were.

"We went to check on the patrol. We found them all dead just like she had told us. Many were torn apart and charred from some kind of fire. She claimed that she had not seen who or what had done this to them. And this in itself is an elusive tale to be told, as we never did find out anything about what happened."

Amanshar paused, as the somberness of that day passed over her face.

"That day, my only two young ones and my mate…all of them impressive and proud warriors, were on that patrol. I was such a young mum at the time." A tear streamed down her face as she relived the deaths of her two first born young ones and their father.

"Sahrya has been doing things that she claims are to bring back our culture and the Old Ways. But some of these ways died for a reason, and they should be left that way. She has been doing it also to increase her power no doubt. The Blackguard adds much to that, especially with their deadly skills. And I fear that she has revived those ancient techniques used by them as well.

"Now, listen carefully, as you must maintain these things and trust no one but yourself. The priestess may have had something to do with the elder's death. I can feel it but have nothing to show for it. Now you must also keep your birthmark hidden, for I think that it is a symbol of the future, of things yet to come. Somehow, all of these things and you are tied up together. But I haven't been able to make complete sense out of it yet.

"My little Zaramagrii, I never meant for anything of this sort to befall you. Please know that I would do anything to keep you safe. There are other forces in the world at work, never doubt that. And never question that everything happens for a reason. But you must be prepared, and this is why I am telling you all of this. So that you know it and accept it.

"Your father passed to me all of the things that I have been passing on to you. Even though I only knew him over a handful of times that we met, it was like we had always been together. And that feeling, that bond or love that was ours, still is. I feel it. It far exceeds the bounds of that with even my first mate whom I had known for all of my life up to his death.

"I am telling you this so that you know there is so much more to this world than we can see or ever imagine. Trust in your instincts and judgment, Zara, and also in what you might see. And not only with your eyes."

Zaramagrii's gaze fell to the ground, her eyes turning into large mirrors of budding wonder and contemplation as she realized the magnitude of what her mother told her.

Suddenly, Amanshar stiffened and turned her head slightly. She sensed a presence nearby but could not put her finger upon it exactly. The surrounding air fell in an ominous and foreboding downpour. Her first thought was to protect her most cherished thing in existence.

"Quickly, come, Zara," Amanshar whispered as she pulled Zaramagrii towards the lip of the ledge, peering over it into the blackness. There, not far down, was a small outcropping of rock.

"Listen to me now. I want you to stay down until I come back to get you. 'Tis probably nothing at all, but it is better to play it safe."

Amanshar carefully helped her climb down to the small shelf, mostly lowering her by her arms. The uneven ledge was not very accommodating, but it had a waist-high rise on the far side that would keep Zaramagrii from accidentally falling over. This made Amanshar yield more easily to the notion of leaving her there.

Even though Zaramagrii was full grown, Amanshar still could not help seeing the little, innocent dark one in those beautifully large pools of eyes. Soon, Zaramagrii's figure was lost to her sight, completely hidden within the murky wash of the ledge.

Zaramagrii simply stared back with welling fear in her eyes. "But, mother, wait. What is it?"

The only response that Zaramagrii received from her mother was the sight of a finger to her lips, motioning for her to be silent.

Amanshar returned back to where they had stood, closer to the stone altar. She looked towards the rough opening that led back to the main cavern. Someone was coming, the occasional shuffling of the steps echoed off of the walls.

The cloaked form of Priestess Sahrya appeared from the darkness, the two elongated designs on the front of her cloak appearing as sinister crimson eyes floating in the dark.

Priestess Sahrya's thin face was wrinkled with a smirk, the timeless headpiece reflecting the torchlight while her purple eyes gazed upon Amanshar. She slyly glanced about as though searching for something, or someone.

"My fair Amanshar. I am honored to see you here this eve."

Amanshar could make out the tall, dim outline of the Blackguard captain not far behind her, waiting, watching.

"My Priestess Sahrya, why I never expected to see you here tonight. What a pleasure," she said almost mockingly. Her eyes flared towards what she considered to be the implement of her father's demise.

Zaramagrii could not really see much above the ledge from where she crouched, except for her mother's head and that of another tall form facing her. But that was only when she dared to raise up ever so slightly for a glimpse. It was fairly dark and the cavern wall that she leaned against was cold and gritty. But she heard voices talking now from above, one voice was her mothers. And then she knew who the other belonged to. The priestess had found them.

Sahrya merely smiled and crossed her arms, one of her hands holding an intricately crafted rod. It was crafted from dark wood, and covered with gemstones of varying colors, and fine gold.

"Well met, my wretched one, why not say exactly what you mean? After all, you do mean that sarcastically…especially for one such as I that has taken your father from you." This hiss of words was violently thrown through the air like daggers.

The rage that overcame Amanshar could not be contained. "You stand here and admit such travesty? You claim responsibility for a cowardly act of backstabbing?"

Amanshar could barely keep still and squeezed her hands into balled-up fists turning pale in color.

The priestess silently looked her over for a moment. "Why, my Amanshar, daughter to the prestigious Elder Tarrne, yesss! I slew him, and I had immense satisfaction in doing so. But…" She stopped abruptly as her lips twisted into a wicked grin. "But not as much satisfaction as I had in doing away with your dark one and two little runts with that patrol so long ago! Their agony is still fresh in my mind, and I cherish it often."

At this point, Mendonytes braced himself for action and readied the hideous pollaxe.

This was too much for Amanshar, as her right hand suddenly began to glow with arcane might. A sizzling, bluish-white ball of energy transfixed upon it while extending upwards.

Amanshar let the glowing missile fly straight towards the priestess and screamed, "You will pay for what you have done, you witch!"

Sahrya did nothing as the missile arced at her, striking and then shattering into a hundred sparks as though it had hit an invisible wall around her. She laughed.

"My little one, why, is that all you have? My dear, I have studied far beyond your abilities it seems, and in the many disciplines at that."

In an instant, Amanshar froze, unable to move. Even her breathing appeared strained. It was as though some unseen force held her completely motionless, helpless.

"Now, tell me, child…and I do mean *tell* me, as my patience for you is gone, where is that young one of yours, Zaramagrii?"

Amanshar spat at her. "You will have nothing to do with her, you bitch! I shall never let you do anything to her!"

"Now, my Amanshar, you mistake me. I merely want to speak with her. But what a shame. I do not need you to find Zaramagrii. Now I will show you true power!"

As Amanshar's eyes went wide with dawning realization that she wouldn't be able to protect Zaramagrii, the priestess' form began to take on a sinister red hue. Strong winds gusting from behind her raged towards Amanshar. A brilliant white explosion burst forth from where Amanshar was held motionless. The crack was ear-splitting, like lightning had struck. All was lost in the cloudy chaos of smoke and heat.

Once the dust, debris, and nauseating smoke began to dissipate, nothing remained of Amanshar but several charred pieces of flesh and bone. The largest being that of one whole foot, which landed near the feet of Priestess Sahrya.

Even the rock altar was gone. A smoking crater lay where it had been. The crater's tail stretched out to where the floor dropped off into darkness. The blast took out a good portion of the ledge itself.

Meanwhile, Zaramagrii shivered from the tension of what played out not very far from her, as the tones turned to grating rage, then her mother's helpless exasperation.

Her mind raced. She yearned for another chance to tell her mother that she loved her. That she could not express what she felt for her mother with words because it was so profound. Other things flashed through her inner focus. Things she had kept from her mother. Things she now wanted so much to tell her.

Then, in a potent roar, everything was silenced by the blinding, stunning eruption of energy that sent her reeling.

The place where the small outcropping had been just below the ledge was completely gone. And so was the thought-to-be frail form of Zaramagrii, tossed down into the blackness of the unknown by the force of the explosion.

But Zaramagrii's life had been far from perfect, the facade of what had been also came crashing down off of that ledge into the darkness. Things not yet emerged to her coherence, secrets buried within the perceived normality, echoes that wanted to reach out and be heard.

Chapter 8:

Dawn of the Eternal

Mother

The whole of the many seek that which is most profound. Even when splintered shall each be the same, and so shall all kinds act towards their others.

–Sixth Edict of Lord Braxis, etched upon the Great Slates, recovered by Arterium circa the year 13 BA.

he squat pine trees lurched and swayed in the blasts of the northern winds. Lofty white birch trees popped as they partially thawed in the warmth of the duo suns after the freezing night. The sound was as loud as the hammer of a blacksmith at work. Winterfall was still a fortnight or two distant, but that did not hold back the icy weather this far north along the eastern Rock Rim.

Nestled high along the upper rim, but still under the crest, sat a small timber dwelling. It rested amongst large, snow covered meadows populated by thick growths of mixed birch and pine trees. Fluffy, white smoke poured out of the stone-laid chimney. A rock wall skirted several paces out around the small place.

The sturdy, hardwood door slowly opened. It swung in to do so, its thickness revealing the large timbers used to design it. Framed against the cozy lighted interior stood a young woman wearing striking gray furs tightly clinging to her figure.

The woman's lean, trim form arched slightly in a stretch while stepping outside. Black leather boots rode to her upper thighs, accenting her toned legs with smooth, doeskin leggings visible. Long, auburn hair curled all around her head. The greenest of green eyes stared out at the snow from a flawless face that appeared even younger than her age of twenty-six summertides.

Rhalwa Jadorthanelle, Wildborn. She was born of Thimoryn Jadorthanelle—Master Ranger under the Emerald Crown once upon a time. A thing that, at least to Rhalwa, now only whispered to her from a very distant past.

Her nose wrinkled briefly as the fur from the fox tail touched it while stretching her arms up in a yawn. Life for her was one with nature, as taught to her by her father.

Not even the fox fur that helped keep her warm was taken solely for that need. Instead, she had waited until the fox passed on from age, watching it every day, as well as providing meat and water when the poor creature could no longer get them on her own. Only after the old fox passed on did she take the hide.

This was the way of the ranger, ever the caretaker, as well as the protector of the creations on Zholryn. Ultimately, being one with the wildlands and those things that thrived there.

She warmly remembered her father, who had passed eight years back now. Even though Aylsh, her father already had been old when she was born. He had been one of the last of the brave and fearless rangers under the Kuhrzothian crown. But that time had been long before hers, long before she set eyes upon this world.

The rangers under the banner of Kuhrzoth watched over the wildlands, especially the Fallen Lands. They took pride in keeping the common people safe.

Most folk in Thaldeia referred to the uncivilized areas not governed or under any kind of thumb as the wildlands.

Of course, most territories were sketchy at best anyways. Not one king or magistrate could draw a line on what they considered to be the bounds of their territory. At least not one that would match up with any other noble or official of the same lands. Sure, a Kuhrzothian knight could tell you all day long that it was a score of days' ride from one end of the kingdom to the other, and an equal amount from north to south. But not a one, king or knight, could go out and clearly mark the line that might be called the border.

In fact, this very thing had been the start of at least one war back in the early days. Kuhrzoth and Ravenkort conducted many a bloody campaign for just this kind of crude squabble over shifting lines of ownership. Many times it was a knight, or cavalier as the knight lords of Ravenkort were known as, getting his breeches in a bundle over some fair lass of nobility from the rival lands.

The Tourney itself came about to be a mediator for many squabbles. Not long after the move of the festival to Longshadows, a proclamation was instituted that most kingdoms accepted. It allowed for any disputes of honor to be reconciled through combat, whether there was any hard proof to the guilt or not. This process applied for all of what were termed *Rights of Honor*. These included the extreme transgressions of murder, treason, heresy, disloyalty to one's lord, betrayal at arms, falsehood, and the disparagement of a maiden or lady. The accuser or dishonored one was required to petition her own kingdom's form of civil regulators. The party who allegedly committed the described acts would then be summoned to add their own voice to the matter. The civil regulators would then determine whether or not to push the matter to the officiating Council of Tourney. If this council accepted the motion, then the event would be set up for the next Tourney. Of course a king could unquestionably dictate such standoffs as he saw fit. Tourney or not.

When the Emerald Crown decided to dismantle the rangers, Rhalwa's father told her that he decided he had enough of nobility and the politics of kings. He was finished with royalty of any kind.

Let them figure it out, he had told her, and let them sacrifice what they know nothing of in their safe, warm little walls. For he—like some other thousand rangers—gave up trying to convince anyone of the dangers that lurked out there, what they dealt with on a routine basis.

These hardened folk—mostly Aylsh, half-Aylsh, even some mixed Akhruuk—all quietly dispersed back into the wild mostly. Some of them found other professions amongst civilization again. And very few kept up the primeval ways of the ranger, at least openly.

Ever since the passing of her father, she reflected more upon what her purpose might be and what to do with her life. Out here, within the solitude of the world. The wild and rugged home that she knew so well.

She pondered leaving her home many times over, but the last words of her father had been for her to follow her heart. And her heart ended up always wanting to remain here, even after the bouts of indecision and doubt.

It had been she who sent her father off on his final journey, a noble pyre set on fire to consume the physical form and join the essence back with the Wild. The spirit fading back to where it hailed from. Such was the way for a ranger.

He had told her carefully what to do for the traditional cleansing upon his passing. The salve made up of ground sage, pine knot, whistleweed, and mountain red flower was to be prepared during his last day. This salve was then painted onto his face, hands, and feet immediately following his last breath.

Then the pyre was to be lit that same day at its final breath. She could still picture how the fire had taken on a strange blue glow just when she thought it might burn out.

This was after the pyre had slowly burned away the night, making way into the dawn of the new day. Then taking off in that bluish brilliance.

And when she had thought it done, it flared to a searing white that nearly blinded her. Yet, the heat could only be felt when she reached very close to it. Even then, it was a relaxing and gentle warmth—not scorching hot as it should have been.

Then it was gone, no ashes or remains left anywhere. There were only the four timber posts that had held the pyre, and these had not been burned to the extent that they should have been. Then, the most amazing thing happened, as the following frostthaw broke and the snows receded. A tiny Oadewood sapling sat there in the exact center of where the pyre had been built.

Rhalwa looked out upon the cold landscape and contemplated her life. Most might consider this way of life full of loneliness, but not she. The woods and the mountains were thriving with energy and she looked to her seclusion as one of necessity and harmony.

She held no craving to be part of a society. There was no need for the company of others. She felt at peace and whole, simply with who she really was and the altruistic forms of the Wild.

The lands were her home, and she was a caretaker of not only them but the old ways of the ranger. She had been taught to see those vital elements as part of the natural order, and these things could never be accomplished from within a community of any known kind of people.

Her father had taught her much about existence. About the different cultures and beings, and the weakness and corruption that most societies bred within their own foundation.

His vast time had made him wise beyond measure, even though he strayed from built-up and populated lands for the majority of his days. He distinctly taught her that many of those within such societies plied their powers to weaken and subject the others to their own selfish beliefs and goals. So that most of these others, subjected to the will of the few, ended up living within a facade—not fulfilling their true purpose. They found themselves chained, both physically and mentally, to an inescapable fate. Ever getting further and further away from what they truly were.

Rhalwa never really doubted all that she learned and was told by her father. But there was never a validation of these unknown or unseen things. Until she found the Oadewood sapling growing in the middle of where her father's pyre had burned.

Her heart had truly felt sick and weak at first when she watched the pyre take flame. She thought that she would not have a grave or a physical place where she could visit her memories of him.

But, as it turned out, that would have been all that was being accomplished with such a meager thing as a burial mound. The essence would not be there, and it would have only been a place where she could hold on to her past with her father.

The fact of the matter was that this was one of life's many illusions. Now she fully understood this, and moved beyond it with the visit of the young Oadewood tree. She had suddenly grown so much more spiritually over the next several years since her father's passing, once she saw that proof of there being more to existence. And more importantly, once she fully accepted it.

She walked back inside where a sturdy table rested against the wall. On the table lay a great-bow of unsurpassed craftsmanship, for it was made of Oadewood. These unique bows were carved from a living piece of an ancient Oadewood tree, and the bow itself was said to be infused with the very essence of that altruistic energy.

Rhalwa occasionally saw it take on a blue glow, but only a handful of times and always late at night. The color of the bow was a swirled pattern of dark green and gray with an agelessly spun bowstring made of the silk retrieved from a giant skar spider. The taking of the piece of Oadewood tree for crafting such a bow was a very ancient ceremony, which most did not know of.

Skar spiders, rare as they were, inhabited subterranean regions mostly. If they did not have a cave to live in, then they were known to dig their own burrows. But their silk was considered to be the toughest, and stronger than even braided rope.

The skar spider had a gray and white speckled wash to the body with black appendages sprouting from it. The tough shell of their body was some of the strongest material known to all folk, at least of Thaldeia. For this reason, there were shields and plate armor suits constructed from the carapace of the spider body. And, when bathed in Faery Fire, this shell then took on another quality. It became near translucent and made the wearer appear blurry when in motion (and sometimes when not).

Of course many sought out these spiders for this very reason, due to the increased advantage of being harder to hit with the sword or arrow. But, last and definitely not least, the notion of acquiring a skar spider intact and dead could be construed as maddening. These spiders grow in size to as large as a destrier.

Rhalwa grasped a specially designed quiver from the table, one that was known far and wide among the rangers. This quiver had a unique harness which kept it positioned a particular way upon one's back. Such a thing provided unsurpassed flexibility and movement if and when needed without having to worry about it flipping over and losing the arrows. The strap system also allowed for up to four of these quivers to be fastened together, which gave the archer four times the number of arrows.

There was only one way to survive out here, and that was to always be prepared, and always be aware. She had been taught to constantly keep her bow and sword at no farther than arm's length.

She also inherited her father's unique sword. It was a longsword with a blade forged from mixed ore and then folded several hundred times. It was sharp on one side while flattened on the other for parrying during swordplay. The weapon was infused with a material unknown to Rhalwa, as well as silver and iron. Thus it made a formidable blade against such things as chanjlyrs and the dead. It was known to be effective against anything not of this world. But the reality of that notion encompassed quite a lot. A subject that very few individuals gave much thought to nowadays.

Now chanjlyrs were peculiar creatures indeed. A chanjlyr was what one became as a result of being bitten or mauled by a Fleshling.

Of course, an explanation of what a chanjlyr was deserves first that of a Fleshling. Fleshlings were unique creatures that had the innate ability to become one of the Wild creations, or animals, at the spur of their own will. Now this transformation could be into that of a deer, a wolf, or even an eagle. But the Fleshling first had to adapt to and practice the particular form of the creature that it desired to change into.

The chanjlyr was one that ended up getting bit, scratched, or mauled to a certain extent by a Fleshling. Of course, this had to be while the Fleshling was in its animal form. Only then would the strange fever take hold.

Once inflicted with this condition, the being could suddenly change into that animal form at the drop of a helm. Sometimes lunar or solar shifts, maybe even stress could bring it on. At least until the being learned to have some control over it. But the question here would be *if* they ever managed to gain control over the condition.

There were tales of Fleshlings actually taking in those chanjlyrs that they created, to help them mature with and learn to control their shifting natures. Usually these tales spoke of such Fleshlings doing so in order to assume more power, and form a family, or a pack for lack of a better term.

Of course, both chanjlyrs and Fleshlings were referred to by most with the term *skin-changer*. This was probably more out of ignorance to the respective creatures than not.

There is not a lot of lore on these things. But, for the most part, the bite of a Fleshling was only known to affect sentient type beings like the Man-folk, possibly Aylsh (although there are no known accounts of these).

Of course Rhalwa never actually had to use the sword against anything of this sort. As a matter of fact, she had not used it in combat at all. There had been no need yet. Even though, as much as she practiced so rigorously, one would think that danger lurked around every corner.

The name *Garghothuul* was etched in Aylsh near the handguard of the blade. This meant *deepslayer* literally, when translated to the Common tongue.

It also possessed the uncanny ability to slice deeper than expected, sometimes even clean through and completely severing whatever it cut into with the one stroke.

She had tried this, but only on dead trees. To her amazement, it had cut extremely deep into whatever it hit, sometimes all the way through. And this was with hardly any more effort than swinging it.

Of course, the blade never had a mark or scratch upon it, and never had to be sharpened.

Then Rhalwa stared down at a smaller table in the corner. This one was constructed from a birch tree stump. It was aged and worn now, the inside of it was actually hollowed out for use as storage.

She had been so young when her mother died, and her mother's face still eluded her to this day. But her father had spoken of her often over the course of Rhalwa's younger years. Her mother, Rawa, was the daughter of a merchant within the Free Lands when Thimoryn had found her. He would always tell her that she had gained the looks of her mother, but with the beauty a thousand times more—and her mother had been a rare beauty indeed.

She stared at the hollowed out tree table, unblinking, finding that old childhood memory. A goblin raiding party visited their home one day while her father was out on a scouting trip higher up along the Rim. Her mother had already been slain when he returned, and in such a brutal fashion.

Memories of this segment in time always came back to haunt her, as she starkly remembered those images even after so many years. Though these images flowed to her unchecked at times, she could not ever see her mother's face. She would be pressed with these other graphic things it would seem for all-time, making her feel cursed.

Her father thought Rhalwa had been lost in the goblin raid also. He searched everywhere before finding her tiny form tucked inside the hollowed out table. This same one that she could not remove her eyes from right now.

Apparently her mother had hid her in there with the first sign of trouble outside. It was here that she cowered silently without so much as a peep, even being but three summertides old.

The horrific sounds of what went on outside and the screams of her mother had quieted her completely until her father found her.

The bloody clothes and the form lying there on the ground, the sitting in the dark for a whole night while her father had gone back out to track the goblins down.

And then she remembered how he looked upon his return the next morning, covered in dark blood that had already dried. But none of it was his own.

Rhalwa fastened the quiver on her back and clasped on the sword belt. She grabbed the great-bow and stepped outside. The invisible hands of the eight winds swept through the house, carrying the fragrance of the lyptun flower incense to her from inside. She had been burning it the entire morning.

The incense of the lyptun flower, when dried and bound with weirweed, was almost like water to the likes of rangers, sages, and druids—all those dedicated to the ways of the Wild. They always had to have it, whether burning as incense, or even dried and bundled hanging from a belt. Many claimed that this incense actually kept evil and dark things away.

The duo suns had already risen past their midday point. Ordinarily she would have been gone already to fill the water skins, but something had kept her home later than expected. It was more of a feeling that did so, but now it was getting late and she knew that she needed to start her trek. Stuck out in the night, away from her home and without the company of the wolves, was not something that she made a habit of doing.

Initially she planned to go the shorter route down to the river, especially since the day was now half over with. Without even realizing it, she found herself at the top of the snow-laden ravine that would connect with the river close to the waterfall. This small pool of water was the best place to fill the skins. Not only did it remain mostly unfrozen, but it offered easy access when compared to the steep, ice-covered banks. But this way was twice as long as the other.

That would be okay, she thought. She could stop and visit the site of her father's pyre.

Even at the swift pace that Rhalwa moved, the day waned deep into the late-suns. Huge boulders loomed ahead, resting where the wide mouth of the ravine dumped into the crisp mountain waters. The cold water frothed as it quickly flowed past her, protesting as it crashed over jutting rocks here and there. The river was wide, but no more than chest deep.

She turned and made her way along the winding course of the cold, menacing clarity of the water. The river's brush-covered banks were frosted with snow and ice. Then she veered back up the slope for a short distance until she came to where the ground leveled out towards a steep rise.

Not far ahead, and near the base of the rise, was a small clearing within the pines. Four old timbers still protruded above ground, the place where her father's pyre had stood.

This was an amazing miracle to her, two tiny Oadewood trees, still not yet as tall as her.

Yes, two trees and not just one. That had been so revealing of the hidden realms, she thought.

There was no way that such a tree could have sprouted within a season of her father's passing. It was definitely connected to him and his essence.

Then, not two score days after the first had appeared, another Oadewood sapling sprouted a pebble's throw from the first. Rhalwa took this as a sign that her father had reunited with her mother. These growths, this Wild display of the higher concept beyond existence, confirmed this to her.

The power of the duo suns began to fade into the east as she spent time at the clearing, slowly passing a bundle of burning lyptun around the two Oadewoods. Then she was off, back in the direction of the river. Now she cut over at an angle to save time, and eventually merged with the river's edge again.

The sound of the waterfall could be heard for a ways before she finally reached it. Her first look was to the top, where the roaring torrent of white froth originated from. So pristine with the enclosing rocks, lightly frosted in snow and ice.

For a moment, her eyes froze in their sweep while surveying the icy fountain of water. She thought she saw a couple of small bluish orbs dart over the lip and out of sight above. It was enough to cause her to stop and scrutinize the rest of her surroundings, especially the upper ledge.

And then, as her eyes stared down to the rock-strewn pool of water bombarded by the falls, she again stopped short—now stunned by what she saw.

There, on one of the driest rocks, lay a young woman who appeared to be sleeping. The rocks did not have even a trace of snow or ice on them.

Peering closer, she could make out the dark caking of old blood on the woman's head and neck. Her sickly pale complexion contrasted against the thick, exquisite matte of golden hair clinging to her face. Her hair took on a dull scarlet hue with the last rays of the duo suns.

The woman was gravely wounded. It looked like something had struck her hard about her head.

Quickly Rhalwa stepped into the basin of water as the raging water crashed away. Now she knew why there was no snow on the rocks. What should have made her shiver with a frigid cold felt as hot as bathing water fresh from atop the hearth.

As she knelt down beside the woman, the rock itself felt warm and radiant. She could now see that long pointed ears rose out of the woman's thick hair. She was Aylsh, or part Aylsh.

At least she lived, thought Rhalwa, seeing the Aylsh's chest rising and falling under very soft and slow breaths.

The water skins would have to wait, thought Rhalwa, as she started to pick up the limp form of the Aylsh. Well, maybe one skin, as she would probably need the water.

Whatever had warmed the water and rocks was obviously gone. She could now feel the cold sting as it quickly turned to freezing.

At least the woman was as light as a feather. Picking up her bow in one hand, and slinging a skin around her neck, she started back towards the warmth of her home.

This time she cut across to get up on the first rise of the high ground. Then she bee-lined towards where she estimated her home to be, attempting to make the trip back as straight—and short—as possible. She had to make several stops to rest, where she also shifted the Aylsh to the opposite shoulder. Eventually she came out fairly close to her home, a little higher than expected. But it took her no time at all to finally reach the cozy interior of the small timber walls.

By nightfall, Rhalwa had snugly wrapped the now naked figure up in a warm blanket atop soft furs beside the crackling hearth. It had taken a while to bathe her, as well as to clean and dress the wounds.

There had been a heavy amount of the dried blood, not only around the wounds but also soaked through her clothes. But there weren't any thick red lines snaking their way across her skin, no obvious signs of infection. And the deep lacerations amidst the blackish-blued bruising appeared to have already sealed or at least crusted over.

Rhalwa always spent the summertide collecting not only firewood, but various herbs and plants, like the lyptun. Each of these had their own unique use. This gathering also included berries and such for the upcoming winterfall stores. Of course, all of these gatherings had to be dried and stored properly as well. If not, then the medicinal properties would be negated.

She had already mixed and heated a paste comprised of bell thistle and muarypop grass. This cool and soothing salve also deterred infection and rejuvenated the body, or maybe regenerated was a better term. Three or four days use of the salve on even a nasty cut would have it looking like a month old scar.

The Aylsh had several peculiar markings on her body though. Rhalwa had noted one above the nipple of her left breast, not very far from where she could feel her heart beat.

From afar it looked like a large *S* with a small blade running up through it. On closer inspection, the gold-colored mark looked like the Aylsh symbol of the Omega, a mark symbolic of the Eternal Lasting. And the blade could have been a feather. Or maybe the feather was set as the background for the symbol. In either case, the blade or feather was white, almost silvery. There was a thick green border around the edges.

Rhalwa knew the Aylsh language well enough, but her father had never talked of this in all of his teachings. He had explained the myths behind the Omega and the Eternal Lasting.

According to the ancient Aylsh lore, and even written in the First Writings, the Omega was a sign of the Eternal Mother, the divine mother of the entire world—not just the Aylsh folk. She was known as Ityarfa Vorjanimae within the Aylsh First Writings, which translated literally to Great Mother of Eternity. This was the reason that many of the Aylsh would refer to her as the Great Mother when conversing on the subject in the Common tongue. But the Eternal Mother was known to most of the sentient races.

The Omega was something that would precede the times when the Eternal Mother would walk upon Zholryn again. She was rumored to one day revisit the lands in worldly form, in order to start the Eternal Lasting.

The Aylsh First Writings, ancient scrolls from the *First Days*, claimed all this and more. Of course, what the Omega was no one really knew, and there were no clues as to the truth behind it. These fine scriptures were brought to the world by none other than Thiliathain Lourendalthemee. By Thaldeian standards, this occurred prior to the year 1900 BA, during what the Aylsh call the First Days. Although the Aylsh system does not align with the Thaldeian one, it records the events of the First Folk well past two thousand years before the current era.

Thiliathain, known as the Father and True King of the Aylsh, went into the *Grypth*. The Grypth was the vast, ancient network of halls underneath the mighty Louren Ghuvruul. These old forests were known as the lifeblood of the Aylsh-kind. It was in here that the legends spoke of him communing with the Olden. He emerged a ten-year later, but more aged than he should have been, bearing elaborate engravings upon thin sheets of metal that were very hard and flexible. It was berlyllum. And these sheets would come to be known as the First Writings. The engravings were finely crafted in High Aylsh and they radiated with the power that created them. Pure strokes etched into the hardest of materials, marks that held a ghostly silver glow.

The riddle of berlyllum was also passed to Thiliathain, but as the spoken word only. This was done so that the First Folk always had an edge over their enemies. He in turn passed this lore on to the royal Aylsh foundry, as well as to several trusted master smiths. And it had been handed down this same way ever since, so that the secret remained with the Aylsh alone.

The Eternal Lasting was supposed to be when the most prodigious Aylsh king ever would be born, also known as *Itharzyr Morwhe*—the Fatherless Son—in the Aylsh scriptures of the First Writings. This Fatherless Son would lead the Aylsh people to their redemption from a blackened and corrupted world.

The First Writings even suggested that the Aylsh king would lead all Aylsh, be they dark, light, whether considered noble or not. And there was even speculation that the verbiage meant possibly other beings. Some claimed it meant all beings, all living things. But, as with the Amethyst Scrolls, the First Writings were elusive as to exactly who the Thirteen Favored Children of Lord Braxis were. It mentioned the creations of the Wild in a similar manner. And the *yuanhad*, meaning lesser beings, also presumptively came to mean those lower things such as goblin, kobold, and the like.

The skin around this mark upon the frail form of the Aylsh was slightly raised, as though it had been branded on.

More peculiar yet were the designs on her back. Lifelike, brownish-green roots started at the top of each buttock. They joined at the base of her spine where the shapely little dimples appeared, just above the spread of her buttock cheeks.

These two roots then intertwined and did so entangling all the way up her back along the spine, closely woven together.

Just below the neck line, they parted again and spread out over the shoulder blades. One of them ended in the shape of a feather while the other ended in the shape of a giant leaf. The feather on her right side was a long, fluffy white one with silvery quills, while the leaf was that of an Oadewood edged in golden trim.

Such exquisite artwork must have taken a fine crafter much time. But Rhalwa did not know what kind of crafter could even make such a thing. She found herself mesmerized and stared at the designs for most of the evening.

This Aylsh, albeit young and ageless, had probably been in existence for many times what Rhalwa's age was. So frail but lean and sinewy strong, the Aylsh-kind surely were blessed by the Initiator.

The Aylsh's ears rose straight up from the sides of her head. They were so long and pointy, yet daintily threatening in their own way.

Obviously this was a near to or full blooded Aylsh. The reason Rhalwa thought this was because she remembered her father's full Aylsh features—and how little she had received of them. Rhalwa knew that she herself was only partially Aylsh, even the barely pronounced ears spoke that fact.

The unconscious Aylsh also had a unique marking around her abdominal area. Where a belly button normally poked out (or in) was an elegant, glittering, and shimmering swath of skin. This region sparked with tiny golden flashes of light under the glow of the fire, as though the Aylsh had been covered in gold dust down there. This dazzling effect widened and extended down to her smooth crotch.

The Aylsh do have a similar thing to a belly button though. Most Aylsh-kind had a small round or square button of skin where a belly button would be. It was called an *ogrou*. This button was either green or blue in color and appeared almost like there was a gem or jewel peering out through the skin there.

Legends spoke of the ogrou having a dull glow to it at times. They also claimed that this thing was of the oldest essence of the world. And it was a reminder of how spiritually connected and attuned these wild ones of the Eternal Mother were to the very creation of life itself.

Those of the Black Clans, or the Aylsh Ismaru, did not have this unique feature on their bodies.

Rhalwa admired the sleeping form of the fair Aylsh and sat by the warm fire well into the morning's pale light. She wondered at what had befallen her and then at what evil in this world could harm such a thing of immense allure. It was just before first light when she slowly slumped over and into a deep sleep that was filled with uneasy dreams of dark things.

§ § §

The Aylsh king regent sat on the royal throne, surrounded by baronial knights clad in shiny plate armor. The throne overlooked the great hall which stretched back far, the sides lined with gallant statues. A high vaulted ceiling rose up, where intricately crafted crystal panes allowed the rays of the duo suns to kaleidoscope down upon the throne and the cold, mirroring quartz floor.

The aged and wrinkled regent contemplated the circumstances that were imposed upon the renowned Aylsh Kingdom. It was not that there hadn't been royal heirs to the throne, but that the three sons of King Daumere Bari Lourendalthemee of Enclave Noblynbindyn had been slain in various ways. Two of them fell alongside the king, in battle with the Great Wyrm in the year SA 1525. The remaining son was slain by forces of the yuanhad in a cowardly ambush, set upon him while he rode alone in the forest. King Lourendalthemee decreed standing orders in case such a thing happened, almost as if he had foreseen it all. He subjected the Aylsh High Court to a named king regent if such a calamity befell the kingdom.

The Aylsh kingdoms, as they were called by most, really only was one formidable one. The plural was added simply because most other inhabitants of Thaldeia viewed them as a conglomerate due to having numerous Trone enclaves, as well as the High Aylsh Refts.

But all of these First Folk, whether Trone Aylsh or High Aylsh, fell under the one king and high court. Truth be told, the oldest and most ancient lineage of Aylsh royalty actually originated under one of the Trone enclaves. And that had been Thiliathain Lourendalthemee, the Father and True King of the Aylsh. It was one of the First Lines, one of only two. The other was the Eternal Mother's line Brinthwoulerieh.

The first of that line, Nephritaryah Brinthwoulerieh, was joined in wedlock with Thiliathain Lourendalthemee. And that was how the purest royal Aylsh line began, as was set forth within the First Writings.

The same year that Daumere Lourendalthemee and his sons were lost to the Great Wyrm, so were those remaining of the Eternal Mother's line. The purest. While the Great Wyrm took many, including Daumere's own wife, another horrific and vile deed was done. Mysterious shades emerged and drained the life from those last ones who held the most pure of the Eternal Mother's line. Every last one of them. Well, all except for one. Daumere Lourendalthemee had enough foresight to secret one away.

There was a significant difference between what was called the royalty and what was termed nobility. This not only applied to the Aylsh, but also to the other kingdoms. While royalty was indeed also nobility, the opposite was not true. The royal lines of any kingdom were the ruling ascendancy, as set forth through primogeniture and by divine right. And there were some lands, like Ravenkort, in which divine right ruled everything. Others did not carry it as extreme in the application of lineage. The nobility boiled down to the aristocracy, the higher class, which could have been titled over to the particular line by the reigning king or even through wedlock with a member of the royal line itself. But this was another separate tangent that could be discussed at length. Since royalty seldom joined in wedlock for such a thing as love, or anything less than affirming and adding to their sovereignty and wealth.

The Aylsh Kingdom was no doubt the most powerful and, more importantly, the most united folk that occupied Zholryn. This endeavor went far beyond the simple daily mechanics of the rule across the lands itself. It exceeded the obvious outer countenance of the Aylsh folk and entailed the deeper meaning underneath which grew their spirit and what could only be called their fusion, their solidarity, as the First Folk. Well, most of them at least.

One must also understand the differences of the various royal and noble lines. The line of King Lourendalthemee stretched back literally as far as the Aylsh race did. Of course there were currently fifty-four other noble families. Of these, only eleven were considered royalty. But they only went back eight, maybe nine, turns. Reft Vuranthegost was now the oldest, dating back to the year SA 155. None of the original and and most purebred remained. So the blood of the more recently planted nobility was nowhere near as pure as that of King Lourendalthemee's royal line. Some of which, four to be precise, were only considered nobility as they were bestowed it by the king. Not born into it. The unequivocal watering down of those first bloodlines was nearly complete.

One of the seven Amethyst Scrolls contained a decree specifically mentioning the Aylsh. It clearly touted that the Aylsh lineage of rulers must stay as pure as possible. If the royal lines that led the Aylsh peoples were not kept so, then this Amethyst Scroll alluded to treacherous hardships befalling the Aylsh, and ultimately their eventual demise.

Of course, the scriptures of the Aylsh, the First Writings, had no such lore within them. This might be the reason that most of the Aylsh had forgotten this proclamation within the Amethyst Scrolls. Forgot? No—they simply overlooked what was not within the First Writings, as little else mattered to them. These were their axioms, the truth of their kind.

One could also consider the deeper intent of having any mention of the mixed lineage within the Amethyst Scrolls, solely directed towards the Aylsh and no other kind. Possibly it had a heavier connotation to it. Did the Amethyst Scrolls apply to just the Man-folk, to Man and Aylsh, or to more?

The only ones that laid claim to the Amethyst Scrolls being of the origins of Man were the Man-folk, and not any other of the beings of creation. Most of such conjectures were more assumptions, interpretations, than simple fact. The reality of it was that none really knew what exactly all of these decrees from higher above actually meant.

Now, of course, one could look at these dictates simply as legend, maybe even superstition. But the Amethyst Scrolls were claimed to have been scripted by Lord Braxis himself. And the Aylsh were the most attuned creatures upon Zholryn. The one scroll mentioned that the loss of the pureness of their lines would degrade the pureness of the race, and this would pull the Aylsh from their close affinity with not only Braxis, but the entire nature of existence itself. So one can see why the whole situation had caused considerable grief and puzzlement with at least a few of the Aylsh, even many of those who were only part Aylsh.

King Lourendalthemee empowered the head of the Aylsh High Court as the king regent if any such ill omens ever did fall upon him. This king regent would rule in place for one hundred years, at which point, if no surviving heir or ancient royal line appeared, then the next oldest line's first born warrior would be crowned.

And it was on this day that such a particular Aylsh waited upon the frail regent. Lord Inshro Thann of Reft Vuranthegost knelt on one knee and tended to the old Aylsh while he drank water from a decanter.

Lord Vuranthegost was a little peculiar these days as well. While most addressed the regent as sire or highness, Lord Vuranthegost always made it a point to title him as king regent, as if to remind the old one that the position was only temporary. But there would be no suspicions about a hero to the Aylsh.

Inshro Vuranthegost was known as one with many lives. By all rights, he actually should be dead. It was maybe around four turns ago that the hill tribes of the Tenargone Steppes decided to invade one of the Trone factions who neighbored to their northeast. Vuranthegost led the majority of the battles against them, and eventually chased them back to their hills. But the fighting had been fierce.

More recently, twenty years ago, he rode the lands to check on the safe-keeping of the various parts of the kingdom. And he did this with few guards, always more impatient with getting to the sudden whim of a task than to be overly concerned about his own protection.

While known for this type of nonchalance, it was after one of these excursions when his guards were found dead. Inshro was not found. The knights of Reft Vuranthegost searched and scoured the land for days hoping to uncover what might have happened to him.

Then, a ten-day after the butchered guards were found, Inshro Vuranthegost rode back into the royal palace on a wild steed. He was dirty and disheveled, but alive.

The story spun was that he had been ambushed by well-trained and well-equipped Man-folk. Yes Man-folk, and not the Tenargone horse lords.

He blatantly overstated the fact that these men were probably connected to either Kuhrzoth or the Black Legion, considering their high degree of combat skill and quality of arms. He claimed to have tracked them until he had the advantage, and then he cut them all down in vengeance for what they did to his kin.

Of course, there never were any bodies of these so-called men, but Lord Vuranthegost was a hero and his claims were not further contested. And the Aylsh folk were even more infuriated towards outsiders, chiefly those of Man-folk. What really transpired that day still is not known to any but Vuranthegost and one particular woman, or at least woman by disguise.

For the deceitful things that go on behind closed doors and sometimes in front of unseeing eyes are many. Even the resplendent Aylsh Kingdom was not immune to that. The attack by the hill tribes was really not the uncoordinated and innocent provocation of savages either, as many of our fair Aylsh were led to believe.

Lord Vuranthegost propped a cushion behind the weary regent and spoke briefly in his ear. Then he slowly bowed while stepping backwards.

He turned to the foremost Aylsh knight. "You there, see to it that the king regent is comfortably moved to his chambers for the time being. Establish the guard there from now on and also prompt the king's healer to accompany him."

With that, the knight immediately barked commands to the rest of the guard as they arranged to move the feeble one. Vuranthegost bowed again, and turned sharply towards the doors of the great hall. The sharp ring of his spurs reverberated with the heavy clacks of his boots upon the floor.

Once outside, he stopped to smell the bite of the wintry air. The wind was also mixed with the briny swill drafting off of the Eastern Waters. While still early harvestspell, colder winds from the north tended to break more frequently across the lands.

Lord Vuranthegost had been the specimen of the Aylsh warrior, ever rising within the prestige of Aylsh-kind. It momentarily flashed through some of the memories that it had absorbed since taking the form.

Even as a young Aylsh, it saw and felt that this one had always preserved the highest degree of dignity. But that was exactly why Livforena had devised this plan involving just such a persona, and the eventual Aylsh king at that. That is, as long as things went according to her plan.

The medallion that the priestess gave to it also aided this cause. The powerful thaumaturgy that it would be subjected to, especially being so close to the king regent and the Aylsh High Court, would otherwise give the true form of the thing away.

This medallion was an exact imitation of the real Lord Vuranthegost's ancient medallion of lineage, a device that no one would even question. But this one prevented any veritable seeing or scrying, so that no one could truly see what now called itself Lord Vuranthegost.

Such a clever plan, thought Vuranthegost, as it chuckled with a smirk.

Lord Vuranthegost walked regally down several oversized staircases and then into one of the many quarters that rested not even a stone's throw from the palace doors.

This was his home for the time being. An ornate gold key unlocked an oak door which was twice as tall as he was. Boastful tables laden with exquisite vases and ornaments filled the central hall.

Once inside, he lightly jaunted up the stairs and then down a long hallway to where another oaken door sat.

The door swung open to find the fiery purple eyes of a masked woman staring at him while lounging on a grand feather bed. The skin tight leather leggings allowed a curvaceous attractor between her thighs, while her top barely contained sun-kissed breasts.

Vuranthegost closed the door and plumped down in a chair alongside the bed. "Well met, my brazen one. Here but a short walk from the Aylsh royal halls themselves. I trust that you at least had sense enough to not show yourself anywhere outside?"

As he spoke, he removed the giant seashell from a semrhaj lamp, placing the shell on the table with a sharp crack. These lamps were made from semrhaj, or glow lichen, found only within the expansive Aylsh forests known as Louren Ghuvruul. While they were not extremely bright, a handful of the glowing roughage would comfortably light a fair sized chamber for the most part of a year.

She fingered the various rings upon her hand. A curt smile played across her face. "Lord Vuranthegost, that does have a ring to it. Now tell me, when will that lord become king?"

Vuranthegost raised his eyebrows and rolled his eyes to the ceiling. "Even now as we speak, the guard is removing the king regent to his chambers. He is on his last breaths of life. I expect within a score of days, maybe two, that the High Court will be forced to declare me king."

"Excellent, my aspirant. We will talk more as we approach that next step," Livforena paused to savor the premonition of success, "now tell me, what is the intent once you are crowned?"

Vuranthegost slowly nodded his head in silence. "The absolute goal, as you have been kind enough to remind me many times over, is the complete separation of the others from the Man-folk. That is, I am to make sure that the Aylsh do not rally to the aid of Man when the tides roll against them."

Livforena stared at the form of Vuranthegost thoughtfully. "Good, you shan't forget. And, more importantly, you will not stray from the course. This work is far too important…vital for the final plan of supremacy. Do not fail me."

"You should know me by now, my Priestess," whispered Vuranthegost with a strange light in his eyes.

"So be it. Till next time then. I also have a small gift for you...more so that you don't take to any...urges, being surrounded by your favorite delicacy, thus spoiling all of our long and hard work." She retrieved a leather pouch from her shoulder and handed it to him. Inside were the bloody hearts of several Aylsh. A couple of them were very small, at one time belonging to very young Aylsh when they still beat with life.

It was too bad, thought Priestess Sahrya, *that these creatures can not permanently keep their acquired forms.* As Lord Vuranthegost, this one might be fit enough to keep around longer than originally planned. As King Vuranthegost, it would definitely stay embroiled in power...at least until she could contrive the birth of the enchanted Fatherless Son.

Yes, Priestess Sahrya knew of all the fables and legends...and she would use every one of them to her advantage, any way she could.

In the end, she would be the one that they all bowed down to and worshipped. This was what was ordained, and what would come to fruition no matter the course...just as the Ancient One dictated.

Chapter 9:

Memories in Black

All shall give Way to the Light o'er the Dark and forfeit any and all bonds of perversion. The Way is the only path from the Omega.

> –Seventh Edict of Lord Braxis, etched upon the Great Slates, recovered by Arterium circa the year 13 BA.

aramagrii painfully emerged back to the world after what could have been days of unconsciousness. The utter blackness engulfed her thoroughly. Except for the random flashes of false light permeating through the darkness of her shrouded vision, there was absolutely nothing.

Her mixed Black Clan form, petite yet tall and supple, lay stretched out over the cold, abrasive rock floor. She could not even see the glistening charcoal hue of her own skin, but it felt as though the pain cried out from the very cores of her bones.

The pain arose from lacerations crisscrossing up and down her injured and bruised physique. They screamed like the welts from a hundred stinging ants amid a dousing of powerful cleansing spirits used for the purification of wounds.

At the same time, entire portions of the rock-inflicted rashes would intermittently go numb and feel almost like a cool burning sensation. This rampaging effect across her body made her feel queasy.

The fall from the ledge had been completely jarring. The subsequent impact, which caused her plummet into total oblivion and darkness, had been abrupt. Both also gave the young dark one new life, a rebirth. Without those, she would have also been put to death like her mother. No, slaughtered or even murdered would be better said of what happened.

Tears welled up. She could feel them roll down her cheeks as the mental replay of what had transpired briskly assumed control of her mind.

It was too much. She softly sobbed as a vision of her mother's face flashed. The warm, caring smile suddenly twisted into agony. It had mixed with a hatred so deep, born from the threat to her one and only precious child. A mother's gift to the world. The base instinct any mother would feel and propagate in protecting her own young.

The priestess had found them and surprised them. Sahrya's mannerisms subtly gave away the true malice and voracious hatred that were boiling over inside. She had known something or had finally divined aspects of what Zaramagrii's mother had been concealing ever since her birth. There was no doubt that Priestess Sahrya brought death with her up on that ledge.

Suddenly Zaramagrii was very alone and afraid, for now she was on the outside of everything that she ever knew. Her kind, those she bonded to, those she thought were family, and what she had dreamed of a future. All were locked inside of Tharasvrul.

Where my life was, she thought.

The offspring of the dark ones did not necessarily dream as others of the world did. There was nothing else except death and absorption into the chaos beyond life. And this was only after surviving the rigorous, but ascetic, endeavors of the Black Clan ways.

Zaramagrii had always dreamt of more, yearning for whatever higher knowledge she could grasp. It was more than that. The questions of what for and why live or die unquestioningly always riddled her thoughts. This was the way most would live their lives, accepting it at face value. Without attempting to determine purpose and reason.

So she had always been different. Just as her mother had alluded to. But her mother's term for it was that Zaramagrii was special and unique. A gift to the world. But what kind of gift to what world? Zaramagrii had never stepped out of the expanse of what Clan Tharasvrul encompassed.

A small pebble tumbling down from above snapped her mind back to where she was. The pitter-patter sounded thunderous to her in the quiet of the blackness.

How far above was the floor of the Great Cavern? How far was the fall? Were the priestess and her servants still up there, possibly even looking for me?

No, for no one knew that Zaramagrii had even been there.

But she knew Priestess Sahrya would be looking for her after what had occurred. There would be no survival now in what had been her ancestral home.

The priestess no doubt would want her dead as quickly as possible, and for what? What did all of this mean?

Her mind was still confused over what her mother had told her, and then what had been said at the confrontation between her and Priestess Sahrya.

By now they would have found out that Zaramagrii was nowhere to be found in all of Tharasvrul. This would probably further incite the priestess to extreme measures. There was no doubt in her mind that the priestess wanted her wiped from existence—ruthlessly, viciously—and quickly.

Here she was, practically naked, except for the now-tattered cloth slip that covered her body from her shoulders to her knees. The supple leather fighting halter kept her breasts tightly against her body. It was solely designed for combat. The tight fit held a female's breasts closely, helping to maintain balance and control.

She was barefoot with nothing else but the studded berlyllum tiara, which had amazingly been in her hand when she woke.

Maybe the memory of her mother giving it to her years ago subconsciously caused her to grasp it. To put a death grip on it close to when the explosion had occurred, before the long fall, and before she had lost consciousness.

The large black gem of some unknown type lay intact and firmly embedded in the center.

Was there a small fracture—a crack in the gem now?

Alas, she was not able to tell, but the gem almost felt as though it had a distinct but barely noticeable seam running across the surface. Maybe more than one.

She remembered her mother telling her that she would always carry her mother's heart with her (meaning the black gem). Her mother would laugh after saying this and tell her not to fret as her mother did not have a black heart.

She would then say that the color stood for their home and birthright—Black Clan Tharasvrul and the ancient ways of Isnuuthghor. A symbol of lineage.

The sensory perception of sight took up so much thought and attention. Once it was gone, her mind coiled itself in the anxiety and fevered apprehension of those things lost to her. Her mother and the altercation with the priestess. Elder Tarrne's loss to what seemed like the simple course of nature but was not. The flurry of this torrent lulled her into an attitude of detached glamour.

Zaramagrii suddenly felt trapped and panicked. A wave of emotion and adrenaline surged through her as she feared that she would never get out of the darkness. She could not deal with the black emptiness any longer, such a dismal void.

Without a clear thought, she jumped up and bolted straight ahead blindly. But she only made it so far before the low hanging ceiling of the cavern put a stop to her burst. It was not until she ran clear into the edge of a hard rock wall that she came back to reality.

In one abrupt impact to her head, she was out again. A jolting white flash erupted within her mind before unconsciousness took her.

Once she awoke for the second time within the darkness, Zaramagrii now had a throbbing pain in her head to go with the rest of the aches throughout her body. Again, she reached up to touch the tiara to ensure that it was there.

Then something large swooped low over her head. The slap of the wind from it nearly caused her to drop to her belly. A strange *Mreek* echoed dully within the stillness and then the sound was gone again.

Recovering from the dazed state of sudden fear brought on by the unknown, Zaramagrii remained close to the floor of the passage. Now she had absolutely no idea which way she had come from or gone, so she crawled on all fours for a while. After she went for what seemed quite a spell, she took a break and squatted on the tips of her toes now that her knees were raw from crawling.

She felt around her and figured that she was in a narrow passageway with a low ceiling, as she could not stand fully upright. Standing up too fast would have added yet another headache.

The floor turned to a softer, grainier dirt. So she must be going in the opposite direction from where the ledge had been. There was no way that she ran this far earlier, when she had been foolish enough to run blindly in such darkness. It also felt as though the passage was sloping downwards. At this point, she had no choice but to continue onward.

Zaramagrii half crawled, half walked at times for so long that she finally had to stop. She was tired and sweaty even in the cool underground climate. She could feel the dried blood everywhere on her body as it tightened about the skin, as well as scabs being scraped open to ooze fresh blood. The smell in the air was stagnant and musty.

While she hadn't gone into the panic that sent her reeling earlier, the gloom brought her mood down and she felt miserably helpless. Finding her way only through the use of her fingertips, she cringed at nearly every touch for fear of running into some dark beast or creature.

Zaramagrii remembered the old tales of Qarradoum, the maze underneath, a vast subterranean world down below the lands. It was known to the Aylsh as the black roots of the world. And their lore told of how it was the thick vein that loosely separated the Endless Chasm and this world. So massive and confusing that folk could become lost for ages. The legends told of it connecting all across Thaldeia, and Zholryn for that matter. They spoke of strange wonders, as well as creatures, that thrived in the darkness.

Then her hand came across a damp and wiggling mass— something living and very slimy. A strange, high pitched whining sound erupted when she had blindly grabbed it. Maybe a kind of large slug? She did not know and she quickly retracted her hand back from whatever it was.

As she sat for a while to contemplate her situation again, she thought that she could hear the sound of lapping waves. Similar to those on a shoreline, but soft and distorted. The stifled, confined air gave it a hollow echo that created a steady and reverberating smacking effect.

She walked farther, now carefully, but still blindly, placing her feet ahead of her one at a time. The rocky surface above her gradually sloped down lower and lower, until she was forced to crawl again.

Suddenly she found herself upright with an unexpected gust of cold, damp air in her face. It carried the scent of dank staleness. A few more steps and her feet splashed through shallow water, which grew deeper the more that she pushed forward. She no longer felt the confining closeness of the walls and ceiling around her.

Stopping, she slowly took in long, deep breaths. She calmed herself for several moments in an attempt to clear her mind. A strange feeling took over her senses. One of balancing awareness. She instantly felt that she was at one end of a vast underground cavern that held a small lake. As quick as the sense had taken her, it was gone again and she was not sure.

As she splashed about, she went more to the side as the water remained at an even level. Then she stopped again, thinking that something had reached out and touched her foot. It scarcely brushed her, but whatever it was had moved.

Before she realized what happened, she found herself face down in the water. A tough, leathery thing wrapped low around both of her calves, whipping her feet out from under her. The thing quickly began to drag her toward the depths.

She struggled to get her breath as her head went completely under the water. Immediately grabbing what had entangled her legs, she felt what could have been a large snake or tentacle with one of its ends trailing off into the deeper water. It grew larger in size as it faded beyond her reach.

Zaramagrii gasped and choked as she swallowed water. She could feel her body being pulled along the soft muck of the bottom.

Now she reached out past her head and tried to claw into the slime for traction. But this was to no avail, and she was already in water that was a couple of foot deep.

One last burst of fearful energy and she kicked both of her feet apart trying to break free. But the thing held her firmly, almost making her feet go numb from being squeezed so tightly.

Then she decided to grasp the tough appendage and savagely bite into it, ripping and clawing the resilient hide. Now she could no longer feel the surface of the water, the comfort of being able to reach air, as she struggled. Even though this was only accomplished at this point by bouncing off of the bottom with either a foot or a hand. But any deeper and this too would be futile.

The thick fluid from the thing mixed with the bitter tasting water as she gnawed her way through the tough hide, swallowing fragments of it as well. Then she felt it go limp around her legs. One last bite and violent jerk backwards with her head severed the one piece wrapped about her.

Quickly she reached down to find the muck as it coated her fingers, swimming along the bottom. Hoping that she had chosen the right direction to swim, she feverishly took off with short, frog kicks. It was not long before her head broke the surface and she found air.

The shoreline was but a few more scant thrusts of her arms. Then she hurriedly followed it for a while, still clutching part of the thing that attacked her. Now she did not stray into even the shallow water, instead keeping to where she occasionally splashed the edge of it with a foot.

She stopped abruptly, as she remembered her tiara. But her hands again confirmed that her tiara had not been left behind in the watery depths. Breathing a sigh of relief, a sudden dizzying wave of malaise passed over her. Her stomach knotted on emptiness.

Almost ravenous at this point in what felt like days since she had eaten anything, Zaramagrii bit into the severed appendage and swallowed a morsel of it. The taste was not appealing to say the least. Just a cold lump of goo that slid its way down her throat.

But more meat from this thing might help her gain some strength back and keep her nourished. It might raise her strength enough to continue through these rigors.

No harm came to her yet after having swallowed so much of the thing's blood and flesh from the struggle. She devoured more of the raw meat under the thick, stubborn hide as she made her way along the edge of the water. No longer caring about the water or what may be in it, she lowered herself down and slurped several mouthfuls of the repugnant broth. While not being any different than that of a mud puddle, the bitter tang at least drowned some of the taste from the tentacle.

Truth be told, Zaramagrii had no idea how long she wandered those cavernous passages, crawling and stooping. What seemed to her like an entire season was really maybe a score of days. But there was no way to tell one day's passing into another.

It was long enough to get extremely hungry and thirsty again, but all that she stumbled across now and then were beetles and large slugs. And these were only by feel—and by luck.

Although not much, apparently the substance and fluid of each must have been enough to keep her alive. Oddly enough, all of the aches and pains from her ordeals slowly dissipated. She took no physical notice of this in the darkness anyways. Her eyes were useless here. Things of the seeing world did not matter where complete and utter blackness reigned supreme. Smell, hearing, and touch became the discriminating qualities for survival in such a place. So things that normally took precedence over others lost their value, such as her injuries from the fall.

The memories of what took place on the ledge, leading her into this plight of attrition, now faded to the back of her mind. She was becoming accustomed to the darkness of this underground world.

The cavernous lake was far behind her, and some of the passages now became so tiny that they scraped her body as she climbed through them. At one point, after what seemed like a lengthy crawl up and down, she found herself in what felt like a fair-sized chamber with a dry floor covered in soft soil. This was a noticeable change, but she did not know if it was one for better or worse.

She knew that there had to be an eventual way out, but now she felt tired and only wanted to lay down. Exhaustion called her out, begging her to rest.

Instead of curling up in the dirt, she slowly lowered to her knees and then leaned back to rest upon the balls of her dirty, calloused feet. She closed her eyes, even though it was hard to tell whether or not they were actually closed or open. Several heavy blinks forced her to believe that they were closed.

Then, as she let her fears go and the darkness take her, she felt something. Or more sensed everything.

It was like the blackness of the subterranean world became part of her mind. And she felt the surrounding area almost like a huge blanket or net of sorts, and everything that stirred or crept could be felt...or sensed.

The unusual ability only grew as she relaxed even more and let the darkness rush over her. It was more like an extensive spider's web wherein things that stirred it even the slightest registered within her mind or hearing, maybe a kind of feeling. It could have been a combination of all her senses, she was not sure.

Either way, she now sensed the small centipede that crawled along the passage floor ahead of her. She could make out the tiny serpentine body without seeing it. There were spiders in various places, spinning their webs. One was eating a small beetle that it had captured, the web slightly swaying from the vibrations.

She could sense exactly where these things were, without even seeing them. And now she began to make out the vague outline of the hole that she was in. Again, without really seeing anything at all. Excitedly, she reached up to where she sensed the low ceiling. There it was, exactly where she extended and traced her fingertips to.

Gust of air, she thought.

Down here, that meant possibly a way out, a hole with fresh air from the skies above.

Zaramagrii began to walk forward at a brisk pace while attempting to stay aligned with the fabric of what she termed her dark blanket.

She attuned to what she sensed and maintained a heightened state of awareness and fluid tranquility. She began to trot faster, weaving and turning as she envisioned the winding passage. Then she sensed the narrow curve approaching and quickly slipped her body sideways while running forward. Her breasts barely scraped the rocky sides through the combat halter.

After what seemed like ages, she came to a split in the passageway. The left went on straight then curved off, while the right one appeared to have a slight rise to it. She stood there facing the split in contemplation.

A soft, but noticeable, breeze crossed her face from the one on the right. That settled it, and she took off down the right side.

She figured that her ability to *feel* her surroundings only appeared to extend out a couple hundred paces from her in any direction. Except for the solid dirt and rock compacted together all around the hollows of passages and caverns.

The extra sensory perception that she discovered flowed naturally to her now in the darkness of the subterranean world. A place where she could not use her eyes even if she wanted to.

After a while, the passage began to steeply ascend, and she had to find handholds to climb up parts of it. She carefully gripped the rough, protruding rock, then following with a foot. Once it leveled out again, a distant but bright spark of light appeared, sending dust-filled rays back towards her.

An opening. The thought sent her mind reeling after all of this time underground. Where would she be when she emerged? What would she run into? Minions of the priestess? Or maybe some kind of wild beast.

But the small dot of light possibly leading outside also renewed the hope of seeing her folk again. The notion sparked thoughts about her mother and about others that she knew at Clan Tharasvrul.

What might have happened to all of them?

As the brightness increased, she found that she could no longer use her newfound sense of things to gain her surroundings. The spiraling streams of light cut through the cloudy cavern.

The dark blanket would come back to her once she closed her eyes. Suddenly, her vision went to a bloody gray haze surrounded by a black trace around the periphery.

During this intuitive visualization, she could see beyond the blinding rays of light shining through and make out the rocky passageway ahead, shaped like a vertical crevasse. But then the extraordinary sense was gone again, and she had to stop and concentrate in order to go back to this new feel of things.

As Zaramagrii approached the narrow, V-shaped crack that exited out of the blackness, her eyes began to tear and sting. She had found the mouth where darkness met the light of the world.

She could no longer even look or see things due to the flood of brightness, as the cold, fresh air pelted her mostly naked body. The feeling of it stirred a newness within her. She squatted down near the opening but just inside, while her eyes adjusted.

Zaramagrii judged the day to be near its end, given how low the duo suns hung in the sky. Her heightened senses picked up the waft of smoke or fire burning not far away. Now she saw why this cave system had remained uninhabited. The mouth was actually concealed by large boulders and rocky projections that were part of a narrow ridge running high up towards the crags.

Even after she exited the cave onto a small shelf, she still had to climb down to get to the ground. She pressed her body into the rocky face while toeing cracks and rocky knobs in order to do so.

Zaramagrii was tall for her kind, but very lithe. Nonetheless, everywhere that she stepped from the ledge down to where the base of the ridge started, she left tiny imprints in the soft soil with her bare feet.

Investigating the smell of fire would have to wait until first light tomorrow. These lands were unknown to her, and she did not want to take any chances with what might be lurking around them. And she had no idea how far she might have traveled from her home territory of Clan Tharasvrul.

A short while later found her up in a fir tree, perched comfortably on a bough. The swaying, needle infested branches concealed her in her hiding place far above the ground.

As she sucked on pine needles to ease her hunger, she found herself closing her eyes and shifting to her newfound sense of awareness. Her dark blanket.

She nearly fell out of the tree after being startled by a high pitched whine. The culprit, a bat, darted around the treetop just above her. Yes, she could feel the wave that it emitted, something most things in the world would never even fathom.

She spent the rest of the night canvassing the land as far out as she could using her dark blanket. This was done more to stay vigilant, but all that passed close by were creatures of the wild. A fox, a pair of mink, and then a large squirrel scampered through near sunrise.

Shortly after the rise of the duo suns, she slowly descended from the tree while scanning the scene around her. Not even the wind stirred yet.

The terrain sloped gently down and then leveled off, extending into the distance to disappear within stands of trees. Then extending again above into another ridge of high ground, doing so upwards into the lofty crags.

Her movement towards the direction of where the smoke came from the evening prior was slow and cautious. Zaramagrii tended to stay just up the rise, zigzagging from one patch of trees to another. Her toughened feet no longer felt the harsh caltrops of the ground that attempted to scathe them.

It did not take long before she came upon another smaller dale that extended away from her. Looking down into it, she could see the faint wisps of black smoke spiraling into the sky. They rose until the morning winds took them away.

Not far ahead rested the remains of a cart or wagon. It could not have been very large but had some sort of leather covering to the back, which was now mostly burnt off. All of the wagon wheels were charred and broken, protruding from the ground like eerie, dead stumps. Several unmoving bodies were strewn about the scene.

Zaramagrii scanned her surroundings to make sure that there was nothing still lingering within the area. Yet she could feel something or someone breathing nearby, possibly within the wreckage. Slowly she approached it, studying the bodies as she grew closer.

The bodies appeared to be those of Man-folk, relying on what she had been taught about them. But all of their heads were missing. The cut had been done with an edged weapon, which left gaping holes of decaying flesh and bone each with its own blackened eruption of dried blood.

All appeared to be males except for one, whose body was fairly obese. She was very curious now, as she never actually saw one of the Man-folk before. Plenty had been taught to her by the clan. All of the bodies had arrows sticking out of them in various places, almost appearing as though the antagonists merely shot them to slow their movement, in play and not to kill them quickly.

Definitely a telltale sign of Akhruuk and goblin, thought Zaramagrii.

The arrows were of a dark stained coloring with black feathers. She knew that the Akhruuk around these lands always dyed their arrow shafts in blood. Whatever blood they could get, but preferably blood from their enemies. Hence the dark stain to them.

Now the headless bodies clearly showed the work of goblins, as goblins loved to keep the heads from their handiwork—trophies of their victories. Of course, they also favored the taste of the brain, which was considered a rare treat to them.

Apparently something brought the two distinctly separate and savage creatures together. It was not completely unheard of to find Akhruuk and goblins thriving near one another and compromising on a peace treaty of sorts for their existence. But for the two types of creatures to actually work together. Now that was significant for these beasts and pointed to a greater collusion.

Of course, she had no idea what. After all, she was merely running off of what she had learned when she was young (which, in reality, she still remained). And this applied to nearly everything at this point, as those of the Black Clans never were allowed out of their clan's territory until they matured. This meant that they were viewed as young ones for the first eighty to a hundred years of their lives.

It would seem that life threw her into the mix of things, ready or not, and definitely not expecting such strife or isolation. Like the Man-folk, she had never actually encountered an Akhru or goblin personally either. Besides the teachings, she only heard tales from patrols that ran across them at times in the past.

There were countless tracks of horse hooves throughout the area, but no horses were anywhere, not even their remains. Horses were probably also prey which the motley creatures had taken for their feasts. Such things as goblins definitely did not ride horse, while the Akhruuk might.

But something stirred within the wreckage. Zaramagrii cautiously approached close to the remnants of the wagon, eyeing the smashed barrels and other potential hiding areas. Most of the objects were too damaged to contain anything of value, let alone a creature of any size.

But one side of the burning wagon did have a degree of size to it, large enough for something to hide in. Slowly Zaramagrii walked around so she could see it from all angles. And that was when she spotted the faint outline of a small door.

This portion of the wagon must have had a storage compartment. She leaned forward to open it. Her body crouched in a fighter's stance, coiled and ready to spring.

To her surprise, as the door fell back against where the fire now burned, a beautiful head of tousled golden hair met her gaze. The large, sky blue eyes brimming with fear and the tiny dust-clad face streaked with dried tears peered at her. The thing looked at her in what Zaramagrii could only describe to be calloused shock.

What Zaramagrii assumed to be a woman...no...a girl, a young one in either case, barely fit into that tiny compartment. She was sheepishly oblivious to the consuming fire as it crept towards her. No doubt the shock of what she went through had left her in such a state. Her small lips were open, locked in a gasp, showing straight, pearly teeth. The others, now dead, must have hid her in here prior to the attack.

Zaramagrii knew the Common tongue but never really used it. "Have no fear, my little one. I intend no harm to you." The words poured out more in a heightened whisper, but her tone played her empathy for the girl.

The girl just continued to stare, possibly even she now looked upon a thing never experienced before. One of the Black Clans, in all of Zaramagrii's beauty. Although roughshod at the moment, this dark one's glowing persona penetrated through the silhouetted form. Together, the aura of this entity no doubt held the young girl in awe.

Zaramagrii slowly extended her hand out with the palm upwards as she did with the wolves of the Tharasvrul Rhaanmri. The young girl had a deep purple gown, which partially fell over brown linen pants that fit snug as tights. But the girl remained frozen in place.

Zaramagrii ended up gently grasping the girl under the arms and pulling her free from her hiding place, before the flames could singe her hair. She was barefoot. This was definitely a girl, maybe in her later years nearing maturity. But she seemed so tiny and frail. So helpless.

As the girl came out, she immediately clasped her arms about Zaramagrii's waist and tightly clung to her. At first, this incited sudden revulsion in her, as she instinctively attempted to pull away from the girl.

Then, she thought, this was not an *it*, it was a she. This was one of the Man-folk, and a babe at that. Zaramagrii thought, here was one not very far behind her in the stages of existence.

Although these beings did not live near as long as any of the Aylsh-kind, this girl must be around seventeen or eighteen summertides in age. Her loathing quickly turned to gut wrenching pity for the unfortunate thing, and she held her.

Then common sense overtook her. "Little one, we have to go. I am sorry for what happened to you and your kind here, but we must go now."

She did a cursory check of the broken mess and determined that there was nothing else of use to them. The speechless girl merely stood and stared as Zaramagrii left her side. Then Zaramagrii held her by her hand and slowly led her up the shallow rise away from the destruction.

At first she considered searching for another lofty tree, but then quickly discarded the thought as she figured that the girl would no doubt fall out of it. They had plenty of light left, but she did not know the lay of the land around here yet.

That left the cavern that she emerged from. Maybe for a short while the cave would be a good temporary shelter, at least while she collected a few necessities. These lands were harsh this time of year, and it was better to be prepared than not.

Returning to the small, nearly unseen cave mouth did not take them long at all. Once inside, they found a small patch of soft dirt wedged between the inner rock walls. The area was well-lit by the ambient outside glow, and concealed from any possible approach. The vantage would allow them to see anything coming towards them.

Then Zaramagrii did her utmost to impress upon the stricken girl to remain exactly where she was until Zaramagrii returned. The rest of the day's light was used in gathering necessities, more so for the girl, she realized at this point.

She returned with an armful of soft fir branches for sleeping on, as well as blocking out the cold winds. A makeshift chisel chipped out of igneous rock enabled her to carve out several pine knots to use for burning. She found flint rock and then retrieved a metal bracket from the wagon for use in igniting one. Before long, they had a low but crackling fire going.

Zaramagrii spent much of the first night up in a fir tree near the cave, so that she could stand watch. Occasionally she would check on the girl and find her still awake, sitting cross-legged, staring into the small pine knot fire.

Zaramagrii pondered the girl's circumstances, now distracted from her own. Although in a very similar situation at the present, both of their paths leading to it were vastly different. She thought of how those people had died, and what possibly could have brought them to such a wild place. After all, those people were obviously not cut out for it or sufficiently prepared to endure such extremes.

For the most part, the dark ones of the Black Clans followed the course of nature with reverence paid to the divine. But they believed that the higher beings ultimately were only the sponsors to and of what existence was. They did not answer the trivial whims of mortals or directly involve themselves within the trite activities of existence.

The dark ones themselves aligned, in form and essence, with the things that comprised the world, and those things were the proxy influence of the divine, or Initiator for that matter. In this way, the Black Clans believed the divinities to affect existence, but never did they actually take a hand in manipulating anything as an entity. Instead, the belief was that any alterations by them appeared as things naturally occurring.

The only such time that the divinities intervened directly, at least within the lore that was taught to her, was a long time ago. It was so long ago that the turo never applied an age to it, not even turns of years. Lord Braxis and his Olden met the ancient evil of the *Thalroan*, an unspeakable horde of dark beasts, upon the fields of Rhekmultaer and defeated them there. This was done before the horde of darkness could ruin all of Lord Braxis' creations, and scorch the world into a charred husk. They beat what remained of the Thalroan back into the Endless Chasm, supposedly locked away forever.

Zaramagrii's mother had taught her about the different philosophies and religions, as well as those that had no belief in the higher powers at all. And those kind tended towards aspects of reality and chance. But these types of sentient beings were predominantly of the Man-folk.

Although there have been others also believing in this way, others not of Man-folk, they generally have been few in number. But they still lived by that shallow concept of basing everything in only what they could see and touch. Nothing more, nothing less. A way of ignorant bliss.

Zaramagrii figured that, almost to the point of a deeply buried knowing, these barely contrived thoughts of reality and the nonexistence of the divine belonged mostly to the Man-folk for one reason. That reason was due to the shorter span of life, a much shorter time spent in existence. Thus, she thoroughly believed them to be this way due to ignorance and a lack of knowledge. The sorrowful lack of wisdom that was cultivated over vast lengths of time.

Really, she thought, *how could anyone actually believe that there were NOT higher powers at work within existence?*

More time spent in existence feasibly would, should, produce a higher learning, wisdom, and understanding of most things.

The Man-folk. What could a race that lives for less than a meager turn really discover in the way of the supernatural, or even the natural, for that matter?

Zaramagrii really did not care what was believed by one kind or another, but she was beginning to feel an insatiable lust for wanting to cure ignorance. That was what was on her mind now, well—maybe most of the time.

One other thing was bugging her. Could all of the Man-folk be this weak? Butchered and slaughtered by Akhruuk and goblins?

And there lay even more of their ignorance, for why would such an ill-prepared, small band of such creatures even consider risking the wildlands?

But she would not know more to this tale unless the girl spoke. Only then would she be able to put the pieces together in satisfying the curiosity playing rampantly through her mind.

This might help to explain the concept of the massive settlements of the Man-folk, their kingdoms, the ones that she learned about. But that began more unsettling sparks in her mind, as she was not a believer in the pyramid structure of such civilizations that she had learned so much about. Especially being one of the Black Clans.

A Black Clan was an organized and resourceful collection of interwoven and prolific essences that thrived on natural order. Better yet, they accepted it. Enlightenment was achieved through attrition and self-imposed abstinence. Ultimately, at least believed by those of the Black Clans, this allowed for a higher degree of self discipline and control.

But what could a settlement full of creatures like this girl ever amount to? How could they even survive this world? Let alone thrive as a people?

The proof of this was right in front of her now. This girl was not physically capable, and not even fundamentally sound in essence. This one event of attrition devastated any semblance of survival and rationality within the thing. Possibly the large settlements of these kinds of creatures were formed merely out of the need for protection. That would explain a lot.

The word *essence* was used by folk to indicate the soul of a being. The substance that provided the moral and ethical framework that guided the material actions and aspects of the being, the unseen force of a being. Of course, it was much deeper than just the morals and ethics, better stated would be to say all of the nonphysical nuances of the being. The term *soul*, at least throughout Thaldeia, was used to label an evil presence or disembodied entity. And *spirit* here referred to the complete being, both the physical and the inner self.

Zaramagrii did not care for the gods. If they would not lift a finger to influence a thing that, of necessity, should be altered, then what good were they? There was no point in communing with them.

She, like the majority of the Aylsh Ismaru, felt no significant loss or sense of guilt from not seeking the comforts of idolization, empowerment through the divine. Of course, this was nearly opposite the view of most of the Man-folk, and many other races.

Most of the sentient beings almost hinged their existence upon the whims of the divine, *and* the fear of what might happen if they did not.

Her mother always felt that one had to rely upon one's self. If one did not, then that individual was not truly their own force.

This Zaramagrii now understood, more so than ever before. Especially after everything that had taken place. She could now see that what her mother always said was true. Having to rely upon another for anything, especially for a necessity—in her mind—now showed tremendous weakness. She had always been taught this, but now she clearly grasped it.

But Zaramagrii, in all of her ways, still had not experienced or accepted that everything was different. Whether physically, mentally, spiritually, morally, or in principle.

Of course, she could see obvious differences, but not those more subtle, especially of the mindset, or of the heart. This cold outlook could also have been due to the austere, martial existence that the dark ones plied their kind to. And possibly only now, other dark and wispy phantoms were beginning to emerge within her character. Within her essence.

Zaramagrii decided to remain at the cave for another three days before moving on. This gave her time to fashion a sharp, wooden spear out of a sturdy branch, with the tip hardened in the fire.

The girl still had not spoken one word. She was a mess, barely even able to hold down the fresh meat of a squirrel without becoming sick. But she did take to boiled white pine tea, which forced Zaramagrii to ascend higher up along the rocky lands in order to find snow to melt for the water. At least the squirrel skin would hold them with a small amount of drinking water while they traveled. There would eventually be a stream or more snow along their path.

When they moved out at first light, Zaramagrii chose to head south. She stayed a ways up from the floors of the valleys and meadows beneath them, using the elevation and the thick growths as camouflage. It also provided her a vantage over the lands below for the most part. She could observe for anything that she might want to avoid.

By midday she already had the girl hoisted onto her lower back. She saw how just one day was taking its toll on the poor thing. But she did not mind, as she had developed an affinity of sorts for the girl.

It was purely a physical need where she felt that higher purpose. Like one that has helped a wounded creature, or like a child that has taken in a stray animal. That first sense of puissance through being able to help something that could not help itself.

In reality, Zaramagrii was beginning to view the merging sense of justice that would eventually twist towards the path of chaos. Neither good nor evil. Inevitably, a thing that cannot govern itself is then destined to be governed by another, even if that other be death. And this was that fine haze that would become all too clear to her.

Zaramagrii saw herself as the protector of this weak and gentle spirit. And part of the feeling still leaned towards the concept of fate, where the girl had been placed within her path ultimately due to Zaramagrii's purpose to be her savior and guardian.

The third day found the pair climbing down from a rocky ledge where they had spent the night. After most of the day was spent walking, Zaramagrii crested the top of a small ridge only to see a familiar sight.

Those mountain peaks in the distance were what she saw nearly every day back at Tharasvrul. So she had slowly been making her way back towards them all of this time. It would also mean that her travels underground had taken her a good ways north. That view, that she now looked upon, filled the sky every time she approached the Great Cave.

Lost in thought, she failed to notice the small figures clad in hide armor over the ridge until it was too late.

By the time she saw them, the girl had clenched her body up against Zaramagrii's back indicating that more were down to their side.

The short wiry creatures had yellowish-green skin. They resembled most sentient beings, except for the shortness and skin color. While their size could have painted them to be Half-folk, the color of their skin said otherwise. Their noses appeared bent and wrinkled, as though they had been very long at one time and then scrunched into the face.

Those in the front of the group were pointing simple, iron, stirrup operated crossbows at them while the ones behind had spears twice their height. One held a long war scythe.

With the girl to worry about, Zaramagrii knew that resisting was futile. Another of the creatures strode toward them, dressed in an animal hide robe and adorned with a large necklace of glistening bones and teeth.

They had to be Hulding, thought Zaramagrii.

At least, from what she remembered, the Hulding mostly were civilized. But their language registered nothing with her as she stared at them. Hulding was one of the languages that she was never taught.

Finally Zaramagrii dropped her makeshift spear and then spun the girl around to her front where she could keep better watch on her.

There were more of the Hulding approaching along the valley floor now. The one in the hide robe spit more indistinct words at them, but to no avail. Zaramagrii had no clue as to what he was ordering them to do.

Then, when Zaramagrii and the girl did nothing, one of the Hulding quickly scuttled over and cracked Zaramagrii across the back with the haft of his spear. The spear's cold iron langet, showing some degree of sophistication to these kind, stung her sharply. It left an ugly, blackened mark along the back of her neck. She was knocked to the ground while holding the girl.

As they rolled downwards, she felt her tiara fly off of her head, only to hit the rocky ground sharply with a fragmenting sound. Quickly she braced herself to keep from rolling farther and attempted to get back up to go and find it. But this just brought another whack of the spear haft.

Then the Hulding were between her and where the tiara had fallen, spears down and bristling.

It was too late as she now wished that she had done things differently. She looked down as emotions surged through her, knowing that the last heirloom, the last tangible thing from her mother left to her, now lay out of her reach.

As Zaramagrii rolled downwards and ended up in a half sprawled position with the dark rising sun of her mesmerizing mark glaring up and out, the Hulding closest to her suddenly tensed and clenched their weapons. Their increased volley of sharp tones in the guttural language almost seemed frantic now, fearful. One hovered a rigid spear with an ugly tip close to the mark below Zaramagrii's taut sheath of muscle.

The Hulding in the hide robe strode cautiously forward, his necklace of bones clattering like reeds in the wind. This one must have been a conjurer, or shaman, for the Hulding. But he seemed more wary, almost deathly fearful about something. The teeth were bared back in a harassed grimace as his eyes swayed to a tortured look. It was as though he did not want to approach her, but was obligated to from his position of power.

Indeed, Zaramagrii did not know it, but these Hulding saw an ancient omen of their own destruction come to fruition with the sight of that mark. The dark, rising sun had been a symbol of many things to many kinds. For the Hulding, according to their lore, this symbol was one of extremely miserable death and world shattering effect.

Hulding lore rested in what they called Thinwyltandinuum, or the Golden Leaves. The effigy of a dark, rising sun would signify that the end was near, and that its bearer was Xulghan, an eternal beast come to rend the world apart. Strangely enough, Xulghan meant *winged shadow*.

The Golden Leaves prophesied that every living thing would die a terrible and pain-wracked death before the essence was freed. Of course, the ruling shamans of the Hulding, chiefly their ancient predecessors, emblazoned their own interpretations of this lore. To this day, their rhetoric still held sway over the masses.

The Hulding shaman now apparently made a drastically fast decision as to what needed to be done.

Spittle flew from his mouth as he vehemently barked. "*Kymaetray. Kymaetray porthaunul!*" His stubby fingers sharply motioning towards Zaramagrii as if to perform the act himself. But he remained behind the circle of bristling spears.

The throng of Hulding warriors, ordered by the shaman, only held their ground and actually cowered. They shrank back while extending the spears out, more as though trying to ward off whatever they saw the dark one to be. All of those Hulding warriors surrounding them went into a mass brimming crowd of babble and anxiety. All, that is, except for one.

After all, they had been told to end it, to kill what might be the beast of darkness come to destroy the world. And such ancient power surely could not be harmed by a mere spear. Could it? In fact, terror streaked through their superstitious minds at the moment.

The one Hulding who did not appear to be overly bothered by this dark-skinned daemun with the mark of apocalypse strode through the middle of the doubtful warriors. He calmly lay his gnarled and knobby staff across the spears as his dark green robe billowed in the wind. His nose held an exceptionally squished look to it.

His voice croaked out, commandingly. *"Tinge da—ghanrak. Toolqwaz, sur kladfrin."*

The spears immediately lowered, but the guarded look of fear never left those round eyes. All of the Hulding recoiled at this intervention by the green-robed one, as a pack of wild dogs would once beset by their alpha.

Even the shaman backed away at the spoken words of the green-robed one. Reverence? Maybe only fear. Zaramagrii and the girl were bound tightly with leather straps and dragged to the back of a wagon. One of the Hulding forced Zaramagrii to tightly wrap a piece of hide around her body, completely covering her birthmark.

The wizened Hulding in green lingered in the area even after the prisoners were bound and taken away.

§ § §

Nearly half a score of days had passed for Rhalwa, and still the Aylsh maiden remained oblivious to her surroundings. There could be more underlying damage to her head from such wounds, but Rhalwa did not suspect this.

Instead, she thought that the reason the Aylsh did not wake from her blackness yet might be more immaterial. A hurt possibly very deep within her essence.

Sometimes the Aylsh maiden would cry out and murmur names in her lost delirium. Rhalwa distinctly heard Mordrid and also what sounded like *Shimmy*, but the names were said with such anguish and pain.

These outbursts led Rhalwa to believe that the maiden had suffered tremendous loss, no doubt the loss of those very dear to her. She came to terms with the fact that her charge subconsciously just did not want to wake up. The Aylsh's misery was so deep-rooted that nothing in the world was worth her returning to it. Everything that she held sacred and special was taken from her. Rhalwa could not help but shed a lonely tear from the thought, the conceived pain.

The once flushed and toned skin of the Aylsh was turning pale from lack of nourishment, as well as water. Rhalwa squeezed drops of cool water on the Aylsh maiden's parched lips, but it did not seem to be enough. Rhalwa continued to care for her, trying different herbal mixes, as well as burning incenses that soothed and drew upon positive energy.

Rhalwa began to have dreams over the past few nights since she discovered the Aylsh maiden. They were ones of uncertainty where it was always dark and cold about her as she carried the limp form of the Aylsh. The dream would always end with her stepping out of the darkness, which appeared like billowing, black fog. Then she would find herself standing directly in front of the two Oadewood saplings. These phantoms of the night made her feel as though she did not sleep at all, like they were real and she was actually awake in them. The tiredness led to exhaustion, as each day she awoke less and less refreshed.

It was late in the night, and Rhalwa lay in her bed trying to fall asleep. But her mind would not let her. The Aylsh maiden occupied it completely. Now she couldn't even close her eyes. *Why close her eyes to a sleep that would not come.*

That settled it—Rhalwa would follow her dreams. She quickly dressed and donned her sword. A water skin was hung over one shoulder as she quietly unlatched the door to peer out. The Oadewood great-bow snuggly curved over her back.

The night air was crisp with a slight breeze blowing. Once outside, the serenity of the dark blanketed her. There were only the scraggly stands of trees breaking up the dim, murky outline piercing the snow-covered lands.

It was now an old snow and her footprints still crisscrossed the ground. She also noticed there were many sets of fresh wolf tracks around the home.

She went back inside and wrapped the blanket tightly about the fair figure of the Aylsh.

The crunch of her footsteps in the snow echoed through the stillness of the woods like rolling boulders. With the weight of both her and the Aylsh, it was going to be impossible to silence her movements much if at all.

She first carried the small form cradled within her arms. Then, when she grew weary, she positioned the Aylsh up around her shoulders for a while.

The small form of the Aylsh was very light, but Rhalwa was a little petite thing as well. Similar to the first time she carried her back to her home, she ended up stopping in order to take short rests along the way. All the while she found even more fresh sets of paw prints from the wolves, but she never once felt uneasiness or apprehension.

The only time that Rhalwa left the confines of her four walls at night was usually during the full moons.

On these nights, she would listen for the wolves to howl. Then she would join them on their run as they hunted under the moonslight.

This was something that her father had shown her when she was very young. She had been doing it ever since. She came to know the pack around where she lived, and they her.

Occasionally she even brought down an elk or stag with her bow in an offering to the pack. Of course, this was only done on the hunt and as though she contributed as one of the pack. The wolf pack in these lands was a fairly large one, although she figured long ago that there could have been two or more of them. One time she had counted twenty-three different wolves. All huge majestic beasts.

And she always found their tracks outside her doorstep, making her believe that they checked up on her now and then. It appeared to her that these wolves may have come to accept her as part of their pack, one of their kind.

About thirteen years ago, when her father was still alive, a huge, pitch-black wolf had approached the home with two little pups in tow. Rhalwa had been young and but thirteen frostthaws, just a little girl.

At the time, she had been sitting not far from the front door while playing with several large pine cones that she had found. The black wolf started to gait right up to her with its head flattened down low, putting such a fright in her at first.

But then she looked over to where her father sat cross legged, quietly lost in meditation. As her wide-eyed stare found his eyes, he calmly placed his index finger to his lips to tell her to remain quiet. His hand slowly moved towards her and motioned for her to remain where she was. And his eyes spoke to her about the serenity and joy of what was in front of them both.

As the formidable beast came to within several paces of her, it did the most amazing thing ever. It sat on muscular haunches and stared at her with gentle eyes—one brown and one deep blue—lifting a large nose up in the air every now and again.

The wolf pups, like little balls of fur floating along the ground, approached her to within reach of her face. Then the two let out cheerful little yips and, with tails wagging, pounced on her, licking her face. She went hysterical with laughter from the tickling of the furry faces. The big, black wolf remained there, ever vigilant, while they played long into the evening.

Afterward, her father had offered them fresh elk meat. Later, when she was older, her father had told her that Aylsh had a special bond with all of the animals of Lord Braxis. He called them Wild ones, sometimes just the Wild. And they all were very unique creatures to embrace and respect.

The Aylsh could understand the animals and communicate with them. He then said that, while she was not fully Aylsh, the animals would still be able to read her and understand her.

Ever since that day with the wolf pups, she went out to run with them whenever the moons were full. And she felt so free and connected to everything when she did so. She felt whole, more complete.

Rhalwa decided to quicken her pace and cut straight through to where the Oadewood saplings grew. But now she thought that this might have been a bad idea.

A deep fog slowly enveloped them as she drew closer to the river. It was so thick that she had to slow down and move more cautiously. She could barely make out the snow beneath her boots. At times, even her feet were hidden from her.

Now she began to second guess how long she had been walking and no longer felt confident in where the river was, or whether or not her sense of direction was true. And all the while that she walked, she could hear faint rustling and shuffling noises from around her. Sticks snapped, the packed snow crunched under small feet, and the thickets rustled softly. Sometimes the sounds could have been at her feet, and then they would fade off to disappear in the fog.

After what felt like an eternity of trudging through limbo, she saw an eerie cobalt glow ahead in the distance. It was barely perceptible at first, an orb that she thought was a trick of the fog. A dim halo within the murky night.

What could that be? Her mind raced.

It amazed her that she even saw the glow, as it took a while longer to get close to its source. But when she finally did, then she understood. There, in front of her, were the two saplings with a pale blue aura blanketing them. In the middle was a soft, round refuge of warmth and solace.

The saplings appeared to be giving off the glow, with it being strongest in the exact center—in between them. The rich color of the center gradually flared out to a pale blue.

And there, along the edges of light, were dimly silhouetted forms. Wolves, lots of wolves, sitting and watching her. More of their noble and stoic forms lumbered out from the fog and into the aura.

So the wolves had been with them the whole time, guarding and protecting the pair for their entire journey from her home. Even the pack leader sat there, his once rich, black fur now tinged with silver.

Rhalwa approached the young Oadewoods with the Aylsh maiden and was surprised to find that no snow existed in between the trees. Amazing! It was not even cold in that circle of light. The air felt as warm and calming as that in front of her hearth.

A thick growth of soft, dry moss spread out beneath the saplings. Rhalwa gently laid the naked form down onto the mossy bed. The Aylsh appeared so pale, yet serene.

As she did so, a bluish-white halo surrounded the Aylsh maiden and tiny things flitted and flared about her. A humming and whirring bolstered the air as the things flew about them and the trees. She couldn't make them out as they moved so fast, but each one left a starry trail of blue glowing dust streaming behind it.

Stepping back, Rhalwa suddenly gasped. The twisting marks resembling tree roots upon the Aylsh's back began to glow a dull blue. This effect slowly grew until the roots appeared to be flaming branches of mysterious light.

The intricate symbol above her breast flared into a golden white brilliance. It became so intense that Rhalwa had to avert her eyes, as ghostly stars overpowered her sight.

Then the Aylsh's back suddenly arched up into the air with her chest facing the dark skies, eyes now white orbs of the duo suns. This lasted for a while with her arms hovering straight out from her shoulders, almost appearing as though a force of some kind was drawing her up.

The fair Aylsh maiden gasped and drew in huge breaths as her tiny breasts danced in the aura. She sat up as though attempting to get to her feet. Then she paused and looked around. Her eyes found Rhalwa's.

The Aylsh weakly whispered, "Rhalwa?" It was more a question than anything else.

Rhalwa quickly leaned down towards her and caught her as she slouched back onto the soft moss.

The Aylsh was barely able to utter, "Please, take me back." And then she was again lost to the conscious world. But her breathing sounded much better now, stronger and peaceful. Her face appeared smooth and carefree.

As the aura surrounding them faded completely, Rhalwa was not sure what the maiden had meant by her last words. Did she mean back to Rhalwa's home as if she had been aware of it the whole time, or did she speak of somewhere else?

Rhalwa shrouded her within the blanket again and headed back towards her home. Now the number of wolves had grown immensely. Many trotted along right next to her, on each side, as she carried the sleeping Aylsh maiden.

Soft, powdery snow began to fall the next day, enchanting all the snow-swept lands within a halo of crystallized sparkles under the bright duo suns.

The Aylsh maiden opened her eyes. They were so huge and of a deep, rich blue that could sink any ship at a glance.

Rhalwa was taken back by such majestic pools of life. She thought, *what creature this is of Lord Braxis.*

Rhalwa had been there the whole time, and had placed a cozy gown made of woven silk over the Aylsh maiden once they had returned from the wonders of last night. She had not yet slept.

"Rhalwa. Your name is Rhalwa," stated the Aylsh maiden as she stared into Rhalwa's eyes. "I am Ephritori." But she paused.

Then her Aylsh eyes sparkled with clarity as she continued, "Ephritori Nephritaryah Bari Lourendalthemee. That name was the one who was cast forth from her folk, ever hidden within the world of Man-folk. But I am Ephritori...now reborn, renewed as the Eternal Mother. I am beholden to you for what you have done for me." She paused several times as she spoke, as though deeply considering things.

Rhalwa tucked a fur-lined blanket around the shivering maiden. The warmth of the fire chased out all but the slightest drafts, however a fever still raged within the Aylsh. "Ephritori, such a graceful name. Save your breath for now, we have to get you your strength back."

With that, Rhalwa produced a basket of specially made corn cakes sprinkled with poppy and lemon seed. She also had an urn of steaming, white pine tea infused with herbs.

A gentle scratching sound coming from outside of the door grabbed their attention.

Rhalwa, sword in hand, approached the door and slowly pulled it towards her. To her amazement, there were at least a score of wolves scattered around the outside of the home. All of the animals turned their gaze towards her as the door slowly creaked open.

Three of the wild beasts stood near the door with magnificent winter lilies clasped in their mouths. One of them was directly in front, staring up at her, patiently waiting.

She stood in wonder as those three creatures slowly ambled inside and cautiously made their way towards Ephritori. They each then laid their flower down ever so gently at her feet, softly touching her toes with their muzzles. Then the wolves paced backwards the entire way out of the door.

Over the next few days, Rhalwa and Ephritori talked about various things. Rhalwa spoke of her simple life out here with her father, and Ephritori reminisced about her time at Tamelyn Keep. Her huge blue eyes welled up with tears as she talked of Mordrid and young Chimy. Those vivid memories of that stormy night at the keep loomed up over her, threatening to wrack her with that heart-rending agony all over again. The terror and the evil that those dark things had wrought upon her.

Then she told Rhalwa of the vision that she had while she was lost to her own darkness. This vision must have been while she lay within the healing aura of the Oadewood saplings, but she was not sure.

She had seen her father clearly in that vision though, and both Mordrid and Chimy stood by his side. As sad as she was even thinking about that deadly night at the keep, she knew that her father had given her the peace and love that were needed to fill that dark void. He was telling her that they were fine now, and that there was more to existence than just this physical world that she remained behind in.

All of this illuminated what had been lost to Ephritori. It had rekindled a deep flame inside of her very essence. One that had been forgotten for so long.

Ephritori also began to tell Rhalwa about her past life. Her past with the Aylsh Kingdom. Her father was of high, noble lineage. His name was Daumere Bari Lourendalthemee of Enclave Noblynbindyn—an Aylsh king. Yes, he was Trone.

She spoke of the terrible fire wyrm, the Great Wyrm, that had come to her father's lands. The wyrm was so enormous, the carnage and destruction that it wrought upon her folk had been unbearable. Her kin were lit on fire and burned away beyond any chance of help or hope, many crushed under the giant clawed feet or chewed apart like mice caught by a cat.

But, as her father prepared the last defense of valiant Aylsh knights, he spoke with her. Mordrid Dlobrak, known as Mordrid the Wyrmslayer, was there as well, but not due to any chance reason. No such thing as random action had spurred the near-perfect timing of such a warrior returning back to where his own mother had been born.

It had been fate or destiny that placed Mordrid there at that time. He had been found by the Trone out along their remote frontier, beaten and near death. They took him in, being the pure and caring folk that they are.

Once Mordrid was back on his feet, and his presence was brought to King Daumere's attention, the king saw it as a blessing. Mordrid's repute passed far and wide throughout the lands, at least in name. His deeds had been whispered in the winds even here within the Aylsh Kingdom.

Her father told her that she would be leaving, going away with Mordrid. Mordrid was to be her escort, her protector—there to take her away and hide her. It was for her own good, to keep her safe.

What Ephritori did not tell Rhalwa was no doubt most important. But not even Ephritori had completely accepted it yet.

The vision under the Oadewood saplings brought all of those memories back, and then some.

But how could she be the one? How could this be true? She thought, *even the wolf spirits flocking to me only made it seem all the more real and possible.*

In these aspects, not only did she not tell Rhalwa certain things, she held pieces of her truth cloaked within the darkness. Feeding off of the true nature of the Aylsh, Ephritori told her that these wolves must have sensed her misery, her demise. That was why they had regaled her in their own special way and had come to rescue her.

Ephritori did not even whisper the real reason to Rhalwa—the unbelievable, hard reality. Not yet—as this still remained elusive even to her.

King Daumere knew that the forces of darkness were ever encroaching upon his line. Not only a high-born line, but one of unsurpassed purity in regards to the Aylsh—inevitably, to all peoples and kinds. It was the last of the First Lines, along with that of Brinwoulerieh. In that same year of the Great Wyrm and the fall of King Daumere Lourendalthemee while defeating it, those remaining of the other First Line—that of Brinwoulerieh—also were mysteriously slain by dark shades that rose up. These shades appeared out of nowhere and right beside all of those remaining of the pure blood. It was said that these shades drained the life right out of them, their bodies wilting like flowers after the first Blustreve freeze.

Under the Oadewood saplings last night, in the strange dream, the old king told her that the cruel wyrm had ravaged the Aylsh lands for her. It had been hunting her. This was ultimately why he had sent her away under the protection of Mordrid so long ago, with her old memories hidden away from her.

The vision of King Daumere also told his daughter that she was of a much more altruistic cause and purpose, one that would bring light to the future.

This wyrm had been the work of the evils within existence in their attempt to put a stop to what she might do, destroy who she truly was.

The schemes that placed Mordrid there were of a higher purpose and involved the Black Legion, as well as someone with the Veiled Ones. Mordrid was more than willing to offer his services to such a mighty folk, though he had no inkling to the profound direness of what he volunteered himself for.

Her father then told her that she was the Eternal Mother, Ityarfa Vorjanimae, now walking incarnate again with purpose. A destiny. And her esteemed purpose involved all of her kind, so she must be strong and accept what had been given to her, as well as all that would yet come.

She remembered the Aylsh lore passed down to her from her father, before the events which separated her from her folk. The First Writings spoke of the Eternal Mother, the mother of all things. It was the Eternal Mother's arrival that the Aylsh prayed for, hoped for. The Eternal Mother was very symbolic for the Aylsh people, for their existence.

Mordrid had accepted her as his charge, to protect with his own life if need be. They would travel and live as man and wife, a guise to all of the purveyors of their doings. With the help of Trone sorcerers, Ephritori's past was hidden to her, in order to aid their newly woven story.

No, Ephritori would have to leave some of the truth out for now, especially with Rhalwa. At least until she herself fully accepted it for what it was.

Rhalwa smiled broadly at her, a smile of whole-hearted adoration They spent time relaxing by the fire, while getting to know one another. Any terrors that may have stalked either one of them seemed to be vague memories lost on the horizon.

Chapter 10:

Tidings from

the Past

Living and waking in the Light shall free one's essence, while falsifying one as such shall cast them down one hundred times.

–Eighth Edict of Lord Braxis, etched upon the Great Slates, recovered by Arterium circa the year 13 BA.

copious figure clad in dismal black plate armor stood alone and resolute against the north wind, atop a high plateau overlooking vast snow-covered forests below. The great-helm was of the same dark coloring and gave the appearance of a majestic panther head with gleaming fangs running downward on each side of the opening where a face should be. A black tattered cape streamed back from the figure.

But what stared out from that helm was no man or beast for that matter. A skeletal visage glared out with cold red orbs for eyes. The huge medallion, a sigil, hung around its neck. The design was a black panther head inlaid with onyx and quartz.

Lord Dulf Janlouk the Black Cat, commander of the Black Legion, contemplated the scene before his resolute eyes.

Soon a new year would be upon him, and the year 1624 would be history. It would be the beginning of his sixteen hundredth and sixty-fifth year in this world. And still he would be here upon this self-induced prison of a rock.

For he knew that he could no longer walk amongst his own kind, Man-folk. Not as the visage of a nightmare—which still held the faded and torn memories of life imprisoned within it.

He was nothing but a monster now. Ever since he traded his spirit for immortality and power. Except, the actual embodiment of what was promised him turned out to be completely different than what he had expected.

The Dark One had promised him the power and immortality of the divine, but there was not enough talk of what he truly would become. He was too brash and careless, too impulsive. Not prying further into the ambitious promise by the Dark One. Maybe he hadn't really cared about what it would do to him.

The dream of an eternal Black Legion had been quite strong. It bowled him over and completely numbed his better senses.

Yes, the divine power was his to an extent, and immortality had stolen his character a long time ago. However, the transformation that followed the fateful day the Dark One turned him would forever churn his compassion and tolerance. Whip it into a cold hard flattened piece of iron.

Living so long does things to the mind and heart—seeing and experiencing so many different things for what they really were warps the altruistic sense of purpose and intent.

The caveat to all of this might be that loss of those basic needs, maybe the loss of the ability to fulfill them.

And now there was a shell filled with egotistical and corrupted dreams, which originally started in the early days of the Legion as a foundation of benevolence and justice. The turns of existence have done their work well, and now the original founder and commander of the Black Legion was left to pulling strings from within the dismal hole of pretense, thought by all to be long dead.

But Lord Janlouk had been old and dying when first approached by the Dark One. And the promises made by it for him to forever command and lead the Legion—his conception, his dream—were just too much to pass by.

After all, his intent upon founding the Black Legion back in the days of old had been based upon righteousness and making a stand against the blackness that permeated through to all corners of Thaldeia.

The only things that had resonated with him were power and immortality, and how to retain them for the cause of righteousness.

He had utterly ignored the warnings by the Dark One of other effects. But there was no grandeur in being turned into a lich. He no longer enjoyed the pleasures of the flesh.

Within a fortnight, his physical body had rotted away. This left him a bitter and conniving tyrant of sorts, only pleasant when he felt there was something to be gained by it. Not that it mattered, as the circle of those whom he interacted with grew incredibly small. Until there were only two.

The woman of the Veiled Ones had been his only salvation. Although she was not entirely what she presented herself to be either. She had not aged a day since they first met, and well, it had been at least eight hundred years.

In any case, this Veiled One could be bought by gold. Though he did not completely believe that to be her only motivation.

And he did rather enjoy her unusually gifted talent at playing her sorange. The music that flowed from it at the touch of her fingertips…and that enchanting voice. She only played the part of a bard, he knew, to hide in plain sight when necessary. But she played these parts so well.

The instrument known as the sorange was one of antiquity, even here in Thaldeia. The sorange was small, maybe slightly longer than an arming sword. It appeared like an oval-shaped canoe. The canoe shape ran the entire length, with one end being much larger than the other. On two sides were up to ten strings of varying lengths and types. These ranged from fine, but rare, shifting spider silk to the braided cords of a hopresyk.

The hopresyk was a peculiar beast that dwelled mostly in the dark forests along the western coast of Thaldeia. The individual strands that grew on them had no tensile strength, but when braided into cord they became resilient and stretchable. At certain ranges of tautness, these cords produced eerie, high-pitched notes when plucked.

Of course, they had to be stretched, soaked in the slime of a gigantic clam, and then installed and left to dry for a lengthy time.

If the gigantic clam was not harvested respectfully, then the slime from it would produce dry, flimsy cord that just fell apart. So folks paid a fair amount of gold for such a thing as a jar of this slime. And from a reputable trader.

Legend had it that a genuine sorange was built with a small piece of living Oadewood inside of it and also that the strings had been bathed under the light of an Oadewood's heart for at least a turn. Many claimed that this was what made the truly haunting melodies possible.

The sorange actually was introduced by the Trone Aylsh at some point during the Revered Times. Those not of Aylsh descent that chose such a fine piece to play were considered most talented and also uniquely gifted. Anyone but the Aylsh found the stringed instrument extremely difficult, if not impossible, to master. While rare, it was quite a treat to stumble across someone playing it.

Janlouk continued to ponder his self-inflicted prison of longevity. The feel for the pleasure of a woman was like a constant itch that could never be scratched, in his current state. *Those bodies—the plump and pointed breasts, the savory thighs—entirely out of his ability to enjoy. What blasphemous cursing it was!*

The unabated longing turned into aggression many turns ago, aggression and plotting towards whatever cause he decided to set the Legion into motion for, or against.

Truth be told, there were now the four distinctly separate companies of the Black Legion in operation, each with their own commander. But he still controlled the one that pulled all of their strings. Although located at various locations across Thaldeia, they were still synchronized as needed and when required. And this was by his sole decree.

The giant of a form strode to one of the many outcroppings of rocks and boulders littering the plateau's surface. This particular one wrapped itself around a small cave which routed back somewhat in the shape of a sickle blade.

Far back in the cave was a stone stairway leading downward, smoothly hewn countless ages ago. The stairs were lined with torches as they curled down in a lazy spiral.

Sephoora would not be long now, he thought.

One hundred stairs led through the narrow passage down to a handful of chambers carved into the rock. The first one was quite large and also filled with assorted furnishings. A large passageway led into darkness on the opposite end.

Of particular interest was an impressive, pedestal-like object shaped as a crescent moon, nearly as long as a horse. It appeared to be made of silver but had an antiquated look to it, with numerous runes littering the surface.

The *Mynrooth* portals were objects of old world thaumaturgy, steeped within unknown origins, and crafted well before the time of Man-folk. The name Mynrooth was Black Clan and meant silvery pool.

These ancient devices were scattered at least across Thaldeia, in various places from high atop mountain peaks to subterranean caverns. Only a handful of their locations were actually known, and these to very few. Most of these folk still did not entirely know the end destination that a particular Mynrooth portal might take them, or all of the possibilities of such a craft.

What was known about them was that they were of another dimension or space. Once activated, the device would take whomever stepped into it to another place. This other place could be within one hundred leagues, or across the entire mass of Thaldeia. And those were just the ones that were known.

The meaning of the name silvery pool may be a bit misleading, as they did not appear to be a pool per say, like a pool of water to swim in.

A Mynrooth portal was more than just the object, sightly as they were. Once activated, it raised upwards in the form of an oval disk of silvery shimmer about as high as a banner staff. A pool, more or less, that sat vertically and had the appearance of melted, liquid silver that rippled when disturbed.

One would simply have to step or jump into this and the individual would be transported to the portal's sister device, whether that one was active or not.

There has been much speculation on these pools throughout the history of Man-folk at least. Most of them appeared to be two-way or set for travel between two devices, while some had multiple points of transference.

The trouble was that no one could ever read the runes and know exactly where it connected to, or even what they intended. What had been learned about them was done so through trial and error. In fact, there were tales of at least one intrepid explorer who decided to test one and then was never seen or heard from again. Not even to this day.

The scholars of Man always suspected that these portals were tied to the Black Clans, and when they dispersed to the four winds and disappeared, so did the knowledge of the portals.

This particular one in Janlouk's fortress did connect with another pool, but it also had powerful crystals associated with it, three to be precise. One could carry a crystal with them and, when needed, then could use the crystal to return to this portal with the simple utterance of a word.

In the case of this one, the word used—*naravim*—translated to the meaning of the first in the ancient Black Clan language.

Of course, Lord Janlouk held one of them. He provided one to the recognized commander of the Legion, Axyander Blackshield the Steelborn. The third one was handed to Lady Sephoora. Thus, he had near incessant ties with the two key figures in his dominion, for all of his endeavors.

It was not long before the Mynrooth portal's outlandish liquid materialized, raising upwards. A fairly young and captivating woman stepped out into the chamber.

Clothing of green leathers clung to her fit physique. A brimmed hat rested on her head with one side clasped upwards by a gold triangular pin with a silver circle of metal at the center. A silver rapier with a jeweled pommel hung at her side, and a finely crafted sorange was slung across her shoulder.

She strode towards him, her sleek green cloak billowing in scintillating colors as she did so. The trailing edges of it transforming from shiny foil as it pulled free of the portal.

Janlouk removed his great-helm as he stood near the table lined by several oak chairs. His blackened skull still showed very small traces of grayish white here and there, and long black hair hung from parts of it. He quickly pulled the cloak's hood low over his bony brow.

"My lord, may your days be bright and promising," said the woman in a soothing melody of a voice as her long, wavy brown hair cascaded around her shoulders with the removal of the hat.

"Lady Sephoora, well met. Hopefully your travels were pleasant." Janlouk poured a tall goblet of her favorite red wine as he spoke. It was the vintage of Charathadour, sealed during the year SA 982.

Charathadour, a tiny desert kingdom within the southern lands of Thaldeia, was known for the rich, rare vineyards.

What made the taste even more priceless was the demise of the kingdom back in SA 1100. After several turns of producing an exceptionally fine mauve concoction from the wrathgrapes, the aristocratic magocracy simply vanished.

All of the material things—cities, villages, even the clothes inside dressers and the linen upon beds—remained intact. It was as though the entire people just disappeared into thin air at the drop of a gold mark.

Of course, of all the lands and structures that Charathadour held, the only thing that remained of the enchanted vineyards were large tracks of open desert, as though they had never existed. This did not sit well with the powers in Rhousthaq, another southern empire to the east of Charathadour.

The Krizna of Rhousthaq immediately annexed the hollowed lands under the banner of neighborly succor. The powers of Rhousthaq were hoping to assume the affluent Charathadour wine production, and to establish new riches out of what had become a poverty stricken land soaked in complete squalor. When the reigning Krizna discovered that the vineyards had literally disappeared, he flew into a rage that sparked a long and bloody campaign of conquest throughout most of the southern desert territories.

Over the next hundred years, Rhousthaq would wage war against and conquer three more territories around them in their struggle for supremacy. The atrocities committed under the hand of the Krizna were beyond horrific. To this day, the Krizna ruled over his empire of routed nations with an iron gauntlet.

Lady Sephoora swayed onto one powerful leg as she paused near a chair, providing the lich commander with a feigned sensual pose. Then she sank slowly into the cushions with a tease of her eyes.

"I trust that all has been well with you?" questioned Janlouk, his imperious frame now also seated on the other side of the table.

Lady Sephoora smiled and let out a light sigh. "Of course, my lord. The lands are mostly quiet."

Their talk went to triviality and some of the past that had so heavily soaked Thaldeia. Whenever they met, counsel always eventually turned purposeful and to their affair. An affair of sordid conspiracy, one that swayed kingdoms and moved armies.

The two of them each held their unseen agendas, as they ceremoniously danced around the small talk while working up to what was important.

But Sephoora saw long ago how fast Janlouk turned to matters at hand, matters of importance to him. She read the surge of angst and bitterness in him, as well as the loss of what had tethered him to doing what was just and right. He always attempted to hide this from her, she could feel it. But every now and again those walls of pure obsidian would have the slightest cracks. Tiny but yet noticeable, only faint traces of barely perceptible flaws.

Janlouk softened his voice. "Pray tell, my tasteful one, what news have you that would surprise one such as I?"

Lady Sephoora paused and sighed. "Things have been quiet of late. But it would appear that the plagues that have struck the lands in the past were actually fermented plans of some evil force at work."

Lord Janlouk stopped her with the raising of a gauntleted fist. "Enough of this talk... Forces of evil...lest you apply a name to these forces of evil, then we can't do much about them, can we now?"

He relaxed again and leaned back in his chair. "I am interested in the comings and goings of essential things around the kingdoms."

As he ended this, his other hand raised a leather satchel and allowed the contents to slowly trickle out on the table. Shiny gold coins and a variety of finely cut jewels of differing hues avalanched out.

With eyes a sparkle, Lady Sephoora continued. "Tamelyn Keep was overrun by one of the Black Clans. All were slain including Eggelstyk. Nothing appeared to be taken or damaged as far as the collections go, but my sources told me that one particular book was removed. And the last line of King Daumere Bari Lourendalthemee of Enclave Noblynbindyn disappeared in this attack.

"Not only this, but there have been reports of new activity within Isnuuthghor. At least one of the clans has returned there, but not the one responsible for the attack on Tamelyn."

"This is interesting. What would any of the Black Clans want to return to that dark hole for? And tell me why this last Aylsh line is so important?" questioned Janlouk.

She looked at him for a moment before beginning. "There are ancient Aylsh prophesies of the grandest Aylsh king ever born coming forth, known as Itharzyr Morwhe—the Fatherless Son. This one supposedly will be carried to his power sometime within the sixteenth turn and will not only unite the Aylsh-kind against some terrible evil, but will also be the cause of the disappearance of the Aylsh."

"Disappearance? But how…a whole people? How and why? This is mere legend. And what would this last line have to do with it anyways?" Janlouk clenched the ends of the table as he worked through this in his mind.

The Veiled One paused while studying Janlouk's mask. "The last of the ancient lines, an Aylsh maiden, is the last of the First Lines. That of Thiliathain and also of the Eternal Mother's. I have it on good word that her father, Daumere, actually cloaked her within the Man-folk. Not even she was left with her memories… Knowledge of her people and herself. Thus, even her father himself had been hidden from her. This was done not long before the Great Wyrm plagued the Aylsh in 1525. King Daumere Lourendalthemee and two of his sons fell in battle with the wyrm. The third and last was slain by forces of the yuanhad."

Sephoora added more to the picture. "Happen chance or not, this same year saw each of the other Aylsh that held the purest blood of the Eternal Mother's line mysteriously slain by dark shades. Their life drawn right out of them. And all nearly at once.

"Well, since uncovering this prophecy, the Veiled Ones have watched and followed certain ones of Aylsh royalty. Indeed, my lord, this last line of King Lourendalthemee—this maiden that has vanished within the attack on Tamelyn Keep—she very well might have been the last of that ancient bloodline. The other Aylsh of royalty—and there are none pure at that—are from within the origins of maybe eight to nine turns. Many merely just appointed as such. Her blood goes back well before recorded history even."

Commander Janlouk raised the tone of his voice slightly. "And what exactly are you saying, my dear one?"

"I am saying that she could have been the one prophesied to herald in this fabled king of her people. But it is much speculation. I am more concerned with the murmur within the Fallen Lands— and the recent activity of the Black Clans," she finished curtly and added, "as you well know, my lord."

Janlouk let out a labored breath riddled with thought. He also noticed Sephoora's eyes, and what he thought was the natural hazel color now appeared more of a golden hued glow. *Interesting*, he thought. This was something that he never previously noted.

"I will have Tamelyn secured soon. Now let us keep watch on the activities inside of the Rock Rim and find out what is afoot. The Akhruuk, goblins, joutuun… The yuanhad. Well, all of that filth contained within those peaks. It has not surged outside of those borders in many, many turns.

"Let us find out what is going on if we can, and my dear, come to me immediately if any of that is connected with the Black Clans. As well as those regions where the companies of my Legion are active."

He paused while running his hand along the edge of the table. "And what of the Purple Bloom? What is behind that? A black moon is not due for another sixty years or more."

A black moon referred to the time when all five of the moons that orbited Zholryn would eclipse at once. The result was breathtaking, as it would present a layered halo of many colors that would last most of the night. Glorified rings of purples, blues, reds, and oranges permeated the entire period of the covering.

The Veiled One pursed her lips while speaking, "It would appear that there is a fluctuation in the Shadehaunt itself…and its correlation with our world that we are in. But I have no facts as to what has spun this yet. All I can say for certain is that this particular oddity is far more reaching than just Thaldeia. I believe that it is across the face of Zholryn."

She continued to share her findings of the recent bloom of the nightmask flower. From north to south, places where the flower never previously grew. They discussed these events well into the late-suns, until the powerful duo suns began to dip in the sky.

Lady Sephoora glided across the plateau as she thought about Lord Janlouk and his intent. She was several hundred paces from the sheer drop off.

But, she thought, *he had almost given away his chief concerns…while still smart enough not to say it outright.* Yes, he had said that he wanted to know the comings and goings within the kingdoms, but she knew what he really meant by that. His use of kingdoms truly only meant one—Kuhrzoth.

The old lich intended to get his bony hands around what has been the power base on Thaldeia for quite some time now. With only a frail king, and that one on his death bed, Janlouk could possibly gain enough leverage himself or through another proxy to assume the crown.

But would that be for the better, or for the worse? She did not know for sure. What was for certain was that the lich commander had changed significantly since she knew him in those early days. There was no longer any doubt to his twisted sense of greedy purpose now. The man had become one of the monsters that he had always tried so hard to destroy.

She did not divulge possibly the most important piece of information that she had come across. Ephritori could indeed be Ityarfa Vorjanimae, the Eternal Mother. And the humble young man of Longshadows was connected to this prophecy of a Marked One, all somehow tied in to the Eternal Mother's return. But what was behind this orchestration of unknown precedence?

Sephoora did not falter as she approached the vast cliff. She continued her pace and casually leaned downward off of the edge and into the air head first, as though diving into a pool of water for a swim. As her form disappeared over the edge and into the thousand foot drop, it transformed into something gigantic. Only the tip of a huge reptilian tail, golden hued green in color, was visible until it disappeared out of sight.

§ § §

Priestess Sahrya stood alone in her inner chambers. Her collusion of both the arcane and the divine arts gave her tremendous powers. The lost arts of the Old Ways, shown to her by the Ancient One, only prominently enhanced what already had been achieved by her with the varied schools of thaumaturgy.

Rarely did an aspiring practitioner of thaumaturgy ever study more than one of the disciplines of power, let alone more than one sphere. For Sahrya, her mastery of the Wild encompassed vast power from all of those disciplines within it. But her particular focus was on the black arts, even though aspects of both Light and Dark tainted it.

She closed her eyes, envisioning the cave high up on the top of the mountain within the Purple Peaks. One hand held out the charred piece of ash wood soaked in the liquid from the eye of an Aunlourey.

Once the perfect vision of where she wanted to be was beheld in her mind's eye, she whispered the words and felt the strange, but brief, multi-directional pull over her entire body. And then she was there.

She could not use her transference spell to get to this cave until she first had been brought here by the Ancient One. The spell only worked when it was used for places that the caster had physically visited and was familiar with.

From what she knew, there was no physical way to actually get to, or even inside, this cavern. The only small passage that connected it with the rest of the world was a very tiny crack, leading through layers of rock. A crack high on top of a jaggedly steep crest.

She always marveled at the cave, as the entire inside surface of it was covered in naturally formed crystal. Using another of her basic crafts, she created a small glowing ball of light in order to illuminate the area. The Purple Peaks were famously known for their hidden wonders. Caves and veins full of gem-infested rock.

Now the entire cave appeared to have hundreds of small lights as the crystalline surface reflected the glowing ball. From purples to reds, blues, and opaque ones. The faint shimmering iridescent glow throughout the cave was impressive. The spark of light hovered freely at the center of the cavern.

Of course, she knew the obvious intent of the Ancient One desiring to maintain their meetings in such a space. Besides there being no way for anything to actually get inside, crystal was rumored to contain many properties of thaumaturgy. One of those known included the preclusion of any kind of scrying attempts through it. Crystal was effectively dead space when it came to the metaphysical powers of extraordinary sight.

Distant memories emerged as she stared at the floor of the cave. She had lain bundled in blankets the very first time that the Ancient One had brought her here. It was right after he had rescued her from the battlefield of woe. After the raiders had taken their turns with her and several other females of her clan.

These dark ones had been known to her, all of them her kin. Not one of them survived the ordeal.

She remembered how she felt that day—naked, battered, and weak. Their seed, Man-folk seed, dripped from between her legs, making her thighs feel clammy. Making her feel futile and worthless.

The Man-folk raiders had nearly done her in, taking advantage of both her ura and her arse. As she lay there dying, she was forced to watch as the Clan Omrasstefor Rhaanmri—all thirteen robust cats—were slowly drawn in and murdered, then roasted for a feast. Their pained, hopeless mewing ever echoing through the haunted halls of her mind.

The mighty beasts refused to leave while members of the clan still lived. The poor creatures always came back to try and save her...save them...sometimes in pairs, only to be trapped and slaughtered.

She had long ago disconnected the torment associated with those memories, filling the space up with the black arts and plans of vengeance.

One day, the Ancient One brought her what was left of those men that had pillaged and destroyed her clan, her cats. Living symbols of the horror that had decimated what she had been, forever changing the inner spirit or essence.

The thirteen that were brought to her had been left bound and tied each to their individual wooden beam.

The Ancient One called this thing, the killing of these thirteen, part of the healing process and also the opening of a very dark portal. It took her thirteen days to butcher them, each of the Man things slowly and carefully carved with razor sharp blades for the entire time. She had reveled in the screams, the screams then eventually turning to whimpers. The whimpers to silence.

The agony inflicted on the Man-folk was as prolonged as she could force it to be. Many times she would carve them right into unconsciousness only to stir them back to their suffering with cold water before continuing on. The once recognizable men were reduced to bloody, bony quivering masses of cut flesh.

A small trail of black smoke streaming into the cave from the small crack brought her back from the ordeal. It was smoke with a sense of form all to itself.

The gaseous vapor was not really like smoke though. It appeared more as a watery substance being moved through the air—as though contained within an invisible water skin, sloshing and moving about.

The mysterious form materialized into the black cloaked Ancient One, standing directly in front of Sahrya. The long hood was pulled far over its head, with just the chin and mouth showing. The skin appeared to be completely blackened, like charred wood, and the chin protruded down into two grayish white rounded points.

For the first time she noted that the teeth in its mouth appeared as glistening, silvery metal, set in a lipless scar. The blackened hands were clasped in front, near the waist. The towering figure loomed well over even her tall form.

Almost immediately the thing began to make deep sniffing sounds and then let out a shrieking hiss of displeasure. "Pray, my child, what have you within your cloak? Something so repulsive? Whatever could that be?"

Priestess Sahrya thought about what she had brought, and then produced the bloody cloth from Tamelyn Keep, wiped in the Aylsh maiden's blood. She had placed it back in the pocket of her cloak after allowing Rosella to acquire the fragrance of it. The scent of what she would hunt.

"Only this, my lord."

Olri Uchrah, the black leather-bound book recovered at Tamelyn, was tucked under an arm.

The Ancient One came closer and sniffed the wrapped cloth. "Yes, so…hallowed. I have not felt that or sensed it in a very long time. It is almost as though hundreds of Aylsh were all together, in one place. And the essence that such an abomination gives off. Whatever could this be from?"

Sahrya quickly recounted the events at Tamelyn Keep, including both the old book and the disappearing Aylsh maiden.

The Ancient One brooded silently for a time. "I believe that whatever thing this blood came from…it walks the lands with a blistering radiant light."

"What does that mean? A radiant light? To what end?" wondered Sahrya, out loud.

The Ancient One exhaled deeply while warning, "I suggest that you find this Aylsh thing, or whatever it is, and put an end to it quickly. Before it realizes what it is and fulfills whatever purpose it is here for."

Sahrya felt the cloth while eyeing the dark form, its eyes now blazing out at her from the blackness in sharp, brilliant red orbs. She knew at the time that something had slipped through her grasp that night when the Aylsh vanished.

Sahrya obediently replied. "As you wish. I will find her and destroy whatever it is…or whatever it has."

"And what of the new breed?" hissed the dark form.

Sahrya thought about her latest scheme involving the Akhruuk. "The trials have gone better than expected. The offspring are extremely strong and agile, and they possess most of those endowments that make one of the Black Clans so formidable. But it will take near a turn to have any numbers worthy of an army."

The Ancient One's eyes flashed out in a red glow. "Then do what it takes to create more. This is important for the final plight against the Man-folk. And ensure that this new breed is solely driven to obey and to kill. Nothing more, nothing less."

Sahrya thought about her intent for at least the first few of these Chosen, the name she had given this new breed. And these were showing an exceptional capacity for exactly that. Killing, mercilessly and fearlessly. Most important to her now, though the Ancient One was oblivious to this extreme determination, was the blinding focus to destroy Zaramagrii.

"Yes, my lord, the Chosen are being lashed and beaten into the Chasm itself with *only* that in mind."

The Ancient One fingered the weathered binding of the old black book. It knew that it was drafted by none other than Siri. But what of the material inside? And how did the Man-thing that she had been deceiving fit into it all? The book had been positioned at the keep to be found specifically by that one. That was certain.

"My child, what is this man that you played with in order to uncover the Lost Scroll? Does it still live as well?"

Sahrya scowled. "Wybur Buttlecut... But do not fear, my lord. For I have my mistress Daemun tracking him as we speak. He will not last long. None of them shall, they will all fall."

Her thoughts briefly flickered to Rosella, one of the more powerful Daemuns. Well, maybe all Daemuns were very powerful, or so she thought. But Rosella was a kind from the lower regions of the Endless Chasm.

According to lore from across Thaldeia, the Endless Chasm was where beings known as Daemuns originated from. There were many kinds of Daemuns.

Supposedly there were a hundred layers to the Chasm, to this place of tormented things. Sometimes it was even referred to as the Hundred Layers. Each of these layers had its own unique kind of spawn. And each of these regions, as one went down, was worse than those above it. The farther down in the layers, the stronger the powers and abilities of the spawns that resided there. Also, the deeper the wickedness.

"Yes, I trust your word on this," hissed the Ancient One. But it really did not. Not at all.

There were now three separate entities afloat in different directions, possibly even set afoot by more than one force of unknown might. And entities that were of unknown quantity, unleashed for hidden purposes.

The priestess did not have enough means to contain them all as well as maintain the other dark operations across Thaldeia. And the Ancient One still needed her—needed to use her for these other dark designs that could not falter.

No, the Ancient One would take pleasure in keeping an eye on these thorns that had been scratching at its plots. Just to make sure that things were taken care of…properly. But it also knew that if too much of its power was unleashed, then *they* might decipher what it was. And that could not happen, at least not yet. Too much was at stake.

Sahrya eyed the dark form while contemplating the tone. "I have fully devoted the efforts of our Windwalker from the light world now. She is of tremendous power, and I think with no living match, at least in the realms of Man. Even now she leads my Thalroan, my horde of darkness. And they are strong."

She reveled in the choice of the name for her army.

According to Black Clan lore, the Thalroan was the dark army that rose from the Endless Chasm thousands of years ago to ravage and decimate the entire world. It was only by the hand of

Lord Braxis and his Olden, as they met the Thalroan upon the fields of Rhekmultaer, that the all-powerful evil force was sent back to its hole. The fields of Rhekmultaer were the ancient flats high up in the Gloomy Mountains, surrounding the dark fortress Isnuuthghor.

"Indeed, Sahrya. It is as I have spoken. All foretold as prophecies. Your destiny, Rha's destiny…there cannot be the one without the other." Secretly, the Ancient One thought about how well these plans had come together, even with what he had done a long time ago to bring such a being as Rha into this conquest. "And have no doubts that Rha will play her part.

"Also know that she is but a dynamism, a pawn, to maneuver and use as necessary. Do not let her overstep her bounds, or deem her more useful than she is. Never lose focus of your final place…as the all-powerful. Or of what still remains to be done, over time, before you can assume that place. We have many things to set forth, at the appropriate time."

Priestess Sahrya slowly nodded her head while tightening her lips. "I will not, my Ancient One. I will not forget that the third plague must be fulfilled prior to the Rise of the Fallen, and the emergence of the Dark Rider."

"Yes, my ravishing one. Yes, indeed," drummed the Ancient One as his thoughts went to other plans not yet known to the priestess. Most never would be known. And his glimmering, red eyes beamed with excitement at the possibilities of what might happen over the next turn.

After the priestess departed, the Ancient One contemplated what it had sensed from the powerful blood on the cloth. And what it had sensed went further back than ancient itself.

The Aylsh were not as old as the Black Clans, but that essence was deeply set in their lineage. Only something more divine, with its very essence rooted within the foundations of the world. This would take more study, and more contemplation. But, in any case, the essence that shed that blood had to be found. The Ancient One feared the possibilities of why Lord Braxis would place such a power back onto this world. Feared? Well, maybe not feared, but it loathed any such intervention in its intent. Possibly the Ancient One's existence might have been detected. Somehow, some way.

The ancient, black leather-bound book contained the original sign of Siri—at that time, the divinity of Chaos, Death, Darkness, and Shadows—of the Shadehaunt. This offered a degree of credibility to what the priestess hunted—the dark child named Zaramagrii. So it was possible that she was of the essence of Siri himself, and maybe even protected by him. But she remained mortal for the time being, and able to be destroyed. If all of this happened to be true, then she may very well be on her road to Ascension.

If Lord Siri's goal was to create another powerful divinity, then the dark child had to be stopped above all costs. It could not be a coincidence that the dark child was roaming the lands freely, as well as this other hallowed thing of the Primordials emerging at the same time. But which one was real? Or were they both real? If so, they both must be eradicated before their Ascension. And the Aylsh maiden really needed to be dealt with sooner than later. Before she had a chance to realize her destiny.

Chapter 11:

In the Company of Death

Those of sentience granted autonomous thought and free will shall walk charged as the caretakers and nurturers of all domains.

–Ninth Edict of Lord Braxis, etched
upon the Great Slates, recovered by
Arterium circa the year 13 BA.

igh atop the soaring barren peaks of the southern spires along the Rock Rim, the wind whistled and whipped around like a living thing. Nothing green could grow up at this immense loftiness. Only the toughest and hardest creatures survived even a night during summertide due to the cold chill that crept along the surface of the crags after the suns went down.

One of the taller peaks rose out of their middle, like a long, curved sword. There were several ledges that ran up this particular one, although each of these was very roughly formed and obviously natural. Or were they?

The highest one, facing out over the south, even had a fashion of a rocky roof that jutted over it. A very dark shape rested on the rugged edge, possibly nothing more than a bush.

But no, it was a figure, crouched forward on the knees and slightly seated on its buttocks. A closer look revealed that only a pair of deeply set but contrasting orange-red eyes stared out coldly. These were the only things that indicated such a being existed there.

The strange blackness about the form, other than the black silk clothing that occasionally flapped in the wind, created an optical illusion with the observer. The blackened material—no, the unique armor—was what was so mesmerizing. It almost entirely warped the figure, blending it into the background as a pale shade, maybe a dim mirage.

Now the white cloud of breath could be seen as the living being exhaled in the frigid cold. This was not the burst of chill-wracked breathing as would be expected in such an extreme place, but a methodically slow and premeditated ritual.

As the duo suns rose higher in the west and opened up the world for life and prospect, the outlandish armor almost appeared to be a hole of blackness. At the right angle, one could note the rune-covered, black metal suit of fitted and fine craftsmanship. It even covered the head and only left a tight oval where the hellish eyes stared out from.

Nimosese, master assassin of the Dhourkuul, quickly stood and looked out indifferently upon the lands. The Dhourkuul, Order of Death, had been around since the existence of the Black Clans.

The Black Clans were known to be the very first of the sentient beings born upon Zholryn, although the Man-folk would not claim this and the Aylsh refused to acknowledge it.

In the glory days of the Black Clan stronghold Isnuuthghor, before its original fall a thousand years earlier than the current era, there had been thousands of Dhourkuul warrior assassins. Most say that the dark fortress would never have fallen to the oppressive hand of Arterium, if his expedition had invaded the homeland back when it was thriving in all of its glory.

These Black Clan warriors were embodied nightmares to their enemies, but they lived the ancient and honored ways of the Thurpazkul. The Thurpazkul was the first of the known Black Clans, and the founders of the ancient order of the Dhourkuul.

The face of the rock wall swung inwards, breaking the perception of a flawless surface with the sharp lines of the secret door. Nimosese strode back into the fortress of the Dhourkuul and the wall returned to its former state, the outline of the door no longer recognizable.

The air inside of the cavern was chilled, but several braziers and torches along the walls kept the frigid bite off.

Nimosese walked back down what was known as the Path of Enlightenment. The Path was a solid piece of iron, wrought with other unknown metals. It slowly rose as it stretched from the center of the chamber and up to the secret entrance. Many runes and carvings stretched across the face.

This old span was the commencement to one of the oldest and most sacred ceremonies of the Dhourkuul. It was part of a rite or, more what could be called, the beginning of a Dhourkuul assassin's extraordinary ways.

Up until the time that a young warrior undergoing the training stepped forward to jump off of the Path, she was only an apprentice under a master assassin of the Dhourkuul. And such a trial as the Path of Enlightenment was what bestowed the legendary armor that the deadly assassins wore. Yet it was more than just some inanimate armorer. It was the final gauntlet of truth that tried and tested the very mettle of such an esteemed warrior. Quite frankly, it made them, or it literally broke them—shattering their bodies thousands of foot down on the slopes. Skeletal remains littered the expanse of sharp, calloused rock at the foot of the mountains.

Nimosese removed the covering from over his head, almost peeling the strange material back, to expose his bald, ashen-colored skin. One of the Aylsh Ismaru. Exotic black runes of different designs littered its surface.

He was the last master assassin of the Dhourkuul, now entering his eleventh turn of existence. Young ones were needed for his order to survive and prosper. Currently there were only a few score of young apprentices, along with only a handful of those that actually completed the trials of the Path. It would take another turn or two before one of these could ever hope to become a master and attain the full reach of twilight abilities.

A Dhourkuul assassin was able to use the powers of the Shadehaunt. But, more importantly, she had to master them. If she did not attain that mastery and stepped forward to challenge the Path for the unique trials, she would not be able to successfully pass to the Shadehaunt upon jumping from the ledge. And the ground was a very long way down from that ledge atop one of the highest peaks of the Rock Rim. There was no chance in surviving such a fall.

Yes, the would-be Dhourkuul assassin would have to sprint up the ramp and leap out off of the ledge as far as possible, then entering the Shadehaunt. This would begin the trials in which even more difficult and unknown challenges awaited. None of these were ever known, and never spoken of by those who had attained such mastery.

Priestess Sahrya was standing within the gloom of the flickering light cast from the braziers when Nimosese returned inside. There were six dark ones standing nearby—all so young—maybe twenty to thirty years along in life. The priestess was dressed as usual in the flowing dark blue cloak with the monstrous red eyes symbolically watching everything. Sometimes he thought that he could see them glow.

"Master of the Dhourkuul. Last shining knight of the twilight. How quaint of you to be so prompt. And do I sense a fading to the numbers within your order?" Sahrya plied with a smirk, toying with Nimosese.

The master assassin knew her kind well, as do all predators who intimately study their prey—and potential threats—with barely a thought given to doing so.

He knew that this one was very meticulous, uncompromising, and exceptionally ruthless in all things under her purview. Nimosese, above all, knew that he was dealing with a viper of a serpent. One who would have no remorse or regret in snuffing him out of existence if it suited her whim in the least.

The only thing that had started this deadly courtship was her promise of offspring, young ones of the Black Clans, whom he could train as Dhourkuul. And raise them in the particular ways of that life to bring honor and purpose.

Ever since their tryst began, he had been hunting for her…and killing for her. Truth be told, he did not much care for such broadly applied use of his violence. But it was survival. It was not the true path of the Dhourkuul.

And here she was, with exactly what she had promised. But questions weighed upon his mind. Her fiercely intense purple eyes burned out from the darkness. Those eyes briefly made him consider his most recent vision during meditation.

But it was more than that, for he had dreamt it as well. This particular dream was now haunting his sleep nearly every night. The future of his order was paved by, or through, a strange, billowing form made of pure blackness. The only thing that stood out on this countenance were the brilliant eyes, the right being darkest obsidian and the left a glowing white. But this was the only piece of such a dream or vision left to him after waking, and the rest remained vague and nameless. Now he saw that dark face, obscured through strange gloomy mists, and those eyes each time that he closed his for meditation.

The master assassin bowed his head slightly, "My Priestess, it would seem that you have graced me with your presence. But these young ones, might I ask…what of their kin? What of their past?"

Sahrya hissed and crossed her long arms in front of her. "I give you the future of the Dhourkuul and you question the plate on which that future is served to you?"

"It is no matter, my Priestess. I merely wished to know their mindset as it is key to their training. Forgive me." Nimosese bowed his head slightly while averting his eyes. The runes inscribed upon his head showing clearly in the firelight from a nearby brazier.

Priestess Sahrya smiled at him and gestured towards the young ones. "This is but a token of…faith." She scoffed at the use of the word, as though it amused her. "And only part of what you will receive upon completion of a new task that I have for you.

"There will be twenty more where these came from, mixed cocks and cracks. You can start your own lineage. And the future will then be yours. All of this for one simple thing that I ask."

Nimosese knew that she did not actually mean the word ask. No, anything directed from her was never a request. It was a demand.

He replied in a subservient tone, "I am honored by you, my Priestess. Yes, of course you have my word. The task will be completed, just name it."

"I knew that I could count on you. My one true warrior, noble to the cause."

She paused while walking behind the group of little ones, then briefly turned her back to the master assassin. "I need you to track down one of my own…a traitor that murdered several of my Blackguard. And I need you to rip her from this world. It needs to be done immediately, and not ceased until your obligation is fulfilled."

It was obvious to Nimosese that Priestess Sahrya tried to stifle the explosive contempt that she held for this traitor, but it seethed under the angry wrinkles of her furrowed visage.

She walked towards him now, while producing a small silver mirror from within her cloak. With the swirl of a finger upon the mirror's surface and a whisper, a form began to materialize within the mirror. It was an exotic and pretty, but young, dark one wearing a black leather halter top—Zaramagrii, though he did not know her by look or name.

Nimosese stared at the image without an ounce of expression. The dark one was dirty and disheveled from some plight unknown to him.

Priestess Sahrya eyed him knowingly. "Look closely, my hunter, for this is the one. She is called Zaramagrii, but the name matters little, at least to you."

Nimosese studied the form in the mirror as it turned and shimmered, from some far off vantage. He could not clearly make out the details of the face, but the reflection gave him enough. "My Priestess, I will need to have access to something that belonged to her as well as possibly a place where she has recently been."

Sahrya did not falter in her words. "You can return to Tharasvrul with me, and everything that you ask will be there."

Then the slender form of another young female of the Black Clans rushed through the archway from behind them. Her long silver hair was held back by a single leather tie. She immediately bowed and fell to one knee. "Forgive me, Master, I did not mean to interrupt."

"It is okay, Llornah. What is it?" Nimosese looked upon the skinny one with pride.

She was the oldest one now, of all of his strays that he had accumulated. But maybe not the strongest. Her slender face had a gray, jagged scar running its length canted from the neck to disappear in the tight swaths of hair. The mark was an ugly reminder of crossing paths with a mountain yeti several years ago. But she had held her own, and this was one of the many things about her that he was proud of. She knew the difference between encroaching upon the creature's habitat, which sparked the attack, and pure aggression. It had been her own carelessness. And she determinedly defended herself without injuring the beast until she could make her escape. Thus no harm befell the creature, as it had been only defending itself and its kin in the area.

Llornah's pure white eyes, surrounded in flames, glanced up at him momentarily before returning to the floor. "The Order is ready for meditation, Master."

The Order of the Dhourkuul meditated every day, as well as practiced their various disciplines. These rigors occupied most of their time, especially when under apprenticeship.

Such was the dedication of the Dhourkuul, and this was what made them specialists of death. Specialists in all of the skills which they honed. But legends of the order were steeped in mystery, surrounded by a haziness of fear.

No one really knew the intricacies of the Dhourkuul, like how it strived for the natural balance in all things. Or that the deadly skills they employed were actually part of study and assimilation into the world itself. For the purpose of understanding, and for existing in such temperance that a Dhourkuul did not upset the natural balance if at all possible.

Most of those with any inkling in Black Clan lore thought that the Dhourkuul died out a long time ago. During this current age though, the majority of folk across Thaldeia had no clue as to even the name Dhourkuul.

Nimosese proudly folded his hands behind his back while speaking, "Today, there will be no meditation. Take our new guests and make them comfortable. Introduce them to the rest. I will be gone for a short while.

"And you, Llornah, will be left as the master apprentice while I am away. Go now."

With that, Llornah quickly gathered up the six that were brought by the priestess. She led them back through the archway, disappearing into the deep bowels of the fortress.

Soon, no one remained within the large chamber, once Nimosese and Sahrya vanished.

§ § §

Wybur made his way through the last of the thick pines along the eastern slopes of the Rock Rim. It had been near a fortnight since fleeing Longshadows. Somehow the lowly and meek lad had made it all the way through the wildlands, staying off the traveled roads the entire time.

Now he was a bit thinner and very haggard. Wrinkles and pockets on his gaunt face were still marked by dark blotches of dried blood mixed with the stain of traveling.

The sprawl of the rock and log wall of Rory's outpost sat before him, visible through the trees. It rose to about the height of three tall men.

The large banner of Dawn's Glory flapped above the crude portcullis where several warriors in gleaming plated armor stood watch. The banner glared in the brightness of the duo suns, its pure white background almost glowing. A gilded rising sun shone down from the top of it, showering gold lightning bolts over a silver four-pronged spear as it pointed up to the sun.

It was a tearful sight for Wybur, after all that he had been through. What took place back at Longshadows seemed only a terrible nightmare that had receded with the break of dawn.

He knew that those men in the watch towers would spot him. They would see him as soon as he broke free of the rough tangle of pine and into the cleared portion of the fortifications.

His stomach had tightened a long time ago, and had been grumbling nearly every day at the various things he ate. Tiny morsels of whatever he could find as he moved through the wilderness. Grass, worms dug from deep inside old dead trees and an occasional bulbous root of a water onion from the bed of a cold stream. That was all. Now his nose was so attuned to things from the lack of them, that he could smell the tiny wafts of meat cooking over fires from within the outpost.

He heard the familiar barks of the dogs as they ran to and fro around the front of the outpost. As much as they were companions, they were instruments of early warning for anything approaching. Sharp bouts of barking signaled the approach of travelers, heralding their arrival to the guards about the gate.

The last couple hundred foot of clearing seemed to go on forever. The hardened crust of the snow took some effort to break through. Now the guards milling about the gate were watching him as he approached.

One of the dogs, light brown except for a white chest, came running out to him, the tail wagging fiercely. This one was named Star and had spent much time with Wybur here whenever he visited under the auspices of the Buttlecut trading company.

It was not long before he found himself in the familiar surroundings of where he typically stayed, parked in front of a cozy hearth with a thick fur wrapped about him.

Rory walked in abruptly, not long after getting word of Wybur's arrival. His thick blond hair trailed him as he did so, bouncing to his brow as he stopped.

"My good man, what in this world is going on? You look like you crawled all the way from Longshadows," said Rory with a concerned tone.

He laid out a tray of hot biscuits and roast venison on the table nearby, and then grabbed a stool beside Wybur.

So Wybur recounted the events that took place since he left Dawn's Glory last time, telling Rory about the horrors that he found at his home in Longshadows. The whole time, deep furrows creased his forehead and the sickened look of disgust upon his face would not disappear. "Rory, I feel just awful. It is all my fault," he ended.

When Rory asked why he said this, it did not take long for Wybur to highlight the uncomfortable tale of his encounters with Livforena and the uncovering of Siri's black book, Olri Uchrah. This, of course, led to his bouts with Rosella, as Wybur completely opened up to the mountain of a man beside him. He even mentioned his recurrent dreams involving the huge snow owl. But Rory Sivercroft was known as the listener, always having an ear for one's problems or worries. And he also held a calming warmth that emanated from his persona. Whether knowingly doing so or not, it soothed those around him.

"Listen, my friend. You were just doing what you thought was right. That is your nature. And this Livforena took advantage of your good nature…among other things. None of that is your fault, things happen. And you could not have stopped what happened to your uncle and his family. You cannot *what if* yourself to death.

"And, the Veiled Ones… I never figured that to be a real group anyways. There is no hard proof that they are out there, other than the history lessons that sages speak of."

"But Livforena seemed so...so...sincere," sighed Wybur.

"Aye, sincere... *and* she gave you what you only dreamed about. I call that enticement.

"Relax, you are safe now. Nothing will harm you here, nor even attempt so without a mighty fight." Rory trailed off as one of the healers came in. The old man was lean and sinewy for one of his age.

Rory stood up slowly before leaning back towards Wybur, while placing a reassuring hand upon his shoulder. "My friend, look to your dreams or visions. Perhaps you are lucky enough to be guided by them. Such a thing as this giant owl—and a white one at that—could only be a force of good.

"There is much mysticism in such beasts. But this owl is possibly what you seek, or should seek, as it is no doubt a harbinger. I deeply feel that. Instead of fearing it, you should embrace it."

Then Rory cracked a smile as he proceeded to the door. "Now you listen to Blarold here, and get some rest. You need it. We will talk in the morn."

Wybur fell victim to a deep sleep, but visions still haunted him. They flew to him and hovered over every sleeping moment. Scenes of horrible carnage, while standing helplessly outside massive, green gates with the colorful banner of Kuhrzoth waving above. And always the white owl, ever lingering inside of his mind. It was nearby in a tree or gracefully in flight whenever such dreams of war and death came to him.

Meanwhile, Rory lay in his chambers sleepless. The interesting talk with Wybur did get Rory to thinking. He gave it much contemplation until late in the night.

There had been a good deal of commotion going on lately throughout Oshghrul, the Fallen Lands. Commotion that normally did not happen, at least not on this scale.

Every day his patrols came across sizable and well-equipped forces of Akhruuk on the other side of the Rock Rim. And this spelled all too clearly that there was some kind of organization in their fettered, unkempt ranks and scattered activities.

The next morning, once Wybur was up and about with several cups of tea in him, Rory grabbed him up and they talked for the rest of the day. Rory wanted to know more details about what Wybur had told him previously. From this black book of Siri, to what Rosella and Livforena looked like.

Within the space of a few days, Wybur was feeling much better and more himself. But now he had different dreams mixed in with the ones that usually haunted him of late.

He would find himself standing atop a towering portcullis at the end of a deep ravine with mountains surrounding him. Below him, he watched hundreds of monstrosities waving about cruel weapons. Off to the side of a ledge, a small dark-skinned girl was running and fighting her way to the gate, or so it seemed.

That was what stuck in his mind when he awoke, the girl making her way through that torrent of evil. And the last things that he saw before everything went to blackness were her shimmering eyes, one piercing white and one onyx black. Both were aglow with such a burning. Those eyes shone out to him, though he could not even make out her features from the distance. As much as he tried, and even with the surge of the day, he could not get the vision of those burning eyes out of his head.

Chapter 12:

Future of Change

A stout purge of the unkempt by the flames of darkness shall emaciate the lands.

Ill tides sweep over the Akhruuk as their blood is meshed with the dark daemuns.

The orbs mark the Time of Blasphemy afterwards. And all will be consumed by that which was thought only of the night.

Though not of the Akhru volition, the darkness will take the offspring of them as well. There will be none unseen by the eye of such judgment.

> –Translated lore from the Khaman, the ancient revelations of the Akhruuk.

omething stirred again deep within the ancient fortress of Isnuuthghor, nestled in the heart of the Gloomy Mountains. Two of the dark-spirited Black Clans, thought to be scattered to the winds or worse, were now back at their home of old.

Deep within, several feminine moans resounded throughout a dank chamber. These were briefly interrupted with bouts of suppressed whimpering and muffled crying, all echoing a subdued hopelessness.

This rough chamber, buried under the world, contained a countless number of hard, flat wooden beds. Writhing forms, shackled about both hands and feet, lay upon nearly every one of them. The air reeked of filth, from the rotten remains of foodstuffs to excrement and piss.

Bulging bellies, from barely pronounced to that of well-rounded, marked all of the females on one side of the chamber. Two of them appeared as though their stomachs stretched tightly over giant eggs. On the other side, the young females were slender and trim, but covered in grimy sweat.

Dim, vague shapes danced along the walls and ceiling within the flickering torchlight. The glistening naked bodies reflected the dark skin of the Black Clans.

One solid iron door, set into the center where the room narrowed, stared at them as the only portal of escape. But it held no accoutrements on the inside surface, other than a little square-shaped hole about where a handle would be.

It was not long before the grating of iron and stone sharply rang out, and a naked monstrous form stormed through the door. The door clanged shut behind it. The bulging Akhru stared about at the Black Clan females as silence set in.

The Akhru was exceptionally large even for one of their kind. Bands of knotted muscle stretched down from the head and neck to contour with its back. The now growing appendage between the legs showed it to be male.

Something had definitely piqued his interest. The skinny ones nearest him began to squirm and yell out, but these sounds just faded dully into the thick rock walls. Iron manacles held their arms well beyond their heads while their legs were pulled apart.

The brute strode up to the first of those without rising bellies. As the female attempted to keep the thing away from her, the Akhru leaned his might into her while climbing atop. His rod slid in effortlessly and then slowly began to pump in and out. As the beast thrust his hips ever harder, he grunted and groaned baring huge, yellowing teeth.

This one obviously relished in the thrill of such power and control. He clamped a moist, grimy hand over the young female's mouth so that those eyes would show him the terror and disgust brimming over within. This one act must have been so satisfying, as it did not take long for him to lose control and violently spray his seed within her.

The Akhru simply went to the next one and began to roughly fondle her breasts and ura. It took no time at all for his appendage to rise again, and he continued his sweaty efforts until he had filled each of the tight, unwilling concubines with his filth.

The door creaked open as the Akhru stomped back out, now with a more relaxed gait. Two Blackguards entered to take up positions on each side of the door.

In strode the familiar cloaked form of Priestess Sahrya. Behind her followed another dark one. This male wore a long black robe of simple design and had no visible weapons as the others did. His long, narrow face held bulbous eyes that appeared to float along with him.

The priestess hovered between the rows of squalor. "Luqfur, how are our seeded ones coming along?"

The dark head of Luqfur, covered in braids of black hair, slightly canted as his luminous eyes swiveled. "As expected, my Priestess. They will give you plenty of strong Chosen ones…over time. I personally have been ensuring the care that they receive," he paused momentarily, "however, there are some of our keepers that appear to be overly concerned with them. More than they should be."

"Excellent. And exactly how many more of the Chosen will this give us?" Sahrya inquired.

"Near thirty within a year's time. Two will come forth this day. If only we had more to work with."

Priestess Sahrya eyed him and then looked back towards those with swollen bellies.

Time passed as two of the captives slowly went into agonizing spasms. These two were in beds beside one another, their bellies so stretched outwards that it seemed they could burst any moment. Their offspring were due soon.

Luqfur stood near the foot of these beds, with two of the young keepers beside him, ready to assist with the coming births. Priestess Sahrya stood behind them watching, a smug look of anticipation on her face.

Before long, one of the young Black Clan females heaved with a fatigued relief, knowing that the pain was gone for now.

But her weary face told the sick tale of disgust at the sight before her. Her offspring was notably large for a dark one. The color of the skin appeared normal, but the head was covered in bone-like ridges protruding around the forehead and the sides.

Just as the Akhruuk had individually unique bony ridges and knobs rising across their heads, these young ones had similar features. The already hulking muscles of these newborns also looked strangely matured. Their bodies bulged with sinewy strength. Straight from the ura.

It was abominable to the young mother. To the priestess, it was amazing.

"Now this is my pride and joy," hissed Sahrya as she knelt by the exhausted dark one. "You have done a meritorious thing for your folk, Eirleh."

Then Sahrya gingerly wiped the dirt-streaked sweat from Eirleh's forehead.

Without taking her eyes from those of Eirleh's, the priestess said, "Now take this fine future champion to the turo's den. He shall make a good addition."

The next one was ready to come forth also. This young Black Clan female heaved in labored breaths while her legs tightly pulled in towards her.

There were gray puffy bags of skin built up under her mesmerizing green and red eyes. Tears, mixed with filthy sweat, streamed down her face as one of the young keepers placed her hands gingerly down upon the mother's ura.

A small head littered with knobby bumps was already emerging down there. It was not long before the young keeper held the newly born thing in her arms, the long, oversized ears on this one very pronounced.

Priestess Sahrya, peering over the shoulders of Luqfur, suddenly narrowed her eyes and grew tight-lipped. "What! Yet another little one with a gaping hole," she cried after seeing that the little one was female. Her words trailed off as she reached to grasp the babe.

In the priestess's mind, she saw the haunting irony of Zaramagrii and her mother Amanshar's tryst of secrecy in every mother and female young one now. Especially in the births within her special Chosen.

The uncontrollable fury raged within her eyes. By now, she had grown temperamentally overpowered by each and every thing considered by her to be such an abomination to her own rise in power.

What the illustrious divine have set forth and commanded, with substance set above and beyond mere mortals. How could anything else even matter, or attempt to subvert that? And how could such unfathomable blasphemy go unnoticed for so long, even under the watch of the Ancient One?

Sahrya relived the tormenting discovery of the lost lore of the Shadow Soul and that the very one destined to become that beast, young Zaramagrii, had been right under her nose the whole time. This was such a magnified point of inner contention within her own visions of the world and her supreme power. A world that was supposed to be hers to do as she saw fit.

The priestess tightly grasped the newborn around the feet with one hand, while the babe laid in her other. As she knelt down to show the mother the creation that she brought forth, Sahrya slowly squeezed the feet and legs until the little one began to wail louder and louder.

"Yes, so precious...but not the little cunts with the holes. They are not part of the new breed. We cannot thin the dark blood down any further by allowing one such as this to spread its legs and ride the rod...ever," she whispered in the young mother's ear.

As she finished, she placed the young face near that of the mother. The babe rested in her hand with her fingers splayed out and extending about the small head and neck.

Slowly, Sahrya began to close her hand into a balled-up fist. The mother screamed in horror and thrashed her chains. But it did not take long for the frail form to go quiet after a series of fleshy snapping and popping noises.

As the priestess walked back out of the chamber, she spoke to Luqfur with a renewed energy, almost like the act had invigorated her. "It is a shame that we slew all those kin to Amanshar and Ghenwari. The females would have provided us more numbers for breeding."

Luqfur merely nodded in agreement.

Then Sahrya abruptly came to a stop while lightly grasping him by his shoulder. "And, Luqfur, stay keen on our little flock of keepers tending to these special mothers of ours. Advise me of any that become more of a problem. Even the slightest whim."

"Yes, my Priestess," spoke Luqfur as his huge eyes held their own while he slowly nodded his head.

On the way out of the chamber, as the door slammed shut, the keeper that tended to the mothers silently stared at the lifeless form in her hands.

One glare from Luqfur brought her back to reality. He ripped the small body from her.

The lifeless form was discarded as a rotten apple might be. It was tossed onto a mounting pile of small, innocent corpses not far on the other side of the doorway, no doubt adding to the stink of the place.

The priestess mindlessly walked off, mesmerized by her own ambitions. Her ambitions and what this plan with her Chosen had become.

She smiled with a frigid warmth that coursed through her being. Yes, the first of these Chosen had already excelled in their training and preparation. And they would fulfill their very special purpose. Of course, it would be very regrettable if she was not able to watch their handiwork when the time came.

Chapter 13:

All Things Must Come to

an End

Let not the weakness of one's fledgling lodestone overcome the essence. Steadfast, those most deserving mature to the perfect reflection.

–Tenth Edict of Lord Braxis, etched upon the Great Slates, recovered by Arterium circa the year 13 BA.

astle of the Wild Reaches, officially named Emerald Rest, literally sat on the doorstep of Oshghrul, the Fallen Lands. Perched upon the eastern side of an immensely picturesque valley that ran south out of the Fallen Lands, the castle had been the southern watch over the unknown terrors of those lands for over a thousand years now.

The valley was lush with large hardwood forests covering the upper portions and crests of both sides, until higher up where the landscape turned to sweeping rocky ridges. The valley floor was mostly covered in fields of long green grass occasionally crossed by a small bubbling brook of cool mountain water. Wild berry bushes dotted the greenery. This visage could be seen far up to the vanishing horizon looking north, a rise of maybe a thousand foot over a couple of leagues.

This region was particularly rife with wildlife, and the castle residents were avidly known for their undying taste for freshly roasted red grouse. The bird was a very elegant and splendid one, but also of exceptional appeal to the palette. It was considered a delicacy.

Emerald Rest received its title from the fact that it housed the main contingent of the Emerald Knights, the legendary and main heavy cavalry of the kingdom of Kuhrzoth.

In the old days, these numbered near ten thousand strong here at the castle with another five thousand garrisoned at the royal seat of Nuuroc. Presently the knights at the castle numbered about fifteen hundred, with another three thousand at Nuuroc. Of course this did not take into account the Emerald Guard and other men-at-arms that comprised the force at the castle. But these forces did not cost near as much to field as the Emerald Knights.

This would not even amount to what the Kuhrzothian martial forces referred to as an *order*. An order was of such numbers and mixed specialties that it could hold a sizeable territory in combat. Emerald Guard, Emerald Knights, men-at-arms, archers or arbalists, as well as skirmishers and even a line of pikes. This would be composed of various lines and ranks that spread out to form the breadth of a good front of ground. More such orders could be established along each side, depending upon how much battle front was needed.

Indeed, times change and fears subside. But many of those who know the way of the sword would argue that it was not change and the loss of fears that created such a lessening of might. They knew it to be weakness and ignorance within the masses that eroded what was once unbreakable. And, of course, this being ultimately led by corruption and greed.

Although the armory was well-stocked, the support ratio for the fighting force at Emerald Rest was not even close to what it should have been. The number of smiths for the knights alone was so lacking that they could not keep up with simple repairs.

Now, mind you, this was for the very basic of routine maintenance and not what was commonly entailed by such a force that regularly conducted drill and training each day. And one that kept up constant patrols and fully manned posts.

This was another sad fact that would have to be dealt with. Without the proper number of smiths, the armory would be depleted in no time if such a need for it ever arose.

But things were different now than they had been even three hundred years ago when evil stirred from within the Rock Rim. These days, knights were more concerned with the local lasses running about and the contents of the casks at the various taverns and inns than much else.

In the days of old, a patrol might have noticed the recent incursions of lesser goblin scouting parties within the area, or at least trace of their sign left behind. If a patrol did not pick up on them, the valiant rangers who used to be employed by the Kuhrzothian throne definitely would have. But there were no more patrols and the rangers were set free from their service a long time ago.

§ § §

On such a crisp late-harvestspell day, not even the guards manning the huge gates of the castle or those walking the parapets above took any note of peculiarities. Such as the subtle shift in the way that the light rays warped the field of view across the valley floor not far from the gate.

The blended edges of the forest distorted and wrapped about the greenery of the grassy meadows as the Aunlourey concluded her netherworld travel and materialized.

Although still concealed by invisibility, the feminine figure flickered briefly a few times as she made her way back behind a boulder near the tree line, while crouching low. Her long purple robe rode back in the wind, covering most of the tall, thin form. She gave off a very unique womanly look. But she obviously was not of this world, as occasionally traces of brilliant white would radiate out of her eyes. Sometimes the brilliance would show through her naked skin, flickering and then dissipating.

Now she only had to wait for the expected actions to run their course. The warriors here were not very adept, and even worse at keeping information to themselves. One young guardsman had divulged all with barely the show of her upper thigh. And that lad probably never even remembered the encounter, for he was too drunk.

§ § §

The duo suns rose high in the midday sky as the guards continued their vigilance of boredom and self-centered lack of enthusiasm while on watch. All the while that these people frivolously went about their activities of wanton frolic, they were carefully being observed by unseen eyes.

Wild boars were roasting on spits as the people prepared for the last of the harvest feasts. A long time ago, there had been only one such feast, during harvestspell at least, and it was at the beginning of Greatfest and not the end of Eavesmarch. For the feast was a celebration of survival, as well as to cherish the fact that the harvest would be fruitful before the snows settled in. Thus providing plenty of stores for the coming winterfall. This was a ceremony of thanks, as much as one of reverence, amongst a group of people who considered one another family.

Now, the cause for a feast was any reason for the patrons of power to throw a festival in order to drink mead and ale well beyond capacity, and to romp amongst as many women as possible.

Thus, the effect eventually pushes forward no matter the circumstances, as our residents of Emerald Rest shall soon see.

Degradation and degeneration always breed weakness and eventual consumption through natural order of attrition.

Apparently this saddened state was not viewed as such by these people themselves, for they appeared to be enthralled beyond oblivious happiness and content. A false sense of everlastingness had settled upon them all.

Now there was one lone individual who was always prepared, and none other than the legendary commander general of the Emerald Knights. As events unfolded, Lord Tyrim Steele was profusely sweating after several rounds of swinging his giant broadsword at the various wooden training dummies. The sword itself was made of the finest steel in Kuhrzoth, Dureq steel.

The majority of arms used by the Emerald Order were crafted from the same. Only the best, forged out of the ore slabs made at the Dureq foundry. Such a fine product cost weapon smiths good gold. Thus they charged their customers more than enough to make up for it. Aside from the Aylsh or Kharaghou steel, there was no equal to Dureq steel other than that of the Nyraltin foundry in Phanduzar. Instead of being formed into slabs, Nyraltin steel was formed into what were called bricks. Of course no alloy surpassed or even came close to that of the Aylsh or Kharaghou, berlyllum or ghalqra respectively.

Part committed to being a perfectionist and part venting accumulated frustrations, the man of over six foot tall maneuvered the two-handed blade back and forth. He wore only leather breeches and riding boots under the cool spell of the duo suns.

Commander Steele had finally persuaded the king to allow him to reseat his leadership of the knights back to Emerald Rest, where it always had been of old.

At this point, thought Tyrim, it was possibly too late. He saw how dismantled the force had become under the decrepit leadership of Mynse Velore, the lord of Emerald Rest. Lord Velore, if one can empower such an individual with that title, had nearly destroyed the order through languor and atrophy. Velore was the appointed thayne for these parts of Kuhrzoth, not that there were many towns and villages out this far. There were none, other than the castle itself. Additionally, any force of the Emerald Order never fell beneath any lord or title other than one of its own. But, in this case, Velore also held nobility. He swayed the king to place all subjects under his thumb, be they martial or populace, even of the Emerald Order. *It was for better governance*, he said.

First he took the reins away from the captain of the knights and then countermanded everything that they historically stood for. The result was a diminished order of knights only reputable by name and now weakened nearly beyond recovery.

Tyrim already realized, after reviewing the force for only two days, that his road would be long and hard if he were to reinstate the Order of the Emerald Knights to even a fraction of what they used to be of old. His first step had been to oust them from under the controlling hand of Mynse Velore, which formally took place yestereve.

Yes, this would be their last day of celebration for quite some time. Commander Steele already had to throw several of the knights into the jailor's cells earlier in the morn due to their rowdy and unprofessional behavior. Many more of the Emerald Guard and also men-at-arms filled the cramped cells.

He sternly returned to concentrate on the placement of his blade and to finish his routine for the day as colossal, purple-tipped clouds glided through the skies on a cool but gentle breeze. This was but the first of the colder drafts to come in for this time of year, surely a mark of the snowy weather that was due soon enough.

Meanwhile, atop the foremost portion of the high stone wall, the scenery was enticing. Only a few members of the guard stood sentry and looked out across the valley and up towards the mountain range. One of them, Huck Mournfellow, now impatiently paced as his comrades joked and acted out the previous night's bout of ale drowned debauchery.

The distinguished banners of Kuhrzoth waved and snapped in the winds, set upon both sides of the gatehouse not far below him. Such an enlivening mix of colors, emerald green with a rich golden border displayed a large shield checkered blue and black. A magnificent crown rested above the shield. A silver two-handed sword sat on each side of the shield, the point canted down and in. This same symbol could be seen in smaller versions either across shields or on both sides of the surcoats worn by the Kuhrzothian forces. In the case where a knight regaled herself also within their own noble lineage, a canton in the corner of their shield displayed such a coat-of-arms. A surcoat might also show this, but only as a smaller device and not nearly as large as the royal banner of Kuhrzoth itself.

Huck was a driven young lad born of the fine lineage of one of the first captains of the Black Legion. Even though his father was a nineteenth generation Legion-man, the family eventually took to farming and also carpentry, in which his old man had spent his last days carving and building things within the walls of Nuuroc.

Now, without any of his relatives alive, Huck had cleaned the past slate by volunteering for duty in the ranks of the Emerald Guard. But instead of achieving some gallant position of knighthood as he had hoped, he ended up assigned to the outpost of Emerald Rest.

The Rest was known for the fact that once one went there, then they were lost and forgotten about. Swallowed up into the dusk of time, as the quaint castle of Emerald Rest was by the overarching loftiness of the Rock Rim.

Such has become of what used to be considered noble duty guarding against Oshghrul, or the Fallen Lands. Back during such times when patrols into those lands took place near every fortnight. When each and every patrol out there always bloodied their blades.

Of course, many fine warriors also perished, on almost every patrol that went out. But that was the chosen life and profession. And yet the people, the masses, got tired and weary of war and death. Tired of young and old alike dying.

So the people ended up complaining about and diminishing action that most of them had no inkling of in the first place. Most have never set foot outside their own little village or town, even the walls of Nuuroc.

And yet they had a voice that eventually influenced a king and his court. Albeit maybe a weak king and court. One that only wished to remain in power, to maintain hold on the reins. No matter the cost or what they must do as a ruling body.

Huck remembered the stories passed down from one of his uncles when he was but a child. The tall tales of his great-great-great-grandfather while adventuring under the name of the Black Legion.

This was, of course, when monsters ruled the lands and roamed paths of terror and death. To him, monsters did not exist at all, and those stories seemed to be tales for entertaining the youngsters and wee ones. He had never seen so much as a goblin or an Akhru for that matter.

Sure, there had been giant owls and eagles, but those were creatures of the wild world, and normal.

And the imposing valiant rangers of old, why they were just myths to keep the newly recruited warriors of the kingdom on their toes. To push them into achieving at least some degree of their full potential.

Huck was staring across the valley floor at what seemed like a brief mirage of the air itself. He almost could have sworn that he saw the scenery blur and bend, as though the view was a mere reflection in a pond and something rippled the surface. Continuing to stare at the area, he attempted to discern any more oddities.

Clenhis, the other guard posted with him atop the western battlements, caught his attention.

"There appears to be a storm approaching from the north. My, I hope that it does not bring the snows already."

Clenhis' rustic tongue drowned everything that he spoke. It really came out sounding like he said *thar appers ta beya stowm approachin frum te nowth*.

Huck snapped his head around to look north up the valley, as he reminded Clenhis, "Did the ale drown yer brain? 'Tis not an angry cloud in the sky up yonder." But he trailed off as he saw what Clenhis spoke of.

Looking up the soaring valley that ran for several leagues to where it opened into the Fallen Lands, Huck saw a tiny murky wall filling the entire breadth of the valley up where it vanished into the Rock Rim. But then, it could not be a wall, or even the black clouds of a storm.

Now he could tell that it was steadily growing as it flowed down the valley towards them. Every now and then tiny glints and flashes shone in the bright sunslight. Sometimes there would be scores, then hundreds.

Realization dawned on Huck as he feverishly ran to the archaic, but reliably deafening, sounding horn posted directly above the gate. That was no storm.

"Mourn, what are you doing? Wait!" cried Clenhis after him, trying to stop him from sounding it. Of course this sounded more like *Mown, what ahh ya doeen? Waeet!* Many of Huck's fellow guards called him Mourn as a nickname.

But it was too late, as Huck sent off one long, thunderous roar echoing throughout the castle baileys and the valley outside. Clenhis tackled him at this point, their armor and weapons clanging upon the stone.

Huck nearly punched him while breathlessly crying, "The enemy, you idiot. That is no storm! That is an army!"

Not far away, one man heard that long blast and reacted instantly. But the majority of the men-at-arms and knights did not. Most were still too enfeebled by ale and spirits, even more were too snug atop or beside whores and lasses to even care.

Commander Steele hurriedly donned his armor and belted his sword. He was on his huge destrier within a short time, headed towards the gate. Always on an edge, he wasted no time in galloping at full speed towards the gatehouse. The huge, emerald green cape whipped in the wind behind him.

Meanwhile, Huck sent another blast from the horn for as long as he could give it wind. The loud burst bawled out through the valley and rang off of the walls.

The voice of Tyrim Steele yelled out from below, "Hoist the gate up and set it!"

"Commander...to the north...an army or something big!" cried Huck.

The commander general of the Emerald Knights quickly spurred his mount outside the walls to see. He soon rode back in like the winds and bellowed up to Huck, "Quick, my son, send three blasts...repeat sets of three! And don't stop until the fields are full of mounted knights!"

A repetition of three blasts was the call or muster to form out in the valley to the front of the walled fortress. It was an imminent warning that danger loomed close.

By this time, the black horde of writhing things had closed the distance considerably. Now the monstrous forms could be seen. Whether man-sized or not, they all appeared menacing and savage. Giant man-like things, striding along the edges, carried huge clubs. Big-eared scrawny creatures with yellowed teeth rode fierce, snarling wolves. But these wolves were like no others.

The seventeen captains of the lines appeared next to Commander Steele soon enough, all hurriedly conversing. Even these men were in various stages of donning their armor. Most of them at least had on a breast plate, but several did not have the time to get their helms or leggings on. Many of the war horses had no armor at all.

By the fifth iteration of the triple-note heralding, over three hundred of the knights had lined up across the middle of the valley floor. As many footmen and archers flanked them nearest the castle walls. They already were setting up a resolute wall of steel.

§ § §

The Aunlourey spied out upon the ring of Kuhrzothian commanders, what she knew to be the head of this serpent forming in front of her.

Her vantage point mattered little with her invisible form. It was now almost time to begin her games.

This moment here and now had been building anticipation within her for six score of days, finally the start to the inevitable. Before long, she would be a power to contend with in Thaldeia. And Priestess Sahrya promised her free reign over all.

§ § §

Both large and small figures could now be seen amidst the approaching blackness of dust and blurring momentum. Akhruuk, goblins, ogres, hobgoblins, and even joutuun were thundering towards the ranks of Emerald Knights and the hodgepodge assembly of men-at-arms and Emerald Guards.

It appeared that Commander Steele, in the center of his ring of captains, was about to disperse them back to their lines with standing orders. The horses shifted and neighed with the tenseness in the air due to the encroaching battle.

The majority of knights roughly formed the skirmish line, but several groups were also still exiting the gate out onto the battlefield. Most were in one form of disarray or another, as they awaited their captains to bark orders at them.

Even though the skies were mostly a transparent blue, a small black cloud formed. A soaring bolt of lightning flashed, raining down directly upon Commander Steele. The resulting boom shattered the afternoon calm forever, and the explosive burst sent armored body parts and sizzling blood flying everywhere.

The bolt of electricity was so powerful that all of the captains near him suffered the same fate, maybe most not in nearly as many pieces. Many knights and other footmen near the circle also were cooked in their own blood.

An instant later, only smoke trailed up from the area of impact, and nothing remained of the core leadership of the Emerald Knights. Or any leadership of the forces at Emerald Rest for that matter. Only seared, armor-clad flesh and bone scattered about under a hot rain of blood and the smell of burnt meat.

More horrific than that was the near perfect timing of the destructive lightning bolt. As all of the knights and the men-at-arms stared in shock at the loss of their leaders, the chanting and yelling black horde was but moments away from colliding with the now stunned skirmish line.

While many of the knights stood their ground the whole time, many others did not, and that was all it took.

Then the horde from the Fallen Lands hit the line of knights, too many of whom had faltered in the wake of the devastating lightning bolt and decimation of their leadership.

As the line was not held, Akhruuk and goblins alike waded through and the men of Emerald Rest found themselves solitary islands within literally thousands of savage creatures. Brawny joutuun, towering nearly up to the height of the walls of Emerald Rest, took out both horse and rider in one fell swoop.

The defenders of the castle did not know, but the horde had numbers to their advantage. The horde attacking the castle was at least in the tens of thousands, almost like a surging wave crashing over a shoreline and absorbing everything as it did so.

The creatures of the Fallen Lands did not care, such was their bloodlust. Sometimes they even butchered their own kind in bloody fratricide, in the extreme closeness of the combat and mixing of forces.

Their eagerness to draw the blood of Man—be it man, woman, or child—was in such a fever due to literally months of this fervor being fed. Like the fanning of a vast fire. They wanted to draw the blood of everything…anything having even the slightest to do with the Man-folk. And, honestly, there just were not enough of the Man-folk warriors here to satisfy the blood lust.

Their mistress commander of a goddess that could throw lightning bolts like skipping rocks had incited this with chants and rallies throughout their training and organization. Endlessly promising them power, riches, and supreme control. All they had to do was listen to her and follow her.

Poor Huck watched in horror as the disaster played out. By now, a line of arbalists with their windlass crossbows had formed atop the wall with him and were finding their marks. But, of the near three thousand knights and men-at-arms that had hurried out to battle, none of those outside the wall could even be seen alive.

Of course, they had closed the gate immediately upon seeing such close proximity of the enemy, all of the monstrosities looming in front of them. And Clenhis had abandoned Huck even before Commander Steele was struck down.

The wave of creatures within the black horde at first streamed right up to the looming gates of the castle, pounding upon it with fists and swords while their archers pelted anyone they could atop the wall. Some of these found their mark, but many more of the motley horde fell under the ceaseless crossbow fire from the men along the top of the wall.

Slowly the horde pulled back into the valley, until they were out of the hail of crossbow fire, and then just out of the range of the longbows. But they continued to chant their guttural sounds of victory and jeering taunts while waving their weapons and fists at the castle walls. Several more of the beasts were felled as cranequin-drawn crossbows were brought up onto the walls.

Then the crowd of misfit attackers quieted completely, ceasing their antics, and the seamless wall of them parted to create a lane maybe ten paces wide within their midst. Some of the creatures turned to look back to where this cleared path disappeared as it led to the far break of trees.

The defenders of Emerald Rest had halted their volleys a while ago to conserve their ammunition. There were now maybe a hundred men-at-arms, none of them knights. These were ones that never made it out of the gate during the initial onslaught.

All of them held fast within the bailey nearest the gate, preparing to face whatever might come their way.

At this point, the people inside of the castle were trapped, and they knew it. Many of the inn keepers, tavern owners, and farmers now watched with fear while cowering amongst various buildings. The good folk also knew that their so-called elite force of roughly three thousand had been overrun and cut down in less time than it took to boil a red grouse. One can imagine that suddenly there were some very religious and faithful devotees with such a sobering experience. Not that this would do them any good.

Looking back up the colossal valley to where it rose into the Rock Rim, Huck now saw nothing but the plunging black wall of more creatures.

Good grace, he thought, *what on this land could possibly rope such a crew together and then keep them that way?*

He saw a score of what he could only assume to be mountain joutuun gather towards the front of where the parted path formed. These huge things, at least twice the height of an Akhru, bulged with muscle and sinew. Most of them wore some form of fashioned iron breastplate, and they carried large clubs the size of trees or monstrously crude iron war axes. While they appeared like large men, their skin was a dark brown and the nails on their huge, six-fingered hands ended in long curved points. All of them had thick black or brown fur hides covering their wide backs. They were so muscular that their whole body appeared to hunch forward from the strain.

Then a surging, crackling pillar of white energy appeared within the cleared path, slowly moving towards the castle. Bright threads of sizzling electricity shot back and forth within the vortex of energy, with little electric snakes snapping out in all directions.

As it grew closer, a figure could be discerned within it. The energy was contained within the shapely form of a tall slender female. But instead of flesh and hair, there was the flaring vortex of electricity. The shape was definitely that of a curvaceous female being. The long legs strode to where the line of the horde extended out from both sides of the cleared path.

The arms of the energy-filled being raised up and a huge bolt of force shot forth towards the wooden-planked gate. The gate exploded into a million burning embers of wood amidst the smoke-filled air, heavily laced with the smell of charred wood.

The energy of the explosive impact sent everyone along the top of the wall flying backwards. Some of the bodies ruptured and were dismembered by the force. Others were flung back onto swords or spears held by the armed contingent below, who were left staring helplessly at the bodies hurtling towards them. That is, those who were not impaled themselves by the flying missiles of wood and stone. Even the defenders' own weapons had turned against them, as the shattered haft of a halberd protruded out from one of those standing in the bailey. The warrior stood staring at it, unable to process what had happened to her, now dead in her boots.

Huck was sent tumbling off of the wall and onto the ground with such violence that he was immediately overtaken by unconsciousness.

§ § §

Huck slowly came back to his senses from what he thought to be a deep sleep filled with pleasant dreams. He dreamt that he was in a freshly made warm bath, the water making soft, comforting, sloshing sounds as he moved about in it.

The reality that he awoke to was far from comforting or pleasant. His eyes opened. Since his head was tilted down due to him being in a seated position, he quickly noted the steaming, chest-high water in which he sat. But the water had a strange reddish hue to it. Then he realized that his arms were tied out to his sides uncomfortably tight, and there were others seated around him.

Several women, two men, and Mynse Velore, lord of the castle and the symbol of the Kuhrzothian crown. But Lord Velore was dead. There was a huge gaping melon-shaped gouge in his head showing a bloody gray mass, no doubt from a club or mace.

Now he began to sweat heavily as the churning water became unbearably hot, even though the air was seasonally cool. He could hear the popping and crackling of a fire somewhere nearby.

Two of the women moved subtly and occasionally moaned. One was obviously dead as her stomach region had been ripped open, entrails hanging out and floating in the water like boiling pasta. This was no doubt mostly the cause of the reddish hue to the water.

The large-nosed, knobby head of an Akhru peered in over the edge of the huge iron cauldron as it swung in a large pole with a pointy end, as though mixing a stew. Huck soon realized in horror that he was in a large boiling pot in which soups and stews were prepared for the masses of folk such as for the harvest feasts.

The Akhru then savagely stabbed at one of the moving women about the chest and stomach while licking its frothy lips, the deeply set eyes flickering with excitement. She screamed in agony for a moment before succumbing to death as blood and organ tissue squirted out.

Huck began to scream now in the crescendo of mortal agony as his skin literally peeled back from the bone in the now superheated water. What seemed like days to him were really only many long moments, and then he finally passed from this world.

§ § §

The small wooded clearing sat nestled over a ridge, within a league from Clan Tharasvrul. It was nearing the witches' light as Priestess Sahrya stood quietly at the clearing's center.

Thirteen small cages—barely larger than the size of the wolf that each one contained—stretched out in a line to her front. The wolves stalked about their confining cages. Each beast already had on a heavy leather strap tightly around its neck, and this with a chain attached to it.

Many snarled and growled at those that they viewed as their turncoat captors, two Blackguard standing in the front of each cage. Some did so from the fear of not knowing what might befall them, most instinctively snarled in anger sensing what would happen to them soon. A few sat shivering even though it was not that cold with their thick fur, the tails of these wrapped underneath them and their ears hung far back.

There was an extreme sadness in the eyes of these wolves, as their heads nuzzled down, staring out of what they knew was unescapable. Animals indeed were the very instinctive and supernatural embodiments of life, ever direct and pure. They could sense things and feel what most sentient forms could not. They had a reason and a purpose behind their existence, and they always maintained sight of those ingrained priorities.

The warriors stood at the front of each of the cages, where there was a small square opening in the center. The chain attached to the straps around the wolves' necks ran out of these openings. They silently stared at the priestess, waiting patiently. One from each of the pairs loosely held their chain.

The priestess looked across to each of the thirteen bodies of the impressive black panthers, one of the dead hulks lying in front of each of the cages, directly below where the small opening was located. Slightly behind her stood another alluring woman of eternal youth. She possessed long, black flowing hair and wore a thin, wispy gossamer gown.

Sahrya uncontrollably smiled in excitement. Three small, pure white foals awkwardly stood near to her, tied to a tree.

It had been several nights since interrogating the keeper Ghenwari. Since then, she had subtly rounded up more of Amanshar's family and, so far, none appeared to be aware of the mark upon Zaramagrii. None indicated any inkling of what the little dark slit could be, might be—even under extreme agony. All the way to their dying breath.

And now, with this hallowed night, she would bring back the ancient rhaanmri of her real clan, Clan Omrasstefor. They would once again walk this world.

She looked down upon the flickering gold basin where the ritual would be done. Methodically, she began to mix the contents of three different silver goblets, each with the blood of an exotic thing in it. One that of a virgin of Man-folk, another of the gelding of a winged stallion, and the last most important one contained the mixed blood from one hundred Pixies.

Now she lit thirteen torches, and each of these had a leather strip soaked in crushed and decayed bone that had been blended with the spinal fluid of several Aylsh.

Sahrya turned her head slightly to speak with the woman behind her. "Rosella, I now need your essence, my love, the blood of a Daemun. Come and partake."

The woman in white stepped forward, suddenly her body transforming within moments into an enchantingly tall naked female. Giant bat-like wings protruded from its back and dully flapped.

The thing stepped forward on monstrous, three-toed feet with wicked, curved talons, while stretching forth its right arm with the palm up. Her, or its, eyes glowed a rich orange. The thing's skin glistened in a darkened purplish hue.

A massive, sinewy tail with a pronged, razor-sharp tip whipped from behind and neatly sliced the wrist area, allowing the dark, thick liquid to spurt into the basin with a splat.

Then Sahrya began to chant as her eyes closed and her hands traced strange symbols in the air. "*Maaruu chertoomna klaanghoot rhu draftagmol wan twujhax pharoom!*"

With that, she quickly whipped out a long, sharp, silvery blade and then cut each of the foals' necks. She let the blood gush into the basin, each in their own turn. The braying and chirping of those young, precious things did not stop until their eyes glazed over.

As she finished with the last bleating and twitching one, she raised her hands to her Blackguards scattered about the wolf cages. Nearly in unison, one of the dark ones by each cage pulled the chain and dragged their wolf up against the end of the cage.

Most of the wolves braced themselves with all fours, but to no avail. Soon the head and neck of each of the wolves was pulled tight out of the small opening in the cage. Then the other Blackguard neatly slit the throat of the wolf and allowed the fresh blood to spurt out onto the body of the panther below it.

Sahrya's voice rose in her feverish chanting until all of the wolves rested, limp and lifeless. Quickly she snuffed out the torches using a ceremonial cup made of green crystal.

The wind began to pick up momentum, whipping debris and brush through the air. All the Blackguards stepped back towards the priestess as a strange eerie wail rang out through the night and the bodies of the black panthers began to twitch.

§ § §

Avrul, the rhaanmri sgoth of Clan Tharasvrul, had slept uneasily for most of the night. She lay awake now underneath the thick furs, just staring at the dying embers of the fire. A deep cold came in, and the winds suddenly picked up, now making nearly everything rattle and thud.

It must still have been a short while before dawn when the mother of the Tharasvrul Rhaanmri slowly trotted in. Daraphyn was quietly whimpering with her thick tail hung down low. She let out the most utterly miserable howling moan. Avrul never heard her sound more pathetic, ever.

"Come, Dara, tis okay. More bad dreams?"

Dara had come in to her home now for the past few nights, always late like this. But she never sounded as upset as she did this night. And she stood looking out the doorway, as if waiting for something, or fearing something.

Avrul jumped up and slipped on her clothes quickly. She grabbed a torch and lit it by the fire, then stepped out into the brisk air. No one stirred nearby at this time. Dara almost seemed to be trying to lead her off to the south, ever growing whinier.

"Go my furry one. Take me, show me," Avrul prompted the old wolf as she began trudging to the south and away from the comfort of Clan Tharasvrul.

Before long, she was stepping through brush amidst the trees, distancing herself from where the clan stretched out. The torchlight played bizarre wavering forms across the trees and patchy, snow-covered ground. The winds of this night were barely perceptible but steadily gaining in strength.

Then Avrul saw Dara rigidly stop with the hair along her entire back raising straight up. Her head lowered, and she was growling.

Avrul could see what she thought had been a trick of the light. Translucent fog with a peculiar blackness to it softly floated around her from the south, even though these gentle winds should have dispersed it long ago.

Avrul felt a dark and ominous presence like she had never felt before. There was something close by that had sinking evil about it. Even the air appeared to shiver and cower around her.

She quickly lowered to the ground in front of Dara and leaned towards the wolf. "Dara, go now. Run and get far away. Quickly, lass… Go!"

Dara looked back at her after several paces, as though pleading for Avrul to follow her. Then she skulked away to the east as Avrul made a face and pointed sharply in an attempt to get her to go.

Avrul crouched low and proceeded forward slowly, the torch burning out in front of her. Something was in the brush not far ahead of her. Soft padded steps could be heard and the brush moved.

Then a loud growling noise erupted from the direction, slowly turning into an unnatural hissing roar. She could see two glowing red orbs coming her way.

As the thing grew nearer to her in the half light of the torch, she saw the bloody, ripped flesh of the huge black panther. But something was wrong with it, for this was no panther or mountain lion at all. Those red eyes stared at her, and she could see bones protruding from various places on the cat's body. The thing was nearly as tall as her. Blood dripped from those giant fangs as the thing menaced towards her.

As she slowly began to back away, she heard more movement along both sides of her. And then the undead cats were upon her, with no chance of escape. And none of those of Clan Tharasvrul who were disloyal to the priestess survived that night.

§ § §

Priestess Sahrya sat on her elegant throne within her private chambers. Rosella stood next to her, waiting for direction. She was now in her form of beauty, once used to lure and hold the ignorant Buttlecut under her spell.

A loud purring erupted from in the darkness, though one that made natural creatures cringe with hair standing on end. Flaming red eyes shone through the dark as the faded outline of a repulsive head turned back and forth to eye the priestess.

Sahrya drummed a knuckle on the arm of her cushioned chair. "My dear Rosella, what are we to do? That Wybur Buttlecut has the unfortunate knack of remembering everything he sees.

"If he continues to live, he may very well script his own copy of the black book of Siri. And I cannot have that."

Rosella's head nodded back and forth, from side to side, upon hearing this.

"Rosella? I need you to hunt the little thing down and put him out of his misery. Can you do that? And I do not care what you do with him, so long as he is torn to shreds. He cannot be allowed to escape."

Rosella jumped up and down for several moments excitedly like a child who was given her first pony. She gleefully clapped her dainty hands together.

Once Rosella was gone from the room, Sahrya looked to her devastating rhaanmri leader, Yhanduur. The cat was twice the size of the others, its torn flesh rapidly decomposing since it was assumed by the ancient essence. The cat read her thoughts and lithely jumped over to her side.

"Yes, my splendid Yhanduur, I do have something for you. Vigorous and deadly one, now back with me. Stronger than you ever were before."

Sahrya produced a small piece of cloth wrapped in leather, the one soaked with the blood of the Aylsh maiden from Tamelyn Keep. "Go, my devoted one. Go and find this thing. Take two others with you."

Sahrya affectionately scratched behind one of the cat's decaying ears while smiling. "Hunt her down, and rip her apart."

Chapter 14:

Becoming One with Fate

Take nor want more than the fruits of the perseverance bear, lest one shall be damned by the ignorance of the self.

–Eleventh Edict of Lord Braxis, etched upon the Great Slates, recovered by Arterium circa the year 13 BA.

everal days had passed since Zaramagrii and the girl were taken captive. They both had been blindfolded and bound after they were captured, even their feet

were cinched tight. Then they had been loaded onto a cart. The ensuing journey felt like it took the good portion of a day.

Zaramagrii's legs were numb from the awkward and cramped position that she had been forced to lay in for so long. If she had not been so beaten down by the loss of her tiara, she might have been able to use her newfound senses, her dark blanket, to keep track of where they were going. But she gave up after a short while, and left off with knowing that they were being taken to the west. The girl grasped her arm firmly with both of her bound hands for the whole journey.

Once the blindfolds were removed, they found themselves within a rocky valley lined on both sides with tiny round dwellings. Rising smoke from fires dotted the sky here and there. The valley itself was vast and Hulding moved about like tiny ants throughout it. The two were immediately taken into a cave that had a heavy vine-bound portcullis set within a gridiron style wood plank wall.

An intimidating ogre slouched within a stall, which was barely large enough to allow the thing to move. The behemoth was caged near the gate where it could raise and lower it using a rope. Heavy balls of iron were shackled to it at both the neck and the feet.

Several guards wielding shortswords and round wooden shields crowded both sides of the gateway. One of them carried a spiked whip, no doubt used in forcing the ogre to obey. Pieces of dried skin and dark blotches covered its length. All telltale signs of its constant use.

As Zaramagrii passed the creature, she noted the subdued and hopeless look in those enormously round, black eyes.

She curiously eyed the ogre once more, since she had never encountered one before. The form must have reached near nine foot tall, and the whole body appeared as heavy muscle. Its rough hide was a light shade of brown. The bumpy nose, although somewhat pointy, flared out at the nostrils.

Once inside, the cave opened up to a high ceiling. Torchlight illuminated the surroundings with flickering schemes dancing along the walls. There were several pens of varying sizes throughout, each one lined up along the sides of the cave. The bases of the timber poles ran deeply into the hard-packed dirt floor.

One of them held several wolves, but all the magnificent beasts looked beaten and famished.

There was an aged man in another, two younger ones and a woman farther down.

Another slim pen contained a goblin. It swayed weakly as it stood, wallowing in its misery as there was not enough room to do much else. Its pointed ears leaned forward for the most part, and the yellow eyes gleamed out of the mottled, blackish-green frame.

She had seen dead goblins before, as well as Akhruuk. But this one was alive still, with a stricken and defeated look to it.

Zaramagrii and the girl were kept together in the same pen for several days. Apparently Zaramagrii was considered some sort of powerful monster, even worse than the ogre, as four to six of the Hulding guarded their pen at all times. The guards never took even a moment's break from watching the dark-skinned fiend. The crazed expression of ignorant delusion always within their look, one of fear and apprehension.

Many times the shaman leader with the bone necklace would show up with others and then proceed to stare at Zaramagrii while ranting and raving. The others appeared to be of higher stature, more elegant in aspect, if that could even be said of such a rustic folk.

After what must have been a tenspell of days, Zaramagrii was separated and taken outside the cave by a handful of the Hulding. She was led to a large rock platform, meticulously chiseled with a multitude of fine depressions littering the surface. Many Hulding in mixed dress were congregating around it, the din of their conversations sounding alien and loud to her.

She noted another similar platform not far away, but this one held an altar at its center. It was carved entirely from reddish-hued rock. A metallic basin rested upon the altar. This was no doubt used for some form of appeasement to a divinity. A small statue of what looked like whitened clay stood aside from the basin, extending over it.

So, she thought, these were mere savages who worshipped one of the lower divinities.

It was a statue of Blaagh, a divinity of the all-encompassing. Her studies taught her that this divinity was one of those favored by more primitive Hulding, and some other beings like goblins, kobolds, and even the hill tribes of Man. But, ultimately, all being more simplistic in nature and ways. Yes, ignorant.

What they probably did not know was that the higher power they so reverently worshipped was really only a powerful *shunmrith* (well, allegedly). Legend had it that Blaagh was only made one of the Myno due to its subservience and loyalty to the more powerful Olden of Evil, Dhanarwey.

Shunmriths were particularly strange creatures and normally only subverted and enticed creatures of the world in their hunger to kill and eat. But they could assume various forms, any of those that they had slain and devoured. This Aylsh term meant *double-goers* in the Common tongue.

Of course, shunmrith were different than the *aledrin*. Legend had it that an aledrin could assume the shape of most lifeless things, from a sturdy table to even a door. This probably depended upon the size of the creature itself though.

A shunmrith's original appearance was supposedly that of an ugly, gray, hairless anthropoid thing. What always gave away such a monstrosity was their insatiable appetite for wild things like Aylsh. The heart of an Aylsh was a delicacy to them, preferably still pumping.

The shaman initially presented himself to the crowd, looking like a deranged chicken as his head canted weirdly back while eyeing the gathered ones with exaggerated round eyes. His hands were down at his sides, but they fanned out rigidly. All this while she was led onto the platform.

This appearance of what was supposed to be might and awe apparently impressed the masses, as all went straight into unmoving silence. Many stared agape at the shaman, full of anticipation.

The shaman then went into long pitched diatribes of rocky, winged words. While Zaramagrii could not understand it, the gathered Hulding surely did. Many of the frenzied bouts were followed by deep rolling murmurs. At times, he would have one of the countless guards raise their spear tip to the mark upon Zaramagrii's abdomen.

All were swayed by this agitator with the bone necklace. That is, all except for one. The same aged Hulding that had been where they were captured now looked on. The green-robed one held an air of disappointment about him.

Zaramagrii finally understood to what purpose she was here for. It was an inquisition. The shaman attempted to steer the Hulding into killing her. That was evident by the gestures and menacing glares.

The tirade from the shaman went on for a long while. The finely attired Hulding, closest to the platform but still behind a layer of bristling guards, now began to raise their hands and roar.

The one with the bone and teeth necklace rattled off constantly to her side while looks on some of those faces in the crowd went from anticipation back to disappointment. Now it was an auction. An auction of flesh. And one that would end with the winner being allowed to torture and kill the dark-skinned Daemun.

It appeared that a chunky fat one, who could barely stand on his own two feet, might win the day—and the dark beauty of the Black Clans.

The green-robed Hulding with the gnarled staff, who had lingered in the area where they had been captured, stepped forward with both arms slightly raised. The crowd shrank away from him as he did this, as though this Hulding was surrounded by an aura of deadly stigmata. And so he had purchased her, with no objections from any of the other Hulding, or even counter offers. But there were many sullen looks that followed him. Stares that both spoke a harnessed urge to fulfill the shaman's notions, and a fear in doing so.

It was not long before the girl was brought out and shuffled onto the platform. Zaramagrii stood watching while held between guards belonging to the green-robed one. The girl was pushed to the center as the bidding started. Now the atmosphere of the crowd was much more relaxed, less apprehensive.

But not one of those Hulding even indicated that they wanted to buy her. This Hulding in the green robe, who had bought Zaramagrii, simply nodded his head once. That was all it took and the girl was brought to him and placed with Zaramagrii.

The one that bought them appeared to be more wizened and calm than the rest, never once giving in to the swelling of vehemence being pulled out of the crowd by the shaman. He had several rings upon his hands, each one covered with glittery gems and precious metals. The Hulding's yellow eyes looked at her coolly before signaling his guards to take them away.

This Hulding had a particularly nice dwelling. It was situated along the very brim high on the western side of the village. The entire place was surrounded by a five-foot fence of stonework and could only be reached by a winding, narrow path.

Zaramagrii and the girl were shown a modest but windowless chamber within the home. There were soft furs in the corner for sleeping and other rudimentary things of comfort.

At first, Zaramagrii figured that they were bought to enact whatever backwards sense of zealotry was invoked. But then she realized that she was as far from the truth as a soaring eagle from the lands.

Later that night after they were brought to the Hulding's home, the old one beckoned Zaramagrii to follow him. He brought her alone into another room, one that appeared to be his hosting chamber. The chairs and table were ornate, along with a crystal window that overlooked the village sprawled out amidst the gorge below. Large, fluffy cushions were scattered everywhere.

The Hulding grasped her by her hand and looked her in the eyes. At first he mumbled several strings of words in Hulding and then broke out in fragmented but understandable Black Clan. "My dark child, I…" He paused many times while searching for the words. "I will not harm you either. You are free to be inside, just not the outside…unless with I."

After several moments, he smiled and then pointed to himself. "Khorpah. Khoorpaah."

He did this until she nodded her head in understanding. Then, unnoticed until now, she saw the small Aylsh rune clasped to the fine chain around his neck. It appeared to be a pair of Aylsh letters set into a circle. What did this mean?

Zaramagrii smiled back and just stared at him, questioningly. At this point, she did not want to give anything more than she had to, and that included conversation.

Then, before they parted and as she turned towards the door, Khorpah gently stopped her. He did the most unimagined but amazing thing ever for her. As he smiled, his eyes radiating warmth and calm, he gently set a bundle of cloth in her hand and then turned to go back to his chair.

As she closed the door behind her, Zaramagrii carefully unfolded the cloth and found her broken tiara resting within.

Her step lightened as she returned to her chambers, now relieved and somewhat elated with this turn of events. There was much more to this Hulding Khorpah than initially realized. But what exactly was his purpose?

Indeed, Khorpah Gathyooram was a very special and unique Hulding. Unlike the majority of his kind, Khorpah was well read in the ways of the lands. His enlightenment, both the learned and experienced paths, was one of vastness.

For Khorpah had been found and raised by one of the disbanded rangers of Kuhrzoth. He had been part of a patrol when he was young. The patrol's purpose was to go out and explore…well, raid…a newly found settler up along the Western Spires of the Rock Rim.

This settler turned out to be more than they bargained for, a courageous ranger who had just been relieved from his duties under the crown of Kuhrzoth. Freed from duties that had been his whole life, and now with an attitude matched only by his prowess.

Back then, Khorpah never realized why this Aylsh had spared his life after killing the rest of the patrol. But, over time, he learned. He learned that the Aylsh read his actions and saw behind the visage that this one Hulding had more depth than most. At least more than those other savage Hulding in the patrol. The Aylsh eventually had spoken of a vision that prompted his mercy upon Khorpah.

The ranger had been watching them all along, even as they crept up to the rudimentary home in preparation for the attack. Khorpah never saw a warrior kill so many so fast. The name of this ranger was none other than Thimoryn Jadorthanelle. But this time was well before Thimoryn had met his kindred spirit Rawa, and the birth of Rhalwa.

Most of the other Hulding were scared of the fact that Khorpah was away from them for so long, and they feared this unknown taint, as though Khorpah had become some twisted and demented monster. These folk feared what they could not understand. He became an alien thing to his own people, an unknown quantity…unknown things become feared. Especially the way that he talked, the way that he thought. Undecipherable. Unpredictable. And this frightened most of them.

The majority of Hulding were a superstitious lot anyways, beset in shamanism. Of course, it only took one or two of the shamans to incite this into blind allegiance...to them, to whatever they deemed could hold sway over the multitude for their own benefit.

But Thimoryn ended up teaching Khorpah so many different things, things that never before made sense to him. These things did not make sense to him because, for his entire youth, he had been polluted by these power hungry and ignorant shamans. These Hulding that used the fear of the unknown to control all. In order to control those they themselves needed to complete their own self-centered existence.

One can be a slave to something without ever realizing it. And this was the result of such close-minded, dominating rule over the Hulding kind.

When Zaramagrii returned to her chambers, she found that the girl had already curled up within the furs and fallen asleep. She quietly sat and gingerly uncovered the tiara again, carefully studying it. The large, black gem had indeed cracked and now appeared with many tiny hairline fractures crisscrossing its surface.

With barely a touch of her finger, to her dismay, part of the gem fell inward into tiny pieces. Then she saw the hollowed out portion inside, and in fact, this was no gem of value at all.

There in the middle, once wedged between the interior edges, was a large ornate ring. It was made of antiquated black metal and had a slew of gems inlaid around it.

Quaint, thought Zaramagrii. So her mother had yet another secret...this ring hidden within the tiara.

But why? What did it mean? Did she even know about it?

It looked fairly large and probably would not fit any of her fingers. She slowly slipped it over her right index finger anyways, marveling at how archaic it looked and felt. The ring radiated with the impression of time, as though it was permeated with history, from many ages ago.

As she slipped the overly large ring onto her finger, the ring somehow ended up fitting perfectly once fully seated.

But then her head swam with dizziness and the room began to spin. She closed her eyes as she tried to shake the feeling.

As they closed, the spinning stopped and she found herself somewhere else...maybe a lucid dream? It was as though her eyes were still open. But the world around her now appeared as a strangely eerie orange-hued darkness. Instead of the abode, she was now out in a large open field with twisted black trees coming out of the ground. Dim wraiths moved about everywhere.

And then she opened her eyes. The familiarity of the chambers surrounded her, with the girl silently sleeping beside her. But she saw strange wisps of what appeared to be black smoke radiating from her skin, about her hands and arms. The gems on the ring held a subtle glow now.

Not sure what had happened, she nearly pulled the ring back off of her finger. But then she suddenly felt so tired and sleepy, she blew out the candle and lay flat on her back beside the girl.

Sleep overtook Zaramagrii quickly that night. Her eyelids weighing heavily, she let go of the struggle to stay awake and closed her eyes. Even though it had the appearance of a sound, peaceful sleep, it was anything but that. The unsettling visions, or dreams, that engulfed her body and mind seemed real.

At first she dreamt that she was running through that strange twilight world again, running and running to reach some place or thing. But she never tired, and not once lost her breath to the exertion. The outlandish, blurred creatures appeared here and there but kept their distance from her.

To her shock, when she looked down towards the ground, she found that she had large, dark paws made of the night instead of her feet. And there were four of them, for she had the body of a huge black wolf. But unlike any wolf that she had ever seen.

And then this elegant beast with fiery eyes that trailed smoke jumped forth from her and separated, now distinctly not her anymore. She stood naked and barefoot—she could see her own arms and hands again.

But she could feel the thoughts of that beast and she sensed its feelings. Though fierce and menacing, the beast spurred no fear at all within her. Instead she was overcome by a different sense. One that she could not at first put a name to.

Like a mysterious deep voice within her mind, it distinctly spoke. *Fear not, my dark queen, for I will come soon. For I am you, and you I. We are the reflections of the perfect essence.*

As these thoughts came to her, she could feel an overwhelming sense of love and care from this beast of an entity. A sense of intimacy.

Then the vision of the shadow wolf was gone, along with the feelings that it projected to her. She was now surrounded by solid blackness, but with that a sensation of peace and restfulness overcame her. And she felt power—the power of twilight and darkness.

Now she partially understood, as she was one with the darkness, one with the shadows. And that coursed pure power within her. The last thing that she remembered before waking was seeing nothing but blackness around her.

Then her mother appeared in front of her, dressed in a flowing white, radiant dress. She was floating through the blackness.

Her mother constantly kept repeating the same string of words over and over. *Never take the ring off, my child.*

Spectacular rays of light shone in through the door and woke Zaramagrii within their warm glow. She felt completely refreshed even with the strange dreams. There were various cloth pullovers, furs, and supple doeskin wraps placed just inside of the doorway.

In the light, Zaramagrii noticed that her unique mark below her navel was now more pronounced, and its surface slightly raised. The half sun and rays were much darker in color. These were contrasted even more against her dusky skin than they had been before last night, before slipping the ring on.

The girl stretched underneath the furs, as her eyes peeked out. Once the girl rose from the covers, she slowly sat up and reached out to touch Zaramagrii's arm. She lightly grazed the wrist of the dark one, using just the tips of her fingers. Then she stared closer at the dark, glistening skin as it shimmered in the rays of light.

For the first time, Zaramagrii saw the girl's lips curve in a quick, faint smile. An honest one of delight.

The girl then tried to mouth words, but all that came out was "Ga…oddesss."

But her eyes bespoke her complete adoration for the dark one, and then Zaramagrii realized that she had become an unmovable rock of solace for the young thing. Zaramagrii had much more on her mind though, not to trifle the affections of the girl.

The next few days were spent inside of the abode, where all doorways leading outside had one of the private guards posted.

The two were expected to do menial things around the place, such as cleaning up and washing the various linens scattered throughout it. In truth, they had nearly the entire day to themselves, as Khorpah was usually gone for the better part of it. Sometimes he would be gone most of the night as well.

Whenever he did return, he would look thoughtfully at Zaramagrii for a short time before going to his hosting chambers.

But she saw a gleam in his eye, a glimmer of insurrection. She could almost feel his resistant spirit to whatever kind of governance was going on within the village by the Hulding shaman. It may even have been his intellect and wisdom that were shining through and attempting to struggle against the primitive savage bounds currently imposed upon the Hulding. Maybe such bonds were more widespread than just this village.

After pondering her newfound ring, and the constantly recurring dreams or visions, Zaramagrii began to feel different. She began to sense her inner form. And, more importantly, she began to feel as one with the dark, almost part of it or it part of her. Now she began to sense that something was growing within her, or maybe emerging, and it was for a higher purpose.

Although not clear now, obviously the cunning shadow wolf running through her mind must mean something. The visions of the mysterious, hazy world, and visits by what appeared to be her mother. All of these had to have some kind of purpose.

The ring was one key. Ever since she donned it, all of these things had come to her. They were like nebulous banks of fog swirling around her mind, concealing something in the dark but now becoming more opaque or transparent.

Or maybe she was beginning to pierce whatever veil concealed it all from herself. Gaining vision...like the new sense of perception that she uncovered in the subterranean world. One that had been shown to her from the ordeal, from the darkness.

One night, deep into its blackness, Khorpah came to Zaramagrii. He said no words at the time, but instead led her to the one room in the place that always remained locked. On the way, they passed a handful of the private guards. The armor-clad fighters were gathered around a table and sharpening their iron swords and spears.

Khorpah took her into the small room and closed the door. Shelves full of various books and scrolls littered the walls.

The books were old and worn. They bore the symbol of the Aylsh rune that Khorpah had around his neck. And many of them had the name *Thimoryn Jadorthanelle* handwritten upon them.

Khorpah sat down in a rickety chair while sliding over an old, burly chest. After lighting a candle, he motioned for her to sit while unlocking the chest.

His scattered Black Clan again came across stuttering and mispronounced. "My child, take this. You and other one go if you want. But one thing...for me... Please. Use it and strike down the shaman. He at rock shrine soon. Then go. I do rest...no worry."

As he spoke these words, he uncovered a long, silver dagger. The elegant blade flashed as it reflected the burning flame of the candle. She loved the look of such things, almost as though finely crafted weapons appeared to her as jewels and gold appeared to most others.

Then the wise Hulding talked long about his life and how he had been found by the Aylsh ranger Thimoryn.

The fragmented words strung together a story that amazed Zaramagrii. One of courage and learning.

He explained how this was the best thing that ever happened to him, as it was a glorious enlightenment. The ranger taught him about everything in the world, not just the closed views of the Hulding folk. And the ranger explained to him the meaning of life and how everything fit into the immense order, a colossal circle. He taught him about the Blue Flames, the Wild Spark.

Khorpah paused and eyed her again. "One more thing. Take this, a symbol from the past. My dreams told me to give it you…and you give to the one."

He had already separated the small Aylsh rune and placed it onto another golden chain. The symbol was that of the letters T and J interlaced together in High Aylsh script.

Zaramagrii bit her lower lip before speaking. "But who is the one?"

"No worry, my child. You will know," replied the Hulding with a content expression on his face, and a look of brimming satisfaction.

As Zaramagrii made her way back to her chamber, she knew that she had read the old Hulding true. He wanted to use her to spark his own coup against this decrepit, no doubt maniacal, ruler of a shaman.

She could sympathize with the wise Hulding. Here was a shaman ultimately practicing witchcraft to threaten his people into conformity. A conformity that was his alone, maybe even a small cult of shamans. But it was not that of Hulding-kind itself.

Zaramagrii's mind naturally worked that way, as she had already given thought to their escape and the release of the wolves.

The time spent inside of the cave the first few days had been long enough for her to watch the activities of the Hulding as they went about their work. Early in the morning there were very few guards roaming about, and only one at the gate to the cave.

A large, iron-wrought ring with various keys always sat upon the small empty keg near the cave's entryway. And this final brush stroke by Khorpah only sealed the plan. She would not betray him, as he had been the kindest to them and actually had intended to free them all along.

She returned to her chambers and woke the girl, who stared wide-eyed at her and the daunting blade as it glowed with the smallest light.

Zaramagrii had dressed earlier, the leather halter partially hidden by a black furred hide tied loosely about her shoulders. A dyed doeskin wrap fit like a short skirt about her thin waist, and she wore knee-high leather boots. The graceful dagger given to her was bound inside her boot, where it would be close at hand when needed.

She made the girl bundle up in thick linen clothing, then wrapped about in furs for extra warmth. The lands would slowly become more and more unforgiving, with winterfall on the doorstep.

Once away from the village, there was no telling when their next rest from the wildlands would be. To Zaramagrii, the wildlands were now home, but the girl remained a frail child.

Zaramagrii took the girl's hand and walked out towards the front doorway. No one stopped them, although the guards, along with Khorpah, simply watched as they walked by. She paused at the door to slowly open it and peer outside. All was quiet.

The night air had a sting to it, but Zaramagrii felt more alive than ever and enjoyed the feel of the cold. Whether hot or cold, the extremes never really bothered her. But the girl was shivering already.

Her main worry was that she had to tote the girl with her, but it was easy making their way down towards the heart of the village.

Once within a stone's throw from the cave where they were initially held, she stealthily pulled the girl into a patch of leafless brush. The darkness falling from a heavy stonework fence draped over them as they crouched low.

Zaramagrii whispered and gestured to the girl that she must stay in this spot no matter what and to wait for her to return.

Once she was satisfied that the girl understood, she crept out along the fence line in the direction of the two rock platforms where the altar was. It was only a short distance away, but she was not taking any chances at being spotted. So far she only saw the one guard near the cave entrance.

At first, the area around the altar was bleak and dismal. No shaman. No activity at all.

But then she sensed him approaching, more than heard or saw. The dull footsteps only then came to her ears.

It was not until he grew to within sight and sound that she made out the shaman's hooded figure. The bones and teeth on the necklace rattled as he walked, and the material of his cloak around his waist swelled out oddly, concealing something bulky.

She watched curiously as he walked up to the altar and began to light the torches around it. Then he reached into the sides of his cloak and pulled several items from about his waist. These were placed around the basin of the altar.

Silently sneaking up behind the Hulding was not difficult at all, the dagger already out but carried so that it strayed within the dark of her arm's shade. She could now sense his breathing, steady and unaware.

As she slipped directly behind him, the dagger's blade quickly flipped out and was run through the Hulding's neck. He gurgled for an instant in his death throes. Then the dark child side-stepped, bringing the blade clean through to the back, and the spine severed completely.

The belt around the shaman's waist held several fist-sized hide pouches tightly bound with oil laden leather straps. She undid one of them and wrinkled her nose at the acrid, peppery odor coming from the coarse powder inside. These were pouches of flash powder, something developed by alchemists in the deserts to the south. But this was only done through the early conquests of the Southern Kingdoms and their ventures to the south. The Thederye were the original inventors of such a volatile substance. They called it *gypto*.

The shaman had indeed rested his iron rule upon keeping the Hulding superstitious and awed by simple tricks. He no doubt used the powder to boost the effect of him supposedly calling down the divinity. She had no doubt that these shamans had other connivance's as well.

As she made a fire in the sacrificial basin, an idea floated to her. Then she placed the pouches on the edge of it so that they would slowly catch fire. There was no such thing as luck, but she figured that the leather of the pouches would take a short time to burn through before igniting the flash powder inside. Time enough to allow her to complete the next part of her plan.

Before heading towards the cave, she smashed the statue of Blaagh to pieces and placed those in the fire as well. The wolves would not become some fur skin to warm any of these ignorant vermin.

The guard near the portcullis was easy prey for her. Now she eyed the ogre, contemplating its temperament.

The ogre stared at her with unwavering, gentle eyes as she slowly leaned forward to place a palm upon one bulging shoulder. She closed her eyes and sensed no agitation. Then she returned to where the rope dangled and pulled down on it using all of her weight. It was a valiant effort, but the gate would not budge. It was just too heavy.

It did not take long before the ogre nodded its enormous head and then grabbed hold of the rope with one meaty hand. In one tug, the portcullis raised up and she was able to wedge a discarded spear underneath the ironworks to keep it from slamming back down.

She again reached across and touched the ogre before proceeding inside the cave.

Carefully she approached the pen holding the wolves. Crouching low, she closed her eyes and saw her clan's rhaanmri running through her mind. Such graceful and exquisite animals.

She gently slipped her hand, palm facing up, inside of the pen while her eyes slowly opened. The wolves just sniffed her and nudged her hand as though in acknowledgement.

Using the set of master keys, she opened their pen and watched as they silently crept outside and disappeared.

The other prisoners stared at her, each of the faces surprised at seeing her, but still filled with hopelessness. She had not intended to release them all, as these other beings in here maybe deserved to be here. She did not know. The wolves were a different story, such magnificent spirits captured, maybe even tricked into it. And that would not stand or go unpunished.

But then she thought that letting all of them go might create even more confusion, in case things did not go as intended.

Within a short time, she had released all the prisoners, even the weakened goblin. Then she made all of them stop and wait near the opening that led back outside. She quickly brought spears and clubs to the ragtag band.

Grabbing the keys again, she made her way back to the portcullis, with all of the freed captives in tow behind her. Their bodies hunched forward as they followed.

Slowly she unlocked the wooden run trapping the ogre in place, then freed it from the shackles as well. The ogre just stared at her.

She secured the vicious barbed whip that had left so many marks upon the giant. Then she handed it to the ogre, presenting it like a ruling scepter.

Recognition dawned slowly in those guarded eyes, and the ogre climbed out of the wooden frame to take revenge against the cruel captors.

Suddenly, several loud booms rang out in the night. Bright, blinding flashes erupted in rapid succession, lighting up the surrounding abodes and rock walls.

Now the village would come to life. Zaramagrii shoved the others out into the darkness and told them, in the Common tongue, to run. But she figured that they already had a good idea as to what to do.

Then she disappeared into the murk and made her way back to where the girl was. It was not long before they were making their way out of the Hulding village just below the edge of the ridge line.

§ § §

Meanwhile, somewhere within the Shadehaunt, still on Zholryn but within a different spectrum or realm, rested a huge ghostly wolf.

The beast shimmered under the dirty orange glow of the twilight world. Trails of black smoke steamed from the wolf's muzzle as it gnawed a bone nearly as large as the beast itself. The astounding flaming eyes set the beast apart, as both were glowing with an orange-red brilliance around the edges. But the right shone like the hottest ember burning white, while the left appeared as an ominous black hole.

The Alpha Omega, Grastharfah il Marilaan the Black, surveyed his surroundings as the bone occupied his boredom. The energetic shadow warg appeared oblivious to everything, but nothing could be more distant from the truth.

Suddenly the gnawing stopped and his huge ears shot straight up from where they rested back along his head. The contrasting eyes glowed with a fierceness.

The glorious beast felt something. Something completely new, and different. It was as though he had a twin, somewhere else, that he could mutually feel and experience through. Or, no…maybe a mate? Whatever the case, he felt an instantaneous draw to the other world. It was more a bond that yearned for him, and it was so strong that he nearly felt he could see and sense what the other entity could.

Wait… The Shadow Lord… Ahh, the Soul. The time had been long since that distant night. Yes, the Soul had accepted part of its destiny and was now unwittingly waiting for him. Grastharfah il Marilaan—Grasfur—was being summoned.

But he could not get over the immense feeling of love and sudden purpose that he felt. And it had taken him so quickly.

In the past, over the countless thousands and thousands of years, he had never felt this before. Not even with those he mated with to create all of the young seeds out there.

The most compelling urge for him now was to go to it and protect it. The giant warg raised off of the ground where he had been stretched out and slowly began to gait.

Then he quickly flipped back towards his bone, snapping and snarling at several lesser shadow wolves that rose from the ground attempting to take it, teasing him playfully.

Chapter 15:

A Mother Returns Home

Sacred life shall be spilt solely for cleansing, and naught for the whim, lest the resultant fervor erode the very essence. Such shall be held against one by the Omega.

–Twelfth Edict of Lord Braxis, etched upon the Great Slates, recovered by Arterium circa the year 13 BA.

he slopes of the eastern Rock Rim grew colder as the wind picked up, swirling the powdery flakes of fresh snow. Strangely, the surrounding area was devoid of the wild spirits that normally romped and roamed throughout it.

There was something else that stalked these snow swept grounds. Whatever it was made the very air ominous and oppressive, sending out the deadly nature of its intent. Not far to the south sat a small home, the white smoke of the chimney staining the blackness above the rooftop.

Eerie growls and snarls echoed lowly across the rocky country, and there was nothing but large deep-furrowed tracks trailing through the fresh snow. Bits and pieces of decayed flesh, long since dead, padded the grooves here and there. Tracks that stalked towards the small home nestled within the rocks.

§ § §

Ephritori found herself running through the dark woods, crunching through old, hardened snow, and vigorously breathing. There was an impending fear of something—a terror—following behind her, or them, as there were the sounds of other things around her. Even though she never saw anything when turning to look, whether a familiar face or some monstrous horror.

The world about her was so vague, as though surrounded within a thick, dark fog. The thing behind her sounded close now as it crashed through the brush, viciously growling. But she felt the crushing evil of whatever it was, like a heavy blanket slowly covering her, trying to smother her. Then she suddenly came upon a large waterfall with a brilliant radiance streaming from within, or through, the cascading water. Then something sharp dug into her back, thrusting her forward. Pushing her uncontrollably.

Ephritori awoke in a cold sweat to the blackness of night. Silence rang supreme. The deafening stillness forced the beating of her heart into her ears. It felt as though only a short time had passed since she lay down to go to sleep.

While the peaceful surroundings of Rhalwa's home soothed her, she was still seized by foreboding apprehension that she could not shake free of. This was the third night that she had this dream. But tonight, the feeling that the dream left her with was utterly overwhelming. It had appeared so real, so raw.

She could hear the wind howl eerily outside as it blew through the trees and swept over the rocky lands. For some reason, the sound gave her chills.

Then she thought that she heard the howl of a wolf in the distance. A moment later, the first was answered by many more to the point where they all blended together. A lonely but edged serenade of the wild. That wasn't just the call of the hunt.

Ephritori instinctively knew that something was wrong, that something was coming. And it was coming for her.

She quickly dressed and found Rhalwa already awake, checking the door.

Ephritori pulled a thick fur about her shoulders. "Rhalwa, something comes this night. A thing of pure evil. Trust my word, we must go soon. These walls will not stop it."

Rhalwa looked upon Ephritori's face under the subtle glow of the hearth's firelight. "Fear not my fair one. For I have only heard those howls of the pack as some kind of warning to the others. The rest of the howls that followed were answers, and sounded of them rallying. Many of them have already gathered outside these walls. They sense something too."

Rhalwa was dressed and had slung her intricate leather quivers crossed over her shoulder. She checked the sword at her side and, once satisfied that it was firmly clasped, picked up the Oadewood great-bow in her off-hand.

The air was brisk, no doubt further chilled by the light dusting of fresh snow. The pair of them stepped out into the cold. The black-furred pack leader sat near the door, his coat streaked with silver from the course of the years.

Then a low growling could be heard, though hard to identify the source at first. The sound became louder, and all of the wolves nearby quickly began to crouch low with the hackles along their backs raising up.

The wolves were all intently focused towards the south where the growling came from. It sounded like a cat making a low, rumbling warning growl. Except it was deeper and more sinister as though from the very depths of the Hundred Layers of the Endless Chasm itself. The chilling sounds lashed out and terrorized the lands.

Both of them stood there in the darkness too long, waiting to see what was making the noise. It was too late when they observed several sets of glowing red orbs approaching, floating along the ground. They flickered up and then down, with the slow stalking movement of their bearers.

The pack leader fiercely stared at Ephritori, as though trying to tell her to go. Then he turned back and leapt closer towards the menace encroaching upon them. Several others joined him to form a line in front of her and Rhalwa.

Finally, they could see dark, shambling forms approaching them in the gusting snow. Three huge black cats the size of horses stood before them, with haunting red eyes that flared in the blackness. The one in the middle, the largest, hung back slightly with the other ones on each side.

They were cats, or similar to a cat, but something was different about them and their presence. This was even noticeable in the darkness with their forms outlined against the snowy background, making them appear darker than they truly were.

Suddenly, one of them leapt high in the air towards where Ephritori and Rhalwa crouched alongside a cluster of rock. The speed was amazing, but a huge wolf sidelined the undead beast in midair, knocking the thing off of its course towards the Eternal Mother. Three more wolves jumped into the fray, while another of the gruesome cats hung low to the ground and crept sideways to flank them.

Rhalwa pushed Ephritori backwards. "Run… Quickly! Do not look back. I shall be right behind you!" She drew the ancient blade of her father while frantically shouting.

Within moments they found themselves sprinting down the side of the ravine, dodging in between rocky mounds and thickets of leafless trees mixed with pine. Snow came crashing down from branches overhead every now and then. Several wolves ran along both sides, waiting for one of the other cats to strike.

A wolf let out a defiant cry and yelp in the distance behind them. Thunderous crashing through snow and brush sounded from where Rhalwa's home lingered. The cozy warmth disappeared with its passing memory.

Ephritori looked back at Rhalwa while slowing down. "We have to go to a waterfall. Is there a waterfall nearby?"

Rhalwa looked at her puzzled, each breath heaving from both exertion and apprehension. She did not know how Ephritori knew of the waterfall, which was hidden until one nearly stepped foot into it. And she had been dead to the world when Rhalwa found her beside it.

She replied. "This way." She took the lead but was only a step or two ahead of Ephritori and off to her side.

Within moments, they could hear a low growling coming from behind them. There was the loud sound of thrashing and snarling along with it. Then another yelp and crash. The cats were not letting up, but neither were the wolves.

As Rhalwa peered behind her, her boot caught under a root buried in the snow. Down she went, tumbling several paces before finally stopping.

Ephritori stopped and leaned forward while looking at her. The huge black form with glowing red eyes was right on top of Rhalwa. The cat had flanked them. While there were many sounds of scampering, padded paws in the distance, the wolves trailing them were just too far away to reach her in time.

To Rhalwa's utter amazement and surprise, the black cat crouched—preparing to spring directly over her and at Ephritori. She could see what appeared to be pieces of skin and hair hanging off of the thing's body, as though it was shedding.

The smell of rotted flesh rolled over her and she knew that this thing was not of this world. And it wanted the Aylsh, even though it would have had Rhalwa dead to rights, being so close and so fast.

Without a thought, Rhalwa swung her blade in a high arc as the supernatural cat glided above her. The blade caught the cat along its middle and severed the beast in two, sending it to the ground with a hiss and roar. Even though split asunder, the cat sounded enraged and still very much empowered. It did not take long before several wolves were at both of the parts tearing and ripping them to shreds.

"Quickly, Ephritori, let us go!" Rhalwa forced herself up and then grasped her by the arm to continue on down the sloping draw.

The noise of pursuit faded and only their own footsteps in the snow could be heard, along with their labored breathing. But they did not slow, and soon enough they were sliding down a steep slope between two massive rock outcroppings.

As the two came to a stop at the bottom where the pool of water rested, they found themselves in front of an extraordinary waterfall. A brilliant wavy line of white radiated out and through the sparkling water as it crashed down.

A large fissure appeared to stretch up within the rocky face of the cliff behind the waterfall. Rhalwa stared at the sight, such a thing obviously had not been there before. This created light patterns around the snow-laden ground and small frosted pool where Ephritori had first lain when Rhalwa found her.

As they both prepared to move towards the fissure in the rock and behind the waterfall, monstrous snarling erupted from a pitch black apparition off to their side.

One of the nightmares had found them and crept up close. The fiery eyes of the dreadful cat-thing appeared out of nowhere. The terror crouched atop a pinnacle of rock, taut and ready to spring. This one was the largest of the three, with glowing red eyes smoldering in billowing smoke and the mangled ears pulled back.

Now, up close, they could see the rotting, decayed flesh hanging in various places off the faded bony form of the cat's body. And then the cat pounced with fangs opening wide, moments before they would have reached the lighted fissure behind the waterfall.

But all was not lost. As Ephritori felt the rush of the air from the beast's surge towards her, proud Aylsh knights materialized right alongside her. A white hallowed radiance shimmered around the shining figures armored in glistening full plate armor, signifying their otherworldly appearance.

The terrifying beast was still in midair as one of the knights brought up a ghostly two-handed sword. The blade arced through the air so fast, flashing bursts of sparkling light. The beast had no time to react and was cut in two. The undead cat's body let out a piercing screech and then both pieces of it hit the snowy ground as parts of the lifeless carcass that it should have been. This time, not a hair moved on the cat's body as it lay in pieces.

Ephritori and Rhalwa proceeded into the white light of the fissure. Both of the knights followed and then held their position just inside, with the points of the immense swords resting upon the ground in front of them. The rock wall was barely perceivable through their ghostly figures.

As Ephritori and Rhalwa turned back briefly, they saw the glowing eyes of the last of the three cats leap towards the entrance of the crack, passing through the streaming waterfall as it did so.

As the unhallowed forelegs entered the radiant light, the huge beast frantically attempted to stop its body in mid-air. Once the cat leapt into that white light, its body instantly dissolved. The cat let out one monstrous growl, which echoed throughout the night, and then it was gone. The unholy monsters of the night were no more.

Two more of the armor-clad knights with flowing golden hair stood before them once they went deeper into the strange cave. One of the knights put up a gauntleted hand, palm out, and stopped Rhalwa just shy of a rough-hewn archway.

Beyond the archway, through a short corridor, they could see the rock tunnel open up into another chamber in which a throne rested. A glimmering figure sat upon the throne, but it was too distant to make out any details. Rhalwa kneeled in awe, knowing that she was presented before the divine, or some force of it.

Ephritori continued on slowly, until she stood directly in front of the silver-haired Aylsh seated upon the throne, her father.

She slowly dropped to her knees in amazement, as her eyes welled up with tears. The once living Aylsh king, Daumere Bari Lourendalthemee, wore a shimmering suit of berlyllum chainmaille and a sovereign jeweled crown. A white dazzling aura emanated from around him and surrounded them both. His kind and reassuring face wrinkled at her with a smile.

To Rhalwa, the white light surrounding Ephritori and the figure upon the throne was dazzling and smoldered too bright to see into.

What felt to her as only moments actually turned into the dawn of a new day. She could not remember the minutia of that time spent, but she eventually found herself following Ephritori back out of the fissure and into bright sunslight. But when they looked back, only the rocky face of the cliff and ledge rose up behind the waterfall. The fissure had disappeared.

Ephritori was different now, in a way, and more at ease. The air about her reflected an all-encompassing degree of serenity, as though she had found an inner peace.

She carried a beautiful rod of ancient dark wood, about the length of her forearm. On one end was an antiquated circular silver orb inscribed with various runes. The other end appeared to have a fine piece of blue crystal embedded within its tip, about the size of an index finger. Tiny arms of the wooden rod perfectly encircled this crystal, holding it in place.

Her form was now covered by a great-cloak of exceptional design. That of Aylsh-craft. The gray color shifted and blended with the surroundings at times.

A polished but ancient necklace hung from her neck. The fine silvery chain dangled a circular, mixed ore trinket in which a dark blue jewel at the center reflected the immense deepness of her eyes. They each appeared as vast, but solitary, oceans of mesmerizing curiosity that drew in the observer.

The late-suns wore away as they both walked side by side south along the lower edge of the Rock Rim. The cave and all the events from the past night were many leagues behind them now.

Ephritori would not speak about what took place in the cave. But Rhalwa was content with the peacefulness that had engulfed them since the appearance of the radiant cave and the ghostly Aylsh knights.

It was nearing the final rays of light from the duo suns that the pair approached a bubbling brook filled with clear, icy waters. Boundless green meadows sparsely covered with snow stretched far to the east, where a line of trees stood tall and majestic, outlined against the final scarlet glow of the sinking duo suns. The peaks of the Rock Rim rose as ominous black teeth to the west like strange and threatening bony fingers, darkening from the fading light.

Rhalwa first heard the sharp but weak whimper emanating from towards the ascending ground, where several rocky islands dotted the landscape. A couple of low barks followed, and then Ephritori perked her ears towards the sound.

Rhalwa drew forth her Oadewood great-bow while Ephritori approached the rocks nearest where they thought the noises came from. Rhalwa saw Ephritori's expression go from one of caution to that of concern. Then the Aylsh disappeared behind the rocks for several moments. When she returned to view, she carried a fairly large, but obviously skinny, old wolf nestled within her arms. Rhalwa ran over to help her.

Ephritori laid the old wolf down on her cloak, sheltered by the rocks. "Rhalwa, this one knows you. This is Daraphyn. She is a rhaanmri wolf." She grasped the wolf's head in both palms to look into her eyes. "This one is an old mother, but she met you when you both were very young."

Rhalwa curiously looked at Ephritori. "A rhaanmri wolf? What is that?" She leaned in towards the wolf, stroking her long silver fur on the shoulders.

"The Black Clans are still Aylsh—hence the name Aylsh Ismaru—though darker ones at that. They are very different than the Aylsh. While the clans do not share the same bond with all of the wild things in the world as Aylsh, they do establish a relationship of sorts with one pack or group of animals—be they dogs, lions, jackals, or even wolves. They call this pack the clan's rhaanmri, meaning pact. Together, the clan and its rhaanmri exist to nurture one another, they thrive together—one depending upon the other. Existing together through a mutual sense of need and sentiment to do so."

Ephritori faded to silence as she poured water out into her cupped palm for Daraphyn to drink. "Daraphyn here was the mother to most, if not all, of her rhaanmri. But something happened and all of them were slain. She came from the west, out of the Fallen Lands.

"It grows dark quickly. Let us make camp. We have nothing to fear for this night at least. Tis a good time to gather things for our dinner and it will help Daraphyn here gain some strength back."

With that, Ephritori started a small fire while Rhalwa hunted. Before long, the night had overtaken them. In no time, they were roasting several grouse and a rabbit over the fire. Ephritori broke off raw pieces and slowly fed them to Daraphyn over the course of evening.

"We must go to the king's seat of Kuhrzoth. Nuuroc," Ephritori stated blankly. "The king will have passed on by the time that we arrive, but there are individuals that I must see. This is important. An ill wind is blowing, and I sense a darkness that creeps across all the lands."

Ephritori then began to unfold the truth to Rhalwa, now that she fully accepted what it was herself.

The encounter with her father settled the doubt within her mind and solidified her past. It had brought those days, along with the memories and knowledge, back forth from where it had remained hidden for so long. She now knew exactly who she was and, ultimately, what her purpose was. They talked long into the night about her true form, the Eternal Mother, the might of the Jahthra Khomar—or Spear of Eternal Light, and what rested in store for the future of most things if existence continued within its current state of oblivion.

§ § §

Castym Steele, commander of the Emerald Guard, silently pondered all that he had been told concerning the fall of Emerald Rest. He was in charge of the might of Kuhrzoth now. Well, maybe second in charge considering that the royal presenter held sway over him if so wished. Of course, this did not really consider the king himself, who commanded all. But the king would likely not rise to even walk again.

Tyrim, his brother, was dead. How could that be? And he, or they, did not even find out about the vile assault until more than a score of days after the fact.

Yet this just could not be possible. For Tyrim was the master of arms, the physically endowed and attuned general of war. He had always been the one that no sword could touch, no arrow could pierce, and no hammer could smote. His tactics never failed him in the past.

And here he was—Castym. Brother to the hero, the legend. The man stared at his form through the image of a nearby silver panel used as an elongated mirror.

The reflection was deceivingly warped, and it made him look tall and stocky, almost menacing. But even the green-hued plate armor could not hide the thick torso and belly, the thin arms and not so beefy shoulders.

No, he was not the specimen of a valiant warrior like his brother…like his brother had been. Almost in his forties now, his once dark hair was thin and receding. The cold, gray eyes bespoke wisdom and perseverance on that clean-shaven face. But he was not his brother, not even close.

Doubt clouded his thoughts as he wondered how such a man as Tyrim could be taken by mere Akhruuk and goblins. And how could he be left to deal with this black army of barbaric monsters, with the entire Kuhrzothian army at his command? Alone and beset with such a meager situation as it was?

He felt as though he was the only one that truly knew what was going on…and what needed to be done. But this lunacy only stemmed from the royal and noble peacocks wallowing in their own lack of competence and foresight. Yes, most of the members of the High Assembly definitely lacked the spirit that was needed to objectively serve the kingdom.

These heavy blankets were coupled with the fact that King Baeynor was on his death bed it seemed, struck down by some ailment that could not be cured. Even the physicians bowed their heads, the weight so heavy on them that they could do nothing to help.

His mind raced and nearly ran away from this horrid din of an overwhelming torrent upon him, his thoughts feverishly jumping to and fro. What would happen now, and what would he do?

Castym did know that one such man existed that could be counted upon, but the king had struck that possibility down a long time ago with such malice. There was no way that the lad would ever appear in Kuhrzoth for the king, or on behalf of the king.

But Castym would keep up his communications with Wullyam just in case there was the slightest chance. The old knight owed him. And who else would rule? Royal Presenter Holcomb?

The kingdom of Kuhrzoth was a base feudal system, but with a touch of justice and equality. Even so, the muttering and rambling of the nobles still swayed any council set forth to govern. Yes, the various royally appointed thaynes who ruled their region of the kingdom (usually named by the thayne's keep) still supplied men-at-arms to the crown at the drop of a helm. But it grew more complicated. Under each thayne was his or her knights, and even lord knights. While a knight might have one or two parcels of land, a lord knight might have a whole plot.

A plot was the amount of land covered in a day's ride on horseback. A parcel was what was covered in a quarter of a day. Note that this was done for both the length and breadth. Of course, this allowed for a wide berth of variance in such surveys. And one wondered why there were so many disputes over land ownership. The estimated size might appear different to each individual that rode the distances measured in such a way.

The thaynes held everything else underneath them in their exercise of power, at least throughout their region of governance. A thayne was more of a martial figure, titled as a lord, but he carried the authority of the king so long as this was used with prudence and tolerance. A thayne would be titled as an overlord if there were more nobles within the thayne's region. A lord knight might herself have many knights beholden to her. And they all carried a force of men-at-arms.

This extensive martial arm of the king, in its entirety—lord knights, knights, men-at-arms, et cetera—swore fealty to the

Emerald Crown first and foremost. Then to the thayne that ruled them. Of course the thayne had to be loyal to the king, as the position was an appointed one. Appointed by the king himself.

To add to this bowl of adders, each town or village was under the auspice of an elected baern. Sure, every baern in a region fell under the thayne. But the baern also had their own council, which held an individual titled as the reeve. A reeve was the lead keeper of the peace so-to-speak. Every reeve held a small force of constables. These civil officials fell to the domestic worries and needs of the townspeople. However, most baerns or reeves also tended to hire on an able-bodied force of men-at-arms wholly committed to their own gold coffers. Many of them did so under a mutual concord.

Nuuroc itself was divided into quarters due to the size and vast number of inhabitants. The castle, maybe walled city would be a more appropriate description, was built upon a concept of huge, concentric rings around the original castle, Old Nuuroc. The rings were more irregular of course, and not perfect circles. Each of the city quarters fell under its own baern with an elected council and all, just like any other inhabited area of the kingdom. While Nuuroc itself fell directly under the king and his royal council's control, there was still the need for the various baerns and their bodies to properly control and regulate the entire walled city and the immediate outlying areas. A thayne was not needed, as the king himself held the scepter of power, but there were many lords titled as first lords who acted as thaynes over each of the quarters and their baerns within the city. Naturally, these first lords were right hands to the king himself. This was done so that the king was not inundated with the countless number of public squabbles and claims on any given day.

Now toss the rest of the aristocracy, like the freeholders and wealthy merchants, into this extensive, flustering wheel. The inner workings and happenings that went around this circle, whether aired or hidden, were fraught with personal aims and convenient interests.

These meanderings twisted and turned, enveloping lord, knight, baern, reeve, freeholder, and merchant alike. Some were officially on councils or the assembly, many more only held secret proxy positions that were lined through gold, as well as the promise of land and power.

In the case of this particular day, the High Assembly included every thayne and lord that could be mustered. This happened to be very few, since the notice for it was only two days old. But another assembly had been ordered within a score of days. This next one would have all of the thaynes at the table.

With a deep breath more self-assuring than anything else, Castym swung open the heavy, wooden doors leading into the council chambers where the High Assembly convened.

All seats were filled except, of course, for the far two on the left, which belonged to himself and Tyrim. And the one on the far right also was vacant, for none other than Royal Presenter Holcomb now sat in the elegant center chair. One only reserved for the king.

The representatives of military matters were always seated upon the king's right in order of precedence. The other side of the monstrous table allowed for those who spoke for civil matters, the royal coffers, general stock, and the guilds.

The other sides of this table branched off to form a very large horseshoe. These seats were mostly empty, except for the first lords and other thaynes that held lands within a day's ride of Nuuroc.

The master guildsman stood for all of the various guilds in Kuhrzoth, and traditionally headed separate assemblies involving all of the guild masters as needed.

And the royal seal sat near the other door, prepared to take official notes and record all that happened during the assembly of the council. The bond to the House of Legends. To officially emblazon it into the history of Kuhrzoth.

Castym paused before entering the chambers, now even more attuned to the snake in clothing. Royal Presenter Holcomb had never been very forceful in the past, ever. In fact, he normally always chimed in as a voice of reason and never attempted to step over Tyrim or Castym, even when the king was absent. Holcomb was always one to sit back and then add thoughtful advice to back up the counsel or plan that was laid out by either of them. But something had changed.

Lord Seth Garten, the most loyal and trusted individual under Castym, immediately rose as he opened the door. "Commander Steele. The High Assembly is seated and ready." His fiery eyes scanned from Holcomb to Castym as he spoke this defiant proclamation.

Castym read it well and smiled inwardly. Seth only did this to show his contempt for what the royal presenter had done—seating himself upon the king's seat in his own presumption of feigned power. Seth was not only unerringly loyal to Castym, but also to the king. A true warrior.

Holcomb smugly frowned with a grimace contorting his long face, one that would have made a weasel proud. "Yes, my good commander. We are quite ready, so please do join us." He quickly refolded his hands in front of him, with elbows planted on the table.

Castym calmly walked around to the far side and took the seat of his brother before proceeding. "I have it on good account that Emerald Rest has been overrun and destroyed, or…at least taken over by a fairly large force of Akhruuk and goblin."

This piece of information created quite a stir of sour looks around the table. It took a small effort to appease and quiet the general clamor of unchecked concerns and fears.

What Castym did not tell them was that a royal messenger had been dispatched, under extreme caution, to go and inspect Emerald Rest from afar. The Emerald Crown discreetly began to use Fleshlings as messengers a long time ago, these unique creatures hidden within the ranks of the royal messengers. The Fleshlings employed by the crown were in their eighth generation, but knowledge of their use was held within the utmost secrecy, and only used by the king himself. Castym did not want to set the Fleshling loose, but it was the fastest way to get at least some word on the situation there. He just had to bide his time until the Fleshling's return. And that should be any day now, or at least he had hoped.

Once the room succumbed to the sound of silence, Castym went into his full report of what was learned concerning Emerald Rest. He then began to outline plans for an advance force to head west, as well as placing the castle into a higher state of readiness in case they were attacked.

The royal presenter raised his eyebrows at Castym. "A question Commander Steele. Has anyone in between Emerald Rest and our city here provided word on this black menace from Oshghrul? Any indication at all that it might be moving this way?"

Castym eyed him, canting his head slightly back. "Not yet, my lord. Just what I have already stated. And this was from the guards accompanying the merchant caravan that was on the way there."

But he already knew where this was headed. The burning pain deep within him yearned to erupt all over this facade of state affairs. He, and obviously he alone here, knew what loss meant.

He also knew the difference between one ignorant with such things and one attempting to sweep something under the tapestry. But Seth also was on his side and could at least feel such an embitterment by what took place at Emerald Rest.

Presenter Holcomb continued with the nonchalant *I am in charge* attitude and smug look. "Well, excellent then. There is no need to rally the army yet. We will send a scouting patrol to…ahh…keep tabs on this black force—a foray of intelligence. We need more information on what we are up against. And maybe this mass of thugs only stopped at Emerald Rest."

Commander Steele now leaned over the table. "That was *our* castle, *our* people that those *thugs* ravaged and slaughtered. I will not sit by while they continue to ransack the lands and possibly even march on our gates. Need I remind you that those of Emerald Rest have stood on the edge of the frontier guarding the lands for over a thousand year now?" He over emphasized the word thugs, plainly mocking the royal presenter.

Holcomb fumed with barely controlled anger and stood up. "Commander, you will do as you are directed. Is that clear? *Need* I remind you who is in charge here? I speak on behalf of the king."

He looked around the table and crossed his skinny arms. "Now, send out the scouting patrol. Then, upon their return, maybe a fortnight or more we will reconvene to discuss the matter again."

After this fairly short bout came to a head and then dissipated, it was back to business as usual. It was as though the destruction of Emerald Rest was but a story in a book with no tangible impact. No real loss of lives, or territory, or forceful tread upon sovereign ground. It seemed that no one could, or maybe wanted to, relate to the real folk who were sliced open and smashed bloody. Maybe worse. At least not the royal presenter, while the rest of the assembly officials merely mimicked their newly perceived puppet master.

And the assembly eventually came to an end for this time. Once all of the members had left, Castym pulled Seth Garten off to the side.

"Seth, do me a favor. Have your men watch our good man Holcomb. And keep me posted on anything out of the ordinary or strange that they may see or hear. Let us prepare the scouting party to Emerald Rest, and double our patrols and their distances around Nuuroc presently."

"Yes, my lord," Seth stated as he nodded his head in agreement.

"And Seth," Castym grasped Seth's elbow at this point, "be careful, at least until we know more of what goes on. And help me alert all of the line commanders so as we are somewhat prepared...but do so discreetly."

Many burns of the candle later, Commander Castym Steele sat upon an old chair in his own chambers for the remainder of the evening. He pulled out the rolled parchment from his tunic and stared at the contents written upon it. There was at least one bit of good news on this day.

It was a ten-day old but clearly written in the old knight's hand. Wullyam, Castym's hidden connection to the Bastard Prophet, had informed him that Rory planned a visit to Nuuroc. And soon.

Chapter 16:

Shadows Emerge

"My valiant people, young and old, large and small. We are all strong and noble. I am here this day to speak of that which ruthlessly forces its mark upon us, and the world.

The Black Clans. The very essence-less minions from the Chasm...ones that claim to be of the Aylsh...and yet also persecute those kind and gentle folk...the First Folk. They have ransacked and murdered an entire village of ours, further mutilating those they butchered for sport. These kin of ours were even gruesomely displayed for us to find, to make us cower in our walls. These dark daemuns struck down that which was most hallowed, representatives of the Aylsh High Court. One being the Aylsh high priest himself—the Red Cloak, servants traveling here rejoicing over the Twelve Edicts of Lord Braxis. Good First Folk that trusted to us for their safety and protection. And then cowardly slain within sight of our dignified walls.

And last in this long list of grievous deeds, but never least, our most radiant beauty. Yours...mine...our queen. Murdered, butchered, raped, and left to slowly die a miserable, painful death.

These acts of aggression towards everything that Lord Braxis has created in his infinite wisdom and grace—they must be stopped. All means must be thrown against them, to stem this ugly, malignant growth before it spreads too far. The dark ones must fall. And they must fall far and in the most agonizing way.

This time in our very existence has marked us as those chosen to enact such a miracle, for us, for this world. Lord Braxis himself has granted the people of Kuhrzoth the power to wipe out this evil from where it has taken root...once and for all.

Now is the time that we take the path less traveled... The road to light and peace. That road must be taken through Isnuuthghor and the Black Clans. We must march there and wipe clean the slate from which they were brought. We must destroy them. And this must be done not only for you, but for the youngsters of yourn waifs. And their wee ones...leaving no doubts to this even well after we all find ourselves at the gates to the Outer Halls."

–Arterium's stirring speech to the people of Kuhrzoth prior to his expedition to the dark fortress of Isnuuthghor, circa the harvestspell prior to the year SA 1.

aramagrii knew that they were high up along the western slopes of the Rock Rim's Eastern Spires. The cold air swirled about them, occasionally speckled with small, fluffy snowflakes.

The day did not drop enough to make those amount to anything, but the night would be a different story. She could see the line of snow, and it was not much higher above where they were now.

They had not stopped to rest since leaving the Hulding village, which was nearly two days behind them. This day would soon dip towards darkness and they definitely would have to be within a place that shielded them from the elements by then.

The girl still had not spoken since those barely audible words at the village, but Zaramagrii could read her emotions from the look upon her face. Frightened, content, hungry, whatever that might be. The girl held up well so far, but her face showed her weariness at this point.

One more league of negotiating the rugged country and Zaramagrii found a nice overlook in the rocks. A stone ceiling jutted out above it and provided fair shelter from most directions.

It was not far above where a small stream cascaded down into a pool of fresh, cold mountain water. Ice lined the edges of it, creating an aesthetic, jagged outline between the rock infested shore and the water.

The wind was constant but the breathtaking view of the lands below provided Zaramagrii with a generous lookout. One that comforted her with the safety of the girl.

During the night, again the dark one practiced and played with the new-found sense she had discovered. Since capture by the Hulding, this had been very limited, but now she could creep about to her heart's content. And all the while she discerned her surroundings and the things that moved about.

While the girl slept, Zaramagrii could sense all of the night creatures as they flew, crawled, or walked nearby. It was nearly daybreak when she finally curled up near the girl and drifted off into a sleep filled with lucid realism.

She also attempted to maintain the special awareness while she slept. But she could not tell whether she was actually picking up on things in her surroundings, or just so focused on doing so that she dreamt it.

Visions of darkness and constantly being in motion came to her, whether she was running or fighting. At the end of it, she was suddenly looking up to see what appeared to be the golden rays of the rising sun trying to pierce a heavy morning fog.

She could see the tremendous gilded spheres of blurry sunlight with glowing rays coming down, shining upon some form or symbol. The symbol appeared to be that of a gleaming, four-pronged, silver spear that rose into the air. The dazzling brilliance was blazing from behind the outline of the hulking form of a figure, a man. But the visage could not be seen due to the streaming rays glaring at her.

At other times, she would see a lofty, stone castle of the Man-folk amidst an emerald sea of tall grass. The huge, marbled walls looked impregnable.

In either case, she was always running from something and towards what was in the vision. Always the scenes of majestic beauty as well as the black carnage of war and battle. Such were the things that were pressed into her memory upon awaking.

Then she broke free of the vision as she sensed a small animal...a fox taking a drink of water at the pool below.

Now fully awake, she quickly peered over the ledge. There it was, enjoying a cool drink. The bushy tail twitched a few times, and then it was gone. She nodded in smug satisfaction at the feat.

An icy kiss, just before the break of day, swept over the lands under the twilight and gently nudged her. The cold never bothered her at all, she felt refreshed by such a frosty bite. But she could see the girl momentarily tremble and tighten the furs about her head.

It was not long before the girl rose and stretched. She smiled at Zaramagrii as she pulled more furs up to wrap about her. Her hair blew in the wind and, for once, Zaramagrii observed the taut skin and muscle on her. Something not previously noticeable.

The past hardships have been good on her, and that meagerly weak look was barely visible now. She had been somewhat hardened through her trials. A little more of such a life, and this girl of the Man-folk would have the makings of a fine warrior in the rough.

Zaramagrii kneeled by her and carefully placed the slim, silvery dagger into the girl's hand. "Now you have to wait here for me. I have to get us a few things, but it will not take long. Do you understand?"

The girl gave her a couple of short, quick nods with a confidant grin. This was a noticeable difference compared to how she was when Zaramagrii first found her. With that, Zaramagrii made her way back down from the rocky ledge.

Zaramagrii spent more time gone than she planned on initially, but they needed provisions. Another animal skin would give them water for their travels.

She also contemplated things and thought about what they should do. The choices were many, and none of it was very clear. But her mother had told her to follow her heart...and what she saw.

Something did stand out from her recent visions. While trapping small game, she finally decided that they would head over the Rock Rim and then move towards the Free Lands and Kuhrzoth. To the seat of power, Nuuroc. At least initially.

As she approached the stream, but at a point much lower than where the pool was, she intended to skin the mountain squirrels. That would give them two skins full of water. This would at least last them a couple of days. But what she saw stopped all thought of this and froze her in her own tracks.

There, along the stream and nearly in line with their footprints from the climb through here on the way up to their ledge above, were several more sets of distinct tracks. Her thoughts briefly flickered back to the long times spent studying tracking, and how those imprints had stuck so freshly in her mind. Soft-soled boots—a group of them. And the marks looked distantly familiar. Similar to those of the warriors amongst her clan.

In the spur of the moment, things suddenly felt off. There was an odd and uncomfortable silence to the air. Now she could almost smell them, and they appeared to be heading right up to the pool just below the ledge, where the girl was at.

Then Zaramagrii's mind raced fanatically as she thought of the girl whom she left alone for so long. She began to sprint along the stream up towards the pool of water, carelessly bursting through the brush. Instinctively reaching for the dagger that was not there.

As she climbed up over the stone-encrusted ground and emerged near the trickle of water that ran over the rocks to splash down into the shallow pool, she froze in disbelief at what she saw. It was more an acknowledgement of what inevitably would happen based upon the scene before her.

Then it was as though she strode forward in slow motion, now crouched and with no weapon since leaving the dagger with the girl. Her mind told her over and over again that she could not stop what was fated to happen here. She was just too far away and the motions already had been put into play.

She recognized all of the Blackguards in the patrol, spread out before her now near the pool of water. There were seven altogether. Three of them were towards her right side. Another three were along the left, closest to the water, and with crossbows slightly raised. The patrol leader stood straight in front of her.

The patrol leader she knew to be Tworrhyx, one of those that jumped at the chance to serve the priestess in the newly reconstituted elite Blackguard. One of blind loyalty and allegiance to the point of utter destruction, with no remorse at any ordered actions regardless of what they entailed.

Yes, she knew this one and the rest, their type not of the true mentality and ways of the Black Clans. They were the perverted semblance of the dark ones. Tainted with some incurable malice.

And they all knew who she was, as no doubt they had been hunting her for quite a while now. The one named Tworrhyx merely stared at her and smiled wickedly, the curved longsword of black-hued steel in his right hand already raised high.

The girl at this point was the motionless center to the rushing crescendo of volatility that Zaramagrii saw and sensed all around her. That look of innocence in those large blue eyes within the shapely face, mixed with blonde hair being whipped about in the wind. Those eyes pleaded with her dark protector.

This was what was most haunting within the inner recesses of Zaramagrii's thoughts. The girl must have come down to the small pond while waiting for her to return. Maybe to get a drink of the cold water. What brought the girl down from the ledge mattered little, as she was now in the hands of Tworrhyx.

What should have been the most heart wrenching burst of raw emotion for any rational living thing was a moment in time that stopped for Zaramagrii.

The graphically torturous scene of the young girl being savagely gutted by the blade of the Blackguard captain—the cruel blade splitting her frail body nearly into two parts. The blank stare and gaping mouth awed by what the captain had done to her body also showed that the young girl's life essence had been snuffed out of existence within moments. Her face contorted in death's agony and surprise by a feeling never felt previously.

The cool droplet of bitterness squeezed free of the corner of Zaramagrii's eye. It briefly sparkled with a soft white glow, as though capturing the sheen from the white orb—then changing, subtly washed in a dark malevolent luminescence. But her features stood resolutely.

Captain Tworrhyx had been spouting cruel taunts while butchering the girl, but these were never heard by Zaramagrii. His mouth just moved in slow motion. A rushing cacophony engulfed her, drowned her.

In Zaramagrii's eyes, the girl was split in two with entrails dripping and bursting forth from the blade's vicious arc. Her blood still remained suspended in the air in several areas, just hanging there as an oddity for speculation. Frozen in space and time, as though Zaramagrii's wish to make this situation better had been granted and time stopped so she could act. Except it stopped several moments too late, after the girl had been disemboweled. Like merciless humor.

Tworrhyx now appeared to her to be frozen with his long blade fully extended after the bloody deed. The members of his patrol were standing motionlessly where they had been. All poised to shoot their crossbows or swing their drawn blades.

That moment standing on edge and portrayed before her seemed an eternity. The pain of seeing what befell the young girl only momentarily visited Zaramagrii. What followed that brief instance of deep pain was altogether something very different with far more greater consequence.

She felt as though, during what could only be called a pause in time, everything from her past burst forth into such a rage.

Injudicious priestess and all of her minions, ignorant, bloodthirsty, and thoughtless cowards!

How could any such living thing or sentient being that exists be so cruel and savage as to do what was just done? Is this what such a long lived, wise, and knowledgeable folk really stood for? What they did with all of that nature and ability? And what legacy and perpetual violence was to be inspired and spread?

She was so angry that she felt as though the very seams of her body and mind wanted to explode into every direction. The rage overcame her and she saw herself moving forward, wanting to do something horrible…no, terribly sinister to these fools who were her kind that she no longer cared to reckon with.

As she moved forward, she felt the very essence of the material and immaterial world around her warp and dissipate within long, billowing black shadows.

If someone were able to view her movement, all they would have seen was a black ghostly form outlined by dark billowing wisps of smoke that had engulfed her. The edges of her body outlined in a blurred red mist like glowing red embers in the middle of a stoked fire. It almost seemed as though the air around her had burst into some unholy red flame filled with darkness, swirling together.

Suddenly Zaramagrii stood next to Tworrhyx, along his right side. Her hand had already wrenched the blade out of his, the tip finding its mark through the neck between the top of his breastplate and helm. Sticky, warm liquid flowed over her and then she was beyond him. His body stood with the head rolling unnaturally backwards, and the eyes still staring where she originally had been standing. The expression on his face barely began to turn to that of shock and surprise.

Everything was happening in slow motion. Everything except for her. She felt very much alive and in complete and perfect form. Masterfully creating the most bizarre and grotesque retribution.

The three nearest the pool of water, with crossbows out, had not even fully turned to view the spectacle that was transpiring. It was as though they had been frozen in their places. One still held his mouth widely open, caught partway in saying something.

Again, Zaramagrii found herself moving past two more of the dark warriors with the captain's longsword, splitting open their abdominal cavities in one long, steady slice. Their eyes had not even the time to turn back to face what had disemboweled them before Zaramagrii finally stopped at her next target.

She had pulled this one's crossbow, which would end up sending its quarrel directly at one of the other three. Then the longsword sailed straight up through the dark one's chin and out the top of his head, gray chunks of brain and blood beginning to spray wildly out, but in slow motion and left hanging in the air about the head area.

Everything except her appeared to be standing still and frozen.

She had come upon where the other three stood, standing directly behind them. All of their faces still barely in the process of turning from where they had first seen her approach over the rocks. One swing that carried with it arcs of both black and red smoky trails sent two heads rolling sideways off of the bodies. The heads slowly spun into the air, still suspended off of the ground.

Then she sidestepped and ended up behind the final living Blackguard, with her left hand resting firmly upon his shoulder. The longsword found a gap under the backside of the leather cuirass and it penetrated straight up at an angle so as to protrude out of the top of the cuirass's front.

Then Zaramagrii held the still living one steady for a moment, on her blade. The quarrel, fired previously, struck the warrior through the eye and sunk deep within the socket, snapping his head back with the barbed point extending out the back. The blade ripped out of the body as it collapsed, grating the rib cage and making thick, dull clunks as it did so.

All that she had done—the bloody, gory work of art—now was spread out across the scene. As though time had reduced to the slowest trickle of its former self. But it continued to churn.

The world around her was normal again and she stared at the carnage. What she had not yet realized was all that she had just done—her movement throughout her vicious frenzy, the killing of the entire patrol—had only been the lapse of a fraction of a moment.

She ran to the young girl and held the blood-soaked body, as the tangle of entrails and chunky organs washed over her lap. The young girl's pretty blue eyes were open and blank, no longer full of the astonishment and fear that dominated them earlier.

Zaramagrii broke down and, for once, wept uncontrollably as she squeezed the frail body. Then she looked up as the surge of rage and emotion attempted to take her again.

Up she leapt, onto the dead captain's body.

The thing named Zaramagrii grasped the severed head and ripped it from the corpse. Zaramagrii began to pummel and beat the body uncontrollably, viciously slashing it until only small pieces were left.

By the time that what was once Zaramagrii finished with the bodies of the Black Clan patrol, she was completely drenched in blood with her hair matted and dripping. Chunks of flesh and organ tissue slid down her body, other pieces of grayish red hung from her hair.

Her eyes remained filled with swirling blackness and deep red surrounding the contrasting pupils. The left one aglow with unholy white brilliance while the right blazed a shimmering onyx hue. This metamorphosis was not as extreme as when she initially started in on the blood spree, but it still would have been unsettling to anyone seeing it. Yet, she was not satiated in the least.

The chaotic scene instilled a strong urge to vent justice where deserved, and yet all of the dark ones involved were now dead. But the need was there to inflict more of her pain and vengeance upon something. She did not know how she had done what she just did, but it had come naturally, and instinctively.

The acts themselves were completely emotionless, the spark that led to those acts was instigated by suppressed raw emotion. Yet the force of her aggression was like a deeply-buried, insatiable urge to do more of it, kill more of them.

But a thing had materialized from the rampage. An old and stifled memory painfully emerged within Zaramagrii as she fell to her knees while cradling the young girl. The twisted scene with the death of the young girl had brought this old nightmare foremost to her thoughts.

But this monster had taken part of her long ago, as she could not feel the emotion that was normally felt between mates, or lovers. Something had taken that, forever buried that pleasure of life in a deep, dark hole. The thing that took this from her had a face and a name, as she visualized the sickening act over and over again. It rushed upon her conscious and overwhelmed it.

It was almost as though the deadly encounter with the patrol and the loss of the girl whom she had come to feel something for had opened a dark door. And then something else forcefully pushed the blackness out of that dark door and into a raging flood, assaulting her completely. And now the injustices crept up through the window to her essence and would not stop. Unceasingly battering her cognizance of the world around her.

Indeed, there are some things within one's life that happen to find a place to hide, possibly instinctively to save and preserve one's rational thought and sanity. But these things never stayed away completely. Instead, the thing resurfaces, triggered by some unforeseen mechanism and then violently returns in painful realization.

If this thing, this monster, has never been sufficiently dealt with or reconciled, then it will tread just below the surface of normalcy. Ready to permeate all thought and emotion on a hinge. Until something causes it to rise, to emerge.

And the surface was truly broken for Zaramagrii, as what had happened to her when she was but a child replayed in her mind. That developing sense of chaotic justice might also have been a culprit in the process, but in any case, the face of her monster appeared fresh to her now. After suppressing it for so long.

The visions flooded through the inner recesses of her mind in bright, clear perspective. Her figment of loathing, one of the turo that had been gifted with the title of teacher and scholar had taken particular attention to her when she was maybe twenty winterfalls into life.

A turo, of which there were only so many, who had been blessed with the privilege of passing on knowledge, wisdom, and history to the young dark ones of the clan. The turo was named Nouryno. Unclouded images with those painful memories flashed through her mind now uncontrollably. The turo, his face, the things that he did to her.

She had been ignoring the looks and advances of her young would-be suitors for her whole existence. The interest in the other sex and their appendage just did not register with her at all. It was as though that sensation, feeling, or even need no longer existed within her. Like it had been carved out of her essence.

The turo had started by secretly taking her to one of the inner rooms of his abode where he would brace the door. He would always stand directly behind her, his hands on the front of her thighs while his thing pressed hard into her backside. As he asked her to speak to him about the things that she had been taught, he slowly caressed her thighs ever going in between them and working his hands under her gown. Dark ones did not bleed as women did, so they rarely wore anything constrictive around their private parts.

It was not long before Nouryno had his fingers inside of her, massaging that little button and slipping in and out. And then he began to force his appendage into her hard and long every time that he took her to the place, feeling as though he was splitting open her ura and making it so wet down there. His breath would be hot and salivating against the back of her neck as he moaned and fondled her barely emerging breasts as well as her ura from the front. At times he would softly bite and pinch her skin while doing so. This would go on for what seemed so long to her, until she could feel his thing inside of her spray his seed deeply and strongly. The whole experience seemed like yesterday now, even though it was more than sixty years ago.

The burning pain and anger of what that dark one did. At the time he had been her mentor and someone that she was to look up to, even emulate. She had been just a young one. The entire thought embarrassed her like nothing else as he had explored her tender body and knew its parts. And she allowed this to happen.

This feeling was why she had never approached her keeper, Ghenwari—not even her mother. Nouryno had confided to her that what they did, really what he did to her, had to be hidden. It was a secret experience in the Black Clan ways.

She was even more embarrassed after she learned what sexuality really was. How naïve she had been under the turo. She somehow had erased it from her mind, until now.

Zaramagrii felt as though many things were coming to light lately, to her judgment. How many other young dark ones of her clan had this turo touched with his wickedness? Now this formed into self-propelling relentless aggression, but more a calm storm that had to be allowed to run its natural course. That course now undeniably led back to Turo Nouryno. That meant going back to Clan Tharasvrul.

Maybe it was the fact that she had been unable to do anything at the time about what the turo was doing to her, she had been powerless. This was physical as much as mental.

Even if she had been able to kill the turo at the time, what would the members of her clan think and do over the circumstances? Would the clan society believe her that one of their extraordinary scholars, supposedly free or incapable of all wrong-doing, could have subjected one of their young to such vile acts?

Who would have been judged as in the wrong then? The perpetrator of the acts that only she witnessed, or her for the blood that stained her hands?

No, there was some other power definitely at play here, as Zaramagrii saw things anew from this point on. And everything that would happen would continue to bring clarity to this outlook. She saw things very clearly now.

As we will see later, this abuse at the hands of one of the clan's turo was yet another facet to her fate. The obliteration of feeling. Of mating. Of loving. The loss of such an emotion generously aided the pursuit of chaos, and that sense of justice born from the wrong that was committed. Without the constraint of love and sex, Zaramagrii was freed from what most carried as baggage throughout their entire existence. Because of this, most were relentlessly battered with it at every step and turn. But not she. Yet even this can leave a permanent scar of untold agony.

What collided with her now was the hardened, but compromised, tier of her clan's ways. Those ways to live peacefully, spiritually, and in commune with all other living things in the world. Now she saw that this was a fallacy, a lie within the bubble of her clan's structure that did not meet reality.

The harshness of realism was portrayed by the currency of its savageness. And this savageness was ultimately just the reality of existence. Things lived and thrived, sometimes by the death of other things. This included not only the creatures and beings of Zholryn, but also the forces of nature and free will that filled and governed them.

Zaramagrii kneeled with her buttocks on the heels of her blood-soaked leather boots. The world around her was spinning and filled with black wispy smoke, like a sweeping wind was fanning a fire set upon the very scenery. The carnage littered the ground around her, and she still could not believe that the girl was gone. The hatred for her people grew and seethed as she went dizzy with rage.

Several soft whizzing sounds could be heard faintly as the numbing rush of the circumstances overtook her. And then one of the blood caked arrows pierced high into her left arm with a meaty thud. The sharp pain pulled her back, her eyes returning to their usual shade. The left now was clear white and the right obsidian black again. No more glow.

She turned her head to look back as she reached up to grasp the haft of the arrow sticking out. There on the knoll, not a hundred paces from her, was a throng of Akhruuk. Several goblins intermingled with them, the green-mottled skin of their bodies, lanky in appearance, and oversized long ears sticking straight out from their heads.

The bows of the archers flipped back up for another volley. She broke off the arrow near to where it penetrated the skin, leaving the arrowhead inside her, then picked up the Blackguard longsword from where she had dropped it. She took up the silver dagger in the other, which was stuck in Tworrhyx's belt.

Quickly she sprung to her feet and began to sprint along the ridge, following the rocks to the south. Another volley of arrows clattered harmlessly behind her against the rocks as she ran. She weaved and dodged while hugging the rock wall.

Then the line of the ridge rose high enough to where she no longer had the choice of getting atop it.

Glancing back, she saw an oppressive, screaming horde of Akhruuk and goblins pursuing her. This was no mere scout party—she had been caught too close to whatever this small army had been up to. There had to be at least a hundred of them now, maybe more where she could not see. She had no choice. Skirting the slowly rising side of the rocky ridge would at least provide some protection. Worst case, she would have a solid wall that she could put her back towards for a final stand.

After what felt to her like a league or two's distance, she came to where the wall of the ridge turned very smooth and steep. It rose five or six times her own height, forming a jagged-toothed line set against the blue sky.

There were several more score of the beasts slightly to her front on horses, and even more behind them. More arrows skipped and clattered around her now as numerous archers lined up while the Akhru and goblin fighters continued on towards her.

Then she abruptly stopped, as her eyes saw farther down the wall. There appeared to be a huge wooden door or gate set into the rock wall several hundred paces from her. Pointy parapets ran along both sides with forms moving about the top. She could not tell who or what the forms were from this distance, other than armor and weapons gleaming in the sunlight.

Another arrow stung her outstretched thigh, making her wince from the sharp tug of the impact. One glanced off her forehead, snapping her head back sharply and momentarily causing her to see a rush of stars.

As Zaramagrii saw, more heard, the chains of that wooden gate open slowly, the horde of Akhruuk and goblins were upon her.

Now she could see that the majority of these beasts were Akhru barbarians, and not just fighters. She remembered the tales of her youth marking the barbarians as those carrying the heads of their victories on a chain around their necks. The barbarians were known for their hardiness and never-ending bloodlust.

Tiny shrunken heads of Braxis knows what swung wildly upon the chains around the necks of these Akhruuk. Their crude instruments, ranging from spiked clubs to rusty scimitars, whipped through the air. She spun as the longsword and dagger both found their marks upon Akhruuk. Four of them went down.

Then, as she backed towards the face of the rock wall, a blade pierced her side. The razor edge grated against her lower rib cage, causing her to buckle slightly. A spear tip pierced her leg just under where the arrow was imbedded. Up came her blades, sending three more of the brutes nearly twice her size to the ground.

Once she found her back against the rock, she crouched and spun her blades intricately about her, thus fending off several more dull weapons while slicing bloody cuts into several of the beasts.

Off in the distance, the line of Akhru horse warriors turned to face towards the gate. It seemed that Zaramagrii was just a passing sport to some of these creatures. They had really intended a battle with those behind the gate.

Now, in front of the gate, were at least three score armored warriors. The first line of them held dignified shields full of colors, shields as large as the men holding them. Behind these were many others with a mix of looming polearms. Farther behind these were yet more lines, one with crossbows and bows.

An armored mountain of a man strode through their ranks shouting orders. His mane of golden hair lit up in the sunslight. She could hear the deep but firm voice from where she fought amidst the din of steel.

Suddenly something made her drop to her knees, lightheaded and dizzy. With a high pitched ringing completely drowning out everything else. A large war hammer had tapped the side of her head as she glanced towards the men lining up. She did not even realize that an Akhru had achieved such a lucky blow. Less than an instant later, her longsword whipped back to thrust through its breastplate and out of the backside. This was achieved without her so much as turning her head.

One of the Akhruuk sounded a bellowing horn and those around her then moved towards where the skirmish line was forming. She saw the huge phalanx of shields lined up and slowly pushing towards the masses of Akhruuk and goblins.

Archers towards the back of this formation let loose what appeared like a black swarm of sparrows during harvestspell, and many of the mounted Akhruuk and goblins fell dead.

On came the phalanx. The chanting black forces now mustered and charged towards it. The screaming beasts hit the shields like a wall, a dauntless wall that held.

And then, with the ugly things up close, every shield in the wall parted in unison about the space of a foot. Sharp spears, pikes, and halberds shot out from their midst through these small gaps. Some of these took two or three of the vermin down.

Then the shields closed again and the tops dipped backwards and down to such an angle that those holding the shields appeared to nearly lay down. This exposed the myriad of arbalists and archers forming the next line, who in turn immediately let loose a deadly hail of fire.

Now the horde turned in confusion, nearly reduced already to a third of what it was. They began to back away from the phalanx.

But the men held their lines and continued to advance, all the while running through the tactics of the shield wall, the spears, and the rain of quarrels and arrows. They spun their line in a huge wagon wheel towards where the dark one weakly stood amidst dozens of bodies.

As everything began fading to black, swirling around her like the night, the mountain of a man with long golden hair and the armada of shields was suddenly there to catch her.

The world disappeared into blackness around her. The golden rays of the midday suns streamed about him and the towering banner trailing behind. The banner had a pure white background. A golden half sun stretched down from the top of the banner above a gleaming four-pronged spear. The spear rose into the air, with gold-colored, lightning bolt-shaped beams emanating down from the golden orb. Her mind flashed to the most recent vision that had filled her dark mind, awed at the crisp colors of it brought to reality before her.

The last thing that she remembered was the deep calm voice of the man saying, "It is all right, my dark child. You are in good company."

Chapter 17:

The Birth of the Harbinger

"The Man-folk upon horse have repeatedly provoked us into protecting only what is and has been ours for all time. These vile yuanhad of the Tenargone do not stop. They have no respect for even words of treatisement. And they do not honor anything other than the drawing of blood, albeit from whatever they deem to their whim. Such a people may truly not be called people, or even beings like you and I. Not even like those of a similar nature within the Free Lands or even Kuhrzoth.

These senseless and repulsive transgressions against us, the First Folk...those imbued with the unique blood, the very essence of Lord Braxis...only speak of the truthful and malicious intent of such ill wrought things. The only answer to such clatter is with the sword and lance...slashed and driven directly into the blackened heart of the beast itself...so that not even their young survive to populate the world with useless abominations."

> –The preceding speech of action given to the Aylsh High Court by Lord Vuranthegost before he led the Aylsh knights into victory against the Tenargone, circa the year SA 1515.

eanwhile, far to the east across Thaldeia, yet another of the ancient revelations would come to life and begin to take root.

The Gathering of Might was just beginning. This simplistic ritual was a ceremonial one that had taken place for more than a thousand years within the hill tribes of the Tenargone Steppes. Actually, the name Tenargone was also the traditional name of these folk of the tribes. The name of these fierce people.

They were mostly known as the Tenargone, as well as the hill tribes of Man. Countless members of the tribes now mingled and mixed together here at the Citadel, although they still maintained large swaths of their own blood. The life of these uncluttered and rugged people was set in the ways of their tribe.

The Citadel was the center of power for all of the hill tribes, as well as the seat for the tribal ruler known as *garuuk*. The most recent garuuk had met his fate, after maintaining a tenacious grip on what could only be called an impossible rein. For the hill tribes were a warring and violent kind, mixed with the likes of Man-folk and Akhru, maybe occasionally others as well.

They numbered nearly three score tribes and lived by sheer physical exertion as the measure of achievement, whether it was hunting or battle. Advancement as a civilization did not mean a thing to these hardened folk, while the spilling of blood determined everything.

The Tenargone Steppes, sprawled across southeastern Thaldeia, appeared as vast and open grasslands amidst rolling hills. Impressive rocky ridges filled much of the region, with large tracts of thick, bristly pine forests. These lands ran straight into the Eastern Waters, mostly bordered to the north by the Aylsh Kingdoms.

A natural buffer, an immense mountain range called the Range of Dulgannor, segregated the likes of Kuhrzoth and the Free Lands from these tribes. But there had never been any known strife between these lands and the hill tribes.

In fact, there was a good flow of trade between them. Most of this trade came and went through the only pass that straddled the Range of Dulgannor, named the Great Vale for how it looked as viewed from either end. On a good day with clear skies overhead, one could nearly see the far end when standing at the other. But that misleading expanse would take at least a score of days to cross, even though it was mostly flat and gentle.

To the south of the Tenargone Steppes, the rolling hills turned to sharp, rocky shores that berthed an ocean named the Roaring

Deeps. These frothed into the Seas of Anarchy not very far to the west, while meshing up with the Eastern Waters to the east. The Churning was a label given to the triangular swath of water off the southeastern shores of Thaldeia, caught between the currents of the Eastern Waters, the Seas of Anarchy, and the Roaring Deeps. These waters were so named for the seething and rushing whirlpools scattered over much of the surface, resulting in the maelstrom of strong currents.

What was amazing about the Tenargone was that there was not one tribe of pure Akhruuk, nor one of pure Man. They indeed were all mixed together and all spoke Tenargone, which was a very rough and simplistic language. Most knew the Common tongue. The Akhru language, even though so many of the tribes held Akhru blood, was not known by many nor used by any.

Yes, occasionally a full blooded Akhru might wander in and join this rudimentary people. Although most of the Akhruuk in these cases were actually wiser and more purposeful ones in regards to existence than the rest of their kind. But the preferred spoken tongue always swayed towards that of the Tenargone.

Ogryk Thundruk looked out upon the masses as they milled about. The center square of the Citadel was marked off with long poles stuck into the ground every ten paces or so. Flaming skulls danced eerily atop them, no doubt the remains from enemies or weaker members of the tribes who were found unfit to breathe.

Ogryk was an ardent massif of muscle, although smaller in stature than most of his kind. His long, shaggy, black hair was greasy in appearance and covered the deformed ears. They never quite extended completely and appeared as short, pointy nubs behind the small black holes of the ear canals. A monstrous nose poked out between sunken eyes, all under one huge, bushy eyebrow that held one too many longer, protesting hairs.

The Akhru features were well pronounced in the large, squared jaw. It jutted out around the thick, blackened lips—the lower one trying to reach up and smother the upper.

Nicknamed the Mongrel, Ogryk was no doubt one of the ugliest and most guileless beings across all of Thaldeia. The fact remained that the hill tribes, being a simple folk, held no bounds in regards to inbreeding. And this contributed much to the obvious physical and mental nuances within their kind.

Everyone was a warrior and shared such burdens, and they took what they wanted as long as one stronger did not stop them. In the eyes of the Tenargone, both man and woman, male and female, were considered equals.

In that same tone, there was no sympathy for the weak, regardless of the circumstances. Thus, man and woman alike had to stand their ground and hold their own. If this was not firmly adhered to, then one would not survive long. And every single tribesman would accept the results of such behavior and actions as those of righteousness in this alienated and dimly lit view.

But one fact remained true throughout the bloody history of this violent people. There had never been a female garuuk, ever. Not that there could not be, there just had not been. So the position of garuuk was relegated to being that of male.

Ogryk knew that the loss of the old garuuk meant a fractured alliance of the tribes, as the old one had barely managed to keep them together during his last ten-year. And the Duraghs, one of the oldest surviving of the tribes, now stood ready to challenge here at the Gathering for the title of garuuk. He knew that they had been waiting for such an opportunity.

Of course the Duragh tribe was also the most prevalent and numbered nearly twice that of any other tribe. Their current tribal head was one called Udath, who towered more than a good foot above Ogryk.

Udath was truly indiscriminate in his rulings and actions, not bothered one way or another by anything in particular. Except for his own power and domination. His gang of supporters were equally ruthless and acted even upon his barest whim.

Tribe Duragh was notorious for killing what they considered to be its own incompetent members, chiefly the elderly and the crippled. If one could not pull twice his or her weight, then the individual quickly became a flaming skull for the Citadel square and sustenance for the curs.

The truth was that they actually made a mockery of this weakness. Huge, muscled Duraghs would take their time in dealing death to the older ones and those crippled or maimed. And they did this killing in front of all as a spectacle for show.

Udath now boldly strutted into the square, flanked by four of his thugs. He loomed over these others with him, even though they were each at least six and a half foot tall.

The act of the Gathering of Might called for one who thought himself competent enough to be garuuk to step forward. To stand at the center of the Citadel square.

This individual was then viewed as the new garuuk, unless, of course, another offered challenge.

This display could also be done with an existing garuuk, if one from the tribes decided that he would make a better one. In these cases, the challenger was extremely mindful. For—even if he was powerful and bold—the gathered tribes might just kill him because they did not like the idea of the individual as their leader. This was known to have occurred in the past even before the challenger had a chance to engage the garuuk.

The term garuuk conveyed the meaning *all powerful beast* to those of the Tenargone. It was meant to befit one that commanded all, whether physically or just by reputation.

In a way, of course, one could consider this to be an immense fear outside of the obvious respect of one administered the title. But this was the way of the Tenargone. The one that led them had to be all-powerful, decisive…and feared.

The Duraghs were known for their use of great-clubs wrapped tightly with water-soaked leather strapping. These were usually laced with pieces of iron or even crystallized rock, sharp as razors.

Udath now carried one such club, resting it upon his shoulder. His rough-cut hide boots rode to his knees under leather breeches. His bare upper body was crossed with simple leather straps, attached to his belt with gangly iron rings. Udath's bald head was littered with the whitened, scraggly lines of old battle scars, the oversized forehead creating dark pits of eye sockets.

Udath raised both of his huge meat pads up to the sky, the club now resting against his leg.

He opened his mouth in a broad, crooked, broken-toothed grin. "My tribes…my strong ones…the time has come for me to be Garuuk." He paused and clenched both giant mitts of fists. "Your Garuuk!"

His four henchmen stood a few paces behind him and just looked on, captivated by the moment. But they knew that a small mob of Tribe Duragh waited along each of the sides of the square, in anticipation of any resistance to Udath's announcement.

But no such response came. The crowds, while not appearing overjoyed, just stood about and watched the center of the square. It may be that most of the lesser tribes already knew the Duraghs would assume control, astride a force just waiting to spring into action at the slightest provocation.

Most knew that there was not much hope, maybe none at all, in crossing the Duragh tribe.

Truth be told, except for the weak lashing together under the former garuuk, there just was not enough kinship for most tribes to put aside their differences or survivalist instincts.

And even those that had held accords now no longer honored them. With the death of the garuuk, so passed all former agreements made amongst any of the tribes. Whether between tribes, or among individuals. It did not matter.

That death sent out the unvoiced break in all prior things agreed upon. It was like everything was anew, and could be started fresh, with no cares as to the former arrangements. And what the majority realized was that it would take many of them to band together in order to defeat one of the size and power of the Duragh tribe.

At this point, even free and honorable trade was limited to but a few of them. And this still created enough tension to draw the occasional blood.

It would take one of more significance and persuasion, one of might and wile, to bind even two of the tribes together to such a point where they would stand side by side. This was lacking, but this was what was needed for the downfall of the Duraghs.

Ogryk stared on at the Duragh leadership as it gallivanted about the center of the square, soaking up the attention of the gathered tribes. Even they knew that Udath would stand uncontested. Here was the opportunity for a crisp, new beginning, but none would lift a finger against the Duraghs.

Ogryk now glowered in partial acceptance of what was happening, the events transpiring like the course of a swift current that could not be altered. He thought of his past and the loss of his own kin, from war and disease. His mother was the last to go, after painfully succumbing to some terrible malady that had struck down many within the tribes.

Across the way, not far from him, stood Imeekrey. The one thing that he had adored since childhood. A woman of his own sort, one of strength and virtue. She was as kind and tender as could be, while also a proficient warrior. Her touch had been his savior from many things. Whether embarrassment at his own lack of forthrightness and will to act, or even his sullen melancholy that he sank into upon the death of his mother.

Imeekrey's long, dark hair danced in the wind as her eyes found his. They displayed that warmth of love and familiarity that he was so accustomed to.

But there was a glimmer of sadness, or maybe hopelessness, in them as well. He knew that she felt the weight of what must come from this change of leadership. After all of the talks that the two of them had, and how he always spoke such vehement words towards doing the right thing for the tribes. And here was a chance that was silently slipping away.

Ogryk felt the sudden sting of that disappointment. He knew that she really was not disappointed in him, or at least never would admit such. But it was there in her face, smile or not. Those captivating gray eyes could not hide it. At least he thought that he saw it.

Ogryk reassured himself by grabbing the haft of the club at his side as he stepped over the line of the Citadel square.

Udath now stood with his back towards Ogryk, all of his goons crooning about their leader. None of them had even noticed the challenger yet.

The throng of people that lined the edges of the square looked on. The noise of the crowd went from mingled banter to a slow, questioning murmur as the Thundruk warrior took yet another step towards the center of the square. Towards where the new and self-proclaimed garuuk loomed.

Imeekrey's eyes went wide with disbelief at what she saw, and then fear set in knowing where this rising scene would lead. Her face contorted, possibly hoping that Ogryk would turn and see her anxiety, maybe even returning back to where he came from.

But he never faltered or even looked, too set upon his decision for once. Folk from all of the tribes now looked on, and Ogryk could not back down. If he did, then he would be the shame of the Tenargone. Not just his own tribe.

Clear visions of the past flashed through Ogryk's mind in those mesmerizing moments of the paces leading into the square. His mother and her undying devotion to him, always lifting him up upon a pedestal. She always saw the good in even the worst, and all of his fallacies appeared as gems in her eyes.

Even in her final moments, she told him to look forward and never back, not even to miss her as she would be there always. With their kind, the wind and the ground would contain their *kafa*, or essence. And hers would be right there alongside all of the rest of those before her, riding on the kafas of the esteemed steeds that had also passed on.

With the dull murmur of the crowd and several of Udath's men now wickedly smiling at the hopeful challenger, Udath slowly turned his stout frame. He did so with only one hand showing, loosely tucked into his belt. His right hand fell behind him, where the club now hid.

The two stood within a horse's length of one another, the very center stake of the square directly between them. Udath maintained his stance and grinned widely at his challenger.

"Why look here, my warriors! I have been challenged! And none other than Ogryk of the Thundruk, the Mongrel!" taunted Udath, leering at Ogryk.

Ogryk rose up slightly as his chest raised with a deep breath. He beamed with pride at what he was doing. In his mind, he would tell this behemoth of a brigand to walk away now or face his wrath, the wrath of the tribes.

But, at first, nothing would come out when he opened his mouth to speak. Then a long exhale and several nervous gulps.

"You...cannot... I mean to..." stammered Ogryk, who never could say exactly what he meant to say. The words felt thick now and his voice erupted with spittle and a high pitched whine. Then he blinked and shut his mouth.

Udath scratched his head with the hand that was on his belt. Then he let out a hefty laugh and barked. "Oh, so you think that you scare me? What was that? I cannot understand you, Ogryk Thundruk. Pull that horse's cock out of yer mouth and speak with some balls.

"Look everybody! Ogryk the *fool* is here to lead you. What say you to him? Is he even worth a fight?" Udath now half shouted his banter so that all could hear.

Ogryk drew his club out in front of him in both hands at waist level. By comparison, Ogryk's club looked to be about half of what Udath held. And it was just a plain, old club with no special adornments.

Udath's concealed hand then moved with a swiftness, which caused Ogryk to pull back his club in preparation for a swing.

Udath had just moved his club bearing hand out from behind him. As Ogryk brought his club around and straight at Udath's centerline, Udath's offhand sprang out and caught Ogryk's club, suspending it in midair directly between them.

The speed of Udath's swing of the great-club across from the side was so fast that Ogryk never saw it coming. It thudded into his side with a meaty whack, knocking the wind out of poor Ogryk.

Then Udath pulled it straight back towards where he stood, with the razor crystal shards slicing and dragging ragged bits of flesh out with it.

This pulled the unfortunate Thundruk towards the towering Duragh, nearly knocking him off his feet.

The pain had not even registered when one of Udath's thugs let loose another blow to Ogryk's upper back, the jagged iron barbs of this club tearing into his back and ripping chunks of flesh as it pulled back. Ogryk fell to his knees, unable to breathe.

Udath slightly turned the club in his hands and then swung again. This time the blow landed across Ogryk's head, knocking him to the ground.

Udath's rough sandal stomped down on Ogryk's hand, causing his club to roll off to the side and out of reach. Then Udath leaned heavily upon the hand, smashing it into the mud with a soft crunching and popping sound.

Ogryk screamed out in agony now, as pain flooded his entire body. Everything was drowned out by a high-pitched droning ring from the blow.

At this point Imeekrey was leaning far over the edge of the square, which had turned into a bloody arena. Her hands held her face as she looked on in horror at something she couldn't stop.

Udath looked down upon his challenger, still stepping on the hand and slowly dragging the sharp crystal shards of his club back and forth across various parts of Ogryk's writhing body. "So you want to be Garuuk? You thought that you could defeat me? How is this even so, my little weakling? And who would follow you?"

Then a rage overtook Udath as his eyes opened wide in a frown that threatened even the ground in front of him. And he began to beat and kick Ogryk back and forth across the square. Ogryk's body violently jerked and shook like a rag doll.

Imeekrey could no longer stand the horror of what was taking place and rushed in to Ogryk's side. But two of the Duraghs caught her and held her so that she was forced to watch.

Udath continued for a long time, until torchlight flickered across the blood-smeared ground of the square. The whole time, all of those gathered around simply watched. Whether this was in disbelief or just numbed comprehension, it mattered little.

Finally, as Ogryk's body rolled to a stop several paces from the excrement trench, Udath slowed to a standstill. He heaved and frothed at the mouth, eyes glaring with satisfaction at his handiwork.

The body was broken in many places, the face and head barely recognizable. But air still filled those lungs, as they sporadically moved. A low wheezing sound emanated from the mangled mouth or nose, maybe both. It was hard to discern one from the other.

With a propelling humph, Udath rolled the beaten body of Ogryk towards the stench of the cesspool.

"I now commit the body of Ogryk the Mongrel to his destiny— that of the great kingdom of all that stinks."

One final kick and the body rolled into the mess with a splash. Udath chuckled loudly and walked back towards the awaiting throng at the square, motioning for his henchmen to bring along Imeekrey.

As the commotion of the crowd slowly receded towards the stairs to the Citadel, the battered bloody form of Ogryk stirred within the pit. The stagnant urine and dung soup sloshed around him.

"Huuuuuuuummmmm," rasped Ogryk, his face twisted and smashed. This ended in a long gurgling sound, as broken bits of teeth and bitten off tongue flew out.

Ogryk's body was in such terrible shape that he could not feel anything at first. Long, slow throbs of agonizing torture began to wrack his form, and then even the slightest movement sent new courses of pain throughout each of his extremities. His twisted legs remained motionless, and only one good arm enabled him to pull his head partially up out of the slime.

The darkness was growing, but he knew that he had to follow the trench. It would lead him around the expansive camp and out of the lower side towards where the impressive River of Tears flowed.

At least he would be able to get out of this cesspool, even though none of his senses could decipher anything in regards to the stench anyways.

The journey to the edge of the camp, where the river could now be heard, seemed an eternity. But now Ogryk felt the cooler rush of air from being so close to the river's bed.

The hole that he was in slowly began to drop and, before he knew it, he was uncontrollably sliding down. He came to an abrupt halt in a gooey pile of what he did not even want to guess was. The fall had turned him onto his back. It took tremendous effort to pathetically roll back over.

Once in the shallow waters of the slow moving river, Ogryk could carefully pull his partially floating body along the shore. The frigid water further dulled the numbing agonies coursing through his beaten and broken form.

His mind could only think of getting far away from these lands, as far as possible, where he could die in peace. After the series of disastrous events, he could never face any of the tribes again.

His only thoughts fell upon Imeekrey. In the burning blur of the pain and misery, he could clearly see the hauntingly beautiful image of Imeekrey's face. This memory, this one good memory, would be what he would carry with him to his end. Blood-filled tears mingled with and faded into the cool water.

The pale light of dawn cast down upon the slowly wriggling form of Ogryk. His one good eye, which could at least partially discern things, took in the haze. The dimmed vision fell upon a small feeder stream that flowed gently down over him. Its serpentine form meandered up and away from the river's edge.

This would be as good a place as any, and probably far enough away from the tribes, thought Ogryk. He could crawl up there and find a sun drenched bank where he could rest until it was time. Time when the mighty steeds of the past came to take his kafa.

As he emerged from the shallow water, he unsteadily glanced down the length of his body. The sight shocked him and made him cough and hack up more blood and fleshy chunks. Tongue, lungs, maybe just blood-frothed spittle. His body was done.

The bony white of several jagged rib bones gleamed at him in the sun, an obtrusive swelling was forming down towards his stomach but a bit lower.

And his legs looked like broken branches partially covered in flaps of hide, with bony white protrusions here and there. New streams of blood squirted out from various places along his body as he came out of the deeper water.

It seemed like the entire day passed by before he found himself at the mouth of a small cave. The feeder stream lazily poured out of it. The banks turned to smooth, packed dirt as it disappeared into the darkness. Faded green grass beckoned to him. This made it that much easier to pull himself along, ever so slowly.

Ogryk could no longer tell if night had returned, as it was already pitch black where he rested deep inside the cave. He remained stretched over the cold, hard ground. His thoughts were lost in the delirium of his near-death state, with his head slightly elevated upon a small mound.

The cold crept up into his very bones, and that seemed to ease the pain and discomfort. But Ogryk knew that he was dying and had accepted that fact, alone and broken. The warmth of Imeekrey floated to him again, teasing him with such guilt.

Consciousness slipped elusively away from him and then the dim haze returned again, doing so several times. His breathing now wheezed and whistled heavily, sometimes slowing to a whisper. Scattering bubbles of blood occasionally formed from the mess that was either his mouth or nose.

There was movement from where the cave's mouth sat, although hidden within the darkness of the night. He vaguely made out a strange, murky bank of mist rolling across the dank floor. But this mushroom of air had a red-hued glow to it, with black tendrils dancing within. As summertide lightning would frolic and play through the puffy evening clouds.

As it grew closer, he could see a dark robed form swaying in the middle. But his weakness caused him to squint and furrow his brows, forcing his one good eye closed again. It must be a figment of his demise, a specter to haunt him for abandoning Imeekrey.

Once he was able to see again, the tall, dark form hovered in front of him, mostly concealed in a large foreboding cloak of blackness.

The red glow shallowly displayed some aspects of this apparent phantasm. A charcoal-colored split chin protruded out from the hooded head. Disturbing hands appearing as large claws were folded at the thing's waist. The skin of those hands made them appear as slender burnt pieces of wood left in an old fire pit.

Ogryk could not muster much to counter the image before him. "Ohhhgruuuuu." He coughed as blood and spittle ran from the crooked, mangled mess of a mouth. He could barely voice words. "Take me...fiend...if ya must and that is my end." He vomited a black glob at the end, as his words came out askew. Fiend really sounded like *fooeeen*.

The figure hissed softly and actually chuckled. The rasping, sharp notes bounced off the mossy walls. The dim echo grated on Ogryk's battered ears, making him cringe.

"Ogryk Thundruk of the hill tribes of Man—the courageous Tenargone. Warriors to the core."

Its hands unfolded and Ogryk could see the long, narrow talons on each finger ending in razor sharp points.

"I am not death here to collect on you." The head canted backwards a little, showing two dull red beads of fire inside. "I am the light in dark places, and I bring untold promises."

Ogryk no longer feared what was coming. "What...you want?" he weakly rattled as more an uncaring response than a question. Already his mind was partly galloping across lofty, windswept plains atop a magnificent steed. He could feel the thick, black mane in his hands as his fingers mimicked his vision on death's door.

"Hear me Ogryk. I am the Ancient One," voiced the form. "You have the power of the beast within you..." The sentence trailed off as an abominable hand passed over the mangled form of the Thundruk warrior.

"Man-thing, hear me, as I have come for you. I can mend you and make you whole again.

"As well as all-powerful... All would fear you—your enemies would be wiped away with a mere finger's flick from you.

"All of the Tenargone would rally to you due to the immense and far-reaching power you would possess."

The Ancient One paused to let its words sink in. "The lore of the Old Ways foretells of you rising up and assuming the dark mantle.

"But heed my words, for you must swear your fealty to me forever, no matter what. To your dying breath and then beyond.

"And do not forsake me or this vow, or you and your kin will forever live in fire and pain. The suffering would be all terrible. So tell me, lump of flesh and blood, what say you? Vengeance upon your tormentors…strength and might to your people…honor and fame to your kind? What is your word?"

Ogryk looked up through his one bloodied eye, and that was but a hazy view of dimness. Blackness was overtaking him and his mind was playing games with him and what appeared around him. Even now the long, green grass of the steppes caressed his body with a soft touch. The sound of the mighty hooves all around him, galloping across the dew ridden ground.

The black form whispered one more morsel to the dying hillsman. "Do not forget about Imeekrey, who you left with the Duraghs. What do you think they will do to her…with her? Already it may be too late."

The Ancient One trailed off to strengthen the intent.

This brought Ogryk back from the brink, in a hazy, fevered bout of both anger and sadness at the thought. He quietly whispered yes to something that he barely knew, but the image taking over his surroundings ever so slowly created an urge to live and to do something about what was done to him. And Imeekrey. If only he had had the strength to do something then, at the time. But what of her now?

As the hoarse whisper of the yes echoed sharply against the cavern walls, the tall form of the Ancient One moved.

Both of its hands hovered over the form of Ogryk as an eerie red glow began to issue forth and downwards towards him. Streams of the black tendrils, basking within red haze, appeared to penetrate straight down into the torso of the mortally wounded Thundruk.

Ogryk began to scream from what those things did to him. The force and darkness that gripped his very inner being started to rip and tear him inside out. Bones snapped and cracked as his stout frame changed.

Such agony was one hundred times worse than that which the Duragh leader had done to him. But sometimes one accepts the price of retribution without really understanding the consequences or, worse yet, what that does to the being itself. The screams pierced the encroaching dawn but were lost in the high winds of the Steppes outside for none to hear.

§ § §

It had been thirteen days since Udath Duragh took his place as garuuk and beat that one nicknamed the Mongrel to death. Or so he thought.

Strong gusts of wind and dirt ripped through the Citadel and the surrounding encampment, causing the loose pieces of the hide shelters to violently snap and crack. The skies darkened with the coming night. Late harvestspell was bringing the first bouts of angry, stormy breaths across the lands.

The Citadel was a simple rock walled chamber that rose out in the middle of nowhere. Surrounded by beaten down and trampled grass, it was large enough to allow for sufficient gathering room where representatives from all the tribes could huddle. Chiseled stone stairs rolled down from three sides of the citadel. These were long and lazy steps, and only rose to the height of a man once they joined to the base of the Citadel.

Of course, the honored square ran straight out from the center set of stairs. This was considered the core of the lands, where the garuuk dealt with his people. But the majority of the tribes maintained their lands and holdings all outside of and surrounding what was claimed as the center of power for the tribes. Garuuk territory. And even these lands were not that distant, each of them within a score of days' ride, at the most, in any direction.

The night was well into its own, and most of those who had taken part in the festivities of the Gathering of Might had retreated to their own abodes long ago.

The tribal heads had already taken their leave, except, of course, for Udath. Garuuk.

He stood at the entrance into the Citadel and looked out upon his lands and his people. All he could see and beyond now belonged to him, and he would ensure that it stayed that way. Tradition claimed that the garuuk's tribe would assume the Citadel, the heart of the Tenargone.

Within a fortnight or so, the Duraghs would pick up and move inwards to where the citadel sat. The tribe of the previous garuuk would be forced to move. They could go out and claim new holdings. Or they could relocate to the lands where those of the new garuuk had just moved from, but this would be at a price. If this was done, then the former garuuk's tribe would be living on borrowed lands.

Udath looked down and saw several of his warriors now positioned at various points that led up to the Citadel. They rigidly stood and watched out into the darkness, which was partially illuminated by the many flickering torches and fires. The high winds of these plains whipped about and scattered tiny sparks of fire as it did so. Large, gaping holes of gloom remained throughout the various islands of dim light as shadows whipped about as fast as the wind itself.

The sharp raining thuds of a galloping horse echoed dully in the distance. At first it had the low rumble of thunder, Udath thought. *Who would be out riding at this time of night? Maybe one of the guards coming in to report?*

But Udath knew that none of the warriors would ride all the way into the Citadel. That would be beyond obedience, and near sacrilegious. They would do as accustomed and leave their mounts near the outer posts. Each tribal camp was set up in a large circle with inner and outer posts spaced apart within all of the hovels and tents, where warriors would stand watch and be prepared to react at a moment's notice.

This semblance was even maintained when the Gathering concluded, but only with a handful of warriors from each of the tribes. This was more as a token showing of the tribe's support for the garuuk.

The monstrously large black horse and rider trotted into the square and to its center, a place normally reserved for only the garuuk. The giant beast looked to be twice the size of a normal steed. The Tenargone were horse masters. But they were accustomed to the smaller Steppeland ponies, although uniquely agile and fast. These wondrous beasts could ride circles around the larger destriers known as Thoerne war horses.

As Udath descended the stairs, he could see fiery red tendrils emanating out of the horse's nostrils as it snorted a chilling rattle of iron chains. The beast's eyes dully glowed a reddish hell. Now the scene before him had his attention, and he firmly gripped the great-club slung over his back as the hairs on the nape of his neck rose in tingling apprehension.

The black-clad rider slowly dismounted and stood at the very center of the square. The rider's mount turned briefly and then faded to a thick stream of ashes into the air.

The huge figure towered well over Udath. The armor was a dullish black color and had fiendish points, edges, and spines all around it. A daunting scabbard hung low at the side.

Udath eyed the apparition as though it did not exist. "You, thing, be gone now. 'For you are cut down to nothing. I am Garuuk, and I command this so."

Then he noticed that what he thought were black gauntlets were mostly the skin of the man, if it could be called that. The skin looked as black as the night, with long, shiny nails extending off each of the fingers. Two red orbs glared out of the blackened helm where eyes should have been. The opening showed little else of the head.

By now, two of the Duragh henchmen had lined up on either side of Udath.

The thing stood completely motionless for several moments. It seemed that even the wind died down.

A deep, guttural voice laced with haunting echoes growled, "There is no garuuk. No king, and no almighty one. There is only I. I judge, I cast, I grant. None other."

The rider in black eyed one of the poles near the foot of the stairs that led up to the Citadel. A slim naked form hung upside down by the feet, lifeless. Even from the distance in the dark, the gorgeous long hair and face of Imeekrey could be seen in the torchlight as it sputtered in the wind. Blood trailed to the ground where it pooled into a dark paste. The body was ghostly white after draining of its precious oil for so long.

The wind picked up violently now, and a tattered dark cape flapped all about the black rider.

Udath nodded his head once, and this sent his four brutes on a slow, methodical advance towards the figure.

Several members of the tribes began to gather on all three sides of the square, awakened by the commotion. They stared on with questioning gazes as the Duragh four stood only paces away from the lone horseman. But they looked like dwarves compared to the rider, all being even shorter than Udath. Their weapons had already been out and were pulled back to swing.

The next move was so blindingly fast that all four of the brutes appeared to continue standing where they had been.

The rider's blade arced out so quickly and smooth from the sheath, that all four of the Duraghs remained motionless. It was as if the blade had missed them. But then all the heads began to slowly slide forward and tumble to the ground amidst geysers of blood. The bodies eventually crashed downwards in crumpled heaps. The black rider remained motionless with the large blade out to his side. The blade had been so swift that it remained clean and free of any blood at all.

Garuuk Udath cried out, "To me, my warriors. Quickly!"

But none so much as moved, and all those that gathered continued to stare on.

Udath raised his razor-rock great-club and defiantly roared at the form, "Who are you that comes into my lands and threatens me?"

The black rider methodically removed the large helm, letting it fall to the ground. The face of Ogryk stared down at Udath, but then it was not the Ogryk of old.

It was different, or maybe twisted. The skin appeared all gray with large black swaths cut through it. The red beads of eyes glowed from more than just firelight. When his mouth opened, the hole displayed large fangs across both lower and upper jaws. These appeared shiny and gray.

Udath now knew that his time had come. "You... You... I destroyed you and kicked you to the wastes of our people," he cried. "You cannot be alive."

The figure looked down and grimaced. "You once knew me to be Ogryk. But I am anew, and I am returned."

In one smooth action, the rider known to be Ogryk stepped forward. As Udath's great-club swung, one of the rider's hands stopped it in midair while the other shot out and gripped Udath by the neck.

The Duragh's feet now kicked frantically several foot above the ground. He gurgled and choked from the tightening grip on his throat.

"Now, Udath, I am known as Ghurvoor Nagam." And with those calm and evenly spoken words, the large hand slowly squeezed until the flesh oozed from the fist like a squashed worm.

The body slowly stopped jerking as the hand gripped the spine of the neck. Then the other hand took hold of Udath's chin and tore it upwards and off, detaching the head completely. Ghurvoor Nagam tossed both bloody pieces far away into the wind.

In Tenargone, Ghurvoor Nagam literally translated to *dark rider of death*. The name was also known in legend of being the

Dark Rider that brought death and destruction wherever it rode. One that carried forth an executioner's sense of diplomacy to the enemies of the Tenargone. Even to those who had never been introduced to the hill tribes. Such a figure in the legends of the Tenargone was a mysterious hero to them, especially as they grew from a very young age. A figure of awe and reverence.

Within a ten-year, this leader of the tribes would become their revered Dark Rider and would carry such as a title that bore a smothering weight across all of Thaldeia. Especially with those of Man-folk within their scattered kingdoms. When, oddly enough, the Tenargone would refuse to trade with them. When the Tenargone refused to honor the presence of any but their own kind on their sacred lands.

The black figure now stared out at the people of the tribes as they gathered around, all silent in the howling wind. "Bring me the tribal heads, here to the Citadel. You have until dawn of a new day to do so."

At the crack of that last word, several groups of those gathered could be seen hurrying off into the darkness. Ghurvoor Nagam quietly walked towards the stairs. He stopped near the body of Imeekrey, silently staring at the carcass with his head bowed.

After several moments of silence, he spoke long forgotten words of an even more ancient language. To the astonishment of everyone, the beaten and abused body suddenly burst into a white hot glow. Then it was consumed quickly and turned to nothing but flaming ash as it blew away into the wind.

§ § §

It was the time during morning where the duo suns were not yet risen but light had been cast all around. None had seen the one called Ghurvoor Nagam since he had disappeared inside the walls of the Citadel under the darkness of the night.

All of the tribal heads had gathered in the square, the Duragh leadership standing at the center. They stood in front of the stairs awaiting the mysterious rider of the night. What remained of Udath's head now adorned the centermost pole. The body of Imeekrey and the others who had been slain were gone, only black stains left around the square to indicate that they had been there at all.

Ghurvoor Nagam strode out of the Citadel and down the stairs. His helm was still removed and all could stare at what he was.

His huge form stood tall, well above even the Duraghs. There were three of them, with the one appointed as the new Duragh tribal head by Udath set forward of the other two. The representatives of the remaining tribes solemnly waited behind these three.

By now, thousands had gathered around the edges of the Citadel square without even so much as a cough. These Tenargone from all of the tribes mixed together freely, but mostly within a heavy cloud of uncertainty that was thick as fog about them.

Koravek, the one appointed as the Duragh tribal head by Udath after becoming garuuk, now folded his massive arms on his chest and stared at the black form with contempt. "What is the point of massing us here this morn, Ghurvoor Nagam...or Ogryk? Whoever you want to call yourself. I am now rightfully Garuuk."

The gaze of Ghurvoor Nagam never faltered and remained fixated straight forward, as if waiting for something. But he did not speak a word. The tattered black cape snapped in the rising winds as though it was alive and trying to escape its master's back. His right hand slowly raised out in front of him, with the palm facing skywards.

Not being able to stand for what appeared as insolence towards him, Koravek breathed heavily with anger. He then stepped forward while gripping the cruelly large scimitar.

But then Koravek stopped mid-stride as Ghurvoor Nagam's right hand slowly squeezed into a balled fist.

Uncomfortable sounds erupted from Koravek's mouth, as well as his head. It almost looked as though he was trying to fight off some evil menace around his temples, both arms now flailing through the air.

Then those gathered around could see his head begin to shrink, as though the sides were caving in. The eyes bulged and Koravek screamed.

With a sickening pop, his head completely collapsed into itself as the skin was torn and fragments of bone and brain burst out. Blood flew everywhere.

The two supporters with Koravek began to act in the same fashion as Ghurvoor Nagam stared on, relaxing his fist and then slowly clenching it again. Within moments, the three were headless corpses laying amidst blood, tissue, and brain.

Ghurvoor Nagam stepped forward now, through the still pulsing pool of slop. He moved directly in front of the remaining tribal heads. His heavy, black boots glistened as they swam through the gore.

Even in the daylight, the eyes of the black rider still held an eerie red sheen, similar to how the eyes of felines shone and reflected light. The blotchy gray and black flesh almost looked as though it had been ripped apart and then sewn back together again.

When he spoke, his voice was low and deep, but reverberated out amongst the entire crowd. "My fellow Tenargone, warriors of the Steppes. There will be no more Garuuk. The age of separatists—of stubborn tribal egotism—is gone, and a new time is before us.

"I am here to take you to your glory and might…as one, not as many. I will not falter, or hesitate. My strength will never diminish, but only grow stronger and stronger.

"You fear me, and you have every reason to do so. For I am death. I am your death…eventually. But you can chose that day, and make it very distant, by following me and taking your place in this world. I will show you what was meant to be for us. Together we will carve out our kingdom and make our destiny."

He paused as he slowly turned to look at all of those gathered along each side of the square, striding through the body of tribal heads. "But all masterful things must have a birth—a beginning. And birth must be done through blood."

His gaze went to the throng off to the side. "Lhofareg Zhanqur, you come forward." And out of the crowd emerged a tall, muscle-bound lad with a large blade hung at each side.

"You are now leader of the Zhanqur tribe. Only we now consider the Zhanqur tribe as the *Ushnere Tyat*. And you, Lhofareg, are general."

In Tenargone, Ushnere Tyat translated to mean *first military order or group*.

Lhofareg's eyes beamed with recognition as he stared in awe at the new head of the Tenargone.

With that, Ghurvoor Nagam went down the line and called out one mighty warrior after another from each of the remaining tribes in similar fashion. He instated these as the new military orders. All except for the Duraghs.

The former tribal heads still lingered about the square, now frantically searching the faces around them. The look upon each of theirs begged some semblance of their former recognition to vault forward. One stepped out and approached the black-clad form of Ghurvoor Nagam.

"My Garu—" he quickly stopped himself with a swallow. "My fearless one. You have left those heads of the tribes with nothing. What are we to become?"

Ghurvoor Nagam calmly stated in a tone that both soothed and ordered at the same time, if that was even possible. "My elders and wise ones, fear not. As I have said before, a mythical birth must be done in blood. It is time to cleanse us of the old." He raised up his arms ardently as he spoke the last words. "And that blood is yours."

As he uttered the last of it, all of those gathered now appeared empowered by the proceeding words of action and inspiration. With a loud clamor and rush, those elders that once were named as the tribal heads disappeared under the fury of hundreds of their own kin.

Not long after the bloodlust had been satiated, Ghurvoor Nagam stood high and commanding atop the stairs in front of the old walls of the Citadel. His look and gaze commanded the silence of all, and within moments one could hear one's own breathing.

"My fearless ones, you have a task afore you now. The first one of many. This one to prove who you are.

"Go now to the Duraghs, and let not one of them survive. For we shall not have thieves and backstabbers amongst us…and that is all that they are. Go and spill the blood of every last one, all the men, women, and the young included. *Butcher* them all.

"Then you will send out representatives to your kin in your lands and all will come in so that we can begin anew…and we will regroup and be even more powerful. Go now and do as you are commanded!"

And then each of the appointed generals amassed his warriors and together they all rode hard for several days to where the Duragh tribe lived. Within a ten-day, not one was left alive and the largest tribe of the Tenargone simply ceased to exist.

What followed that massacre of their own was an elaborate reorganization. Ghurvoor Nagam brought in all of his people to live as one in a huge circle. He called it the Wheel of War and labeled his people as conquerors. He now commanded more than thirty thousand Tenargone warriors.

Within two score of days, one man or possibly thing, did more with the hill tribes of the Tenargone Steppes than any other throughout history. And the tribes grew, as he declared that every capable woman would stay with child for the next twenty or more years. He also brought new and previously unknown tactics to the training camps, as well as creating master forgers to craft unbreakable weapons and armor.

And this would not be the last that would be heard of these people, not by the mighty shot of a longbow.

§ § §

The cold winds of winterfall now crept throughout most of the reaches of Thaldeia. Snow was blowing higher up towards Oshghrul, but only a particularly dry chill covered the vast valley near the ruins of Emerald Rest.

Rha the Lightwalker stared out across the valley at the thousands of glimmering fires of her huge army. Her tall, lean form now appeared mostly as that of a woman. But what could be seen of her skin radiated a subtle white glow under a nearly translucent sheen. She stood within the shattered remains of a tower, the jagged remnants of the walls rising and falling against the moonlit backdrop.

No army would ever prepare to march for war at this time of the seasons, with the frost and snows setting in. Any reputable martial contingent would be at winterfall quarters. So it would be fair to reckon that none would ever suspect such a thing either.

These creatures, *her* army, worshipped her like a goddess, and they would do anything for her.

Rha's emotionless, methodical thought process now careened down the road of conquest and her sole purpose, to raze Nuuroc from existence. This was what the priestess stated as the first act in a very long and enjoyable play.

Since her banishment within the elemental realms, particularly the one of light, what were normal feelings and emotions became warped. Instead, she saw only the need to exact pain.

But what she saw as pain was, in her truth, a final act of mercy. For the extreme agony that she had spent years enduring, before it swept her clean, now remained only as a cold, wicked callousness of its former self.

Rha considered what Priestess Sahrya had promised her. An eternity of subduing and inflicting agony upon everything in her path. Sahrya had granted her freedom from the realm of light and brought her back to Zholryn.

Albeit somewhat changed, she now felt as though she was a savior, the savior of Thaldeia. The priestess had confided in her the secrets of the lands, and how the ancestors of Kuhrzoth had imprisoned her—banished her to her elemental prison. All for her trying to do the right thing. Everything that Priestess Sahrya said made so much sense.

In truth, Rha's mind was so warped from her experiences that even she could no longer remember what she had been banished for. It had all disappeared somewhere in the two turns that she had endured in worlds where a thing of flesh and blood just cannot exist. She had to rely upon what Sahrya told her, the gaps within her own memories filled in by the priestess.

As her past vanished, her physical form began to adapt to the rigors of the new environments. She became more a being of energy than of life itself. This transformation stole her mortality as well.

It had been the year SA 1280 when Rha, formerly known as Rhadelle Yorrow, was thrown into banishment. She just turned her twenty-fifth year and had studied the arcane arts for nearly her entire life, already a powerful wizard.

What she did not know was that her father, also her teacher, had sealed a vow with a powerful creature known as the Dark One when she was much younger. It was a promise of untold arcane might granted to him, and thus to his daughter. But this came back to haunt him as the vow came to pass on the morning of Rhadelle's twenty-fifth birthday.

The Dark One returned to collect on the vow and took Rhadelle away. But before it did so, it whispered the designs for the girl to her father. And this made the man mad with such hate, both for the Dark One and also himself for foolishly agreeing to the deal. And then, what was a father's life—his heart—vanished to another world.

This caused him such grief that he lit himself on fire through his arcane abilities and slowly died in mortal agony. It appeared that this act was to punish himself for what he had done and somehow purify his essence within the hellfire.

But this was fate, and had been foreseen and planned all along. For this was what forged Rhadelle into Rha the Lightwalker, the one who would lead the Thalroan—what the priestess called her horde of darkness. And this had been the intent of the Dark One all along.

No conscience now. No fear or knowing of any kind of pain or misery. Just the being of energy that pulsed with an essence. But an essence that no longer was governed by mortal power. One that was as hollow as her physical form had become from the elemental realms.

She needed a powerful entity to shape and direct her drive and need to purify or cleanse the seeds of man. And that entity was Priestess Sahrya, the one that pulled her from worlds immersed in air, fire, electricity, and light.

Here in this world, where nearly everything was somehow tainted, she was the sole beacon of guiding energy who could set all of the tainted ones free. This was what the priestess had confided in her, and now held her up high and potent to go do. It was her duty. To save them all. According to the priestess, this had been foretold by the divine. Her task at hand was divinely inspired and was written within the very fabric of existence.

The valley below had a fairly high wall of felled trees that ran from the corner of Emerald Rest out and across to the other side. Here it tied in to more roughshod log barricades. The towering joutuun had accomplished all of this work within half a fortnight, stripping the trees and then planting them top first, deep into the ground. All were lashed tightly together.

Now her dark army had a genuine advantage from this fortified structure, as it led all the way back into Oshghrul. The long valley running all the way up into the Fallen Lands was like an extensive highway where the foot soldiers and weapons of war could easily move.

A large figure strode down below, heading in the direction of the crumbled tower. The monstrous right hand of Rha appeared near the top of the rampart leading up the wall. It was not long before Gauth the Bloodmonger stood at the top of the stairs.

Now Gauth was a cross between an Akhru and a mountain joutuun. It was known that his father died in the violence of his conception, such was the tempest of the rapture between a joutuun and an Akhru. His mother perished from his birth, due to such an enormous newborn.

And nothing satiated his bloodlust it seemed when engaged in combat. There had been no rival, not even a group of them together, worthy enough to defeat the Bloodmonger.

Standing slightly over ten foot tall, his muscle-bound frame was lithe as a cat. He always wore the lightest traces of armor so as to exploit his vast speed and flexibility while fighting. This night, he wore a simple leather cuirass that covered his upper body. A skirt of scaled maille panels hung down to just above his knees. A cruel double-edged sword, the size of a lance, was strapped on his back.

"Lightwalker, the main force is ready." His growl echoed throughout the walls as he spoke.

Rha turned towards him, her eyes slightly aflame. "Tell me, General Gauth, how many comprise our army...that are ready?"

"Near one hundred ranks, each from seven hundred to a thousand strong. This does not include our engines of war and their crews."

"And what remains? We will not give up our foothold here."

Gauth scratched his side with one clawed hand. "No, my Light One. We leave many behind, a good fifty ranks here. And there are many more back up the valley."

She nodded slightly in approval. "Remember, Bloodmonger, the tactics of the field that we shall use."

"Have no fear, my lady, the orders are given. The march will be split. One third as vanguard, with the majority behind. Several skirmishing groups will foray along the edges with occasional long range probes. Our movement will be secure, as you wish."

"Excellent, then we march for Nuuroc at dawn." Rha stared down at the glistening fires.

She reveled in knowing that soon she would be casting her own judgment upon the impure spirits of Kuhrzoth. *It would begin with those.* A smile slowly raised the edges of her mouth and the translucent glow brightened.

Chapter 18:

Premonitions Prove

Themselves

"The lands, the people, all must be protected. We have amassed our fortunes of gold and gems through the glory of the sword and axe. We have had the fortune of shaking the very foundations of this land with the thunder of our horses, and our boots.

Now there comes a time when the burden falls upon us to protect that which we call home, the very lands that have provided us the base to go out and do what we do best. I for one will not allow the evil that I have sought out to destroy for gold and glory to come back to my very home to lay its own violent wastes. And I will not tolerate that evil laying waste to those homes of my brethren. You now must stand up with me. Together we can instill a peace that these people, our people, have never really known. Our past has brought that gift to us for this day, a gift that we can give to our people. What say you all?"

> –Lord Razorrock, the very first
> Knight of the Wild and the initial
> formation of the Wild Order, circa
> the year 135 BA.

Zaramagrii woke to the sight of a gray-haired woman silently looking upon her with a radiating smile. While the woman appeared to be a caregiver, she also wore a thin bladed longsword strapped to her side.

Her bed was a cozy softness unknown to her, but tiny, feathered plumes rose every now and then to give away the goose down. It was a fair-sized room with the door partially cracked open. The towering oblong windows allowed the light of the duo suns to brighten its features through miniature crisscrossed designs that were carved into the shutters.

It was difficult to open her eyes at first, even slightly. She still had to blink repeatedly while they adjusted. Tears filled them from the effort as well as the light.

Then the memories of the battle with the Akhruuk and goblins came back to her. The innocent young girl butchered indiscriminately by the Blackguard. These memories appeared vividly, and yet seemed so distant now. And she was famished beyond belief, with a thirst to match.

Zaramagrii was dressed in a light linen gown and nothing else. The blackened ring still rested upon her finger.

Then she remembered her wounds. Instinctively she winced, realizing that she may have moved too quickly to touch those areas. But all that she found were bruises where they had been. No wounds or protruding arrow shafts. Not even a scar to show.

"Are...you...all right?" The woman slowly articulated her words, as though she was speaking to a young child.

Zaramagrii stared at the woman's face, carefully reading her countenance. "I understand you perfectly. And yes, I am fine." Then she looked over at a chair beside the bed, which contained a pile of clean clothing. Her leather halter was laying on the very top, and the hafts of the Blackguard blade and silver dagger poked out from underneath.

The door swung fully open and the large man with the golden hair walked in. He wore dark leather pants with a hauberk of padded chainmaille over his muscular upper frame. The bulging strength in his neck made it appear as though he just finished strenuous exertion, but he was very relaxed. A big furrow creased his brow while his face lightened with a wide smile.

Zaramagrii noted a strange sereneness within his countenance. The face could give off a false impression of cretinous idiocy to some, but she saw beyond this and into the crisp, stark mirrors of his powerful sea-green eyes. A gleaming battleaxe hung at one side, an exceptionally long dirk at the other.

The tone of the man was almost soothing, "My dark child, how are you? You had quite a few wounds when we found you. I am Rory, and this is Mena. Welcome to Dawn's Glory."

Zaramagrii looked intently into his eyes at first, as though struggling to discern something. But her eyes, as well as her thoughts, were still cloudy from the deep sleep.

She flashed her eyes quickly and looked away before speaking. "Tell me, what does the banner…your banner…mean?"

Rory thoughtfully stared at her while he lowered himself to rest upon the side table. "Why, the banner of Dawn's Glory is a symbol of a free and united people. Those who choose to live of their own free will and accord…with autonomous thought…as individuals amongst the whole. Together in the more noble effort for all.

"But the four prongs of the crowning spear… Well, they each mean a different thing and add together to form the stronger, unmovable wall—honor, sacrifice, righteousness, and clarity.

"These are the base values expected of one another here. We are a living, breathing power that is made up of the many."

Zaramagrii pondered this for several moments, then pushed her hair back along both sides of her face. "I am Zaramagrii. Your banner, I have seen it before. The sight of it came to me in my dreams before we even met, almost like a vision. You were also there, not that I knew it was you. But your form."

"Yes, my dear," eased Rory. "Truth be told, you have been out for days now—eight to be exact. The wounds that you suffered were severe. While we have good healers, there are none that can make such wounds of that nature fade so quickly."

Zaramagrii looked upon him questioningly.

He scratched his chin briefly and stated, "You are, indeed, touched with the Affliction. Feel blessed by such a thing and be empowered by it. But many who go about with this gift also find that their minds are clouded and filled with certain visions both while awake and asleep."

She vaguely remembered learning about such a thing when she was younger. When one was touched by the Affliction, as it was known, most thought that the individual was literally touched by the divine. Those with the Affliction were known to be capable of healing themselves of even fairly serious wounds.

It was not that the individual could actually heal their injury through some form of thaumaturgy or unique power, but that their being instinctively did so. And this was done by simply going into a deep state of sleep, maybe more akin to a meditative trance.

In any case, the individual would succumb to what appeared to be deep sleep, but never really determined to be self-induced or just naturally occurring. The claims were that this state would last from two or three days, up to a ten-day, depending upon the severity of the injuries.

Of course, most did not know the real truth behind this strange boon, not even those learned scholars. Whomever possessed this Affliction was really on the path of Ascension, to immortality, or the divine. While they could even be slain prior to their actual Ascension, the time of Ascension would indeed force them to experience death before they gained immortality. But immortality still remained an imperfect state, as there were things worse than death that could befall even the immortal ones.

In walked Wybur Buttlecut, as Zaramagrii finished stretching into her black leather halter. Once she turned back around to face both Rory and Wybur, the young Buttlecut's attention appeared to be fixated down towards her stomach and abdomen. It was bare of anything and fully displaying her strange birthmark of sorts.

But her glowering frown after a moment of him doing so obviously implied something completely different to her. She no doubt thought him to be staring at the alluring shape between her thighs.

Wybur caught himself, as well as the stern look upon her face. "Ahh...no, forgive me. But it was the mark...there...that I was staring at."

He appeared flustered for several moments and turned as red as the glowing horn of a succubus.

Then he peered at Rory with only the movement of his eyes. "Rory, my good man, by chance can we talk? I shall meet you outside."

And with that, the little misshapen lad was out the door.

Rory was smiling as he held up both hands. "That was Wybur Buttlecut. Forgive him, for he is perhaps a bit odd around the social things. But his heart and intent remain true.

"I will return. There will be plenty of time to talk, so rest and gain your strength for now."

Then he lightly bowed as he departed.

Mena returned shortly afterward with a medley of fresh venison, yams, and a soupy mix of herbs and vegetables. "You must be famished. Enjoy this and there is plenty more if you should want."

Zaramagrii wasted no time digging in to the array of steaming fares set upon a simple wooden tray, but with a curiously elegant silver fork.

§ § §

Meanwhile, Rory and Wybur retreated to a balcony off the upper level hallway. One side of this hallway opened onto what was considered the great hall, where several long tables and rustic chairs stretched across the floor below. Here was where the people of Dawn's Glory gathered in feast or counsel.

The other side of the hall was littered with numerous doors, all being accommodations of sorts that could be used as needed.

Rory was calm, but Wybur could not be contained and immediately spoke. "I saw this same mark upon the old black book... The one that also laid claims to various things which would befall existence by one such thing that bore that mark. All of this material appeared as though it was produced by Siri himself."

Wybur emphatically trudged on. "This book also tied together a lost Amethyst Scroll, the Lost Scroll, that would only be uncovered by Haqnimemza...or through Haqnimemza, or whatever the intent had been. More a riddle I would expect.

"And Livforena, the one that I told you had enlisted me in this grand scheme, always saying that I would be the savior of Man-folk and such... Only now, I think she fooled me."

Wybur caught his breath. "For she was very intent upon finding this book, and she became very strange when I spoke of it, especially when I said that I could recite the whole thing. The girl Rosella, then what happened back at home in Longshadows… My poor nieces, my aunt and uncle. All a trick, and I was such a limppod! Deceived within the very intent of doing good."

A limppod was a large, clumsy, and stupid sea creature that normally was found clinging to the bottoms of wooden ships. They had a terrible suction to their circular mouths, which they could use in addition to their axe-like teeth to grind holes into the hulls. The things were more or less long, ugly eels.

Rory folded his arms on his broad chest with a smirk. "Now calm down and take a breath for a moment. We already discussed this *making a fool of you* business. And you know that this woman who claimed to be with the Veiled Ones played right into who you truly are.

"Look, Wybur, I am sorry about everything that has happened to you, but all of that might *even* get the best of me. So no more lost feelings of letting anyone down, not even yourself. You are indeed one of the most brilliant ones that I know."

The mountain of a man paused and took a swig of his mead. "In fact, *you* are now the one that has uncovered the whole plot, more or less. That is actually something that one should be extremely proud of. Revel in that knowledge."

"But what for and why?" queried Wybur, more to himself than anything else. "And to tell who? Ahhhh, what good will come from any of it?" He hopelessly slapped one hand on top of his head.

Rory grabbed Wybur's shoulder with a gentle squeeze. "My friend, I believe that Zaramagrii, as well as you, were both steered here together for a reason. That all of this happened through the reckoning of some order—not just chance—a higher purpose. The two of you were meant to cross paths.

"It seems to me that this dark child, while sure-footed and knowledgeable beyond belief, might be a bit confused or maybe just wayward. And unknowingly finding her way here, through the clouded path of Affliction dreams. Well, that is more than luck.

"But she has a higher purpose behind her. And you might help her with that. This is what was meant to be... Face it and accept it.

"All of this sounds as though there is more going on than just random chance. As you know from our past counsels, I am not a believer in such random things. Everything...and I mean *everything* occurs for a purpose."

Wybur thought for a moment. "But the book, the talk of dark things inside of it...the Marked One may be the one that brings those things to the world, well, according to this lore or legend what have you. She may be the one. What possibly would I do about that?"

Then Rory smiled warmly. "That is exactly what you must do."

Wybur grew impatient, now obviously confused by the giant. "What? What specifically do you mean by that?"

"Why, help her gain clarity of this stuff all tangled up inside of her. What you know from this book, and what she may be.

"I believe this one to be very even tempered, although youthful, and mixed with an astute, sharp mind full of the learned ways. But she still is young for one of the clans, and apparently gaining the experience and wisdom to match. Assist her, help her find her way. Help her find her path, my good man."

With that final thought from Rory, the man then firmly gripped Wybur by both shoulders while looking him in the eye. "But do it subtly."

After a couple of days, Zaramagrii allowed Wybur to make small talk with her. She found him to be very peculiar, especially since he spoke of what was most important to him.

He spoke of such rudimentary things, but ones of pure benevolence to her. The things that he talked about appeared to her as valiant notions stuck in a world that would not, or could not, live up to them. The good in things, in people, in Aylsh, maybe in all beings. And the idea that mostly things were meant to be good, or inevitably become good.

Instead of falling sway to the mix of his misleading physical appearance and the initial awkwardness, she began to see his inner light. The one that yearned for knowledge and truth, and a higher calling. Zaramagrii perhaps saw many of the same things within this unsightly young man that she herself valued. And his ability to retain nearly everything that he had come across—whether book, song, or talk—was beyond veneration.

Then one day, she watched as he sat with one of the dogs that lived here. Wybur sat alongside the furry creature, as though it was a friend or even a child. And he held a conversation with it while wrapping one arm about it. As the dog leaned its head into Wybur's neck, the tail wagged up a storm and a huge tongue-flailing smile split the muzzle.

She keenly saw how these simple, unblemished acts gave away the dog's perception of the man. It uncovered the real heart of such a sorely taken in sight of a thing. The countenance of the dog glowed with pure happiness just from being next to Wybur, and

Wybur reflected that light. He definitely was one with the animals, and they to him. For they were the true and pure reflections.

Many of the conversations between them began to linger into the evenings. And the stuff talked about shifted towards Olri Uchrah, the black book of Siri, which Wybur had uncovered. Zaramagrii was now engrossed in these parleys, especially when he went into recitals of the book's content.

Wybur pointed to what he thought to be the purpose for the book's existence. "In short, that book clearly implied that the Shadow Soul, the one with the mark of the dark half-sun, and what was called the Alpha Omega, together would signify an incredible change in the world as we know it. A horrendous one.

"The writings claimed that these two beings would bring darkness to the world, and the Shadow Soul would rule all with a hand of chaos. And there was much talk of chaos being brought forth as an all-powerful force, for more balance to existence.

"But much of the lore was supposedly within this lost scroll. The book did allude to something taking place whether this Shadow Soul completed its destiny or not…clearly claiming either way that the world would be consumed by the darkness.

"The book appeared to be a clue from Siri, as if intended to be uncovered at some point, maybe even in conjunction with this Soul and Omega coming into being. But I do not know."

Zaramagrii sat in silence after he finished, her eyes studying his face. "Clearly, Wybur, I see there is much to this black book. I really do appreciate your grasp on all of this.

"But is there anything that explains where the Soul and the Omega meet or come together at? What exactly is the Shadow Soul and what is the Omega?

"And what about the event that sends the world into darkness?" She held forth her hand with the unique ring upon it, now allowing Wybur to stare at the blackened shape. "And you also know that the Aylsh scriptures mention an Omega, and the Mother, within their contexts. Could these be one and the same?"

Wybur scratched his head briefly while staring about the room. "I know not, but possibly more will come to light. The book that I found clearly stated Alpha Omega, while those Aylsh scriptures contained similar references between the Omega and the Eternal Mother as most know her by. I was hoping that maybe these dreams of yours would reveal more about the whole thing. More tangible fact."

He wiped his forehead in exasperation. "But all this that we speak of is mere conjecture anyways. We may only be stringing together false effigies based upon our own wild imaginations of what we have read and seen. Like loons come home to roost."

They spent many more days talking about their visions or dreams that kept reoccurring. And both realized that the dreams were indeed visions of things yet to come, always revealing another possibly important act or part to be played out.

After an endless amount of counsels with Wybur, Zaramagrii began to practice her new sense of darkness well into the morning frost. Gradually, she became accustomed to keeping her eyes opened while doing so. This training turned towards the half-light of dawn, and then under the morning light, where she could hone the transitions until they became instinctive. Before long, the ability was second nature to her.

She never realized it before, but the initial emergence out of that subterranean realm had created the subconscious block when in daylight, or light. Chiefly whenever she was aware of her eyesight. For it had been the lack of her sight, in that dark and utter blackness of Qarradoum, that initially brought the dark blanket out. That had given birth to it.

All that time spent searching to get out from the underground caverns, she no doubt had her eyes open the entire time. But it was just too utterly dark for her to realize it. Now she could invoke the strange sense of her surroundings at will. And transition back and forth to the Shadehaunt was now with only a thought.

The blending of her Shadehaunt power with the darkness of the current world she was in was what was most impressive, allowing her to warp time more slowly or maybe speed up her movement. Either way, the results were the complete decimation of the entire Blackguard patrol within a moment's time—and before they even knew what had overtaken them.

That night the visions returned to her. This time she found herself in a rocky corridor, as though within a cavern. Every time she dreamed this vision, it would end at a naturally illuminated, cavernous chamber. A tall, armored skeleton stood near the far end, watching or waiting. It held something in its right hand, but it was still too far away from her to make out whatever it held. The slender frame of the skeleton always seemed to be familiar in some fashion to her. But she just could not place the feeling, the intuition.

When she grew closer to it, the eyes began to glow. The right one, as she stood facing it, was the darkest obsidian while the left appeared as a shining diamond. Both were surrounded by a strange, thin, reddish haze that widened and appeared to be filled with tiny strands of blackness. More like unraveled filaments of a garment. In her dream, she instinctively thought that she looked upon a mirror reflection of herself and those unique eyes.

Then it suddenly dawned on her why the form was so familiar, for it was she. But a darker and more sinister version of herself. And then the vision would fade and she would snap awake to the darkness. This happened each night, and always before she was able to fully see what the thing carried, or the hidden face.

But every night that she awoke, she would find herself already in the uncanny state of her dark blanket of sense. That strange ability uncovered within the subterranean realm suddenly, and now instinctively, at play without a thought to spark it.

Upon conversing with Wybur every day, Zaramagrii began to understand what he was doing. In explaining the content from the mysterious black book, he had tied together many things that initially appeared vague to her.

One day, while she discussed her most recent dream or vision, Wybur referenced what he knew concerning the Nook of the Reach and its possible location.

Of course, this came from what he had read and memorized within the black book of Lord Siri. But to her, it immediately became apparent that this was the place she was being led to. It was like instant recognition upon Wybur saying the name of the place. And that tied itself to the familiarity of those dank halls occupying her dreams.

Rory personally began to lead the scouting parties out at dusk. Zaramagrii would refuse to stay behind, even though Rory walked the fine line of telling her to stay and continue resting, and that it was for her own good. Her doe eyes would just glare at him as she crossed her arms. In the end, Rory always swayed to her will.

The first couple of nights doing so ended up with no luck in crossing paths with any of the motley forces of Akhruuk, goblins, and whatever else ran with them.

The third time out proved to be very different. This particular night was black as ever, especially once they descended out of the lowest snow line. Nothing had been found while they extended their hunt along the highlands in both directions from where the gate stood.

The decision was made to go out deeper, thus descending into the thick pines. The patrol of ten went from being able to observe one another within the contrasting snowfields to tightening up their distance to an arm's length. They could no longer see even three paces out once below the snow line.

Of course, Zaramagrii had no difficulty whatsoever, and she immediately began to sense and feel the surrounding area, as well as take the lead. Barely a rustle could be heard as the group moved. Such was the typical discipline and skill of Rory's warriors.

Then Zaramagrii froze and pushed her arm backwards to stop Rory, who stalked behind her. He nearly blundered right into her.

She turned to him, whispering, "I hear many of them moving ahead of us—traveling away. Quick, stay close and we shall surprise them."

Rory turned around to pass word to those behind him after telling her to wait. By the time that he returned to the front, she had already disappeared. Silently cursing, he quickly crept forward trying to discern her form up ahead.

Then, within the space of a moment, he could hear groans and cries in the guttural language of Akhruuk, and steel or iron clanging. Speeding up now to close the distance, he and the others came upon Zaramagrii and the ground littered with a dozen dark shapes. Rory saw those glowing eyes in the darkness staring at him, a strange reddish hue surrounding her entire outline.

When more sounds erupted from behind them, he found that she had disappeared from where she was in front of him. Within what seemed a moment, there were more brief sounds of groans and thuds, then silence.

Again, Rory found her after edging towards where he thought these other sounds originated from. There she was, amongst more freshly slain bodies littering the ground.

As she approached him, whipping her blades through the air to clean them of blood and gore, her eyes glowed still with that red flare highlighting the white and the black orbs.

"Zaramagrii, you must stop. We can no longer see to fight," Rory whispered while leaning forward to discern her.

She stared at him, saying, "Have no worry. That was all of them, at least here." Then she headed off, back towards where they had approached from.

Rory had never seen or heard of anything like what he had witnessed this night. What Zaramagrii could do.

The western skies glowed with the rising duo suns before they returned back to the camp. Now he could see wispy, black traces subtly emanating from the skin in various places along her body. But her eyes were crisp and clear, very lucid, almost like a keen predator always in the game of the hunt.

After that night, Zaramagrii began going out alone, beyond the gate, once the duo suns disappeared. She would return after sunrise, only to eat and rest for a while. Then, once darkness fell, she would slip quietly out again. This went on for the next fortnight.

The time that she spent with either Wybur or Rory grew shorter and shorter, as though she was slowly weaning herself of their company. When she did sit with them, it was only for breakfast, and only for a short time.

Then one morning they awoke to find her room empty and her belongings gone. She apparently never returned from the darkness of the last night.

When Wybur learned of this, he instantly knew that she had gone to Clan Tharasvrul to seek the justice that she craved. The justice that had been driving her. But was it to take vengeance upon this Priestess Sahrya as well? He knew in his heart that they would cross paths again.

As for Rory, he took it in stride that Zaramagrii was gone. While never really accepting that she was gone for good, he kept about his usual routine and refused to speak of her. Even with Wybur.

But Rory knew some of what she was going through, especially dealing with being marked as an outcast from your own kind. He could easily sympathize with her—as well as give her some space.

Even Rory had fallen under Zaramagrii's spell. Sure, he would not talk of her, but deep down inside he sorely missed her presence.

Rory had also known about being touched, or having the Affliction. For a long time now. Ever since his attempt to tame the wild, to bring what he termed his *like-minded* people out here to the rugged lands.

The very first day that they began to secure the narrow passage leading into the Fallen Lands—well before the first log was ever placed for Dawn's Glory—they had been attacked.

The waves of Akhruuk and other vermin did not cease until they had the sturdy portcullis and barricade constructed. But he had been one of those gravely wounded during one of the attacks. The fighting had been fierce and bloody.

The blow of an Akhru axe had cut deep into his lower side, and everyone thought that he was lost. Rory turned into an inferno as fever from the ugly wound took over his body. It did not look good, and the healers could only watch and wait.

But nearly a fortnight later, shock and surprise overwhelmed the people of Dawn's Glory. The wound had sealed and appeared as no more than a bad bruise with a long, fading scar. Not long afterwards, he was walking around, albeit a little stiff.

He had guessed early in his life that he was one of those touched, but this confirmed it. The little things that happened to him throughout his life, falling down and scraping a knee to falling out of a tree. He always seemed to heal fairly quickly no matter the injury or malady.

Even though there has never been recorded proof of what actually happens to those touched with the Affliction, it was considered a known miracle beyond any thaumaturgy. Of course, none knew exactly what ensued when such an individual actually died either. How could anyone? And any diviners of the black arts that might have unearthed such knowledge never revealed it.

It was about this time that Rory Sivercroft, the Bastard Prophet, began to have dreams himself, or what he took to be visions of things yet to pass.

There was a sequence of things that would permeate and haunt his restless bouts of sleep. They would never pollute his sleep all together. Instead they would take turns dancing with him at their own accord, one each night. As time wore on they became more translucent and real.

In one of the dreams, he found the familiar face of his father on his deathbed. The old man would appear so feeble and pale, and each time Rory found himself unable to move. Unable to move or to speak, even though he wanted to go to his father and utter those words that had been lost for so long.

In another dream, he would find himself helplessly sinking into deep, dark water, with all of his battle dress taking him down faster and faster. The surface would grow farther and farther away as his lungs threatened to burst.

And then there was the ghostly vision of a radiant white form of a woman whom he thought to be his mother at first. Even though he could not ever picture his real mother's face. It remained elusive to his memories.

Rory knew that he would inevitably confront his father…and that confrontation would require some thought. He despised the man that gave him life, and facing him again for any reason left a gnawing, burning emptiness at the pit of his stomach.

Over time, the more thought that he gave to the confrontation, the less hate boiled through the seams of his being.

Now Rory's spirit instinctively turned to what he always did best, seeing the inner light or the good in everything no matter the terms.

He eventually began to see that his father had been cheated out of having his son by his side—in his life—for the past twenty years, maybe more. And, no matter what had been done or said by either of them way back when, it was always in heated rage or anguish. But most of all, it was done through scarred pride. Yes, even he himself was guilty of that.

He would not listen at the time to what his father's reasoning had been for acknowledging him, at what was really an attempted apology by a man who could not put words to his own mistakes. Ever. An attempt at doing so in the only way that he knew.

The anger gone, Rory pondered this new feeling for a while. And he saw more clearly now, after the past couple of ten-year where he and his kind had carved out their own niche in this savage world.

That was another point, sharp as a razor now to him. Life itself was so precious, and could dissipate in the fleeting time it took for a harvestspell leaf to fall to the ground from its perch in a tree.

Time did not allow for short-sighted squabbling or grudging, ignorance, or misguided judgments.

It could be gone within the blink of an eye, leaving no chance to ever do what was intended but had been put off.

His father also had been cheated out of spending his days with such a woman as Rory's mother. Rory's mother, who died giving him life.

Now he saw the pain and misery that such a man as his father no doubt held inside and concealed, trying to show the world that he was strong and invincible. He had to portray this.

He perceived a cloud of guilt that harangued his father over the death of his mother. No doubt such a noble as he could not openly concede a mistress like her even if he had wanted to.

Rory's heart nearly leapt out of his mouth as he suddenly realized that he had done to his father what he had been trying so hard to teach others not to do.

Forgiveness, if and when one seeks it forthright. That was the step to acceptance for who one was, for their essence, their spirit.

And one needed to acknowledge this in another, if that other stood up and said *here I am, I make mistakes, please forgive me but I am trying my best.* If they genuinely reach for magnanimity.

Tears welled up in the corners of his rich, green eyes. Yes. He would go to Nuuroc, and he would speak with his father.

Now he saw what was always in front of him, so simple and deep-felt. All of this time, it had been easy enough to bury it within whatever he could—to control the emotions from spilling over and making a mess out of his rationale.

§ § §

The gaunt lord of the Black Legion sat and stared at the raised Mynrooth portal. He had given much thought to what he was about to do. But it was time, his time. And the time of the Legion.

Before long, a monster of a man walked through the portal to stand, staring at Janlouk. The jagged white of a large scar ran across the side of his cleanly shaven head. His pitch black, bushy beard gave him the look of some wild thing.

The overall blackened complexion of his regalia gave him a very menacing air. But the long, black cloak with gold trim and a large silver scythe emblazoned upon its back marked him as the commander of the Black Legion. The visible commander at least.

Axyander Blackshield the Steelborn bowed his head slightly as he spoke. "My lord."

Indeed he was a brooder, as nothing seemed to erect a change to his demeanor. Ever the cold and unreadable visage.

The bony lich stared at his first chosen for a while, beaming with confidence. There was one thing that only he, and of course the Steelborn, knew as fact. And that was Axyander's background, in particular, his ancestry. When he had first learned of it from Axyander himself, the plotting lich could not contain himself with the near perfect scheme. One such as Janlouk himself, with the look of death, could never legitimately play the Legion's master.

Now Axyander claimed that he was born to an Aylsh mother, though he had no such visible attributes whatsoever. Those within the Black Legion were of the race of Man-folk only, and no others were allowed to join the ranks. This had been the way of the Legion ever since its inception. A force of Man.

Janlouk had his reasons for choosing Axyander, not only to hold over his head if need be.

The real commander of the Legion also knew that Axyander would live for several hundred years, with a little luck. The Steelborn was just entering into his fortieth winterfall. And this would provide some continuity to the operations, not to mention some stability for Janlouk's trust.

This longevity could always be explained by thaumaturgy, a spell or other such thing. And they could continue to leave his true heritage hidden.

But not even Lord Janlouk knew the full truth behind Axyander and what he really was. Axyander claimed a renowned warrior lineage. However, everything known about him stemmed from his word alone. There was no other Blackshield across the lands. Nor had there been since at least the beginning of the current age. No one could possibly know this though. There were no recordings of inhabitants within any town, village, hamlet, walled city, or castle anywhere. Minus a gold-struck maeyur or hoodpick of a thayne, only the tax and tariff collector had a need for the counting of the masses. But these were mostly rough numbers, not necessarily names.

Janlouk offered his hand and pointed to the chairs not far away. "My Legion Commander, what news do you carry?"

Axyander poured a goblet of wine as he spoke. "My lord, I have dispatched five score men from each o' the companies at Tornspire and Longshadows to take control of Tamelyn. And word has it that it is secure there now.

"Recruitment has begun across the lands, and I hope to have at least a thousand green swords by frostthaw. With no setbacks, we will have the fifth company of the Legion up and running at Tamelyn by summertide.

"But there will have to be some modifications to the keep, or around it, to allow for all o' the Legion-men and other things like training grounds, stables, and fields—to name a few."

"Excellent, excellent. I knew that I could count on you, Axyander. And I made no mistake in placing you in command." Janlouk now poured some of the red wine into a goblet.

He swirled the surface of the wine, pausing before taking a drink. "And how many mages are there now?"

"Each of the captains has three to four with him at all times. At least two of them are able to use their powers to travel. We can maneuver at will for the most part. But there are limits to the powers. The numbers of men and equipment that are able to be moved are hemmed up."

Lord Janlouk rose and retrieved the long tube of a faded scroll, shrugging off the small banter. "Axyander, the time has come for us. There are opportunities at hand."

Janlouk unrolled a dried parchment of a map displaying the known lands of Thaldeia. "I must be able to count on you—lean on you for this next task. Only you will be able to pull it off. And it is very crucial for you and I...and the longevity of the Legion.

"A king is about to die—the Kuhrzothian king. I have it on good terms that the illegitimate son of this king will set foot within Nuuroc at or before the king's death.

"Also, and I might add, most important to this endeavor…an endless black force of rabble from out of Oshghrul marches on Nuuroc even as we speak."

The lich paused in order to let his words sink in, as the piercing, red eyes stared out at Axyander. "Now, all of these pawns have been set in motion and can undoubtedly provide a possibility of power to us. But it will be up to us—you, my good crusader—to take the advantage and allow that power to fall into our lap."

Axyander continued to stare at the map and ponder the spoken words of his master. "Yes, my lord, but where does this power come from? Precisely what will deliver to us more than what we have at the now?"

Janlouk smiled, if such things as skeletal remains could. "Yes. Put the pieces together. All in good time.

"Understand that this horde from the Fallen Lands is very large and well-equipped, organized if you will.

"Kuhrzoth will need our assistance in this matter, they will nearly beg us for it. And we will be there to place certain demands on those terms in order to bring our forces into play."

Axyander nodded his head dramatically. "Ah. Terms at the crucial moment whereupon this horde is bearing down upon Nuuroc. But what can they possibly give us? Besides blood to whet our blades."

Janlouk let the exhilaration about the air soak in for several moments before replying. "Generalship within the Kuhrzothian forces, the title of royal commander in the Emerald Order."

Axyander's eyes sparkled slightly with gaining comprehension. "Yes, a position within their military might, thus the Legion would be part of that might. A contracted, yet fully fledged army of its own. Capable…empowered throughout Thaldeia and backed by the Kuhrzoth banner."

"Yes, Axyander, you get it but you are missing the major point. With you granted such a title within the Emerald Order, you would be within reach of the failing monarchy's crown itself. And the power that goes with it."

Now the eyes of Axyander truly shone with awed respect for his ages old leader. He knew that, if the Kuhrzothian king died without an heir, the next line would go down to those in command. That would be one of the royal commanders—the most senior one.

Kuhrzoth was no democracy, nor was it an oligarchy. It was a monarchy with rulings set forth that have not been changed for more than ten turns. The kingdom thrived on military might and efficiency. The crown would always stay within the Emerald Order, even if the royal family for some reason fell away from it. The Heir de Facto decree was an emergency decree enacted after Arterium's time, for Arterium himself never would have allowed such a possibility.

That decree set into place the proclamation that the senior commander of the Kuhrzothian forces would be the next heir to the throne, if no such actual heir existed. And now there was only one such commander left alive, at least since the fall of Emerald Rest.

Janlouk strode around the table and stood next to Axyander. "For it to take the right shape, one must form the appropriate pieces to do so. The companies of the Legion must be set in place and prepared, you must be at Nuuroc to set the terms when this black horde descends upon it, and those terms must be met by the Kuhrzothian king—no exceptions."

The lich commander eyed his most trusted right hand while pausing. "Now listen carefully, as the companies must be properly arrayed as well. All four companies must be positioned to the south and west of Nuuroc. Understand that your primary concern will be to make sure that this black horde does not deviate towards Longshadows. We will not let it descend upon Longshadows, period. But, for this to work, you must ensure that those companies are within half a day's march or less of the walls of Nuuroc."

Axyander understood what was being asked of him. It was a masterpiece in the works. A scheme that no doubt had been devised by Janlouk over much lonely time.

Axyander was a true Legion warhorse. He knew the game being played, and all of the stakes that were at risk.

Such a man as he was. No longer attached to anything in the mortal world other than war and death. And both of those were inevitable, one way or the other. At least for most.

Then Janlouk folded his arms, the bones grating together under the maille. "And, Axyander, make no mistake. Even if this illegitimate son claims the throne when the king dies, *you* must be the only one in place to assume that crown. Do you understand?"

Axyander slowly nodded with complete understanding, and for once, he grinned broadly with a look of omnipotence creeping through his dark eyes.

Chapter 19:

Path of Vengeance

"Times are great! Wild beasts and creatures of the darkness roam free across the lands. Men... Men that chase such things for sport and challenge live high and mighty now. And gold and notoriety, not that they are the most valued, but they flow like ale from a cask that has a broken spigot. Even more enthralling are all those lasses and wenches that pay tribute to those such as us."

–Whil Ketori, adventurer and hero extraordinaire from Orondyraq circa the year SA 32.

he cold air was swirling and fluttering through the pine trees around Clan Tharasvrul. There was no quiet to this dark night where it seemed even the very flames could not cast long shadows, nor their warmth very far.

No wolves of the Clan Tharasvrul Rhaanmri remained, no howls could be heard from them in the surrounding lands. Their haunting calls sounded only in memory now.

Priestess Sahrya sat in her chamber next to the one reserved for meditation, high and imposing upon an oaken throne of self-justification that was encrusted with gems and precious metals. Several Blackguard stood motionless inside and outside of the doorway, at the ready. The air tensed with anticipation. It reeked of mixed energies that threatened to ignite the seams of reality.

Low feline growls of an eerie kind emanated forth from the doorway leading into the dark meditation chamber, no doubt where the once regal cats now stayed. The rhaanmri of old Clan Omrasstefor had been resurrected by Priestess Sahrya, in all of their newfound unnatural glory, to assume that of Tharasvrul.

Sahrya rested patiently with her delicate chin on a thumb, propped up on the side of the ornate chair. She looked to the dark, unlit corner where she could make out the form of Nimosese, but only because she knew that he was there. His unique armor allowed him to blend in with the dark, rocky wall.

She knew—no, she felt—the young one coming. Although not entirely sure of anything specific, her scrying told her that the dark offspring of Amanshar was indeed close at hand.

Good, she thought, *let this be the end of it.*

The timing had been near perfect. With Nimosese already here at Tharasvrul, Sahrya decided to set a trap for the little bitch.

One that was of her own device, one with the Shadehaunt. And the master assassin would not fail her.

Nimosese stirred ever so slightly, causing his black armor to silhouette against the wall in the glow of the torches. He stood still as a statue, waiting, patiently arrested in the stalk.

Sahrya eyed him subtly. *Yes,* she thought, *perhaps your timing here has been preordained.*

§ § §

The wind blew throughout the abodes, crevices, and rocky outcrops within the hollow of land, stirring debris and such up into the air.

But more than the wind swept through Tharasvrul that night, as the storm approached, bringing even more oppressive gloom to the foreboding azure miasma hanging so heavily. The first cracks of black-laced lightning sent many who were still gathered around fires fleeing indoors. Energy seethed throughout, and a strange tingling feeling erupted across most living things as though the air thrived with an electric zeal.

Nouryno, the senior turo, was one such dark one forced to retreat to his large home.

His home was littered with lavish furnishings. Here was where he provided each of the orations and teachings to the young ones of the clan. He relished the thoughts about such things, especially the little females who were always so naïve to his advances.

But these acts were in the name of Lord Braxis himself, he sternly thought as he chuckled softly. *Oh, the joy and pleasure of feeling each of those young ones.*

Lightning cracked nearby, booming directly overhead. The flash sent tiny flickers of blackened light through whatever cracks and holes would feed them into the dark confines of the turo's own private home.

The massive door was double-bolted now as he approached the far wall deep in the back of the home. This was where he spent most of his time with the young ones.

The flint sparked, and up rose the thin flame of a torch within the wall bracket.

Upon turning back from where the torch rested on the wall, Turo Nouryno jumped from the haunting set of glowing eyes barely two paces away. They were reddish hued, one being pure, snowy white and the other the deepest obsidian.

He was so startled that he nearly fell back flat against the torch that he had just lit.

The ghost must be an illusion, having materialized directly in front of him. It was she...and he knew it. But she was different, as he could unmistakably tell from those glowing, dark-hued orbs piercing through him. She was no longer a child, or at least the child who she had been.

He blinked, but the black form remained when he reopened his eyes. The torch was hot against his neck now, as he began to finger the shortsword at his side.

Dark blotches of something streaked her face. Dried blood. From *what* he could only guess.

"Turo, wise one... The one that is held above most others as sacred and righteous to us of the clans. He who should be looked up to and revered...ever giving to the young of the dark, so that they can continue the ways of the Black Clans."

The cold, detached hiss of her words slapped him sharply as he suddenly grew more than a little concerned. Now he fearfully studied this calm and cool dark one in front of him, as her form gave off the glows and hues of some blasphemous radiance.

As he took his chance with the short, sharp blade of his sword—never even expecting this small one to be capable of thwarting his move—things happened in the blur of a dizzying moment. Not even knowing what had fully transpired, he suddenly found himself pinned to the wall beside the torch with his own blade.

This painful realization fully kicked in, and he knew that the blade ran through his upper left shoulder and deeply into the wood behind. She was close to his face now, those glowing orbs keenly visible.

The turo suddenly feared what had returned to haunt him, and he shook with panic at what he saw staring into those cold, callous embers of eyes. There seemed to be an outlandish, wispy black smoke rising off her skin.

"Let me finish," she whispered as she wiggled the blade ever so lightly, sprouting waves of pain through his body.

He cried, maybe from the intense pain, possibly from the fear of what was in front of him.

"How many more besides me? What have you done to us? Tell me... I need to hear it, and then I shall make the pain stop."

He closed his eyes in an attempt to make the night disappear. "Too many for me to count... Over the turns... Too many. Forgive me!"

Then he whimpered as he struggled to balance the weight of his body upon one foot to prevent it from agonizingly sliding farther down over the sharp blade.

She did not even blink. "Perhaps you can bring one good note to this... Tell me why I cannot feel the Rhaanmri...and Avrul is nowhere to be found."

The pain caused him to spit his words out sharply. "Dead... They... *Err*... All dead. Part of the cleansing... Priestess Sahrya said it was necessary."

Zaramagrii barely contained a new course of emerging rage. "What? What do you mean cleansing?"

He pleaded to her with his eyes now. "Priestess Sahrya claimed all of them had conspired against her, along with you. Against the whole clan... They threatened the existence of the Black Clans themselves...our survival. Our future."

Zaramagrii had heard enough. She whipped his arm up against the wall and held it there. Her other empty hand now went low on him—slowly trailing down the front of his pants and loosening them. "Forgiveness is but a word... A word apparently used when one seeks sympathy from another."

At this point, she allowed his breeches to slip down below his knees. Her hand found his manhood muscle, or in their language, his *raham*. It grew hard even with the stress, as though he thought that this encounter might go another way.

"Do you enjoy that? My Turo?"

With that, once his raham was as hard as it would get, she tightened down on it to his surprise and savagely ripped it from his flesh. The meaty tearing sound would have made any nearby creature cringe with intuited pain.

He screamed in thorough agony with his mouth wide open and canted towards the skies above. More black lightning crackled outside, the thunder raging along with Nouryno's terror.

With another quick move, she shoved his own instrument into his mouth, lodging it deeply into his throat. Nouryno gagged and choked amongst all of his spittle and tears.

But she was not finished yet, and while one hand held his mouth closed, she tore away his ball sack in one fingernail clawing grip. This trophy also went straight into his mouth. With the turo shriveled and profusely bleeding, he was no longer concerned with his impalement upon the blade.

She slowly leaned in closer to him as her leather booted foot spread his legs apart. One hand grasped the long, silvery dagger as she whispered into his ear. "I have no sympathy, and I do not forgive. But soon you will be freed from your pain, as I promised.

"When you pass, I wish an eternity of unbearable agony upon you—the darkness *take* you."

With that, her hand swept steeply and viciously upwards. His body lurched and raised as his eyes widened, until the blade impaling him through his shoulder stopped his tormented flesh from being pushed any higher.

She had rammed the silver dagger so far up his arse that the pommel barely poked out amidst the bloody tissue and gory stream flushing down onto the floor. Thus, she left him in such a state to pass from this world in an agonizingly slow and miserable death.

While this appeased her sense of justice to a point, she was too close to another one with whom she needed to deal with.

§ § §

Mendonytes emerged from the torrents of wind driven rain outside and approached the priestess as she sat perfectly straight, basking in her own glory.

"Priestess, the skies crackle with black lightning and strange black smoke has been seen countless times about Tharasvrul."

He paused for a moment while looking at one of the intricately crafted black bracers on his forearms. "It almost seems as though the Blackguard bracers grant more power this night."

Sahrya looked at him and scoffed. "Yes, my bold Khamatiri. The powers of the Shadehaunt are strong this night, and they do so for me…as foretold. Be vigilant and double-check your guard."

Secretly, to herself, she swore her oaths to the Ancient One. She knew that what was happening was another sign of what would eventually come in the not so distant future—when she assumed the reins of Thaldeia. To crack and whip everything into submission.

But what she thought she knew as the truth was nowhere near the actuality of things.

It was true that the Shadehaunt forced its powers around the breadth of Tharasvrul. But this was not because of the priestess, or from her, as she vehemently stated and believed.

Instead, the fabrics of the different dimensions shifted and melded because of the violent rage and unsatisfied vengeance for justice of the emerging Shadow Soul. The one that would lead by, and rule through, chaos—the true power of chaos. It was the presence of Zaramagrii that created such a rift where the Shadehaunt provoked the very form of the material world about this region.

§ § §

Zaramagrii moved through the cold, mysterious realm of the Shadehaunt. All about her were strange, grayish forms, drifting in the orange-purple hue of an aura.

Here, things were different. But she knew where the Great Cavern sat in relation to the turo's home. It would only seem a moment in reality when she emerged there.

The power and rage overtook her during those final moments as Nouryno's essence faded away. She suddenly was filled with the thought or want of a more complete vengeance—the priestess.

Here she was, but moments away from running a blade through that witch. There was no way to let it go, no matter how hard she tried. She was too close, and putting an end to Priestess Sahrya would only do more good for this world.

Her Shadehaunt powers allowed her to peer back into the material world of Zholryn, where she now saw the familiar surroundings inside of the Great Cavern.

Even though within the Shadehaunt, everything appeared murky and blurred. Everything mixed with the dull haze from a hellish black light somewhere overhead.

Blackguards were posted everywhere.

All of her being called for the blood of the priestess, as she was so near. She thirsted for it, and this was her opportunity. But the priestess would know who was going to take her life, and Zaramagrii would make sure of that.

She was now through the main walkway from the Great Cavern, and she could see Sahrya seated upon some kind of elegant chair cast as a throne. Her face was set in a smug look of determined satisfaction. It held the air of one playing cat and mouse, waiting for the right moment. But Zaramagrii was too far gone to realize this or even break free from the yearning bloodlust.

Now only paces away from the last door, from gliding past the last two Blackguards near the doorway. It almost seemed too easy.

Maybe seven paces away, she was preparing to step back into the material world to reveal herself before running that bitch through with the Blackguard longsword.

Then a dark, smoky form was alongside her, just before she transitioned from the Shadehaunt. The figure caught her completely off guard, as she had been so focused on the priestess.

Her eyes could barely discern the exotic, black armored figure. But it held a wicked double-edged blade, thick as a whip, pulled back and high to the side. She saw the partially exposed, bald head covered with various black runes.

This dark one's eyes, orange-red flames, stared her down harshly. But this look instantly turned to one of perplexed amazement and dawning realization.

By all rights, this unseen warrior would have had her if he had wanted. She probably would never have even seen it coming. But he held his blade and froze.

Then she saw one of the various runes upon his head, which looked very familiar. It had a small crescent sun with rising rays coming off it, all in darkness.

The mysterious dark one yelled at her in Black Clan. "Flee quickly. It is a trap!"

With that, she lowered herself, never slowing her movement. Then she was gone, back the way she had come, running through the Shadehaunt as countless Blackguards rushed the door.

§ § §

Nimosese intended on cleanly severing the head of this treacherous dark one that the priestess wanted dead. And, of all places that she might have appeared at, it would be here this very night.

He sensed the movement of something coming in through the doorway and knew that it must be her. But such speed and absolutely no disturbance within the air about him.

What was she really? Or what was she doing to accomplish such stealth? Even his abilities had limitations that curbed such total illusions of secrecy.

Nimosese moved to intercept the thing that his senses told him was nearing the priestess. His keen blade was poised and ready. As he sensed the presence immediately in front of him, she began to slowly materialize.

He suspected her of transitioning out of the shadow realm itself, but his abilities allowed him to sense such things as well. Though he usually was not able to fully see them.

As he prepared to whip the blade in a perfect arc, what he saw stopped him in his tracks and he froze in awe.

There in front of him, as in his numerous recurring visions, stood the dark female with her form silhouetted by the strangely hued glow.

What stopped him were those eyes, the glowing white on her left and the obsidian on the right.

And in that instant he understood that this was the progeny of Lord Siri, and the solidification of the legends of old.

He had followed the false prophet for all of this time—the priestess. How could he have been so blind?

He quickly yelled to the dark child that it was a trap and to flee. How could he have let the falsities entice him into nearly slaying the one born of darkness? The one that will eventually rise and conquer such abominations of righteousness in this world.

Then, after those piercing eyes met his, she vanished. But he swore that he saw something in them as well—a recognition. A truth to everything.

Nimosese glanced briefly towards the priestess as he pressed closely into the wall near the doorway, in order to blend in.

And the master assassin appeared to vanish. Priestess Sahrya screamed at the top of her lungs with spittle flying everywhere, "Noooo… Impossible!"

Even the terrible undead cats stirred in the chamber nearby, at least the ten that remained with the priestess.

Nimosese watched as a flood of Blackguard ran into the room. Once they cleared the doorway, he silently slipped out past them and through the length of the Great Cavern. Then he disappeared into the grim line of trees.

The priestess' rage ran unchecked at the failure of her plan to kill Zaramagrii. In her blind haste and presumable omnipotent ignorance, she had failed in her assumptions.

The Order of the Dhourkuul followed Lord Siri and none other. Such was their discipline to him and their order that nothing else could sway it. It merely took Nimosese this confrontation to see the reality of his recent visions, and of his misguided servitude to the priestess. With that, he had steered back towards his true purpose and ways.

Much to the chagrin of Priestess Sahrya, this night did just that, and she learned a valuable lesson in placing way too much confidence in the plying of her power and assertions. The master assassin had betrayed her, even after everything that she had promised him. And this would not go unpunished.

Priestess Sahrya's anger slowly subsided. *Yes,* she thought, *the little shadow bitch might have escaped this night.*

But she knew that it would only be a matter of time. Her first born Chosen had gained incredible strength and tenacity. With the ultimate weapons in their hands, they would exact her vengeance upon Zaramagrii.

Chapter 20:

The Reign of the Prophet

The pleas of the Mother will be refused unto the

morn of the Thirteenth Passing,

During which those same number o' orbs of flame align.

The righteous one shall fall amidst an oppressively

dark but tremendous victory.

Afterward floweth the light of times,

To mark the coming of the Fatherless Son,

A period of remittance shall fall,

Before the heralds of the Eternal Lasting.

And the seals shall be opened,

Allowing a future of untold night.

–Excerpt from the First Writings, the
Aylsh scriptures, circa two thousand
years before the current age.

The magnificent castle of Nuuroc sat amidst the open grasslands and rolling hills, a flawless, picturesque sight distinguishing it as the seat of Kuhrzoth. It was on a fairly wide plateau with many long, steep fingers of draws and ravines crossing throughout the grass swept expanse. Lush forests sat nestled along most panoramas, but these did not encroach within a league of the walls and battlements. And the line of trees to the north was much farther away even than this. The grand Mhisimik River rushed down and through this green expanse, but at a distance off to the west. It was known for the deep and clear waters that usually carried the golden sheen of the rising duo suns.

The grand range of the Dulgannor sat picturesque against the southeastern skies. This mountain range was known for the bronze glow that it presented when observed from afar, or even close in at times. These peaks were famous for their richly mined veins of gems and ore, hidden deep within their bowels.

Of course the Kharaghou were those kind that found the most wealth there, as they were the ones that thrived within the Dulgannor and called it home.

The Kharaghou came to be known as such by the Black Clan name given them in the ancient days, as most things. Kharaghou translated to *little fiend* literally in the Common tongue.

Now in their own language, the name by which the Kharaghou called their kind meant *first chosen*. There have been many legends concerning the meaning of this, but only one has taken root and stuck. And this was mired within the Black Clan lore itself.

According to most ancient legends centered within Black Clan lore, the Kharaghou were named for their disposition as well as their appearance. It was passed down that the name was given to them when their kind emerged from a smoking, fiery crack in the ground. Said to have come out of the Endless Chasm.

In Black Clan, the Kharaghou name originated from the tale that these things were the first chosen to be bred with fiends from the lower layers of the Chasm. There was no indication within the lore of what the fiends had been bred with, but the semblance was that closest with the Man-folk. At least in upright appearance.

But the Kharaghou were an odd sort of beings and mostly kept to themselves. There were always wild tales about the various trading companies throughout Thaldeia and their experiences with these reclusive ancients.

Sometimes it was claimed that even familiar merchants venturing into the territories of the Kharaghou went there and then were never seen again. Occasionally survivors would return crazed and disheveled, babbling incoherent things. Most of them kept repeating how the wild things went crazy, killing everyone and destroying everything. And it seemed that there was ne'er an explanation for it, as it was lucky that there was even a survivor to talk about it.

Baeynor Sivercroft, king of Kuhrzoth, lay on his death bed high in the Emerald Tower. King Baeynor the Amiable was the title that most were accustomed to knowing him by, as he had always been a very personable king. One that urgently wanted his people to truly want him as their sovereign.

Of course, he treated his men—his loyalty—no better than a pack of wild dogs. And this was where the reins upon his forces had loosened considerably. Especially in the case of the Emerald Order, particularly the Emerald Knights.

It was only recently that King Baeynor agreed to allow the commander of the Emerald Knights to retake his position as such at the fortress of the lofty order, Emerald Rest. And this was only due to the sudden illness that had taken hold of him, which only gave birth to his lack of enthusiasm over defending former decrees.

The Emerald Tower was named so because, historically, the king had always been the true head of the Emerald Knights. In the old days, the king actually commanded the order from this tower. It was the stronghold of the Emerald Knights, well before Emerald Rest was made the symbol of their power. This was before the present royal hall had been built.

Thus, it was forever known for this seat of high respect. For the Order of the Emerald Knights was considered the mightiest force in the history of Thaldeia. At least Kuhrzothian history claimed this. But most of Kuhrzothian history fell to the likes of the proclaimed royalty that desired to make the Knights of the Wild acquiesce their power and lands a long time ago.

Construction of the tower had been started under Arterium, but only finished well after his death. It sat within the original castle, what was considered as Old Nuuroc. The tower overshadowed one of the very first establishments erected upon the grounds, the original temple to Lord Braxis.

The original seat of Kuhrzoth rested at Venlour Keep, now an aging ruin, but once a bastion of hardwood defenses. This relocation took place under the hand of Arterium around the time that he revealed the Great Slates, or Twelve Edicts.

The Twelve Edicts were presented by him to the world after he claimed that he had a vision, not long after one of his many bouts of exalted learning and studies.

Initially, when the first bands of Kuhrzothians moved into what is now present day Nuuroc, many spoke of the entire land appearing as though an unbearable fire had swept over it. The land was burned down to the soil, and only sparse vegetation sprouted as these first pioneers began to construct the massive castle. The early ones also spoke of there being several buildings already standing. Arterium's palace, the original temple to Lord Braxis, and the base to what would later become the Emerald Tower. The royal engineers had marked what would become Nuuroc (at least at that time), which spread out far and wide from around the existing structures. Even though this was only the first of the numerous rings of baileys and grounds that would eventually follow. This was the start to what would be the most prominent example of a concentric castle.

So King Baeynor the Amiable wheezed and coughed while his physicians looked on helplessly. No one could cure what was ailing the deteriorating lungs and heart. Such severe onsets of bodily failure usually ran their course until death.

Until now, he had held on stubbornly for many seasons. But not a score of days ago, the illness took a dramatic turn. He began hacking up nasty, blood-filled fluid. His skin assumed an ever darkening hue of red, as though the king was always in a full blush.

Although none would speak it directly, many would claim that King Baeynor was being paid back in full for his wanton years. And most would also say that no one could ever even attempt to reclaim the integrity and honor that one such as he had trifled away for so long. Especially the disgrace that he had shown so many.

But what most did not know, and probably never would, was that the sole instigator of this malady was none other than the royal presenter of Kuhrzoth.

The royal presenter was actually one of high title and power. As a matter of fact, the official position actually enacted many powerful dictates throughout the kingdom. And this individual maintained a very tight hold over judiciary findings, if not even swaying them one way or the other. After all, he headed the High Assembly of Kuhrzoth.

The current one, Royal Presenter Holcomb, was a slim and lanky man in his mid-forties. He had a very tall face which gave the impression of a weasel with long, unkempt hair. But appearances, as well as titles, can be deceiving as we have already found out. For the king's malady started to become apparent around the crowning of summertide. It was about this time that the behavior of Holcomb had changed slightly.

On this particularly cold day, half way through winterfall, King Baeynor could see the tall Green Gates. These gates were the main gates leading into the city from the north, and still remnants of the very first gates that led into Old Nuuroc.

The positioning of the Emerald Tower allowed unchecked views of both city gates south and north by merely looking through different arched windows from the same vantage point. And it was on this one day that the last vision of the Amiable King would be of those gates opening up, the oversized hoists and chains rattling away to chase birds from their roosts.

As King Baeynor raised his upper body enough to fully look out upon those opening gates, he went into a contorting spasm that wracked his entire body. This continued, even as the light faded from his eyes, and the rattling breath let out in a long, uninterrupted murmur that was never taken in again.

It so happened that one such individual disgraced by King Baeynor the Amiable was riding through the Green Gates even as the old king forcefully passed on from this world.

The Bastard Prophet, Rory Sivercroft, rode into Nuuroc astride a graceful Thoerne war horse. The beast was decked out in glinting plate barding—shaffron, crinet, peytral, flanchards, and crupper—polished to a mirror's brilliance.

The last snowfall did not stick, but a couple of warm days created a slick, muddy soup out of the Emerald Road and the grounds within the outer baileys.

Twelve of his entourage, gallant warriors from his fortress of Dawn's Glory, also flanked him on each side. These were more talented than the finest knights, all of them clad in heavy plate armor with either sword and axe or sword and flail at the side.

Behind this followed ten more warriors, adept not only with the sword and spear but also the longbow. The duo suns gleamed off the armored figures, both horses and men. The banner of Dawn's Glory flying high immediately to Rory's side.

In fact, the approach of the party was so pristine and captivating, the city guards simply began to open the gates as they drew near. Not a word of challenge or question.

Each of the gated quarters had a fairly large bailey once inside. These eventually led to another sequence of gates, totaling three on the northern approach and four on the other. Of course there were other smaller gates and passages also, as the vast walled city was steadily built outwards in rings of fortifications over the turns. Nuuroc spread out in eleven quarters.

This methodology was for sound defenses, if ever there was need to hold the ranks and stop some encroaching monstrosity from reaching the actual inner walls where the heart of the city fortress thrived.

Rory's group stayed within formation as they halted in the middle of the first bailey, not far from a man watching them intently. The man was a curious figure in flowing, dark green robes that appeared way too large for him. His long, unkempt hair hung over the golden jeweled necklace with the Kuhrzothian seal that titled him as the royal presenter.

His crooked smile greeted Rory's company as an open-palmed hand extended out. "Greetings and salutations on behalf of King Baeynor. I am Royal Presenter Holcomb and will host your arrival. Might I ask who has arrived?"

At this time, a much smaller pony appeared from behind Rory's mount to display the short, stocky man atop it. His humpback and pudgy face poked out from within a thick, gray cloak. A hawk-like, crooked nose wrinkled at the cold. The odd and misshapen lad coughed several times.

The demeanor of Holcomb immediately changed to a tense agitation at the sight of this short and squat man.

A whole armada of Kuhrzothian soldiers had trailed the royal presenter and now stood silently in attendance, like statues.

Holcomb's face twisted and quickly took on the appearance of a conniving rodent who just lost his cheese wedge. "You there!" cried Holcomb.

"I know *you*," he shouted while pointing a finger. "And you are a marked man, wanted for the barbaric butchery of your own kin in Longshadows—little ones at that!"

Spittle flew from his mouth now as he recanted what one of his irksome nature simply reads and retains for later use. "Guards! Arrest that man. He is Wybur Buttlecut."

The man had that estranged gleam of hypocrisy in his eyes and tone. His mannerisms became so rigidly animated that Wybur thought he would end up poking out his own eye.

Rory glared at the man in hearing such things about Wybur.

"Stay your words, my friend." Rory gripped the handle of his two-handed blade. "This man, a merciless cold-blooded killer of even babes?

"Beware what you accuse and seek. For this is a heroic knight of mortality...for all of you that cannot see that through your unfathomable ignorance, then be damned, and I will smite you down myself.

"Go from my sight before the path runs red with your blood! Correct this dirty blemish upon the lot of us, to make such disparaging filth against one so good. This man has been the target of an evil and sinister plot...because he uncovered it.

"In fact, *that* very evil now marches towards you and your home. They will be here within the fortnight."

Rory's blatant threat and what was perceived as direct insubordination to Holcomb's position was just too much. Possibly what was an even more eloquently pitched speech pushed him over the edge. Holcomb's uncontainable fervor exploded through his writhing visage and he could barely restrain himself.

"Do not move—any of you. Or you all will die here!" Holcomb continued to goad, elevating not only his own mannerisms but also the already taut nerves of the scene.

His pre-staged guards along both sides of the yard raised their crossbows, while the foot soldiers drew their swords. The agenda of Royal Presenter Holcomb was now evident. He no doubt had been expecting this particular company to enter the city today. Like a snake that coils in wait for its prey.

The tension increased and movement began towards armed action on both sides. Then a figure clad in green-hued maille strode through the middle of the armada of soldiers—from behind Royal Presenter Holcomb. The newcomer's forest green cape whipped behind him. A booming voice shouted out.

"Stay your weapons, men. Stand down now!" Castym Steele, commander of the Emerald Guard, forced his way to the front with arms out to signal to his men.

Holcomb's face turned red in anger and he wobbled back and forth while his feet rooted to the ground. "Commander, are you committing high sedition and going against my authority? I am above you—I am *the* Royal Presenter!" His voice raised to an uncomfortably high screech.

Once weapons were partially lowered, Commander Steele strode in front of Rory's magnificent beast. Then he removed his helm. "Stand down, men. Here before you is Rory Adnan Sivercroft, the only living heir to King Baeynor Sivercroft the Amiable, now passed onward to the Outer Halls."

Castym dropped down on one knee. "Your people need you now, sire. I am at your service as are the forces of Kuhrzoth. King Rory Adnan Sivercroft, sixty-ninth king to the Emerald Crown."

At this, a sullen cloud played across Rory's expression, as his eyes narrowed and cast downwards. Rory would not get the chance to reconcile with his father. Time had stolen that from him, partly a fault of his own for being so ignorant a fool for so long.

Wybur Buttlecut looked up at Rory's flowing golden hair in awe, never before comprehending the significance of the man whom he thought he knew so much about. He never put two and two together. And he never gave any thought to the family name of the king of Kuhrzoth, only the famous name of King Baeynor the Amiable.

In the glory and wonder of the moment, Holcomb was livened with rage and edged closer to the newcomers as Castym professed the new king with distinction.

Fast as a cat, the wiry man, now frothing at the mouth, jumped at Wybur. In his hand was a long, sharp dagger dripping some dark, sticky substance from the blade. Holcomb's robe flapped in the wind madly as his body vigorously arced directly towards the now unhorsed Wybur.

But Rory's gauntleted hand drew forth his battleaxe hung on the saddle pommel and swung even quicker. He did so without losing so much as a breath—even though his expression was still lost in saddened reverie.

The shiny, double-bladed axe struck into the bony section between Holcomb's neck and shoulder, causing the body to nearly split in two with both arms flailing harmlessly to the sides. The dagger scattered off to the ground.

As Castym's men jumped on the twitching form, it began to vent glowing, white steam into the sunny skies.

The appearance of Holcomb's body began to change, and the oversized robe moved about, like a bunch of mice scurrying into all different directions underneath it.

Before long, the exposed head took on the shape of an odd, grayish thing with bulbous eyes and large teeth. It was hairless and smooth-skinned with knobby ears poking straight out of the sides. But the thing was dead and no longer moved.

"Some type of poison on the blade, no doubt, my lord. But I have no idea what that thing is or was," one of Castym's men reported.

Castym, his sword drawn, looked back to Rory and Wybur. "I fear that this thing has taken the life of King Baeynor as well."

Wybur, still dumbstruck and in shock at seeing the lanky form spring at him so fast, murmured as though reading from a book. "A double-goer...*erhum*... That appears to be a shunmrith."

Wybur knew the look of a shunmrith from all of his studies of course, not that he actually ever saw one. But there it was, there could be no doubt. These creatures were elusive as well as mysterious. The question would be how long had this one assumed the form of Holcomb? And what other mischief had it created while doing so? Then the undying question would be—now that one of these beings had proven itself to be real—were there more of them hidden within their everyday visible world here at Nuuroc? Across the lands?

He finally drew in one deep breath and seemed to regain his composure. Then he sighed heavily.

The body of the former royal presenter, or what he had become, was removed for further study and research.

Over the next couple of days, Rory Sivercroft was officially crowned as king. One of the first things Rory did as king was to send word to Longshadows as to Wybur's innocence.

Along with this word, the party that went also brought back Shab the mule. This was much to Wybur's relief.

Over this same amount of time, Rory began to hold counsel with Castym and the other persons of influence and power in order to prepare for the inevitable. The coming tide of the black forces that ransacked Emerald Rest. Even though most of those within the walls of Nuuroc still doubted such a thing actually happened.

§ § §

The last master assassin of the Dhourkuul stepped back into his ancient fortress to find a small, lifeless form upon the rock floor not far away. One of those young ones brought by Priestess Sahrya.

It was now four days after he fled Clan Tharasvrul. Nimosese felt his heart flicker as he noted the feet and legs of another laying halfway through the inner door. This one had been cut down from behind, and so had the other, he noted once he carefully stalked closer to the doorway.

There were no sounds at all coming from deeper within the stronghold, just eerie silence. He slowly peered around the corner to look down the corridor. Two more of the young brought by Sahrya lay dead, along with two of his own that he had brought here some time ago to train.

Dark ones who he brought here to care for, and show the ways of the Dhourkuul. To provide a way of life. All of these young ones now lay butchered, mostly from cowardly angles and with much more force than was necessary.

He maintained his slow gait as he stalked farther into the labyrinth of the fortress, carefully scouting for signs. Once he turned into the meditation chamber, he saw the body of one more young female, that of little Vufarnah. She had been coming along so well in training, especially in the disciplines. Now only a bloody mess of tangled clothes and flesh. A dead Blackguard lay just beyond her body.

What he had figured to be the work of the priestess was now confirmed. And apparently her brutal rats came through when least expected.

Until now, it had not looked like a fight had been put up against the intruders. But this Blackguard body had a clean, neat slit through his eye.

As Nimosese rounded the last corner leading into the quarters, a lonely, crouching figure wobbled on one foot while bent down on the other knee. Llornah's look of piercing determination even amidst her tattered, bloody clothes rang keen over the edge of the slim longsword pointed at him.

Upon seeing him, her eyes returned to that lost, youthful look that he remembered when he found her among the trees. Then she was so young, such innocence and desperation in those wide eyes. Letting out a voluminous sigh of relief, she fell forward towards the bodies of two more of the dead Blackguard.

Nimosese quickly ran to her and caught her before she hit the cold floor. Her tiny form, battered and cut, felt light as a feather in his arms.

"The rest are safe, Master…behind me, there." Llornah weakly motioned towards the hallway behind her before going limp in his arms.

He gently swept up her small form and walked towards where she had pointed. There, far back within the quarters, were those remaining of his order. Their small bodies were huddled together with drawn weapons of various sorts protruding forth.

§ § §

The slender figure silently crept through the dim passages of the Great Cavern at Tharasvrul. The light of a flickering torch briefly caught the partially cloaked face of the female dark one.

Her huge, piercing eyes studied the corridor ahead before she began moving again through the obscurity.

It was not long before she passed through the meditation chambers and then the reception hall. Now the new section, sealed by a locked door, beckoned her. This was where Priestess Sahrya retreated to, where she lived, where she planned the details of her devious acts.

Nerathurya knew that she only had a short amount of time to play with on this venture. And this would be the one and only opportunity presented to her, at least for the time being.

It had taken so long to even get this far, as the priestess always kept Blackguards or her pets guarding these chambers. There was no way to tell when or even if there would be another such chance. And that waiting was near unbearable to her.

She thought about her task and knew that the object she sought had to be somewhere in here.

Once beside the door, Nerathurya produced tiny metal tools from a leather pouch.

Picking the lock on the door took no time at all. But she was careful to make sure that no wards protected it, as she closed her eyes and sensed the space around the doorway.

Once inside, she moved across the room to another door. Again, she picked the lock and kept going.

Now she was within the inner chambers of Priestess Sahrya. There were several more doors along the wall, as well as large cabinets on the opposite side, and a table and chairs in the center.

After searching the remaining doors, she finally came across one room with an ornate, locked chest inside it. There were other furnishings as well. Mirrors, clothing, and a plush, velvet-covered lounging chair.

Nerathurya carefully bent over the chest and studied it from every angle. Then she closed her eyes, feeling the surrounding space. Nothing.

One last thing, she flicked a small pinch of sparkling dust up in the air and watched it. But it did nothing spectacular that would indicate special wards or glyphs.

This lock took a while longer to pick, but eventually there was a sharp, metallic click. A shimmering, purplish glow permeated the small room as she slowly opened the lid of the chest.

There, resting at the bottom and in the center of the chest, was what appeared to be a scroll completely encased within purple crystal. Ancient Black Clan script flowed across the parchment.

This had to be it. Sephoora mentioned an object of value that held crucial information of worldly consequence. And of ancient origins. The outlandish scroll reached out to all of her senses.

She reached into another leather pouch and produced a blue gem that fit snugly in her hand. It was shaped like a pyramid, although not a true one, as one point was higher than the rest.

As she held this over the glowing scroll, she recited the words and there was a faint blue flash.

These seeing crystals could capture an image of whatever was wanted inside of the tiny pyramid. Of course, only when in the hands of a trained practitioner of the arts. Then another string of words would produce an exact glowing replica of the captured image above the tallest point of the pyramid.

Their use was an old technique. One that eliminated any taint of the information sought, especially on the part of the thief. There was only the cold, hard genuineness of the document replicated by the crystal, for such information as a written document.

Nerathurya began to painstakingly place everything back into the position that she had originally found them. She was methodical as she retraced her way back out of the inner chambers to the meditation chamber.

Once she was content that everything was as it had been, she began to cautiously make her way out of the Great Cavern and back to her quarters.

She thought about all of those dark ones whom she had secretly gathered in preparation. Priestess Sahrya had intentions to relocate Clan Tharasvrul to the ancient fortress Isnuuthghor in the near future. This scheme of hers was one of power, of reviving the Black Clans of old, along with a newfound purpose of conquest.

With Nerathurya being so close to the priestess' inner circle, she was privy to most of what was discussed between her and Khamatiri Mendonytes. And those things raised the hairs on the nape of her neck. Dark times would come for many if Priestess Sahrya was allowed to complete her plans.

Sahrya's plans would eventually reposition all Black Clans that she could locate back into Isnuuthghor. She would reclaim it, if she hadn't already done so. And it sounded as though she had at least four of them there now.

But many of Clan Tharasvrul came to see the light after Sahrya's path of cleansing, the return of the Blackguard, and the resurrection of the black panthers. The killing of the clan's rhaanmri had broken those of true heart and mind.

Those here that had good sense and enough wit to see through the priestess's sheen of wickedness did not want to go to Isnuuthghor. Nor did they even want to be under her power at all.

Using several others as a buffer between her and this growing group of dissidents to the priestess, Nerathurya managed to put into place a plan for them when the time came to move. But the more that were involved in such intricate workings, the greater the chance of being exposed. And exposed meant certain death.

Of course, she could not dare risk being discovered and forfeit her position as an agent of the Veiled Ones. Feeding information about the priestess' plans was ultimately most important. But she would help this group as much as she could.

The night air was chilled, and a blanket of snow covered the ground. But, by the middle of the night, this seeing crystal would be on the way to Sephoora. Its precious cargo would be delivered to the hands of one that could do something about the evils that plagued the lands.

Chapter 21:

Finding Shadows

"There is nothing like the open seas to yer front, the high winds to yer back. All mates at the posts and a whole lot o' saltswords onboard, full deck onward o' sails. And yern enemy settin' into the wind tryin' to run, but all the while just closing the distance on the spit-frogs."

–Unknown privateer captain along the Frostsea.

he lone, slender figure glided along the soaring, rocky path that switch-backed up the tallest peak of the Reach, located along the western spires of the Rock Rim.

The Reach was named as such due to its appearance. These peaks resembled an enormous hand with fingers extended towards the sky, narrow and higher reaching than their surrounding siblings of the Rock Rim.

This particular path was of ancient inception, and it was designed along this approach due to the constant high winds. Even during the most frigid periods of winterfall, the winds would sweep the path endlessly and keep it free of any snow buildup. Thus allowing use of the path all of the time, regardless of weather.

But the truth was that it had not been used for a very long time. Not since back in the early days when Arterium reigned.

This middle peak within the Reach was named Crystal Peak due to the opaque icy formation at the pinnacle. The oddity was unlike any other summit within the Rock Rim. Even from a considerable distance, it appeared as a shiny gem or crystal shard glinting in the rays of the duo suns.

Zaramagrii felt the cold sting of the icy air. The frosty blasts were constant at this lofty height of the Rock Rim. But amazingly, her breath was strong and unhindered by such scarcity. The winterfall storms of ice and snow had subsided, but probably not for long. The season rarely mattered up here as far as the elements were concerned.

Not that such a thing would stop her, nothing would. Her resolve was beyond any possible constraint at this point, and she deeply felt that she was being guided by some unseen force of immense magnitude. Preordained. Whether a being or other worldly creation, a thing yet unknown, but one of a higher affirmation.

She still could not forget what transpired at Tharasvrul. The priestess had been within her grasp, and so close to getting justice from her blade. And that smug look on Sahrya's face as she sat on her throne with such an arrogant air of indifference. The opportunity to close that vengeful chapter slipped through her fingers as the master assassin called out to her. If he hadn't warned her, then things might be different now. The priestess would no doubt have finally succeeded in her quest to butcher Zaramagrii. Even if the master assassin failed in doing so, Zaramagrii learned that Sahrya had other traps devised once she grew close enough to where Sahrya sat. No, Zaramagrii would surely have been slain one way or another. Possibly even captured.

But her interest was piqued by what the master assassin had told her. She had waited outside the Great Cavern and well away from the frantically searching Blackguard patrols sent out after her. It was not long before Nimosese appeared, sprinting from the mouth of the cave nearly in a straight line towards her, unbeknownst to him at the time.

Zaramagrii naively thought that the legends of the ancient order of the Dhourkuul and Clan Thurpazkul were only stories of myth. Stories created to bestow awe and interest in one's past, to build the mystique. To inspire the rhyme and reason behind certain aspects of the Black Clan way of life and death. But, after she met Nimosese, and they had talked for a while, many parables turned to reality.

What he explained helped her to understand herself even more. And it all directly connected and wove together into the counsels that she had with Wybur at Dawn's Glory.

Those visions of the skeletal apparition within a cave became even more lucid over the past few nights. Just when sleep tried to take her, she would drift off into bouts of what seemed so real and clear. The skeleton had something in its hand, but what? That was the one piece that just never materialized within the visions, ever. It had to be significant.

Zaramagrii's mind returned to her conversation with Nimosese, as it so often had done since they first met outside of the Great Cavern. There was just too much left unfinished. Incomplete.

No, when all was said and done, she would visit the Dhourkuul master in his mountain fortress. When all of what was said and done? Now that was something that needed to be further reckoned with…and unraveled.

In any case, she would revisit him at some point and continue with the revelations of her past—the Black Clan past—everything concerning the past. All that he was willing to share and expound upon.

It was he that had shown her the ancient ways of the Mynrooth portals, one of which was nearby Tharasvrul. Then another one that was within a day's march of Crystal Peak. Using that old, lost art had allowed her to quickly emerge near the Reach. These ancient portals were old world thaumaturgy from an even older folk and time. But she now understood them, and what they could do. She wondered if the priestess had any inkling of them.

Her concentration was broken by the edges of a jagged, gaping hole in the path ahead of her. The path had fallen here, possibly after so much time and weathering, or something had shattered it.

Without so much as a thought, she eyed the distance and then leapt through the air. As she glided across the chasm of unknown leagues below her, she somersaulted feet over head so as to look directly down the hole before landing gently on the other side.

The distance was a good thirty paces, but the strength of her sinewy body easily carried her across it. Or maybe it also meshed with her Shadehaunt abilities. She was not sure.

Then she knew, or realized, what now was missing from her essence. Fear. She had not felt actual fear since the confrontation between her mother and the priestess, and then the aloneness of the dark, subterranean world.

It almost hit her like a slap across the face. She never really had an actual shaking fear of anything, but now it was like there was not even the slightest inhibition. Even for such harrowing acts as leaping over a chasm that must fall straight down at least four leagues to hard, rocky lands below. No fear from being in the middle of a sprawling Hulding village, all alone. Just an urge, or instinct, to act and influence the world around her. But the events of the patrol and what she did to it or them appeared to further drive that fearlessness. Maybe it was just plain confidence in herself and what she could achieve.

Instead, such dire circumstances almost made her more sharp and lucid. More calculating and meticulous in her thoughts and actions. What was considered perilous by most simply honed and sharpened her like a finely crafted blade forged by a master smith.

Zaramagrii climbed for nearly the second day straight, and what appeared before her only increased her eagerness to discover what had been driving her to this old place.

The archway and doors of the ancient fortress known as the Nook of the Reach were broken and appeared blown inwards by some unimaginable force. Fresh fragments of pulverized stone lay strewn everywhere. The destruction was recently done. Someone or something had already beaten her here it would seem. The cold, dark hole spoke nothing but gloom, yet it beckoned Zaramagrii inside as an ominous, enchanting chest waiting to be opened. Somewhere deep within her, those dismal wraiths found a kindred entity. She felt a detached, sterile warmth of sorts, completely free from that sense of strangeness of an unknown place. Calling to her. Inviting her. Almost making her feel like she was returning home. And then she was inside the ages-old fortress.

Prior to whatever had breached these walls before her, this place had not seen a spirit for maybe over fifteen hundred years.

Yes, she remembered what she had learned about the history of the Nook of the Reach, resting high atop Crystal Peak. Tales of an old lich, a powerful wizard, who held an undead army at the mountain post. The lich was always reputed to have unleashed some of the terrors running through the world to this day. Experiments and wild tampering with things unknown. With dark things that most knew better than to stir and pry at.

The most prevalent one was that this place was the spark to what created things like the Akhruuk, as well as other creatures. That it had been some sort of gateway opened up by the lich and used to bring these things in from other places or even worlds. Or that the lich had bred and created such monstrosities.

Even Arterium's men had explored it back in his days, whether to quiet the myths, or maybe to prove the fallacies one way or the other to himself. But what remained of their findings, at least in written annals, provided no answers.

All of the walls and doorways inside held intricately inscribed runes and designs of different sorts. Depictions of various creatures and objects also filled these spaces.

The only open passage led straight back through what seemed to be a long, vast chamber. The high, arched ceiling stirred with billowing cobwebs that hung like sheets.

Then the passage narrowed and passed through several places where other corridor junctions had long ago been violently closed. Many could have been from the worn hands of time itself.

A familiar face stared down at her from above an ornately carved, square archway. Once there had been huge oak doors that could be barred, but now they lay in their own state of repose. No longer able to either hold out against an attacker or contain those inside the now quiet halls.

Above that entrance was the ancient, blackened half sun rising up, with lightning bolt rays shooting away from it. The bottom oval of the half sun held a distinct, darker portion.

Each of the upper corners of the doorway's arch held an exotically large gem. One was black and the other white. Even in the dimly illuminated darkness, they appeared to have a subtle glow to them.

But what would the old symbol of Lord Siri be doing in such a place? A place known in recorded history to be the retreat of a powerful lich with an undead army at its command.

Her footsteps barely made sound, but they echoed like thunder down the passageway to her. After several hundred paces, she came to another collapsed intersection. But this time, one side had been reopened recently. Again, there were freshly strewn rocks and pieces of the ornate wall tiling everywhere.

This passage led back and down several flights of exceptionally long steps. It finally brought her to a smaller chamber that had also been blasted into by some force. The stone slab doors lay in fragments.

There were more corridors leading off at several points, but each of these went only as far as the eye could see—before running into collapsed ruin.

Zaramagrii was mesmerized by what she found in that chamber. The old and now withered form of a man lay at the center of it. Rich, lavish clothing covered the bony remains. A jeweled pendant hung around the neck, one of exquisite craftsmanship and exceptional value. The royal crest of Kuhrzoth held her gaze for a moment, as it dully glowed. The rich emeralds, diamonds, and pure silver created a mesmerizing glitter, even in the dark.

So this was the fabled wizard Haqnimemza, the strength and right hand of the legendary King Arterium.

Not far to the side was another more recent victim of foulness. It was an old, fragile man with ragged wounds suggesting that he was stabbed in the back. His robes also signified some degree of wealth or nobility, maybe just in title.

She studied Haqnimemza's hands carefully and determined that something had been grasped securely in the one. After some time spent contemplating the scene, she tucked the arch-wizard's necklace into her pouch and then returned back to the main corridor.

Those that penetrated this place before her were no ordinary thieves or even adventurers. Such characters would not have left these valuables in place, like the gems set in the doorway or this ancient crest of Kuhrzoth.

Now the passage opened up a bit more, both in height and width. A being ten-foot-tall could walk here comfortably, as well as could three dark ones abreast.

But this also appeared to be a dead end, as it meandered into a large square chamber that resembled some sort of cathedral or temple possibly. There was a cleanly built sub-level center to the floor with numerous runes across it, as if it had contained a pool of water at one time. These sides rose up to where the floor ran out to the manicured walls.

Markings and symbols covered the interior of this place. One in particular caught her attention, located at the far end on the floor. Once again, the most ancient symbol of Lord Siri was carefully carved into the floor here, and of very large size at that. It nearly extended across the entire width.

But the lightning bolt rays only partially extended away from the half sun, running right into the wall as though the builder ran out of room.

This far wall had two large orbs, one black and one white, imbedded about the height of one's eyes. Their design was from some material unknown to her.

She was drawn to these globes, which appeared to give off a faint glow at their centers. As her booted feet planted on the blackened half sun, elation washed over her body.

The deeply inspiring feeling was like discovering a new thing, one of powerful significance in the way of one's own uniqueness and profound depth. Like the first time that she learned to commune with the wolves of the rhaanmri—just one of the many things taught to her by Elder Tarrne, gently and with much patience. It was beyond explanation, but felt as though it emanated from outside of her. Yet it completely saturated her mind, body, and essence.

Within moments of her hands finding their place on each of the orbs, the deep, heavy grating of rock on rock erupted from inside of the wall. A portion of the wall began to slide slowly to the side while rotating inward.

An immense hallway, cast in deep gray and carved into strange black rock, extended back. Small tendrils of wispy darkness crept out as though opening the hidden door broke a seal and released some gaseous specter from within.

A dim glow further down the passage caught her attention. The smell and texture of the air within this area changed from that of a timeworn, dusty crypt to one of crisp coolness. It was as though the air was alive and moving about.

The sound of her boots appeared muffled, as she calmly proceeded deeper in.

Not far into the corridor, the far end began to show itself as a sweepingly large, carved chamber. Small metallic cones holding a flame or light illuminated the entire corridor right into this other chamber.

This light was no ordinary flame, for it glowed a dull blue with black hues swimming about it. She thought that there was a faint red or scarlet-colored aura as well outside of this black border.

The light made her comfortable, like the feeling that she had when she spent time with her mother. That flood of warmth and love where her mother made her feel like the center of the world.

This sensation circled about her and gave the appearance that someone or something felt an extraordinary love for her. She could not fully explain it.

What at first she thought to be two more of the strange wall lights, now stood out as eyes of a dismal form seated upon a decidedly large chair. No, a throne...made of large bones. Blackened bones. In the center of the carved chamber.

The thing seated on it was an armored figure. Even in the dull glow of the outlandish lights, the armor shone with a brilliance unsurpassed. A great-helm with an open visor rested on the bony head. If it were not for those eyes, one might think that this statue was just that, a statue.

As Zaramagrii drew closer, a gauntlet-clad bony hand twitched and gripped the arm of the throne with a soft grating noise. The head dipped slightly. The other decayed hand clanked in the steel gauntlet as it dragged a massive two-handed sword up from where it had been resting along the side of the throne.

Now Zaramagrii stopped to stare at the apparition as it slowly rose from the throne. All of the various metal pieces that were fitted and cast into the heavy plate maille armor clanged and chimed as it did so. The suit was of an exceptional quality.

The old knight brought the sword forward and planted the tip upon the floor in front with every step. The thing's footsteps echoed loudly throughout the chamber.

But not one thought of danger or alarm rose within her, not one fiber of doubt as to what the skeleton might do.

The eyes nearly flamed outwards now as it grew closer, small points of red deep within them.

It came to a halt directly in front of her, not three paces away. The animated suit of bones and steel rose two foot taller than Zaramagrii.

With the huge sword off to her side, several moments passed as the eyes confronted hers and appeared to sweep through her body, her essence.

Then the grand knight of the dead dropped hard to one armored knee with an echoing ding. Its head bowed slowly as the free hand brought forth a uniquely crafted blade.

It was a khopesh styled sword. The scabbard alone held an exquisite air, the pommel ablaze with various glowing gems. A blackened, leathery material was tightly wrapped about the handle. This work of death's beauty must have indeed been old. *No, ancient.* She sensed an ethereal presence about the curved weapon that roused the surrounding air.

Zaramagrii stood astounded at the act that just took place, now gathering that this knight served her. It knew her, or knew of her, what she was. *Who she was.* This venerable entity had waited and endured the test of time to fulfill its sacred obligation.

Its head never raised as a deep, smooth baritone echoed forth to her. "*Volkura Drakna*…my Dark Queen, behold your destiny.

"*Volkura Naux et dha Volkura Throk*…the Shadow Blade, the Impaler of Shadows. Know that it will bind with your eternal essence, as it always has been. Now the physical manifestation."

The skeletal knight gently set it within her palm until she firmly grasped it.

With a nearly silent *shhht*, she drew forth the blade and admired the design. The blade was unique as it ran straight out from the handle for the length of her forearm, then curved deeply as a crescent moon out to the tip. Her grasp of the oversized handle instilled her with a new sense of purpose. The rush was so powerful that she had to momentarily close her eyes in order to keep her sense of balance.

Strangely, the blade somehow wrapped its own form about her, about her spirit, her mind. About the essence. She could feel it thriving. Now part of her in some way.

There was a strange trinity between the sword, the ring, and her. But the sense of this feeling was immense, and, like a surmounting, cresting wave nearing the break, it continued to soar farther.

The new found sense that began with her expulsion into the subterranean caves sprang forth and she felt the entire chamber. She felt everything around her, as her eyes closed. The equilibrium of this surge placed things into perspective and a thousand scenes flashed through her mind's eye. Most were scenes of the old world, even before the Revered Times.

Now Zaramagrii fully comprehended that she had a much higher purpose, and that purpose was to find what was called the *Larunwyr*. That was what would lead her to answers.

Larunwyr was ancient Black Clan, which literally meant void in the Common tongue. Hopefully something would make this clearer to her. Something more to show her path to it. And then what she must do once she found it.

Once Zaramagrii's eyes reopened, the glorious hooked blade had an aura to it that shimmered and moved. A blackened, red hue surrounded the blade, tiny wisps of dark smoke emanating from the edges.

Instinctively, she grasped the perfectly crafted handle in both hands and slowly separated them in a widening arc to the sides. The sword became two dark beacons of smoky energy that moved as fast as she could think them to.

They smoothly glided and cut through the air, faster than what was possible. And Zaramagrii danced through the darkness with the duo blades, as though they were extensions of her hands.

As she twisted the blade in her hand and looked back to the apparition, she discovered another billowing form sulking behind the skeletal knight. Two leering eyes slightly higher than hers—haunting eyes that glared at her. Familiar eyes.

And it was as though she stared at a reflection. One of her own body. For the large eye on the form's right side was like a shiny diamond, while that on the left was as black as an obsidian. The visage appeared to be a mirror image of herself, she thought at first, now awed. Maybe this was but a dream or another vision.

But the shimmering outline of the form was definitely not hers, nor like any Aylsh or Man-folk. It was a giant thing, a huge beast.

And then the voice hit her, or more empathy than actual vocals. While no sounds were produced, she could almost feel everything that the form displayed to her...through thoughts? Feelings? Possibly a mix of both, but the understanding of this telepathy was crystal clear. And she could sense the immense depth of the thing's aura, the wisdom of an unfathomable being.

As the soothing warmth of long forsaken now reacquainted instinct overtook her, the form began to materialize into the largest black wolf that she had ever seen. But it was near opaque and trailed dark, sooty smoke whenever it moved—even slightly.

A strange red hue or glow permeated from around the edges of the furry outline.

You are the Dark Queen, the Shadow Soul…and I am yours. We are reflections of the higher purpose. My name is Grasfur, or, in the Old Ways, Grastharfah il Marilaan. I am the first wolf, the first warg, the Alpha Omega. The first of many things in the world now. And I am here to serve.

Both the material world and what had to have been other realms appeared to swirl about her, taking her to dizzying heights. Until it all disappeared in a smothering black haze.

Later, Zaramagrii leaned against one of the pillars and rested near the crumbled entrance to the Nook of the Reach. The comforting feel of Grasfur lying next to her gave her both reassurance and acceptance. His soft coat and methodical breathing eased her mind. Now he was the likeness of a large, black-furred wolf, although the contrasting eyes betrayed his hidden nature.

The intense realizations of her recent discoveries, coupled with the lack of sleep while traveling to the Nook finally inundated her. She lost herself to the overwhelming weariness and succumbed to a deep sleep.

Within the drowning slumber, visions of the pristine emerald banner of Kuhrzoth flying over a massive, walled city leapt over and around her as though she stood high upon the wall. At first, the image of Rory being draped with a rich green mantle settled easily within her. Then she turned to look out across the view atop the high walls. A blinding white form flew through the skies throwing flashes of lightning towards the walls. And, below this being of presumable light, a black throng of Akhruuk and other wicked things swarmed as far as the eye could see.

Zaramagrii bolted upright, completely alert. The abruptness of her stirring caused Grasfur to snap his head up and stretch his forelegs out together while yawning with a slight chirp. She could feel him sense her thoughts. Then the huge warg jumped up, now melded with her sense of urgency.

There was no time left. She must get to Nuuroc. No doubt she would be able to find Rory, or Wybur, and gain more insight as to what was coming to her through these visions in her mind. But there was something going on and, whatever it was, it was not good. But it was what must come to pass. The road to the future. And she sensed that this was something that included her. A deep rolling omen of unstoppable might.

§ § §

Rory stared at the man before him, standing so gallantly there in an armored pretense of condemnation. This man stood against all that surrounded him, and it appeared as though he commanded all. Even the Emerald Guard protecting the king of Kuhrzoth stared at the Legion commander with the look of both awe and respect.

The look of pompous arrogance, which this particular man managed to turn into barbarous elegance. His deep black beard accented a shiny bald head full of scars, and those eyes were cold from many a hardship.

The gaze was reserved yet demanding, almost enticing action out of those who fell under it. Now King Sivercroft knew why most, if not all, succumbed to the will of the Legion commander.

"So why does the commander of the Black Legion call upon the king of Kuhrzoth?" mused Rory as he rose from the ornately carved throne. But his eyes suggested clarity in deciphering the wiles of what most plied before him.

Axyander the Steelborn walked proudly towards Rory. He rested his forearm upon the pommel of the large blade hung at his side, like it was a chair.

"My lord, it brings me great honor to present to you this day. I come upon the drafts of a very large black army from out of Oshghrul."

Using the word *present* played the entire lord and subject game, with such obvious flattery.

The term army was a curious thing, in most parts of Thaldeia. But what did an army actually entail? Most would rightfully say that any group of warriors numbering thirty-five or more was indeed an army. Fewer than this was called a band. And if there were between four and seven such warriors, then the proper term would be thieves. Anything less than that was left to the whim of the perceiver. Of course, these morsels of information spurred from the appearance of either the army, the band, or the thieves actually engaging in threatening behavior.

But Axyander's cool gray eyes denoted no warmth except only when he deemed it necessary with a slow, wry smile. This man had the icy cold of conflict within him, and that was what he thrived upon and lived for.

Rory canted his head and eyed him thoughtfully. "Indeed, my commander, this I already know. But I commend you for your forewarning. You are indeed a man of honor."

Axyander stood now with his expression that of stone. "I knew that you had word—warning—as the might of Kuhrzoth would not be trifled by typical rabble and brigands. But this one is different.

"My scouts have reported peculiarities with this army. It is not your average ragtag band of quarreling goblins and such."

"Well, I am aware that there has been some unification of these vermin...by someone or something. What specifically do you know, Axyander?"

The Black Legion commander now folded his sinewy arms upon his chest with a deep breath, while flexing his muscles for show. "My lord, there are mixed together Akhruuk, goblins, ogres, joutuun, wargs, possibly others.

"There is leadership structure within this array of mud figures, as well as siege engines. A powerful wizard of some kind leads them. You should know that this has been unheard of for a thousand year. The fall of Emerald Rest concludes that...and amplifies the possibilities—as well as their pretense."

Rory nodded his head slightly while listening. "Yes, something has been going on within the Fallen Lands. But surely you bring more than news of gloom? What is on your map here?"

Axyander now sounded incredibly succinct but polished. "I bring you the Legion, my lord.

"Twenty-plus thousand of the Legion at the back door of this unsightly horde. Unification of effort and allegiance, in the name of Kuhrzoth... Like the days of old when there were no lines drawn between the forces of Kuhrzoth and the Legion.

"Together we can defeat them and drive them from existence." His eyes were cold and emotionless, even though his ardent speech was unmistakable.

Of course he spoke of days long ago, even before the Legion was named as such. The days of its predecessor, the Knights of the Wild—the Order of the Wild. Before the royalty of this day had planted its origins through gold and wicked seed. A time when the noble warriors of the lands stood for a common cause.

"But such things never come without some cost. Albeit a hidden one. A grand verse of polished oration leads to the frills of the coffers no doubt," Rory tested.

Axyander spoke the words as though a polished statesman, direct as could be. "Royal instatement, my lord. That is all. No monetary compense."

Rory raised his eyebrows. "You want to fall under the Crown of Kuhrzoth? Nothing more? Surely you jest?"

"Nothing more, my lord." Axyander produced a gold sealed, rolled parchment at this point, handing it eloquently over to the king. "I have preordained a certain contract for you…if you so deem to accept and honor the terms."

Rory slowly grasped the parchment and held it without pulling open the tie. "That will be all, Axyander."

The Legion commander swayed from one foot and stood equally upon both, slightly bowing forward. "Yes, my lord. I will await your decision. But *know* that at least one hundred thousand march on your doorstep even while we speak.

"I will await in the quarters with my mages for another day. Obviously, the more time the better with which to implement any plans. Good day, my lord."

With that, Axyander bowed low and then walked out of the royal hall, his boots loudly echoing across the walls as he did so.

Rory sat back down now deep in thought, as he slowly digested the contents of the parchment from Axyander. All the while he couldn't help but wonder when the Fleshling would return with news.

Chapter 22:

A Kingdom

Prepares

Masses of our kind throughout the lands of remorse,

Taketh these ways to be the rise of our might.

One such of the heavens shall step forth to lead us to the path.

Amongst an orgy of the ones with swarming aberrance,

Our kind shall wash upon the scourges of time,

To vanquish that which holds unjust reins o'er all.

The mark of the night sun rising and the skies darkening,

With the fall of the green spires,

Shall set forth the era of the faithfully blind.

> –Excerpt from the Khaman, the Akhruuk divine lore, as protected by the Oracles of Chevron Ruuk. These date to an unknown time before SA 181 when they came to be known to the folk of Thaldeia.

King Rory Adnan Sivercroft sat upon the Emerald Throne of Kuhrzoth, deep in thought both of contemplation and puzzlement. Each of his visions had led him, or others, to something tangible. Not only that, but almost always something of uniqueness. And of importance.

But now he was bothered by what he saw in his own mind at night, before he would awake in a cold sweat. Every night, his mind raced to a deep, gloomy sea under dark and melancholy skies lit by a nebulous, orange glow. Rory would find himself immersed within the waters, the surface but two foot from his head. The weight of his armored body drew him from it, pulling him farther and farther down. And always down he went, forever sinking before his lungs burst with agony from holding his breath. Until he could no longer do so, then his frantic, ill-rested mind would snap awake.

And even here in his real world, there was no let up to the drowning, the sinking. There was no bottom to the murky waters.

No chance of survival it seemed. Nightmares while sleeping, dark insurmountable adversities while awake.

And on top of this, he had much to ponder as well. From the rigors of going over his phalanx tactics with the Emerald Order to the demands of Axyander and the Legion. The drills out on the training grounds went on endlessly, all the while watching the workings of the heavy horse as they lanced the quintains while maneuvering around the bristling phalanxes. The largest of these fields inside of the walls was known as the Manors, since it was in the Manors Quarter. It was large enough for the entire force of Emerald Knights to assemble for parades and ceremonies.

There were other wartime preparations—the tedious counsels of all plans and defenses with each and every line commander. And on top of all this, there were his routine kingly duties. Although there was nothing routine about settling lineage disputes between siblings, or attempting to appease those beset by end-of-times prophecies. There just seemed to be no rest.

The royal messenger had returned during the night, and his words did not present a very good outlook. He called it an endless black army that not only occupied Emerald Rest, but also the entire valley that ran up into the Fallen Lands. There were no survivors from Emerald Rest left living.

The force that had been dispatched to scout what befell Emerald Rest was recalled as quickly as it had been sent out. Other small probing parties went out to assess the disposition of the black army, but no word had come back yet. All of these forces were ordered to weave their way there, in order to check the huge swaths of the kingdom between Nuuroc and Emerald Rest.

Then there was the mysterious, yet troubling, mark upon the handle of the blade used by Royal Presenter Holcomb. Or what had become Holcomb at least. The alchemists still did not know what the dark, sticky liquid was that coated that blade. But the substance felled a full sized ox immediately, when just a dab of it was placed upon the ox's tongue.

At the time, the mark upon the dagger seemed to be nothing at all. But then, when the body of the shunmrith was hauled off, a mark of the same exact design was found tattooed upon the thing's chest.

But what did the mark mean? An octopus with a curved dagger running through the middle. There were marks, possibly runes, upon each side of the dagger. The blade of the dagger definitely was shown to have a dark liquid dripping from it, most clearly thought to indicate a poison of some kind. But this sigil or crest had never before shown up anywhere of note. No history or lore had it emblazoned within their confines. At least none known to the legendars of the House of Legends.

One thing that did not sit well with Rory was the fact that the royal presenter was the sole officiating body over the awarding of lands and titles. Yes, the king was ultimately the one that decided the benefactors of such things, but the king did not have the time for the countless banter of tasks like this. The awarding of lands and titles, as with many other aspects of governance, were relegated to other royal appointees, like the royal presenter. The king still proclaimed and blessed off on these things, but these were armloads of scrolls nearly every day. And there was no physical way that one man was capable of handling this and all of the other kingly responsibilities.

Now Rory was lost to speculation that there very well could be other titled individuals out there, whether landholders or others in official capacities, that might be connected to the schemes of what Holcomb had become. There was no telling just how long the shunmrith had assumed his being. Of course this was just the tip of the pike. It did not begin to question all of the other dealings that the royal presenter was involved in.

His day dreams were shattered by the large wooden doors of the royal hall creaking open at the far end.

In strode Castym in his green-hued armor, with two figures wearing cloaks in tow behind him.

An aged, but lovely, white and gray-speckled wolf trailed them in, bouncing on all fours.

The one in a scintillating gray robe was also carrying an ornate wooden rod that added a certain glow to the form. Her hood was pulled back to reveal one of distinct Aylsh features, the pointed ears poking out of the thick golden hair kissed by the suns. This Aylsh maiden's face was beautiful—alluring, and she seemed to glide across the floor to him.

Awed by an apparent mystery confronting him, Rory silently stared as he slowly took in the presence before him. His weary expression softened lightly, like the casting of rejoiced light from the rise of the duo suns in the morn.

As the aura surrounding Ephritori gathered weight within Rory's cognition, he quickly rose to his feet and stepped towards her, mouth slightly agape. But his eyes sparkled with knowing now. He quickly kneeled at her feet and gently pressed his lips to her hand after grasping it.

Rory knew who this persona was, as he was so pure himself, and so righteous. He instinctively saw the brilliant radiance surrounding her form, hidden to most.

And his heavily weighted essence lifted up with virtuous rapture, the feeling coursing through him and rejuvenating every tingling nerve within his body.

Huge tears burst forth from the giant's eyes while he looked upon her, the words stretching out as he cried. "Forgive me, Mother, I had no idea that you were here. I had no idea that you walked this world. 'Tis true."

At this point, the hood on the other woman's plain cloak fell back to display her pretty face mixed into her auburn swirl of hair. A great-bow sat in one hand, a bow that glowed a dull blue. She just stared and smiled at the sight of them standing before the throne.

Ephritori's warmth enveloped Rory. "By Lord Braxis, may the power of the suns light your way into darkness."

Rory let out a quick laugh, now freed from the mire of doubt. "And may the five moons guide you through it, my lady."

Ephritori smiled. "You are puzzled, my lord, but do not be. For all will be known in good time. Take things in stride, as you have your people to be concerned with now. Your visions will become more clear to you, let them go and wait. Deep down within, you know what must be done."

Rory, still upon one knee, looked up at her with eyes bespoken of weariness. "Yes, but the more recent dreams… They have been ominous, hard to see. So dark."

She gently caressed his cheek and wiped a lock of golden hair from his forehead. "Yes, when one such as you is open enough to actually see things for what they really are, they can be overly burdening...much with self-driven worry and guilt.

"Remember that fate has its designs, and they will come to pass as such, regardless of attempts to thwart it. And sometimes it gets darkest just before the light. This abides by you as well, I myself, and each of those here.

"Have no fears. Go with your heart. Know that your actions guided by such will inevitably shine with calming warmth and strength, no matter what the circumstances. Trust in yourself and in that which freely flows to you. It has carried you thus far."

Now Ephritori's figure took on a subtle blue glow that softly radiated outwards. "Behold, my lord. For I am Ephritori Nephritaryah Bari Lourendalthemee, last heir and line to Daumere Bari Lourendalthemee of Enclave Noblynbindyn. The most pure of Aylsh lineage. That of the True King and Father of the Aylsh.

"My father long ago hid me from the forces of evil. He hid me out in the open with Mordrid the Wyrmslayer as my protector. We came across a small child while traveling from the kingdom to the Free Lands, and Mordrid devised the clever scheme of wedding me and taking the child as our own. With none knowing the difference. Alas, they were both slain.

"My father did so to protect what he knew to be the future of his race, possibly of the world. For I now know that my destiny was to carry forth as Ityarfa Vorjanimae...the Eternal Mother," she stretched out the small, ornate wooden rod which began to lengthen and glow blinding white, "and behold Jahthra Khomar, the Spear of Eternal Light.

"My time here will be short for I have binding purpose in the Aylsh Kingdom. What I do there will have more far-reaching consequences, many years from now but still will directly embolden what you have started here. It is just not one people or place that shall be cast into the darkness.

"Your place is here, Rory Adnan Sivercroft the Bastard Prophet," she gently touched his right shoulder, left shoulder, then top of his head with the blazing spear, "the Righteous One."

Fine, shimmering blue sparkles cascaded around Rory as he looked up with renewed determination.

And Rory now saw the light behind his purpose of being. There was no worry or fear for what might be or could happen. Whatever it was would happen regardless of what he or anyone else did, but he was destined to walk this path and could not be led astray, not even by himself. "Mother, I will not fail you."

Ephritori looked deeply into his eyes while speaking. "You cannot fail, that is not possible. But you, along with all of the others, will be tested. For an epic battle is coming. In truth, it will only be the start of things. But it will ever be so dark, and darker times do come."

Rhalwa joined them and the three of them talked for the remainder of the day, well into the dark of the night. One important note that Ephritori made Rory promise to was that he would have Wybur scribe an exact replica of the black book of Siri as soon as possible.

§ § §

Before the next day passed, with the setting of the commanding duo suns, Ephritori and Rhalwa found themselves departing from the Emerald Tower. Once down the winding stairs, the path took them past an antiquated stone structure. The impressive, high arched building was the very first structure built here when Old Nuuroc was first established by King Arterium. And here it was, the first temple to Lord Braxis, nearly as elegantly intact as it was back then. The decay had been slow.

But Ephritori had no time to admire it, for she suddenly felt nauseated and nearly fell down to the ground. Such misery and tremendous sadness struck her with the weight of a thousand stone slabs. It hit her so hard and fast that she faltered in her steps. Mountainous tears streaked down her face. Rhalwa rushed to her side and held her as she sank to her knees.

"What is it? Are you ill?" asked Rhalwa. She stared intensely upon Ephritori with a look of concern. Then she hurriedly searched about Ephritori for sign of an injury.

"I...do not know exactly. A darkness just descended upon me from nowhere. It was so sad and forlorn," whispered Ephritori with a look as though she stared at something a thousand leagues away. She gently rested her palm upon the old stone wall of the temple.

Ephritori could not really fathom the depth of what she felt so keenly that day. It was a feeling that was never felt before by her or even pondered.

But it was the din of a thousand voices, the very first primordial essences. Attempting to grasp onto one last hope, the

Eternal Mother. Alas, to no avail. At least not in this early portion of the tale.

It would be another near turn of time before Sephoora uncovered enough of the ensuing madness. Madness that not even the scholars throughout all the ages had been able to foresee. It would be a long time before she would begin to piece together what the legendary Arterium had set into motion so long ago.

§ § §

As the day drew to a close and the shades of night began to play across the regal walled city of Nuuroc, the royal seal and Castym arrived as requested to the throne. The royal seal was a lean, white-haired man wearing fine spectacles that added to his archaic look. But his eyes sparkled with clarity and perception through those thick, translucent lenses.

Rory eyed the royal seal thoughtfully. "Do you have parchment and ink, my good man?"

The royal seal, whose duty it was to record official decrees and proclamations made by the king, fumbled with his satchel at his side. "Of course, sire. Always."

"Then let us get started." Rory took them both into the council chambers off to the side and closed the heavy oak door behind them with a rattle and click of the old lock.

§ § §

The night air blew its chilling tale across the forests, but naught stirred with a murmur beyond the scampering of a fox or the snapping of an old branch by a stag. And even these had their own silent charms about them.

No one would have guessed that near twenty thousand warriors sat in their makeshift camps strategically spread out for leagues.

Those of the Black Legion stood their watches, no light or fires, no clatter or racket. Such was their discipline. And they waited for word, the word to lunge out and do what they did best. Even earlier, scouts had reported the masses of the black horde as it burned its way towards Nuuroc.

The clamor of their lines could be heard even by those of the Legion, the stink drifting to them on the winds. And all the while they remained silent. As quiet as the cold, wintry forest itself.

§ § §

King Rory Sivercroft spent the entire day striding about the parapets and battlements of Nuuroc, stopping at each one to look out over the distant scenery. Nuuroc was so vast. Without his horse, this might have taken a fortnight.

He also attended to some final plans for the upcoming defenses. Nuuroc had a cavernous, but hidden and well-guarded, lower gate that actually dropped down into a large tunnel. This ages old tunnel traveled under the huge city and out into a ravine to the west. This trap door of sorts was heavily built with iron and metals so that no fire could be lit from underneath to destroy it. This portion of Nuuroc also held several fresh water aqueducts and cisterns that flowed in from the Mhisimik River. All of these were underground and also heavily guarded. The subterranean labyrinth that nestled under the walled city held many such places for water, but these were mostly communal. Such an engineered feat allowed an uninterrupted source of water, even if the city ever fell under a prolonged siege.

The tunnel really did not travel all that far underneath Nuuroc. The trap door was very close to the western walls to begin with. This opened into the tunnel that eventually became a wide ravine, leading out to the open meadows and grasslands.

A fairly large force could ride either north or south from where the ravine dumped out into the flats. This could be done in a very short amount of time, and was specially designed with the defense of the castle in mind. Kuhrzoth could have a sizeable army out of the walls and upon an enemy before they even knew what was happening to them. This tactic had been played cunningly throughout the rich history of Kuhrzoth's past.

The forces of the Emerald Crown took well to the new tactics of the phalanx. Practice went back and forth throughout the day, sometimes even during the night when one could not see one's own hand near one's face.

As the late-suns waned, Rory returned to the royal hall again, now resting his eyes upon Ephritori and Rhalwa. Daraphyn stood at their feet, showering Rory with an inquisitive look.

He had attempted to convince Ephritori to remain at Nuuroc, but she had a mind to depart for the Aylsh Kingdom. Except, she kept telling him, there was one more individual that she had not met with yet. And this individual was extremely important. When questioned who and why, there was no good answer from her but *I'll know when I see her.* He eventually gave up on his attempts at trying to persuade her to stay.

It was not very long after this that a dark line of smoke materialized towards the center of the chamber, not far from them. Daraphyn stood and began to rapidly wag her tail. The air within the area swirled and blurred.

Soon the shimmering form of Zaramagrii appeared, silhouetted by strange vapors and trails of dark smoke. Her eyes were clear as she stepped towards them.

An enormous, dimly lit form lingered not far behind where she had appeared. When looking directly at it, nothing could be seen. The shadow could only be seen from the oblique, when not trying to actually see it.

"Rory? Excuse my sudden interruption. But I rushed to get here." Zaramagrii exhaled as she kneeled to accommodate the rush of Daraphyn. The wolf leapt up to place her forelegs around her as though giving her a hug.

"Zaramagrii—what a surprise indeed!" cried Rory as he strode towards her. "Interruption? Never even think such a thing."

They briefly embraced with Daraphyn caught between them. For once, the weariness in Rory's face left him completely.

"I beg your forgiveness, Zaramagrii, this is Ephritori Bari Lourendalthemee and her companion, Rhalwa Jadorthanelle. And this is Zaramagrii Nus—" Rory was stopped in his tracks by Ephritori, who picked up the words for him. His eyes giving away his lost sense of direction.

"Zaramagrii Nusthafay Tharasvrul, the one of the Black Clans, destined to wear the ring and wield the blade. Yes, I know this one." Ephritori swayed closer to the stunning, lithe form of Zaramagrii. Her arms outstretched in a radiant pose.

Zaramagrii's questioning eyes flamed towards those of Ephritori. Ephritori looked deeply into that contrast of black and white.

"Come my child, here," whispered Ephritori.

Zaramagrii had been slowly gravitating towards her.

She slowly raised her hand to Zaramagrii's cheek and held it there, as a mother might to her young in an attempt to console them.

Zaramagrii's eyes flashed quickly many times and shone out at the Eternal Mother, as they somehow comprehended a larger scheme. And those eyes did something that they had not done for some time, as a tear trickled down each cheek.

Ephritori grasped the slim, dark body and warmly hugged her, more holding her. Zaramagrii went limp in her arms. The Eternal Mother whispered something into her ear so inaudible that not a one could make it out.

Zaramagrii closed her eyes while tilting her head upwards. Her taut frame relaxed as though a grievous, but unseen, weight had been lifted from her. The air about them had a faint aura to it, a spectrum of white, blue, and purple. It seemed to be a globe that encased them both as the Eternal Mother held Zaramagrii.

Once they had parted, Zaramagrii fluttered her eyes briefly while opening them. Ephritori grasped both of her hands now, and stood staring at her admiringly.

And all beheld that the beautiful, blue necklace that adorned Ephritori's neck had split into two distinct pieces of equal size and shape.

Now Ephritori slipped one of these from around her own neck and allowed it to fall over Zaramagrii's head. The necklace appeared to shrink itself about her neck, as the glowing blue gem hung just above the top of the leather halter that peeked out from the furs.

By this time, the large form had come into full view. It was that of a monstrous black wolf surrounded in billowing dark smoke.

Rory stood in awe, shocked as he noted the reflection of Zaramagrii. Those astounding eyes! The beast had the opposite of Zaramagrii. The right eye was glowing white, while the left was deep black. Both of these held a rich, purple background.

Then, within the blink of an eye, the monstrous thing shrank down to appear as a large black wolf with a shiny coat of fur.

The beast slowly pranced up to the Eternal Mother, showing off with his eyes flashing. The huge ears, appearing way too large for the head, now flattened back completely as the wolf dipped its head down. His muzzle dropped low in a fang-baring grin.

And then he crouched to lay near Ephritori's feet, waiting for her to touch him. She reached her hand out and stroked the thick, coarse fur.

The wolf stretched as she did so, and sprawled belly down upon the floor at her feet. Daraphyn snugly warmed up to the significantly larger wolf with a deep sigh. Then she nuzzled his neck lightly.

Zaramagrii thoughtfully looked upon Rhalwa for several moments. Slowly she retrieved the golden necklace with the small Aylsh rune upon it, then strode towards her. "Rhalwa... Rhalwa Jadorthanelle... I can only guess that Thimoryn was your father?"

Rhalwa stared at her in surprise, trying to comprehend what she just said. "My father, yes... But how did you know that?"

Zaramagrii carefully placed the necklace over Rhalwa's head while displaying the symbol. "Your father meant much to a

Hulding of considerable power in the Fallen Lands. Your father took him under his wing a long time ago and taught him many things about life.

"He gave me this to give to you. Well, he did not say as much, but said that I would know who to give it to. And now I see clearly."

Rhalwa's eyes welled up as she saw the symbol of her father and heard such a tale of his endeavors. The symbol was that of their family.

Zaramagrii continued. "Your father was a steadfast one, and what he did for this one Hulding may have profound depth much later on."

Rhalwa hugged Zaramagrii. The only words she could muster were, "Many thanks to thee. May Lord Braxis forever light your path and grant you his strength and wisdom."

Ephritori looked on, smiling radiantly. "Now we can continue on to the Aylsh kingdom."

Even Wybur appeared, framed in the doorway, as all of this was going on. The first sign of his presence to most of them was his cry of joy as he stepped in. "Zaramagrii!"

Meanwhile, Rory was about to begin explaining his presence here in Nuuroc to Zaramagrii, but muffled steps sounded from outside.

Just then—the doors to the royal court already flung wide open—in wandered another imaginative and spry figure wearing a shimmering green cape riding low upon her shoulders. She was dressed in rich black and brown leather attire, from the wide-brimmed, forest green hat with one side clasped upwards, to her high leather boots. A thin silver rapier with an elegant jeweled handle hung at her side. Some kind of stringed instrument was slung across her lean back.

As the woman entered and closed upon Rory, both of the wolves jumped up on their feet with their hackles raised high. Neither one indicated a threat with growling nor barking, but something had definitely piqued their interest about the newcomer.

The young woman flung back her lustrous, russet-colored hair from her face as she removed her hat with the curious triangle and circle metal clasp.

Deep hazel eyes sparkled even in the dimming chambers. "My lord, I am Sephoora. And I bring news from afar."

Castym walked in then, much to his astonishment. "My lord, where did all of these," he paused while looking at the wolves, "guests come from? I saw no one come through…"

Rory spoke over his trailing words. "Do not fret, my friend. They all have reason to be here. All is as it should be."

Castym just folded his arms and stared from one figure to the next. His eyes spoke his intuited acceptance of those around Rory.

It took quite some time for Sephoora to explain herself and tell her tale. Especially since Wybur initially let out, "Hey, you are the bard from the Straefyrshir Inn…with the sorange!"

Sephoora told them that she was a servant to the benefit of all, and part of a group looking out for the common interests of the lands and all of its dwellers.

Deep down inside, Sephoora wanted to speak of the Veiled Ones, but she decided to hold that for Rory's audience alone. At least for now.

Ephritori's stoic eyes lingered upon Sephoora, with a slight smile. For she knew what she saw. But what she saw gave her much delight, at least inwardly.

She did not want to shed light on Sephoora's secret, or secrets. So she held it in, knowing that this room was filled with such spirit and power of good—of the Light. All she could do was beam with immeasurable pride and adoration. One could not ask for moments such as this very often. It was indeed special.

While everyone sat and discussed the various things going on, Sephoora dropped the most clattering thing in their midst. She told them about her profound discoveries after thoroughly analyzing the Lost Amethyst Scroll, or the replicated version of it brought to her through the gem of seeing by her agent hidden in Tharasvrul. Just the acknowledgement of it existing brought on immediate silence and looks of disbelief. Even Grasfur and Daraphyn stared at Sephoora as though she held a dangling piece of fresh meat.

"After much deliberation and internal debate, I have come to realize, and accept, that the Lost Scroll holds ancient codes, or runes, that may lead to yet another one such as it. This might mean that there is a series of them."

A dull commotion arose as everyone in the room started in at the same time.

Rory scratched his forehead. "But how could that be? History claims that there could be a missing eighth. That was because seven were found. So, natural speculation placed that there might be an eighth."

Sephoora now swept a portion of the cape over her shoulder. "That is an interesting thought, I think that most—well, most of those that wish to be called learned—agree to the possibility of eight Amethyst Scrolls from Braxis. But this Lost Scroll may not have been scribed by Lord Braxis.

"There is good reason to believe that more such lost scrolls may be out there, and none necessarily worded by the Initiator himself. For what purpose? I know not, but I am working on that."

All the while, Ephritori stood smiling at them. "Lord Braxis wanted the greater good of everything to be key. His designs were to push, subtly, those of sentience into the right direction. So as not to dictate or force the direction of eventual progress of an order or race, even a creature.

"There were his commands, all the Twelve Edicts of Lord Braxis. And the Amethyst Scrolls. But were these solely for Man? For the Black Clans? Just because they were initially held by the clans at Isnuuthghor, and then secured by Man-folk, does not speak such a thing as truth.

"Now, what about the First Writings—the Aylsh. And the Golden Leaves for the Hulding. The Khaman of the Akhruuk, as protected by the Oracles of Chevon Ruuk.

"And there are the Xuthur, or Slates of Thunder, for the Kharaghou. And all of these are just the ones that have some depth to them, a fair degree of certainty as to their origins…somehow tied back to Lord Braxis."

Mute silence and dumbfounded looks prodded Ephritori on with her thoughts. "Do you think that one Initiator would have need of so many different—separate divine edicts for such folk to live by? For so many beings that shared the same world?

"And we speak of only Thaldeia, as we know not concerning farther east, south, and west…even north." Ephritori trailed off, lost in her own thoughts for a moment.

"In truth, we look at ourselves—Thaldeia—as though it was the center of the world. While all along it could be but a small part in a much larger world than we know. And when I say that we look at our own kind, I mean individually as a race—separately, Man upon Man, Aylsh upon Aylsh, Black Clan upon Black Clan, etc.

"And I for one am not truly sure that *this* was exactly what Lord Braxis intended when the world was created."

Of the entire party, the lady Sephoora had an eyebrow raised. There was a look to her face that showed her mind at work digesting what was said. And her eyes shone, as though something finally dawned upon her. "Separation."

Rory now looked at Sephoora puzzled. "What was that? Separation? Of what?"

Sephoora now stood more on one leg than the other and half turned as though posing for a dance at a royal ball. Her lean silhouette displayed her well-figured form. "Yes…separation. Why, do you not see? Why did I not see it before? All of the folk, groups, have all maintained their own selfish ways.

"They have remained lost within their own kind as far as we can go back through the known history. That might be the key.

"That the edicts and scriptures for each of the folk of Thaldeia are all possibly linked. The higher divine, possibly both the Olden and the Myno, would only want unity and peace, at least one would think…among creation."

Now Rory had the look of a horse chewing on grass. "How could they be linked? What are you trying to say?"

Sephoora continued. "At this point, all that I really am saying is that the scholars and historians—for each of the kind, Man, Aylsh, Kharaghou, Hulding—might have had blinders on this entire time. Like ignorant asses plowing away at their own little fields all day long. And still they do so."

Now Sephoora apparently had too much going on in her own mind to want to put words into further explanation. "I have much more research to do and in many more places."

Zaramagrii revealed the ancient symbol of Kuhrzoth that she found at the Nook of the Reach, slowly explaining her travels there. She spoke of the man found with the relic.

Afterward, she handed the ancient Kuhrzothian crest over to Rory. Sephoora raised an eyebrow all the while, but remained silent. Talk went on for a while longer, but without much avail. The momentum slowly dwindled down to conjecture on the coming black horde and the activities of Priestess Sahrya.

Much to Rory's dismay, Ephritori and Rhalwa spoke their intent to depart early in the morning for the Aylsh kingdom. Nothing he could say or do, again, appeared to sway their course in the matter. He finally gave up trying. Nor would Ephritori accept any kind of escort or protection for their travels.

Eventually everyone but Sephoora retreated to their quarters for the night. None knew where Zaramagrii disappeared to, along with the shadow warg.

Sephoora still had words for Rory, or so she claimed, before she parted. The two of them stole away to the council chambers where they could hold further counsel over wine and cold, roasted beef.

It was in these last few moments with Rory that Sephoora disclosed her association with the Veiled Ones.

In fact, it initially took some time to convince him that they even existed, as he figured that they were just a myth. But she explained many things to him that had taken place over the past few turns to bolster reality of the secretive group.

Rory also discussed Wybur's tale of his run-in with the mysterious Livforena, who claimed to be of the same group. Sephoora confirmed his suspicions of Livforena being a fraud as far as the Veiled Ones went. She speculated that it could be a disguise of Priestess Sahrya, or one of Sahrya's minions. Although she did not know this last thread for certain, she was fairly sure of it.

Rory then also offered the mysterious blade of the shunmrith and the strange mark upon it. He explained what took place with the death of the royal presenter and how the same mark upon the dagger was also found tattooed to the body of the shunmrith.

Of this, even Sephoora had no clue. But it would be one more thing that she would further explore, along with the other recent discoveries.

Before they went their separate ways for the night, Rory vowed that he would never tell a spirit about her involvement with the Veiled Ones. And Sephoora promised to work together on the future courses of action, especially once she further studied the various divine edicts scattered across Thaldeia.

§ § §

Axyander the Steelborn stood stoically within the inner courtyard below the Emerald Tower. The moons climbed high. As he stepped backwards to turn about, his boot caught on something and he momentarily faltered.

Blasted rocks, he thought, as he glanced down.

The moonlight cast a pale glow upon the courtyard scenery. There, protruding from the packed dirt floor, was what appeared to be a cold, dark rock.

He kicked at the old blackened rock. Then the Steelborn bent down and lightly grazed it with his gauntleted hand.

Except he knew that it was no rock, as he looked closer at it.

There it was. A haunting reminder of the old days…and his ancient ways. Who he was. What he was. The brush of the cool, black, burnt surface took him back in time, if ever so briefly. He thought about the days of Arterium.

But days long gone. Then he casually glanced at the ground about him.

Strange, thought Axyander, *that such a thing would still be able to touch the air after so much time spent buried. Even in death, the blasted things attempted to grasp at life.*

And the cold, calloused one turned about, brooding deeply as he made his way back to his chambers.

§ § §

Axyander silently opened the door to his chambers. He quietly moved to the corner of the room. A burning torch that hung there cast menacing wraiths from his silhouette. One of his mages named Solistra sat on a nearby chair, facing towards the covered window.

Solistra's hands grasped his knees as he sat unmoving, completely rigid. His eyes were closed and his breathing was extremely shallow and light, almost indeterminable.

After a long time in such a state of weightlessness, Solistra emerged out of it with a sharp gasp, eyes glaring and wide open. It was like he just came up from a long, underwater swim.

He caught his breath and regained his composure for several moments before speaking. "It has been done, my lord. The king has granted the Emerald Commander Castym with right of heir to the throne. The royal seal has scribed it officially."

Axyander thumbed the pommel of his blade, while eyeing the mage. "Yes, my friend, we expected him to do something along those lines. Indeed, this changes things a bit once I get instatement of the Legion."

"But, my lord… What if the king does not agree to your terms?"

"My dear Solistra, he has no choice. Why, it is too good of a deal *not* to. After all, he gets the whole Legion. And for simply giving me the title of commander. He cannot refuse once he sees the black horde camped in front of his gates. No, the only question will be *when*."

Solistra acknowledged with several quick nods of his head. "Yes, I see my lord."

Then Axyander turned to him. His eyes aflame and his voice filled with simmering malevolence. "Now Solistra, we must be prepared once the king sends word. We will immediately have to go to the companies and place them into action. Then we will return here with a token force. And we will ensure that Castym does not assume the throne if anything were to befall the king. Do you understand me?"

Solistra's eyes darted about the chamber. "Yes, my lord, clearly."

§ § §

The next day proved to be bright and sunny well into the late-suns, but cold enough to keep the partially snow-covered landscape from turning to mush.

Sullen expressions filled the ranks of the people of Kuhrzoth as they counted down days from when they first heard of the encroaching black army. It felt as though each new day wrapped the tension about them even more snugly than the previous one. While preparations continued to be made, and people went about their daily grind, the atmosphere grew heavy and grim.

Over the last few days, many of those thriving outside of Nuuroc, to the west, were wandering through the gates. Most of these were ragged and tattered, some wounded grievously.

All these people would speak the same doom, that the black army had burned and ransacked all of the towns and villages in between. That it was headed this way.

People had fled, a few to the walls at Nuuroc. But many more fled to who knows where, they just left. And this did not include the ones that had disappeared or could not be found as the black army swept over their communities.

Of course, Ephritori and Rhalwa had departed even before the first light of the duo suns. Daraphyn had been astride her own horse, riding behind the two.

The royal hall was filled with the presence of many different types, from Castym and his line commanders, to Zaramagrii and Wybur quietly speaking to one another near the throne. Rory and Sephoora sat near the throne and were deep in counsel.

In the middle of the hubbub, a royal guard ran in. "Sire—it is here! It is here!"

The light from the duo suns was nearly gone, only shrouding everything in an orange-red haze.

Rory, Sephoora, Zaramagrii, Wybur, Castym, and others all rushed to the height of the Emerald Tower to look out upon the south and west. Out to where normally a line of dark green could be seen joining the dirty, snow-swept grounds to the cloudy blue skies. Where dark things had not been for a long time.

There, along the whole view of the south, were thick, black clumps dotting the horizon slowly moving to and fro.

As with the coming of night, the moods and spirits darkened deeply with the showing of the black army.

Chapter 23:

Besieged in Darkness

"These folk are mere peasants, slaves to our whim. All those not of noble blood simply exist to serve those OF noble blood. Now bring the finest damsels up from Henchote. And make sure that you run them through the bathing house. If any of the men say a word, then chain them as well. We shall make them our servants this night. Indeed, they will pour our mead and ale whilst their trollops spread their legs for our lances."

-Stated many times by Lord Unsric
Gardemoor, the first born of the
Gardemoors of Ravenkort.

T he arrival of the black army created a degree of panic, and almost no one could sleep that first night. As the next day became long, the small line of black figures way out on the horizon still remained where they were. Never closing in, never departing. Several large fires went up but the black army made no move yet. Long, slow blasts from horns echoed from their distant lines throughout the day and night.

Now the weather turned downright cold, with old crusted snow still scattered across the lands. The nights became clear and fell even deeper into the frosty swirls of winterfall.

Towards the end of the third full day, hundreds of structures could be seen moving around the black line way far out. They had to be siege engines of some kind. Many were obviously belfries. These tall, wooden siege towers were easy to distinguish.

And then the volleys began. The loud swooshes could be heard even inside the walls of Nuuroc as those engines of war fired their deadly loads.

That first night of the bombardment, massive rock projectiles were launched into Nuuroc and at its walls with every burn of a candle or so. The dark nights were peaceful and quiet. Then, with the violence of a landslide, huge crashes and screams resounded throughout the noble city as hundreds of the rocks impacted at one time.

Like a vast hailstorm, the volleys would arc into the walls, then they would strike as a wave within one section of the city, then another. And this went on throughout the night. While there were not that many lives lost, the terror of the firing kept most awake in deranged bouts of impending gloom.

With the rising light of the following day, it found most with little to no sleep from the previous night. Now a token force of the black army appeared off to the north and west. Once a sign of freedom to those within the walls, looking to the north brought just another ominous cloud darkening the sky. This force intensified the projection of impending doom considerably, if such formations were within the schemes of the black army. Maybe they were just the advance of a larger one still on the move. There was no telling at this point.

The following night, a new horror mixed in with the fear of the rock missiles. There had been many settlers and farmers outside of the walls, the once peaceful lands askew with them. Most of Kuhrzoth was a densely inhabited land, at least centrally. The expanse of the kingdom blurred into the rugged and unkempt wildlands. But truth be told, nearly all lands held the possibility of danger and terror lurking about, no matter whether in the heart of such a land as Kuhrzoth or not.

The countless villages, towns, and hamlets along the way to Nuuroc, that the horde of the Fallen Lands flooded across, paid their shield money. In blood. Quaint, lazy settlements like Omsbrow and Culhaven. The small village of Winbrake, known for the flaxen, blanketed lands of corn and wheat that surrounded it. These hard working people were now being returned back into Nuuroc by way of being strapped to the rock projectiles.

Of course, they already appeared to have suffered some horrible fate, but these bloody, mangled corpses landed like sick bags of butchers' scraps throughout the city. Their dead countenances, frozen in twisted agony, now taunted the living.

This strategy did not help the morale whatsoever. When it seemed that the black forces ran out of people to torture, they began to douse ropes and wood affixed to the rock missiles with oil. These ingenious contraptions ended up as huge flaming balls, flaring up even more as they rode the winds into the city. When they hit their mark, the screaming balls of inferno splattered and lit everything on fire wherever they impacted.

Every day, when the early light dawned, the Emerald Guard would attempt to target the siege devices with their own, but this was more a waste of ammunition. Even if they were lucky enough to hit one of them, another was brought up in its place.

§ § §

What kind of army or force besieged a place or even considered beginning a campaign just as winterfall was getting on? Rory pondered this and other things for many a day now. Regular armies of any kind usually went to winter quarters just prior to the first snowstorms of winterfall. Obviously no army of any size could sustain itself within the deep shadows of the icy weather, let alone conduct triumphant martial operations. It just was not feasible, especially with the supply lines. Even foraging during the harsh cold was hopeless at best. And an army of any size that conducted warfare away from its base needed to forage whether there was a fair amount of supplies within its baggage train or not.

Of course, one that had no intent of achieving anything from it. One that intended to endlessly ram itself into the enemy's strength until it won…or battered itself out of existence. He had answered his own question posed, it would seem.

Siege usually meant some kind of terms, even if those terms were complete capitulation. And yet, no word of terms or sign of any dissolution at all. Except for the constant bombardment.

So this black army had a purpose to grind away at Kuhrzoth until one or the other was ruined?

He stared at the agreement handed to him by the Legion commander, merely awaiting his mark and seal. Twenty thousand well-trained warriors right at the back door of this black evil blemish on the land.

§ § §

Two days had passed and still there was no word from Rory to unleash the Legion. But Axyander held his air about him and waited.

Near the end of the sixth day, with bombardments at almost a constant, there was a loud knock on the door. Rory strode in immediately as the mage opened it.

"Axyander, tomorrow is to be a glorious day. You are now a commander within the Emerald Order—the Black Legion under Kuhrzoth," Rory stated while handing Axyander the agreement. It was signed and affixed with the royal signet. Rory added, "Just one last thing…tell your men to kill as many of the bastards as they can."

"It will be our honor, my lord." Axyander bowed his head subtly while speaking. "Solistra, let us go now, we must complete the preparations and give the orders."

§ § §

The journey into the Aylsh kingdom was not without its own hardships. It seemed that none of the Aylsh wanted anything to do with them—Ephritori in her stunning gray cloak, and Rhalwa with her simple one of forest green.

Most Aylsh, common folk and warriors alike, stared solemnly at the pair while they passed by. Others hardly even gave them a look, as though they did not see them at all. And Daraphyn silently bounced alongside them for the most part, foregoing her own mount, which now trailed behind Ephritori. The wolf was undaunted by any of it.

It was about the time that they first arrived at the Aylsh city of Eleghwulmaryk that Ephritori began to have strange visions. Each night, she would drift off into a deep sleep to find herself in the bed of a muscle-bound man with flowing blond hair.

At first she thought that it might be Rory, but then the face never revealed itself. The face was always just a blurry reflection, like looking at it through several foot of water. But she was always with this man in bed, naked except for the skin between them. And he would ride her all night long, until the duo suns rose through the windowed panorama set in the stone wall.

Both of the glowing orbs would be flooding over their bodies through the window, amidst a reddish-hued sky. She could even feel the sheen of sweat on their bodies as they lay intertwined. And the pleasure was something that she had never felt before. So intense, so full of the pure and raw zeal of life. Every night would be this same dream, for thirteen days.

The first day that Ephritori and Rhalwa stood outside the large ornate doors of the Aylsh Royal Hall, where the High Court rested. They did so in the freezing cold and sleeting rain. The noble guards standing post, proudly cast as metallic statues in their regal suits of gleaming armor, would not even offer them the space of the tiny covered alcove at the entrance. They just went about their duties, oblivious to the trio nearby, as the foul weather soaked them and froze into a crackling coat. Various other Aylsh, all of which had to be noble or within the upper tiers of Aylsh society, also passed them by. These just occasionally took to a raised nose or a scoff of indifference whenever one actually paid the trio any attention at all.

Ephritori approached the pair of guards again. "I beseech you, my lord, I must see the High Court. It is very important—of the most urgent nature."

The guard cast a slow glance towards the other one with a smirk. "I see, and what is of such importance? What would two beggars such as you bring to the Aylsh High Court?"

Now Ephritori stood tall and held her head back, canted slightly to the side, as though the burden of the denial grew heavy. "My lord, we are not beggars. We come from the lands of Kuhrzoth. And I bring serious tidings."

The Aylsh stiffened in his suit of plate maille armor. "Oh no... The lands of Kuhrzoth... The Man-folk. That *must* be important. Get out of here now, the both of you."

And so they were forced to leave and go to an inn several leagues back, nestled within a small Trone village.

The fourth day of diligence at the doors to the Aylsh Royal Hall finally brought some allusion of promise. One much older

Aylsh, wizened in silver hair and wearing tiny spectacles, approached the door. He actually paused while entering the halls and then stopped in front of Ephritori to hear her out. He did so even as one of the guards proceeded to inform him of the two unruly beggars camping out.

The Aylsh, with his glittering robe of varying hues, scratched his head briefly before he spoke. "My dear ones, you say that you have word from the lands of Man-folk? Kuhrzoth? Well, you have been out here for some time. Are those features of the Aylsh?

"Well, at least you have some of the special blood within you. Come in and tell me what is so important."

Once he led them inside and into the chambers of the High Court, he was the only one present. The table from where the Aylsh High Court governed was made from a deep black wood that had been treated with a coating of crystal. The crystal surface reflected such depth and color, as it enhanced the texture and grain of the underlying wood while radiating a rainbow of changing patterns. High-backed chairs ran along the outer edge.

The huge serpentine table ran in a lazy arc, in front of where a jeweled throne rested upon a raised dais. Both inside edges of it abutted to where the dais of the throne began. The throne sat in the heart of a black, shadowed pocket of the hollow of a giant tree trunk. The still living tree displayed a variety of changing colors depending upon where the observer moved to.

This was a Lyshmarouk tree, unique in its own special way, but hailed by the Aylsh as the Beacon of the Wild. While these trees were rare indeed, those still found out in the forests of the Louren Ghuvruul were nurtured and protected by all Aylsh. There were occasions where these trees held hundreds of tiny sparkling particles of light flying about their branches and trunks. Not just one tree, but all of them at the same time. The Aylsh claimed that this took place whenever the Light of the Eternal Mother was needed to shed her special rays upon the world, to renew and affirm the strength of the Wild.

The aged Aylsh plumped himself down at the end of the unique table and looked at Ephritori through his spectacles. "Now, tell me what is so important?"

Ephritori proceeded to explain the events that happened in the west, from the black army of the Fallen Lands to the besieged Nuuroc. She told him about her own history and how she came to be here in the Aylsh Kingdom. Why she had been led there.

Then she began to refer to an imp amongst the ruling body of the Aylsh, although she was not allowed to completely finish the explanation for this last remark. Not very long into this elaboration, the old Aylsh just held up both of his hands with palms out towards her.

The Aylsh looked upon her with his mouth partially open, not able to immediately find words. "Yes, yes… The Eternal Mother, I bet you are. Why," he paused to look around and then at the door, "this is a grand scheme and must be brought before the court immediately. A dark priestess… Akhruuk, goblins, joutuun, and the other yuanhad monstrosities all working together. And all handed over to the proud Aylsh folk by two beggars and a mutt, of all things."

Then he shouted towards the doors that they had entered from. "Guards!"

The doors clamored open, sending echoes through the chamber. Two Aylsh warriors, decked out in plate maille armor, marched in directly towards the ensemble.

The Aylsh lifted his spectacles, as he spoke. "Guards, escort these two out, and see that they do not return."

He proceeded to throw his arms about in huge, animated gestures while cantankerously spouting his harangue. "*This* needs to be heard in front of the high court—my, my—such prepostery. And you, my dear, may have some of the Man blood coursing through your body...or perhaps too much.

"Why would we lift a finger for Man-folk in the first place? Such as us—the High Aylsh Kingdom? Who those murderous, barbarous horsemen have been aggravating for so long?

"Take them from my sight."

At this point, the Aylsh guards made to grasp both Ephritori and Rhalwa. But Ephritori held up both of her hands and eyed Rhalwa. Then they slowly headed to the door with the guards close behind.

The next morning, they found themselves even farther out from the Royal Hall, not allowed so much as inside the front gates leading into the palace. Aylsh-kind coming and going just passed on by, ignoring them.

Twelve such days passed fully where the Eternal Mother was refused entrance to the Aylsh High Court. All the while she attempted to reason her cause with those passing by. But none heeded her.

Chapter 24:

A Parting of Ways

"My fine men and women of Kuhrzoth, I am truly humbled to be your servant. I cannot do enough for you. But a better suited land has been found, and one that will provide a position of grandeur and glory. Tomorrow we shall begin preparations to move. A new home is being planned and laid even as I speak to you here, a place that shall be the mightiest castle of all times. One so large that everyone can live within its walls, protected, safe, elegantly comfortable. And not even a wyrm will be able to harm it."

-King Arterium's speech prior to moving the people of Venlour to where Nuuroc would be built, circa the year 13 BA

The long, black line of Akhruuk, goblins, joutuun, and other miscreants stood amidst the speckled snow-scape and distant tree line. Their lines lay south of the walls of Nuuroc, like swarms of tiny ants. They stretched for a league, maybe more, across the expanse.

Behind this first one were more long lines, along with various contraptions no doubt devised for warfare. The once distant line slowly began to grow in size as it neared the outer walls. The march had been slow and deliberate, nearly taking the entire morning to move closer.

It was midday. The approaching lines of the black army came to a halt just out of the range of missiles, whether arrow, quarrel, or catapult. The line parted at the center and let forth a strange glowing beast, in likeness to a small wyrm but made of pure white energy. Geysers of steam arose with each of its steps through the old, foot-deep snow. It was difficult to stare directly at, but another being of similar make rode atop it. The beast slowly rambled along on two legs, strutting back and forth until they were slightly in the lead of the motley force.

The rider was none other than Rha the Lightwalker. Although not known to the forces of Kuhrzoth by name, she had been reported many times to the Emerald Crown by scouting parties as the black army's wizard commander.

The long line of Kuhrzothian warriors held ground far out from the wall, although not seeming as extensive as that of the black army. It had formed rather quickly and was near six deep, varying in sorts of warriors. Another similar line had formed closer to the walls.

Rha raised her arms up, staff in one hand. With a loud and resounding crack of thunder, dozens of small black clouds appeared in the sky and loosed as many bolts of lightning down upon the Kuhrzothian front line.

While the bolts themselves were not all that powerful, they achieved the ruin thirsted for by Rha.

The energy struck up and down the entire line. Some even went deep into the ranks, as bodies and limbs flew through the air, weapons and pieces of armor clanging into one another.

At this same time, the line of the black army charged towards the Kuhrzothian lines, even as the forces of Man-folk broke off and closed up within more than a hundred phalanxes.

The dark rush of Akhruuk, goblins, ogres, and joutuun broke into the mass of bristling phalanxes. Monstrous wargs with goblins leapt through the air, and Akhruuk riding hairless, horse-like beasts with heads similar to a vultures sparsely backed those on foot.

As they did so, the phalanxes went to work, shields parting slightly and skewering most of the first wave. Then the shields canted back and black swarms of feathery death flew out from over the top of the makeshift wall. The wave of the black army momentarily faltered while many of them fell back, many more fell dead.

Loud, thundering rattles and swooshes sounded from behind the black lines as their siege engines loosed a volley of fiery rain. Soaring rock missiles and giant fireballs flew through the air, many striking home within the phalanxes.

All it took was one hit and an entire phalanx crumbled. In some cases they did and the remaining warriors rushed out brandishing swords, joining in with the fighting close at hand.

Many of the war engines were aimed into the walls of Nuuroc, smashing away at it and spraying rock everywhere. And rolling up next to these were scores of belfries, shining in the light of the duo suns since covered with animal skins freshly soaked in water in preparation for the assault. These huge towers had three or four levels to them, with the top one containing a platform similar to a drawbridge. Once the tower was close enough to the castle's wall, this platform could be dropped and then a screaming mass of invaders could charge forth.

Rory stood undaunted amidst his warriors, facing the onslaught of blackness as it came again at the Kuhrzothian line. Their far line was nearly a quarter of a league out from the walls, now battered and disheveled.

The dark scourge was nearly upon them again, relentless and not letting up. There—off to the west and from down in the folds of the hilly landscape—rose three thousand gleaming lances. The last of the Emerald Knights steadily trod abreast as though they were on parade and not a care in the world, secretly birthed from the lower gate. Their full plate armor and the plate barding covering the mighty Thoerne war horses gleamed and dazzled, reaching out to all of their brethren who were fighting. The sight was one of such high inspiration, all those fighting under the banner of Kuhrzoth cheered and yelled.

As they rode in to flank the black menace, they began to thunder to a gallop that echoed across the rolling grass.

Of course, the rise of the lands did not allow the black forces to really take note of them until the knights were bearing down upon them. Such a clash of steel and flesh arose, mixed with yells and the adrenaline charged snorts and blusters of the magnificent Thoerne war horses.

And the black army was battered and run through from the side. The disciplined phalanxes had tightened up during this epic charge of destruction and ceased their volleys so that the knights could work their talents back and forth across the field of death.

Then, in a vast sweeping arc and formed in many lines, the Emerald Knights wheeled around and behind the first line of phalanxes. The phalanxes opened up and took ground, while the knights rode through cleaning up where needed.

The general of the black army rose from within their ranks as a towering behemoth concealed behind the shimmering aura of the snow covered ground.

Gauth walked forward in the midst of the death and destruction, those before him clearing out of the way, while clashing and killing went on all around. His blackened, serrated two-handed sword hung low in one hand, a long spearing point protruding backwards from the grip.

Gauth even towered over his own forces. The behemoth slowly stalked towards the king with the flowing golden hair streaming around the edges of his helm.

Rory saw Gauth emerge, the impending standoff now clearly taking shape. One of Gauth's arms, around the biceps, looked about the size of Rory's upper torso.

Rory began to stride towards the goliath. He brought up his two-handed blade with both hands to his oblique, elbows bent and tucked in, prepared to cleave.

The forces were now mixed all together around him as he moved through the thick of the battle, parrying back and forth. All the while, Rory attempted to challenge one of the beasts.

But Akhru and goblin alike simply eyed him as he walked by them, and they left him unharmed. None would raise a weapon towards him. Apparently their giant commander had marked him for himself.

Several of the Kuhrzothian phalanxes had brought their formations up close to where their king was at, as he moved through the fray. The silhouetted array of belfries had paused out in line with the farthest stand of Kuhrzothian forces.

Gauth smiled a wicked, curved-tooth grin as his large, deep-set black eyes wrinkled. "Man-king, your day has come!" he bellowed out.

They had now closed to within striking distance and Gauth began to sidestep.

Rory simply stood his ground and rotated his giant blade horizontally. Rory spoke calmly, but forcefully, as though he was settling a petty squabble. "You have come to the wrong lands. Not one of you will leave the field alive this day. Take your black scourge back to the depths while you can."

"I have your mark and will be your demise, Man-king. What you say or do matters little. We will prevail. This has been ordained, and all of your kind will waste away." Gauth breathed out heavily, his form towering above that of Rory's.

Rory rotated his body as Gauth moved about to the side.

Rory flashed a grin at the beast. "You are like weeds, the only thing that will prevail are the blades that cut you all to ribbons, and pluck your roots so you cannot grow back."

With that, the black army's general heaved and swung his blade out. Rory's arced up to meet it, and sparks flew as they forcefully stopped together.

Rory held up against the might of a looming tower that appeared much larger than he. And he held his ground, slowly pushing Gauth's enormous form back.

In lightning speed, Gauth turned his blade and attempted to drive the spear-like haft into Rory's chest. Rory sidestepped and knocked it aside with the shining cannon on his forearm. Then Gauth pounded a huge elbow into Rory's face, knocking him hard as he staggered back.

All the while, the forces of the black army appeared to slow their advance since the start of the battle between their commander and that of the Man-folk. But many had already closed in towards the Kuhrzoth line closest to the walls, attempting to weaken the defenders in preparation for the arrival of the towering belfries.

§ § §

Meanwhile, Wybur Buttlecut stood high up in the Emerald Tower, watching the arrayed forces down below. He could easily tell the opposing sides, as one was near black in color and the other was silvery and glinting. The lines were just forming, neither side the aggressor yet.

A remote, familiar sound came to him high in that tower, floating in on the winds. Such an enchanting sound, or no—*a song*. He had to follow it. But where did it come from?

Moving as though in a stupor, Wybur followed the stairs down and outside of the tower halls. He sheepishly walked through the inner bailey where his mule Shab was tethered. Shab merely turned her head and stared at him while munching lazily on a clump of long grass. There appeared to be no worries in the world.

Wybur took no notice of the frantic people running crazily about everywhere. He just shrugged them off.

Before long, he was riding Shab out of the north gate, where no forces of the Fallen Lands had converged as of yet. There was just a sinister black cloud of them, hovering off in the distance.

The watchmen manning the gate barely argued with him, and cracked those huge, oak double doors just enough to let him ride through. He immediately went west and followed an immense, flat ravine that wove in and out of the hills and plateaus.

The ravine narrowed and turned away, with the walls of Nuuroc slowly fading and no longer visible. Wybur slowed to a stop, confronted by an intimate sight.

There, in the same glowing white gossamer gown that he knew so well, was Rosella. Her face lit up with a radiant smile and she noiselessly walked towards him—barefoot in the crusty snow.

It was like a distant dream. So peaceful and happy now that Rosella was here. It had been her voice that he heard, calling out and mesmerizing him.

Then his hand came across the light, airy spines of the giant snow owl's feather clasped to a silver necklace about his head. The soft ripping sound of his finger running the length of the tops of those spines snapped him back to where he was. And it was as though he did not know how he had come to be there. He blinked several times, then noticing Rosella closing the distance. Getting closer.

Finally regaining his senses, Wybur cried out, "Stop! You! What are you doing here? You tricked me—" He never finished his sentence as the form of Rosella began to change.

Her beguiling features twisted into a tall, hairless thing with huge, membranous wings that stretched out far to the sides. The end of each of the wings had a vicious talon that could easily have been mistaken for a dagger. And the razor tail rose up and down like a whip behind her—or it. Now the thing had grown to twice the height of what Rosella had been.

Large, protruding eyes sat above a black hole of a nose, and the mouth was now a perverted, fanged chasm with a black, forked tongue slithering around. The sagging breasts were nearly covered by their ugly nipples.

He could smell the putrid odor from where he sat on Shab. Even the mule was tense and fidgety. Shab's long, folded ears pushed far back across her neck.

Then the creature lunged at him, and he dug his boots into Shab's sides—turning hard to avoid the thing. But Shab needed no goading whatsoever to move, and was quick to leap and gallop away.

The snowy ground did not help at all, giving the creature an advantage. Rosella was able to slice the mule deeply along her side, spraying a fine mist of bright blood as they passed each other.

Wybur heard the crackled hiss of its voice trail off behind him as he spurred Shab deeper into the ravine. "You cannot escape me now!"

§ § §

Rha looked down and across her black tide of motley vermin as the wyrlroc lifted into the air. The strange beast was also of the Light domain, brought forth along with Rha by Priestess Sahrya. The mix was easy to see as hers mostly were covered in dark armor with either blackened or rust-dulled flashes of weaponry. And the forces of Kuhrzoth gleamed and shined in her eyes, as though all of their inner essences were just waiting to break free from their molds.

The contrast of the black and shiny glimmer with a wash of snowy white as the backdrop appealed to her. She smiled as she envisioned the large canvas waiting for her brush strokes. And she was here to set them all free, liberation. There would be no holding back, and her loyalists needed some provocation.

She looked farther back, over the snow-swept plains, towards the direction they had approached from. Her other dark wave awaited her command and then they too would march into the fight. This would be spectacular as these other reserves could not possibly be seen by the Kuhrzothians…not yet. Not even from their wall. And the attack from the north would begin soon. There would be no stopping until they were inside the walls and ransacking everything. No pause, no mercy.

It was time to show the Thalroan, now *her* horde of darkness, what kind of power she had. Her lightning flashed through the sunny skies and left plummeting eruptions of white smoke and haze, as well as broken bodies everywhere. Now many of her own were mixed into these paths of destruction, for it mattered little. The blood and bone of all combatants now mixed and churned together.

She knew that eventually even her minions would have to be freed. There was no difference, as she was sent here to free them all.

And thus she began her divinely inspired work. Her mount, nearly as bright and blinding as she, swayed and screamed with every blast as it maintained its place hovering above the ground, maybe a little higher than the walls of Nuuroc. She destroyed large groups of the skirmishers, those of her army and those defenders of Kuhrzoth locked so tightly in the confines of mortal combat.

Her shimmering wyrlroc then swirled and swooped as she unleashed triple bolts of energy, striking the gated area. Bodies flew and one side of the wooden doors burst into splinters large and small. These struck many situated behind and inside the first bailey, some falling to the ground as a result of being impaled.

The elaborate portcullis already lay shattered on the ground, all twisted about the walls and bailey. Now, no barrier but that of flesh remained to stop the encroaching menace.

Archers nearby, along the top of the wall, failed to unleash their misery upon anything at all. A swathing rake of white fire erupted from the wyrlroc's mouth as they took aim. The blinding spout washed over them, turning all of them to ash.

And Rha sat high and proud atop the bird of prey as it arched a long neck and held form like a hummingbird. The wings could only be seen as steaming blurs. Rha again raised her staff and arms, saddled firmly with legs wrapped around the belly of the beast.

This time bolts of lightning arced out from Rha, across into the broad stone walls, bringing fragmented rock and stone tumbling down upon those below. Various sized rocky meteors flew into the masses all around the front.

Her eyes blazed with her fiery glory and she appeared to be untouchable by any worldly thing. Even when several arrows found their mark on the Lightwalker, they simply were incinerated before even striking the body of energy. Such was the power of the Lightwalker.

Then Rha noticed an older man of some reverence and stature. He stood defiantly in wrinkled robes with a particularly large staff just inside of the shattered gates. His look was one of intent, all of the frantic figures running throughout the background seeming a blur. The thick gray hair and beard spoke wisdom as he raised the staff skyward. She knew that this one had power and was no doubt a mage or wizard of some magnificence.

Memories of her father flooded back to her, and she saw him within her mind's eye from the view of a little girl. Something that she was at one time, had been. Her da. He had been so strong...and he always wanted what was best for her, his little girl.

This old man now before her had incited such welling thought of this, she nearly lost her glow for several moments. Her eyes suddenly hurt from all of the light about her. Her father, her father had been destroyed in his own abysmal fire. And this raged such anger within her.

Before the old mage could bring his might to bear completely, Rha cast such a potent bolt of energy toward him that it disintegrated everything else as it flew past them, all within several foot of it. Some farther away were actually pulled into the vortex and lit on fire by the searing heat.

As that brilliant ball of energy soared streaming towards the old man, one small figure raced behind him. That of a boy but only half the man's size. She could clearly see the boy's contorted mouth, dirty and sweaty from the carnage. This was enough to cause the old man to briefly pause and turn towards the boy, again stricken by the ever present weakness of emotion. Of *love*.

The boy silently mouthed the words *papa* to the old man, as though the boy saw what was going to happen. She could see this. She stiffened and, in her mind, recalled the roaring ball of inferno.

But such things do not happen. For many moments, Rha the Lightwalker fell to extreme agony over her own father and what power had done to him, to her. She now saw this very thing play out in front of her. And the boy was too close.

The ball of energy struck directly in front of the old man, nearly obliterating all of his being instantaneously. There were many others nearby as well that were reduced to ash.

What remained of the tall, wooden doors became whitened husks that blew away with the wind.

And the small boy was nowhere to be seen.

What was left of the little girl in Rha froze as she stared at all of the carnage that she was creating around her. And she realized that she was not meant to save anything. It was all an illusion, the priestess merely dangled the tidbit in front of her just to get her to perform. But there never had been a point to the conquest of Nuuroc. No, it was the use of just another weapon in the arsenal. And, when it was depleted, then it was no longer useful.

Suddenly the blanket of darkness that surrounded Rha made something crystal clear. The Light. Her Light. And that small speckle of Light was all that it took, as it pushed through and amplified her true self. One that had been buried amid the agonizing turns of time.

Then she saw the dark angel, all obscured within its own smoky trails of blackness. It was a beautiful thing, and its eyes now found her as she sat upon her steed. And those eyes, so mesmerizing, one blazing white and the other black as the deadly night. Rha now knew what she was supposed to do and exactly what she had been designed to save. Herself. This dark angel was here to help her with that, to save her from her own self. To save the rest of the world from her grief and misery, and that which they devastated.

§ § §

Amongst all of the carnage and chaos, a billowing, smoke-hued form materialized off to the side of where the gates once stood. The sleek beauty was duo-wielding black, shimmering blades in her hands.

Zaramagrii noted the waves of blurred motion all around her, and even more across the distance, threatening to force their way in towards the walls and gate. All of it lay strewn about in ruin.

Her own kind, the warriors of Kuhrzoth, appeared to her as minuscule rocks and breakers standing tall in the black froth as the dark army poured towards them. It raised forth larger than life, engulfing all as it came. She could see the glowing blond head of the tallest man on the field of death this day.

There was Rory, King Sivercroft, facing a bulky thing nearly twice his height. He was out of her reach, so far out and dancing with the giant of a thing, going even farther away.

Amazingly, all of the black forces around these two combatants stood their ground and maintained their distance from the two brutes as they squared off.

Zaramagrii swayed left then right as she cleaved her way through the swarming wave, leaving brutes twice her size felled and gutted. Every step took her into the frenzy of slaying more and more, as the swirls of red hue around her eyes began to fiercely glow.

Those that she slew occasionally froze in their tracks upon seeing the shining contrast of her white and black eyes. But she could not cut through enough of them to get to Rory. She knew that she should go straight to him, and quickly. But the whispers of the twilight world beckoned to her. And the thirst for the methodical vengeance that she now inflicted with her blades only grew.

A billowing outline stalked not far behind Zaramagrii. As several goblins and Akhruuk atop snarling wargs bore down towards her, the shimmering outline showed itself as the huge mouth breathed fiery red and the eyes glowed brilliantly with hellfire.

At that, several of the wargs immediately turned with tails between their hind legs and cowered off, flinging their riders hard into the ground.

Only a couple of the wargs actually stood their ground. But this was their last mistake. As they did so, it appeared that a near invisible apparition silently leapt around ripping them apart before they could move.

The mighty Grasfur gave no quarter as he flew and slaughtered, a thing born and bred for such a purpose. And he had no remorse for those of his kind that disobeyed him. It was the reckoning of the Alpha Omega.

While moving from one warg or wolf to another, the powerful shadow warg ripped off the occasional head of those dismounted riders as well.

And yet, Zaramagrii could not break free of the bloodspell.

§ § §

Rory knew that the time had come, as he parried with Gauth the Bloodmonger. The king knew that the time was right, he could feel it. The part Akhru, part joutuun beast brought its huge blade straight down hard atop Rory's, the blackened edge clanging against Rory's helm and knocking it off.

In a surprising burst of speed, Gauth whipped the long blade from side to side, lashing against Rory's breastplate. The clangs of the vicious attacks echoed through the rest of the hellish din, knocking the king back each time. Amazingly, the fine mirrored steel took the blows and only dented inwards.

The force sent Rory reeling backwards out of control. Even on his back, his two-handed sword behind him and stuck in a tangle of dead bodies, his look was still of calm deliberation. He eased himself back, resting partially against another dead Kuhrzothian knight, appearing not to be able to raise up in defense.

The Bloodmonger charged with all of his might towards Rory, sword high and whirling down from overhead for a killing blow.

As the blade swept near to cutting Rory's body into two, the giant of a man rolled slightly to one side. The blackened blade of Gauth rang as it cleaved through the armored bodies and forcefully into the ground.

Quick as a cat, Rory was spinning his body back towards Gauth with the battleaxe in his hand.

As Rory completed the arc, the blade of the axe dug deeply into Gauth's unprotected side with a loud, bony thud. The beast of a thing looked up and howled with rage as he tried to raise the bogged down sword.

Rory spun again and, now on his feet, he freed the axe in the one movement and arced it back into the center of the general's back.

Gauth raged in pain, freeing his sword in one grinding yank. He swept back across with a determined swing at the same time that it came free. The lithe Bastard Prophet ducked low as the blade nicked his breastplate with a ringing *clang*.

This allowed Rory enough of a pause to jump up into the air and bring his battleaxe heavily down into the crease of the bulging neck of the Bloodmonger, just below the head. The fountain of dark blood sprayed in bursts and Rory was completely covered by it.

This whole time, not very far away, several Akhruuk and goblins watched the valiant fight. They never lifted a blade to help, but now they tightly gripped their long, cruel spears.

As Gauth fell to his knees, facing away from the Man-king, Rory gripped his axe with both hands and bent back for another blow. He began to swing in a horizontal arc straight for the neck. The Bloodmonger had no chance to turn around and look his slayer in the eye. The huge head rolled slightly. Then it dipped down to the side, hanging on by what remained of the toughened hide with the bleached white of the spine showing.

As Rory completed the arc, half a dozen blackened spears pierced his armored back, some even emerging through the breastplate.

The force caused him to look upward toward the heavens, his blood-spattered golden hair flowing still. And his deep green eyes caught sight of the white fire of a mount and Rha the Lightwalker.

The spears seemed to hold him upright for many moments. The light in his clear eyes still sparkled there to see the devastating effect of the Shadow Soul's power as it raged in agony from the scene of his demise. But, ultimately, his glory.

And Rory smiled in deep satisfaction as he glimpsed the full power of Zaramagrii. He knew that he had impacted yet another of the restless spirits, even in his death. That notion made one of his nature as complete as such an individual could ever be.

As Rory was impaled, the endless skies darkened, as both duo suns shaded to a dull glow by moons equally large. The landscape turned into a twisted scene of gloom. Most looked up, shocked and stunned by the blackening of the late-suns light. And many thought that somehow the black army managed to sway the skies to its path of death and carnage.

It was the rarest of the rare, as a duo eclipse transformed the world into a writhing haze of shadows. The profane effect appeared like a foreboding warning of what may come in the distant future.

Suddenly the air and sky itself turned with the uncontrolled and soaring rage of Zaramagrii as her outstretched arms reached skyward. She was now beyond mortal angst and agony at the sight of what transpired.

A dark purple, hazy hell birthed within a vast area surrounding her as her eyes began to glow brighter and brighter.

Colossal, eerie bolts of blackened lightning shot down and seared the ground in many places as the ominous, sullied skies churned with chaos. The clamoring of the thunder skewered the ears of all that were caught in the immediate vortex.

The dark lightning raged downwards to her, through her, as it then arced out from her eyes initially.

These arcs first caught the Lightwalker and her mount, as they froze in midair and then simply vanished. The two beings of light disappeared into a million ashen particles from so violently clashing with the negative energy.

It almost appeared that Rha was in a silent moment of tranquility, as she leaned forward waiting for the energy to engulf her and destroy what she had become. Both arms spread out as wings ready to take flight.

Then, the dark energy of purplish black crackling hues arced out with a thunderous boom in all directions from Zaramagrii, as she stood alone in the swirling maelstrom of hell and chaos.

The wave of black energy snapped out for a league in all directions, before dissipating. As it came to any living thing, it turned them into dried out, blackened husks of what they once were. It destroyed friend and foe alike, such was the power of the Shadow Soul. As luck, or design, had it, the strange power appeared to only lightly knock at the walls of Nuuroc. It did not sweep through the walled city.

After the torrent of chaos and carnage subsided, Zaramagrii knelt beside the fallen body of Rory Sivercroft and wept. She did not weep for all of the dead, not even those Kuhrzothians who died within her wrath of darkness. For these individuals were not innocent, they were warriors fighting and killing. They died as they lived, and to her were a very small price to pay for the defeat of the Lightwalker and her black army. There was no remorse there whatsoever.

And this was what made the essence of Zaramagrii different, the calloused mediation of all events broad and narrow within her scope of judgment.

But, make no mistake, it was not the ignorance and assumption of societal established and biased judgment. Rather it was the tempered balance of true right and wrong built upon the pedestal of righteous chaos.

Such was the power and will of the spirit of the Shadow Soul. Such was what the essence, will, and mind of Zaramagrii were honed to through all of the previous experiences and actions.

So the Shadow Soul came unto her own finally, within the dark culmination of the vanquishing of evil and wrongdoing in all of the facets of existence. Not for Braxis. Not for Siri. Not even for her own satisfaction or empowerment. But for that which attempted to subdue others.

The consequence of all of it was that it was, and is, done under the banner of sympathy. The unequivocal, evilest evil of evils being simply apathy. Thus the Shadow Soul struck it down with its polar opposite at every given opportunity. No matter the cost.

In the end, the concept of good and evil rested solely on the mantle of perception, as viewed in the eye and mind of the beholder. But either way, the momentum of violent action must overcome and consume all wrong doing.

Zaramagrii continued to kneel, bowing her head as she silently and tearlessly wept. Not even for Rory, the intrepid man, did she weep, but for what the individual stood for.

For Rory took a stand in his beliefs and stayed fast to them until the end, true to his form and never faltering. In his blind faith last brace against impossible odds of force, he stood solid even as he was physically overrun. And this was extremely kindred to her as no other entity in this world.

He was the beacon in the middle of the darkened night, and he held no fear for those things that attempted to subvert him, or others. And she had been dragged to him, like a moth to the flame.

Then she no longer displayed her impassive form of grief over the loss of such an essence, as she sensed that he was gone. The small, petite form of Zaramagrii, soiled and bloodied from head to toe, simply vanished from the field.

Some folk that overlooked the scene of ruin and destruction claimed that they saw the ghostly image of a giant, black wolf linger amongst the field of bodies near to where Zaramagrii was last seen. But then they stated that the huge form simply disappeared or faded, as if it had never really existed at all.

§ § §

The Black Legion commander waited around the bottom of the tower, as he knew that Castym would be coming out any time now.

There he was, along with his first captain, stepping off the spiral stairs and out of the archway.

Axyander had one of his men with him, partially turning and running as he shouted towards Castym, "Commander Castym! I need help at the lower gate. Come quickly."

Castym eyed him hurriedly, so intent was he to get to the south gate where most of the fighting was taking place.

Castym spoke over his shoulder as he turned to follow Axyander. "Seth, take over for me and see to it that the lines hold. Keep an eye on the king, he is way too far out in the lines and oblivious to being swarmed. I will be along shortly."

Axyander filled him in while jaunting to the lower gate. "One of my men just informed me there is something going on at the lower gate. I figured that you needed to know what this was, in case it is another attack. My Legion-man also said there were ones and twos that had somehow managed to get through the gate before it closed. But we do not have a sizable force down there."

"Indeed, Axyander, good thinking, as we cannot afford for them to come at us through the lower gate. It would be a wonder that they even managed to find it. But let us see what is going on so we can prepare," Castym replied, slightly out of breath already. He took the lead now, as they hurried onward towards where the passageways began that led to the lower gate housing.

Axyander, face dirtied from the fighting, gleamed through his steely, gray eyes. Those orbs seemed limitless amidst the darkened face and midnight beard. The Legion commander and his man picked up behind Castym, armor clinking and rattling.

It did not take long for them to reach the lower gate, after many turns through baileys and inner passages that meandered down into the perpetually cool air of the lower passages. The gate was still raised into its resting position of being closed. The huge door lay flat and nearly blended in with the flooring.

Its massive ironworks had no wood whatsoever within its design. Equally sized chains used to lower and raise the far end rested, dripping oil. All that could be seen were several men wearing large, billowing black cloaks with the mark of the Legion upon their back. They stood facing away from Castym.

Castym stopped short, his hand still resting upon the handle of his sword. He slowly turned around, more than slightly out of breath. "Well, my brother, it seems that this was a false alarm."

He momentarily lost his words as Axyander was there near him, huge blade drawn and pointed.

Axyander spoke calmly without faltering in either his words or the smooth thrust of his sword. "Yes, maybe so, my lord."

His broad blade pierced directly into Castym's sternum area with a crack of bone and a meaty thud. The bright blood gushed out around the edges, quickly staining the green-hued scaled armor. Thrusting the blade upwards at an angle had easily separated a portion of the scales.

Castym stared into the Legion commander's eyes with a look of surprise as life slowly trickled away from him. The might of Axyander held the form of the Emerald commander up for several moments before letting the body fall to the ground in a heap.

"All for a better future, my lord. You have been relieved of your duties. Go now, and be at peace."

Axyander withdrew the blade, flinging it to clear it of blood, before turning to his men. "Drag up and scatter a dozen more of the dead black scum…and lower the gate. Make it look like he valiantly held them off until we arrived. Now be quick."

Of course, they had already taken over the gate house earlier and positioned about two dozen dead carcasses of the black army outside the gate and out of immediate sight. It only took a short amount of time to create the artwork of bravery that would bolster the people of Kuhrzoth, and also cement Axyander's position for the throne. And so ended Castym Steele, the last of the Steele brothers.

§ § §

Wybur urged Shab the mule up the steep embankment, now slipping and sliding in the crusty snow. The ravine ended, and the only way to go was up.

Poor Shab was already considerably weaker. The blood had coagulated thickly along her side now, but bright red still spurted out. Wybur could feel the wobbling in the mule's legs. Not even half way up the side of the ravine, Shab collapsed onto her knees. Then she laid over on her side with a soft bray.

Wybur rolled over and into the snow, now worriedly looking Shab over. The poor beast then let out one long breath with a slow, rattling bray that trailed off to silence.

"No! No, Shab… You cannot… Ohhh," moaned Wybur, tears welling in his eyes as he stared at the blank open eyes, the head and neck slowly coming to rest fully on the snow-covered ground. He gently leaned his cheek in close to the mule's neck.

Then Wybur looked back the way that they had come and began to run up the ravine, finally clearing the top. One last look down at his beloved companion, and he was off to the closest tree line.

Of course, Wybur was by far no warrior, let alone champion pugilist. Now he was tired and could not catch his breath in the cold of the day. He knew he should be going towards Nuuroc if he expected help. But alas—he felt that he would never make it there.

The fiend was upon him. Now the nightmarish thing was over the top of the ravine, bounding through the air low to the ground.

The barren hardwood trees beckoned him in with their long, bony fingers, while the bristly pines swayed in the north winds. Such a day as this, with the bright light of the duo suns at play, he might just be out for a stroll through the countryside. But this was not the case.

The scenes from his uncle's place in Longshadows played through his mind. The bloody mangled bodies, their fates probably met by this same thing that now chased him.

After running a considerable distance, his chest heaved and he could no longer maintain his pace. He had just broken out into a clearing with a small mound at the center. He ran-walked towards it as he felt his legs give out.

He could hear the rustling flap of the giant wings now. Then a sharp, stabbing feeling hit him and pushed his upper body forward.

Again it hit him, almost knocking him over, as the thing called Rosella hovered just behind him. He could hear the hiss of her laughter.

The razor sharp tail, or maybe the tips of the wings, began to mercilessly point and tear into him, like nails being hammered into the flesh across his entire back. And the sweet fragrance of what he once knew as Rosella floated down to him all the while.

For an instance, he thought about the irony of it all. Now being brutally stabbed by what once was his passion, his fever and thrill. Maybe this was his punishment for falling into such a scheme that he failed to see through.

Everything became a hazy blur, with dots of red splattering the snow all around. The mound was only a few steps, but he still had no idea why his mind saw it as anything at all. There was absolutely no protection there. Just a slight raise in the lay of the forest clearing, similar to a tiny barrow.

Then, suddenly, his mind flashed in the flurry and haze of the pain and mortal inflictions to a time long gone. He distantly thought, did he lock up Buttlecuts when he left Longshadows way back when? It was like his mind wanted to escape what was going on.

Before long he collapsed onto the mound, which caused the snow to give way to lush, green grass. He rolled over on the raised surface and lay on his back, now fully seeing the wicked monstrosity that was tormenting him. Even with the passing of a few moments, he could see the deep red stains widening throughout the soft, cool snow around his body.

The talon things drove in again and again, impaling him in the chest and stomach now. The face that once was beauty and seductiveness now appeared like a hideous mask of some nightmare with glowing red eyes.

Wybur wept, from the severe agony and futileness of his predicament. His vision was weakening fast.

Then the vast skies suddenly darkened and the duo suns were covered by huge, black orbs. The nuance appeared to make the fiery eyes of the thing called Rosella glow as beacons of their own now. Dismally bent upon flaying the young Wybur alive.

Yet, within the darkness, a strange white glow appeared up above and behind the fiend. But he could not be sure as to the distance away, with his weakened sight.

The radiant, white glow began to take the form of a large figure with majestic wings to the sides, slowly flapping. The brightness hid any details. But it had a very alluring and womanly shape to it.

He could plainly see the dazzling form now, even though such brightness should still be blinding him. And, as the wicked spears ravaged his body, he became at peace while staring at the apparition behind Rosella. His expression turned to one of benevolence.

Then Rosella noticed it. She, or it, turned to look back at the glowing figure, momentarily ceasing her assault on poor Wybur.

The glowing white figure appeared to send forth a white hot lance of light at Rosella, hitting the creature directly in the center of its chest.

Rosella let out a screech that would make an aged wyrm cringe, as her form began to disappear in the white light. It completely encased her body, and then the wind blew it away as dust or ash.

Wybur weakly looked up at the glowing form.

"Fear not, my good one. The pain will pass, and so will you. Worry not, for it will be soon, and it must be allowed to happen." The voice was feminine and cradled him in its soothing tone. It lulled Wybur into his last few moments of life with peace and tranquility.

And then Wybur let out his last breath, with eyes still staring lifelessly up at the radiant being.

His frail and beaten form slowly began to lift up with arms and legs dangling underneath. The body disappeared up into the glowing light, which also vanished not long afterward.

§ § §

The coronation ceremony for the new Aylsh king, Lord Vuranthegost, was indeed tremendous. Representatives from all of the enclaves and the refts made a show for it. For many, the recent passing of the king regent signified a return back to an older way. One stronger and more aligned for the good of the Aylsh.

The heir to the Aylsh throne, by tradition, must be crowned beside the Ikhshaymra, or Tree of Endless Light.

The Tree of Endless Light was one of the last Oadewood trees existing here in the Aylsh Kingdom. As a matter of fact, it had been around since the First Days, as the Aylsh called them. A picturesque waterfall that cascaded down several hundred foot in three separate torrents loomed beside the enormous tree.

The fine mist playing over the ceremony set within the snow-dotted, lush green reeds was mixed with a light fog from the cooler air sweeping over the water. Altogether, it was a very dazzling scene. A near contrast to the wintry chill.

Then, as the crown was being placed upon Vuranthegost's head, the entire sky fell into darkness. As what was transpiring around the walled city of Nuuroc, so here too moons aligned and blotted out the duo suns. And all the lands fell into the dark gloom.

A hushed, dull rumble could be heard from all around as most did not realize what truly happened. Many Aylsh, be they Trone or not, assumed ill tidings from the foreshadowing event and its timing. A sign of ill omens at the exact moment that Vuranthegost was crowned as the Aylsh king.

Once the crowning was completed, the new king was escorted by the Aylsh Royal Guard through pompous parade on horseback all the way back to the royal palace outside of the city Belenhaanra. Aylsh in their finest regalia, be it armor or ceremonial dress, lined the countless towns, villages, and roads. They stretched all the way through the courtyard leading into the royal hall itself. And all of this happened within the darkened times.

Somewhere along this route, two cloaked figures on foot joined in with the procession. This party stepped in near the king's personal entourage, but slightly behind it. And no one seemed to notice or think anything of it. A noble wolf trailed behind the two.

King Vuranthegost sat upon the throne, finally—now with a very accomplished look of arrogance on his face. The smirk was both conniving and wicked, one holding a dark light that was no longer able to remain hidden.

"Nobles of the Aylsh High Court, esteemed ones. I, King Inshro Thann Vuranthegost, of Reft Vuranthegost, now call upon you. I call to you for order and advisement. As your king.

"Do you hear me? Do you heed me? Do you all, the First Folk, obey me and place forth my word as law and order?" spoke

Vuranthegost in the traditional premise going hand in hand with the first time a new king sits upon the Aylsh throne.

The twelve noble Aylsh appointed to the High Court sat in their elegant chairs with heads held high. Even the first ones seated upon either side of the king—the two that had just been appointed to the court by the former lord Vuranthegost.

But, as the newly decorated king spoke those words, most of the attention went to the two cloaked figures, as they strode down the center of the royal floor from the opened doors.

Not an Aylsh had stopped them the whole time, not even those guards at the final doors that led into the palace.

All of the First Folk seemed frozen in place except for the three figures, one being a wolf. Possibly the scene was just too bizarre for any to immediately react.

One of the figures stopped short with the wolf, while the other continued onward. Straight towards the throne.

Ephritori's face could be seen from under the darkness of the cloak's hood. Her gray cloak was now partially opened at the front where it appeared that she was naked underneath. The archaic wooden rod was grasped in her right hand.

She stopped within ten paces from where the center of the unique crescent table formed upon either side of the royal dais.

As Ephritori's hood slipped back, she spoke. "Nobles and lords of the Aylsh High Court, I—Ephritori Nephritaryah Bari Lourendalthemee, last heir and last of the line to Daumere Bari Lourendalthemee of Enclave Noblynbindyn, last of that of the True King Thiliathain—come before you as the bearer of what has come to pass.

"And what will come to pass if you allow this imp to clutch the crown in his claws."

At this point, Ephritori's hands were slightly out to both sides, with the arms rigid and palms facing the Aylsh High Court. The strange rod in her hand was held straight up and down, as though it was longer than it really was.

But, at the mention of King Lourendalthemee, more than one set of those uniquely long ears seated at the High Court perked up. The name of the last exalted Aylsh king, considered by most to be the mightiest of all times. And the direct lineage to the True King of old.

The look on their faces went to one of renewed wonder. Many expressions showed a deep contemplation on whether this could be true or just a dashed hope hanging in front of them like a carrot.

King Vuranthegost stared at Ephritori without so much as losing his smirk. "My, my, you do have some bold words for one such as you. *You* are the imposter!" cried Vuranthegost as he snapped his fingers. "Guards! Kill her now! She is an evil thing here to destroy what the proud Aylsh have so valiantly fought for."

The next amazing thing happened. Not one of those Aylsh royal guards so much as moved at those commands. But each of the nobles seated immediately to the side of the king grew fidgety in their chairs, their eyes darting to the king and then back and forth to one another.

The Eternal Mother did not pause, nor even hesitate. "Vuranthegost! Stop your lies! You must now show your true self—expose yourself, you self-serving and loathsome thing!"

As she spoke those words, her voice changed to a more sinister and deeply haunting tone. The words resounded with the effect of a vast amphitheater. Thunderous cracks of lightning rang out across the skies.

Her arms slowly raised higher, and a strange blue aura appeared from around her silhouette. The glow formed a giant orb with her in the center.

Then the unadorned rod in her hand jumped to life and extended into a flaming white staff, burning within the strange hue. And it burned as though it held the radiance of the duo suns themselves.

The clothes upon Ephritori flamed into ashes and she stood naked in front of all those gathered. Her lithe and provocative shape bare for all to see.

But every single one of those bright-eyed countenances went to the stunningly twisted designs on her back, running up her spine, as they began to brightly glow blue.

The curious symbol upon her left breast lit the eyes of the Aylsh High Court aglow with its golden splendor so bright. And her eyes took on the blue glow as well.

While no wind blew inside, it seemed that she was caught in a magnificent tempest as her hair flew about wildly.

And all before her now knew the truth of what she was, for the Aylsh-kind were very much attuned to creation and existence. Many even fell to their knees at this point. Their heads bowed low to the Light, that of their Mother.

And, with the showing of the Eternal Mother, the skies suddenly filled with the untold brilliance of the duo suns again. It was almost to the point of blinding everyone, causing tears from the pain of just looking within the light of day.

Suddenly, Vuranthegost cried out in agonizing pain, and black smoke began to erupt from around the openings of his sleeves and neck. Within moments, his form burst into a searing bluish-white flame with only a long, dragged-out yell from him.

What his form turned into during that brief instance was something hideous and bestial. A gray, hairless thing. The thing, calling itself Vuranthegost, showed its true form.

Each of those nobles sitting nearest to the burnt husk of a form began to stand up, frantically looking around. Worriedly.

"Behold, my fair Aylsh…a shunmrith had assumed your crown. And alas, even some true Aylsh fell sway to its power—to the power of greed and corruption." She pointed Jahthra Khomar, the Spear of Eternal Light, towards the two nobles nearest the throne.

Their eyes told all as the windows to the blackened, corrupted greed that they had succumbed to.

Those two nobles began to scream in mortal agony as their flesh and bone burned from the inside out. The intense, white light that burned out through their forms was so devastating and yet serene to the First Folk gathered about. Their skin began to wrinkle and peel off the seared meat, as parchment placed into a fire.

It was a horrible sight to watch as both were consumed into blackened husks of nothingness. Only a long hissing, splattering sound like water trapped inside a log upon a stoked fire, and this eventually tapered off.

"And all of those who have succumbed to such evil will pay with their essence…their lives. Let these three be the first…and the warning to the rest."

Ephritori, now Ityarfa Vorjanimae incarnate, turned about so that the gathered Aylsh could see her, behold her, and listen. The golden, sparkling sheen upon her lower abdomen now visible, almost showering down from where her ogrou was.

"Know ye all that not just Man, or those of the Black Clans, or what you call monsters such as Akhruuk, Hulding, and all of the yuanhad—joutuun, goblin, and others—know that not just these beings are subject to corruption. Loathsome monsters and wicked beasts are many. All those that concede to such darkness. You have allowed such stink into your midst.

"You would have blindly let such an abomination misguide the First Folk into the next turn. And I speak not only of Vuranthegost the shunmrith, but also those two nobles that were bought and paid for to do the same. And possibly others that we do not yet know of. There may be others hidden.

"This sets forth that both good and evil exists, and either is the choice that each and every thing makes for itself.

"Know you that these were designs of a much larger and sinister plot to spiral Thaldeia into oblivion. Maybe more of this world than we know…into the darkness.

"And it may not yet be over, for even now as we stand here, Kuhrzoth deals with a mortal enemy, a vast black army encroached upon her doors. So, lest you want to end in such a fiery death, do not cast yourselves higher than the rest of Lord Braxis' creations… That was definitely not what he intended for his special children— the blessed Children of the Light—all of you."

All that the entire gathering could do was stare in awe, and then drop down on their knees, if they had not done so already, toward the radiant figure. More of those standing outside now wanted to see what was going on, and the royal court became very crowded.

The old Aylsh with the spectacles, the one that had initially taken Ephritori in to hear her pleas, now stepped forward from behind the high table. "Mother, we are humbled by your presence.

Please forgive us for our idiocy and ill ways. Lead us, lead us. We are your people. We see you now for who you are, as the Eternal Mother, our divine queen. We stand before you, we stand behind you… We serve you, as has been done since the First Days. We beg your undying pardon and ask repentance in our ways."

Ephritori Nephritaryah Bari Lourendalthemee was crowned queen of the Aylsh Kingdom. They could not necessarily crown the Eternal Mother due to obvious divine prohibitions. But Ephritori could be crowned, and thus she was. The last of the most pure lineage, now back on the seat of power. To lead the Aylsh.

Another amazing feat took place, one that baffled all of the Aylsh that found out about it. Not more than a fortnight after the events surrounding the death of Vuranthegost the shunmrith, Ephritori took to being sick each morning.

This happened every day, until finally one of the royal physicians was hailed to make sure the queen was okay. The first physician was so distraught at what he found from examining her, that he called another in to perform the examination again. But he would not tell this second physician anything that he had found. Of course, this one also could not believe what he uncovered, and so a third one was summoned in.

After two days of going back and forth, the three physicians finally concluded that Ephritori was, indeed, with child. There could be no mistaking it.

Of all things. But what was so mystical about that? Well, the part that they could not grasp, or believe, was that she held every sign of being a virgin. That is, her sex organs were still sealed, and the barrier not yet broken or pierced. Yet, she was with child.

neck. Within moments, his form burst into a searing bluish-white flame with only a long, dragged-out yell from him.

What his form turned into during that brief instance was something hideous and bestial. A gray, hairless thing. The thing, calling itself Vuranthegost, showed its true form.

Each of those nobles sitting nearest to the burnt husk of a form began to stand up, frantically looking around. Worriedly.

"Behold, my fair Aylsh…a shunmrith had assumed your crown. And alas, even some true Aylsh fell sway to its power—to the power of greed and corruption." She pointed Jahthra Khomar, the Spear of Eternal Light, towards the two nobles nearest the throne.

Their eyes told all as the windows to the blackened, corrupted greed that they had succumbed to.

Those two nobles began to scream in mortal agony as their flesh and bone burned from the inside out. The intense, white light that burned out through their forms was so devastating and yet serene to the First Folk gathered about. Their skin began to wrinkle and peel off the seared meat, as parchment placed into a fire.

It was a horrible sight to watch as both were consumed into blackened husks of nothingness. Only a long hissing, splattering sound like water trapped inside a log upon a stoked fire, and this eventually tapered off.

"And all of those who have succumbed to such evil will pay with their essence…their lives. Let these three be the first…and the warning to the rest."

Ephritori, now Ityarfa Vorjanimae incarnate, turned about so that the gathered Aylsh could see her, behold her, and listen. The golden, sparkling sheen upon her lower abdomen now visible, almost showering down from where her ogrou was.

of a vast amphitheater. Thunderous cracks of lightning rang out across the skies.

Her arms slowly raised higher, and a strange blue aura appeared from around her silhouette. The glow formed a giant orb with her in the center.

Then the unadorned rod in her hand jumped to life and extended into a flaming white staff, burning within the strange hue. And it burned as though it held the radiance of the duo suns themselves.

The clothes upon Ephritori flamed into ashes and she stood naked in front of all those gathered. Her lithe and provocative shape bare for all to see.

But every single one of those bright-eyed countenances went to the stunningly twisted designs on her back, running up her spine, as they began to brightly glow blue.

The curious symbol upon her left breast lit the eyes of the Aylsh High Court aglow with its golden splendor so bright. And her eyes took on the blue glow as well.

While no wind blew inside, it seemed that she was caught in a magnificent tempest as her hair flew about wildly.

And all before her now knew the truth of what she was, for the Aylsh-kind were very much attuned to creation and existence. Many even fell to their knees at this point. Their heads bowed low to the Light, that of their Mother.

And, with the showing of the Eternal Mother, the skies suddenly filled with the untold brilliance of the duo suns again. It was almost to the point of blinding everyone, causing tears from the pain of just looking within the light of day.

Suddenly, Vuranthegost cried out in agonizing pain, and black smoke began to erupt from around the openings of his sleeves and

Chapter 25:

A Peaceful Facade

"We can no longer fear that which strikes terror into us. It must be completely annihilated from your mind, your essence. Without the bonds that such a thing as fear imposes upon your physical and mental prowess, then you can surpass all hope and expectation. YOU can accomplish the impossible!"

–King Arterium, circa the year 24 BA.

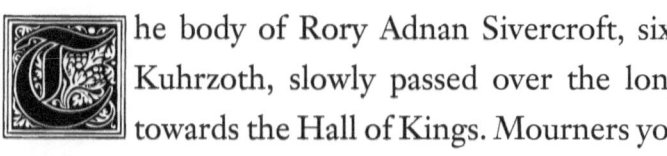he body of Rory Adnan Sivercroft, sixty-ninth king of Kuhrzoth, slowly passed over the long Emerald Way towards the Hall of Kings. Mourners young and old alike lined both sides, from where his carriage began the journey to where his final resting place would be. Not even a stray cat could have squeezed anywhere in between those who stood in woeful silence to show respect for their fallen king. This unity stretched the entire length.

The war drums beat this last march of the king, slowly leading the movement of the procession. The deep reverberations were only achieved through multiple taut membranes. The unique and very distinct *beat-beat*—pause—*beat-beat* carried the king and his knights into countless battles over the past turns of time. Now their haunting rhythm boomed out to honor this final march of Rory Sivercroft the Bastard Prophet. The warrior-drummers rode monstrous Thoerne war horses all decked out in the glory of the Emerald Crown.

Besides the loud war drums, silence reigned supreme as the clip-clop of horse hooves and the creaking of the iron-clad wooden wheels lulled those it passed by. Many lamented a king whom they had known but a very short time, and yet had come to love so dearly.

He was dressed in all of the splendor and regalia befitting his stature. Atop the lordly breastplate, covering the now still chest, rested his sword and axe crossed over one another. A banner placed along each of his sides lightly flapped in the cold breeze. On his right was the one of Kuhrzoth, while the colors of Dawn's Glory flared out on his left.

His body had been left untouched by the disruptive, negative energy that the Shadow Soul unleashed in her moment of anguish.

Maybe it was more a moment of bitterness and pain. His stark countenance rested forever asleep. But his face appeared to have a look of contentment. One of peaceful repose that held the trace of a carefree smile.

Once the carriage with Rory's body reached the entrance to the Hall of Kings, the war horses came to a gradual halt of their own accord. Several knights unhitched the beasts, and they trotted off to a trough full of freshly placed greens. An honor not only to the fallen king, but to those noble mounts that bear his kind.

The knights then picked up the ornate silver and green chains, each grasping the end of the blemished gold bar. Slowly they began to pull the carriage into the hall where so many waited. Each step carefully placed with the beat of the drums.

Inside the courtyard of the Hall of Kings stood scores of Kuhrzothians, King Axyander and complements of the royal orders under the Emerald Crown.

An Aylsh contingent, headed by Queen Ephritori herself, stood in glinting rows of Aylsh steel off to one side. Such a showing of Aylsh sentiment towards the Man-folk had not been seen since the days of Arterium.

The carriage slowly passed through the center of all those who were gathered. Silently, the knights then positioned the carriage in front of a huge emerald slab that rose to the level of their waists.

An immense iron vat rested behind the slab, with a fire licking the undersides of it. The gold-hued vapors rose and danced along the hallowed walls.

The knights gently shifted Rory's body onto the emerald slab. This slab rested beside the one that bore his father, now forever glorified within the gleaming layer of gold. And down the great hall were sixty-seven more such pedestals of kingship.

All had entombed kings upon them, except for the third place from the far side. This was a golden statue standing upright, the resting place of King Arterium. Appearing to be larger than life, the likeness was completely accurate in its modeling of the man himself. He had been a giant of a man.

King Arterium's body was never found. Only his battered helm had been recovered and brought back from the site of his demise. A statue of him had been completed and placed within Nuuroc's Grand Garden where all could see it. All those who knew of him, the countless many, could honor and pay their respect.

Oddly enough, this statue was made of him without armor and weapons, or any other adornments, just a loincloth. So the statue was moved to the Hall of Kings and fitted with his actual ceremonial plate armor and the dented helm. It was then covered in gold. The high rimmed crown of pure gold, speckled with the rich green of jewels that caught every ray of light surrounding them, was then placed upon the head. This was decided to be the honorable way to personify his glory in the absence of his physical form.

Kuhrzoth did not begin using the emerald slabs until the tenth king had passed. So, the first nine tombs, with the exception of Arterium's, were giant circular disks made from the base of the largest ash tree that could be found. This was then covered with paint made from the gaupers berry, which dried to a bright, but deep, green. Those slabs, designed after Arterium, were also inscribed with the divine words from the Twelve Edicts of Lord Braxis. The scriptures were eloquently written over and over again across the entire surface. Of course, this was done in the Common tongue, and not in the language of High Aylsh as they had been found scripted in by Arterium himself.

Gold was the shining symbol of Lord Braxis' virtue, as set forth by Arterium himself. Not the value or monetary worth of the precious ore, but the rich color was what was considered sacred. At least in the name of Lord Braxis.

King Axyander gave the tribute that day. Standing out in his shiny black plate armor, as a dark rock facing an oncoming tide of flesh and steel. The king's mantle of deep green was the only contrast that adorned his dark, foreboding visage.

King Axyander Blackshield the Steelborn, seventy-first king of Kuhrzoth. In honor of the valiant Castym Steele and all that he sacrificed, Axyander decreed that he be named as the seventieth king. He did this even though all of the members of the High Assembly cautioned him against doing so, while they softly referenced the royal proclamations and ages old codes. King Axyander drew his huge blade and threatened to behead them on the spot, if they did not do as he commanded. If they did not honor such a noble man as Castym, a hero to the lofty kingdom of Kuhrzoth.

Castym's internment would be the following morning at first light. This old ceremony could not be changed or adjusted even slightly. It had been the tradition since Arterium that Lord Braxis took up those warriors at first light following their fall. And so the ritual to send such brave ones off must also be at first light. This was the first step towards proceeding into the gates of the Outer Halls, at least in Man-folk lore.

King Axyander's words brought to life Rory's extreme heroism and bravery, forever casting him as a distinguished king. And as a remarkable man, more importantly. As King Axyander himself stated, the markings of a renowned king were not those of time—but of benevolence and propriety, of courage and sacrifice. The man, as the king, was marked by those who make him. And by those actions and consequences done in light of those he was charged with.

But Axyander also used the height of this bravado to bolster a common cause amongst those present. His call went out to all others, who were not present or able to be within earshot.

The call was a promise to carry forth the unity and the strength of the individual to the tremendous good of everyone, just as what Rory strived so hard to accomplish. Even though his tenure over Kuhrzoth was short-lived.

But this effected some amazing and profound things in the hearts and minds of the people, at least for a while. And Kuhrzoth prospered. Things that, for the most part it seemed, Kuhrzoth had left behind many, many turns ago.

The forces of the Fallen Lands had destroyed Emerald Rest and ransacked the lands all the way to the gates of Nuuroc. Before long, Axyander built up such a military might among the Emerald Knights, the Emerald Guard, and the Legion. This showing was so strong that all the people again felt safe and secure within their homes and hovels.

And fewer hovels at that, for Axyander incorporated several new concepts throughout the lands. An important one was an attainment prospect called *Rising Champions*. The people could send in their fledglings, as young as six years, to one of the garrisons of the Legion for training and higher learning. All of this was at no cost to the parents. It merely required a contract with the young one that stipulated an oath to join the Legion, or the forces under the Emerald Crown, for a period of service at some predesignated point down the road.

Of course, all the material presented within this schooling was completely orchestrated by and through Axyander or through his hand. But those that participated could even go back to their homes when they were most needed, such as for Tillers-break and the harvest during Greatfest. All in all, it was an invaluable arrangement. One that contributed to the might of Axyander's forces, as well as to the kingdom's economy and communal strength.

Emerald Rest remained lost and continued to be retained by the forces of Oshghrul. The castle was so ruined and fouled by the monsters of Priestess Sahrya's black army that it was never even attempted at being reclaimed. Instead, it remained its own grisly headstone attesting to the fact that so many had died there.

Both the Legion and the Order of Emerald Knights continued to harass and maraud any remnants of the black army that they crossed paths with. For the most part, the black forces remained within the bowels of Oshghrul, the Fallen Lands. Never flooding past the makeshift wall that they had built across the valley in front of Emerald Rest.

What came to be known as the Black War came and went, with the breaking of the black army. The war only a distant memory, ever fading, always receding into the curtains of night.

The kingdom of Kuhrzoth continued to reign supreme, although still not as strong as the old days. At least for a time afterwards.

Of course, with the fall of Rory, the mysterious symbol carried by the shunmrith posing as the royal presenter was lost and buried under politics and campaigns. This would sit on the dusty shelf for many a year—until cause brought it back up again. That is, as far as most folk went, but not those who stalked within the shadows.

The Emerald King, Axyander the Steelborn, ruled with an iron fist, both as the negotiator of royal duties, as well as wielder of bloody carnage. But he was strangely fair…and just.

King Axyander still led the Legion as a formal entity under the crown. And he managed to significantly increase the force's size. Each of the companies eventually numbered close to eight thousand. There was a fifth company of the Black Legion that occupied a much larger territory known as Tamelyn Keep. This expanse of land was ordered and decreed as sovereign to Kuhrzoth, even though it sat within the Free Lands. And it was now considered to be the base for the Black Legion, flying the banner of Kuhrzoth—highest of course—and also that of the Black Legion.

Over time, he returned the Emerald Knights to a semblance of former glory. And, amazingly, over the course of even sixty years, he appeared to age very little.

When Axyander took power that fateful day as the skies darkened, few folk—if any at all—noticed the grim, dark warriors that silently entered the castle walls to live among them. Ninety-nine to be exact. Sure, they appeared to wear the great-cloaks of the Legion, though faded and tattered beyond ordinary age. Their long hoods were pulled far over their faces, concealing the features. Maybe most took no notice because these mere shadows of Man all slipped into the gates under the cover of the night.

And what of Wybur Buttlecut? Well, he remained within the thoughts of many. Ephritori could feel his essence, but she could not see through the veil that covered him.

So, of course, she said nothing about what she could not clearly define, and she joined in with those mourning his loss. No one knew exactly what happened to him.

The guards at the gate on the day he rode out could add naught to the mystery. Within a ten-day of the epic battle, one of the patrols discovered a dead mule confirmed to be Shab. Shab's body was a short distance from a scene filled with blood and old tracks. The snows had not yet covered the story within its icy touch.

Of course, this just sealed the mystery of Wybur's fate, even though his body could not be found. Truth be told, many bodies were never found in all of that carnage, many more too mutilated to be identified. It took quite some time for the folk to collect all of their loved ones, whether identifiable or not. Eventually most were buried in several very large burial mounds within the Fields of Mourning, inside of Nuuroc. The vast numbers of the dead Thalroan were removed farther out from the walls and then either dug into shallow ditches or burned.

Wybur Buttlecut was laid to rest, at least in essence since there wasn't anything physically to bury. Wybur's mule, Shab, was actually buried there also, although only a handful of folk knew about this. But those that knew Wybur best also knew that the mule had been his constant companion.

The memorial was not nearly as regal as that of a king, but it did have its own unique signature. The people of Dawn's Glory created a statue comprised of three animals. One was Wybur's best friend, Star, at least as far as dogs went. Another was his mule. Overlooking both of these two was a very large, white owl. The elaborately designed details for each of them could not have been more life-like.

Of course, both Ephritori and Rhalwa knew the reality of life and death, in that way of the Aylsh. But they took part in both of the remembrances, more as the ceremonious tribute to each, though.

Such talk might leave one to consider yet another question. What of Buttlecut's family trading company? It was well into the next frostthaw by the time the property and other assets of what Wybur's uncle had accumulated actually sorted itself out. Rather someone assisted the sorting.

Once the death of Wybur was confirmed, several rather esteemed vultures swooped down upon the Longshadows chief magistrate's office. Their intent was to rightfully claim the whole caboodle.

Now most would think that the written word was required to guarantee such a thing. But, here, most things were done without such attestation. Most of the time, folks just did not learn to read let alone write. One's word was considered to be supreme unless proven otherwise. This was something that still carried forth from turns ago.

There were no more surviving relatives or potential heirs to the Buttlecuts, so the magistrate was lost in confusion on how to handle this particular case. Especially one so noteworthy and within the eye of the people.

These vultures all claimed to have been verbally bestowed the entire owning if misfortune were to befall Groelhof Buttlecut and his kin. Most of them were actually rival tradesmen that ran lesser companies. Ones that had been in competition with the Buttlecut's for the longest time. All of which were not nearly as successful as Wybur's uncle had been.

Well, the chief magistrate was unclear as to what to do until one bright, sunny day. It happened to be the last day of frostthaw. The magistrate came into the council chambers and blatantly announced that all matters by, with, and through the Buttlecut family name and business were exclusively bequeathed to a man named Wullyam. Secondary to this man, if he should fail to present himself, was the entire outpost known as Dawn's Glory. Or the duly appointed representative of Dawn's Glory. He also added that there would be no further speculation in the ruling.

Now this sudden inclination to acquiescently spur the matter into conclusion caught the attention of the other officials. And several of these squeaky members were known to be in bed with said vultures.

Also, when the chief magistrate arrived that morning, he had looked so unkempt. His hair was a mess and his clothes were those he wore from the previous day. Truth be told, he had not slept a worthwhile wink the night before.

When pursued further, the magistrate produced a very neatly scripted parchment with all the details spelled out. It had been signed by Wybur Buttlecut himself, and under witness of Rory Adnan Sivercroft. The blazing crest of the king of Kuhrzoth glared back at those greedy eyes that had meant to reap the labors of the departed Buttlecuts.

When broached as to where this claim originated from, the chief magistrate would not speak a word about it. Instead, he just declared its legitimacy unquestionable and that the matter was closed.

Now this magistrate confided in very few. The one man that he did tell his innermost thoughts to was none other than the head of the Lord's Initiates at the temple in Longshadows. The

Lord's Initiates was the religious order throughout Thaldeia that was dedicated to following in the ways of Lord Braxis.

According to the head initiate, the magistrate had been paid a late night visit. The magistrate told him that a mysterious woman, concealed in a large cloak and hood, woke him from a deep sleep. She was right alongside his bed, not a pace way, giving him such a fright. He claimed that the darkness surrounding her was even blacker than the night itself. She handed him the parchment concerning the Buttlecut estate.

Afterwards, she told him that the contents of that agreement would be honored no matter what. She swore to him that she'd return if it was not. And, when she did return, she promised to wade through Longshadows and make any of those guilty of the wrongdoing pay in blood...it would start with him, the chief magistrate.

He was so fearful of the daemun with the glowing eyes that he had to confide in the head initiate just to make sure that he had not consorted with a beast from the Chasm. When asked about the eyes, the magistrate told him that one was white and one black. Both were glowing some abysmal light. Even though it had been pitch black, both gave off a glow of sorts that could scare all the dead kings right out of their graves.

Now no one can confirm that Zaramagrii indeed showed up in Longshadows that night, but it would be safe to say that she had the inclination to do such a thing. It would definitely have been within her nature. A peculiar storm, thunderous but abrupt, had rode in the winds late that night about that same time.

In all cases, this generously benefited Dawn's Glory. Wullyam had taken over in Rory's place, and also appointed a small council to oversee the outpost. He did so because he wanted to make sure that Rory's belief in equality was never overtaken by ignorance and greed. With the council, there would always be a trusted governor-of-sorts to look out for the best interests of the outpost. Even if something were to happen to Wullyam.

Once the acquisition of the Buttlecut's trading company was completed, Wullyam took a small contingent of the able-bodied folk from Dawn's Glory to set up new activities in Longshadows. This group then ran the trading company, adding a shiny cog to the existence of Dawn's Glory. Now the outpost had its own way to provide for whatever was needed.

Wullyam maintained the original name of Buttlecuts in honor of Wybur and his kin. He claimed that there would never be a more noble and pure essence born than the likes of Wybur.

The trading company also opened up other ventures, sparking several trades from some of the talent within Dawn's Glory. One such individual was a mason-turned-sculptor. He could make the most amazing things out of a slab of stone. Stone, granite, and nearly any other kind of natural formation.

In fact, this sculptor was the one responsible for the special marker placed at Wybur's final resting place. Interestingly enough, it was one of his ancestors that had sculpted the statue of Arterium.

The name Dawn's Glory spread out and became even more widely renowned than previously. Now for the skills, expertise, and determination of those within it. Those that had flocked to Dawn's Glory in the beginning were not just a cast of harlequins who couldn't survive in their own society. They were masters at various trades—cobblers, jewelers, physicians, and agriculturalists. Even the famous master sword-smith himself, Selrence Vanduraag. And these professionals had families, and even apprentices. More folk passionately eager to learn the trades and skills. Buttlecuts allowed such wares to be sold far and wide.

And what of the Aylsh Kingdom? Well, Ephritori instated a high order of Aylsh rangers. She placed Rhalwa as the master ranger in charge of bringing them on line, completing their training, and organizing their equipment as well as the doctrine that would govern their actions. Of course, Rhalwa eventually had a daughter of her own, but that will be part of another story.

Jorle Itharzyr Morwhe Lourendalthemee was born not a year past all the chaos at the end of that year. His birth was heralded in by a moons' reach, which was where all five of the moons that orbited Zholryn were full at precisely the same time. It lasted through the entire witches' light. Aylsh historians and high priests alike murmured about it since one was not even due at the time.

But Aylsh lore also dictated that the Fatherless Son would be born during the time of the dark soul. He would raise the might of the Aylsh-kind and brandish redemption. His birth would mark dark times and his will would face a mysterious sect of Darkness.

Of course, none of the Aylsh really knew what all of this meant. But many aspects of the ancient lore already came true, whether this was recognized or not. The Eternal Mother had returned to them, and the Fatherless Son had been born. So many anxiously awaited to see what else might come to fruition.

Of course, news of the Eternal Mother slowly dwindled in awe throughout the rest of the Man-folk kingdoms. And this was only if word had actually reached them concerning the events of the Black War.

It may be worth noting that even the populous race of Hulding benefited from what Zaramagrii did for Khorpah, if you remember back to her captivity and eventual liberation within the Hulding village. Khorpah realized the dark sign that Zaramagrii bore and what that meant to his people. Taking advantage of this, he dispelled an ages old superstitious mantle that rested upon the Hulding kind.

Within fifty years, Khorpah rightfully became the supreme ruler after accomplishing a complete unification of the various Hulding tribes. He literally brought the Hulding out of the blinding darkness of superstitions and taboo to one of existentialism. Sure, thaumaturgy still existed obviously, and the shamans had power, but the Hulding were not subjected solely to religious zealotry.

And where was Priestess Sahrya during all of this time, with war waging…her war waging? Why, she was biding her time, and building the might of Isnuuthghor. She did not care whether or not Rha and the black army—her Thalroan—succeeded. Their sole purpose was to deteriorate the strength of Man, weaken Kuhrzoth at the least. And that was it, to batter the kingdom of Kuhrzoth and fracture its foundation.

Not too long from now, another time of reckoning would come. The true reckoning for Man-folk and any of those who stood alongside them.

While Rha and the black army battered itself against the walls of Nuuroc, Priestess Sahrya was busy organizing Clan Tharasvrul. Preparing the clan for its relocation to the fortress of Isnuuthghor. The priestess had already managed to find five other clans and bring them to their homeland of old.

And many of the more venerated of those clans went all the way back to when Arterium invaded Isnuuthghor. Some of these were the clan elders now, leading their kind. And all of them wanted nothing more than to exact revenge against the Man-folk who had destroyed their homeland and what was most precious to them.

It was not very difficult for Sahrya to convince them to move back to Isnuuthghor. Back to their ancient fortress of old. And to begin preparations for a war like no other. A war to be waged beyond even the most prolific imagination. All efforts to be set up and put forth—to be directed against the Man-folk. Those evil and unscrupulous beings that had invaded *their* homeland first. And many of those old and wise Aylsh Ismaru in these clans still remembered that savage assault of so many Man-folk. Each of the clan elders had been there to see it firsthand. Way back when. When the tall, dark man known as Arterium had stormed their home and then brought it down in a crumbling heap of death and destruction.

But Arterium did more than just slay and butcher, kill and maim. He desecrated the most sacred of the Black Clan symbols. One of their future. He slew the Many Eyed One…and forever cast what should have been the *Phaunim Throth Kharnwul ut Yulpaarah*—Triad of Legends—into the Chasm. This Phaunim was destined to unleash and unite the powers of old through the Larunwyr, with the aid of the Many Eyed One—the last of its kind.

Truth be told, the Black Clans thought that all had been lost when they fled their fortress so long ago. Even the Larunwyr. But Priestess Sahrya made another amazing discovery once she reclaimed Isnuuthghor. The Larunwyr had not been destroyed after all. And this was a powerful binding of the majority of the Black Clans to the might of Priestess Sahrya.

Zaramagrii was another that had vanished. Most thought she had perished in her own devastation. Those who saw the ghostly image of her and the shadowy wolf knew better. For generations though, at least throughout Kuhrzoth, young mothers would scold their wee ones and warn them that the dark soul Zaramagrii would come to get them of they did not eat all of their beans. Or perform their chores, or whatever other shortcomings such little wee one scullions were able to devise.

And those who actually knew her, like Ephritori and Rhalwa, simply let the conclusions abound. For they knew she was still out there, possibly even lost to herself. Yet it would be eighty or so years before the lands might hear of her again. When she did appear again, many would see it as an omen of ill tidings.

Zaramagrii knew something happened to Wybur, possibly something had even taken him. Grasfur had imparted a good deal about what he found at the place where Wybur had last been. Especially of the strange divine presence that still resounded within the air. She now carried the lone owl's feather found by the shadow warg. The dark stains still upon the spines.

Of course, there were countless members of Clan Tharasvrul who did not want to go to Isnuuthghor, nor remain under the wicked hand of the priestess.

Zaramagrii went back to Tharasvrul initially and helped those who stayed behind—those who hid from the priestess. With Zaramagrii's help, all these clan members managed to get to the fortress of the Dhourkuul where they joined with Nimosese. From there, Zaramagrii remained in the mountaintop fortress and began to study the ways of the Dhourkuul under the tutelage of Nimosese. Lost to the current times and happenings.

And what of Lady Sephoora? No, she was not forgotten about. But she disappeared within a flurry of studies and treks that might even astound the most arduous explorer. She fell away from the view of most during that time following the Black War. A feeling of impending fruition overtook her. One of doom.

There was something missing from all of the pieces that had come unraveled. And it felt to Sephoora like an enormous monstrosity. Not that she had an inkling of what it might be. So she searched the twelve corners of the lands hunting for that elusive centerpiece. If she only knew the future, she would have been able to see that *centerpiece* was just the term to use. But the wheel of time would turn and life would flow across the arid lands, forever following old ruts and occasionally twisting along a new spur. It would be another near turn before those things that had been lost for so long began to emerge, like bleached fossils slowly uncovered by the relentless winds.

So the year of the Purple Bloom came and went. Nothing changed, and the effects of the nightmask flower endured beyond the time when it usually faded away. Many folk said the mysterious flowers actually grew larger in appearance. And the strange vapors became even more pronounced. But things like this gradually became an everyday occurrence for types like the Man-folk. Most of their suspicions, as well as the rhetoric of the doomsayers, all subsided as they always did.

All of the sentient beings remained as splintered as ever, even before the black army descended from Oshghrul. Each, from Man to the Aylsh, Kharaghou and the Hulding, worried only about their own little worlds. Their concern did not stretch forth to wrap around others of their sister kind, who were also threatened whether knowingly or not at the time. The future would fully determine this and it would bring each of their own little worlds crashing down around them.

And so the prophecies foretelling the rise of the Shadow Soul had been fulfilled. The Soul had joined with its true mirror, as well as the destined artifacts—the Impaler of Shadows, Volkura Throk and the Binding of Shadows, Volkura Naux. To unite together as one harmonious regulator immersed within Chaos, as was designed and precipitated by none other than Lord Siri himself.

All this under the very nose of Braxis, at least perceived so far. Truly though, all beings carry their own malice and bliss, their own burden of pain and remorse. And they all harbor inner workings and schemes that might surprise even the most astute ones.

But now what? Have no fear, for the story is far from over. The adventures will continue. But that is for another day. This tale does not end here, for it is only beginning. And many possibilities await those caught in this epic struggle of Light and Dark.

The end of Book One

APPENDIX 1

KUHRZOTHIAN LINES

Time Period   Reigning King   Notes

*Pre 69 BA: the Wild Knights, Order of the Wild, maintained an indiscriminate hand of justice across the frontiers. This lasted for about a turn, until Raurick Nuuroc formed and stood up the nobles of Kuhrzoth.

Time Period	Reigning King	Notes
69 - 51 BA	Raurick Nuuroc	–Poisoned.
51 - 17 BA	Athion Nuuroc	–Slain in battle by Akhruuk.
17 BA to SA 1	Arterium Nuuroc	–Fell in battle with the Many Eyed One.

Beginning of current age SA, *in the year of our King*.

1	Cedric Wolstayne	–First of the Emerald commanders crowned after the death of King Arterium. Slain before the year's end and all of his staunch supporters were *cleansed*.
1 - 5	Sevier Oakbroud	–Slain by the Dread Flayer.
5 - 13	Nyth Molgrayf	–Commanded a raiding force into Isnuuthghor and was never heard from again.
13 - 38	Oleg Thembrult	
38 - 54	Oleg Thembrult II	–Slain at Tourney by the Crimson Cavalier of Ravenkort. Sparked the Eight Year War.
54 - 89	Oleg Thembrult III	–Poisoned.
89 - 129	Braq Fairecloud	–Began the Tenyear Campaign.
129 - 133	Braq Fairecloud II	–Slain at court.
133 - 140	Erle Dundragon	–Slain in the battle of Kinsfolk Rings Ridge, against forces from Ravenkort.
140 - 147	Saud Ryncrest the Inflated	–Slain at Tourney by the Silver Scimitar, a champion of the Krizna.
147 - 151	Zahn Valancourt the Pronounced	–Slain during the Wedlock Rebellion.
151 - 165	Zahn Valancourt II	–Slain in the battle of Bloodwater Lake, against forces from Ravenkort.

165 - 186	Ryne Valancourt
186 - 198	Tinis Bellzarig –Slain during the Tremborle Hamlet Uprising.
198 - 223	Vederic Drazdenelm the Defiler –Slain in battle of Ethrun's Fords, against forces from Ravenkort.
223 - 280	Molt Ruknirril
280 - 297	Molt Ruknirril II –Slain in battle of the Ascheyd Plains, first of the Alignment Wars, against forces from Ravenkort.
297 - 334	Arnt Ruknirril the Red –Slain in the Alignment Wars against Ravenkort.
334 - 361	Jared Fenholme –Slain in the Alignment Wars against Ravenkort.
361 - 373	Kreeg Oumshield the Encrusted –Slain while on expedition into the Purple Peaks.
373 - 394	Graegur Chadrick the Oakenleg
394 - 427	Graegur Chadrick II –Led an expedition into the Icefall, never to be heard from again.
427 - 441	Graegur Chadrick III
441 - 486	Rakinoh Chadrick –Slain at Tourney.
486 - 533	Hurwar Jouvanwuld
533 - 562	Seve Jouvanwuld –Slain in battle. Started the War of the Gallows.
562 - 595	Tam Jouvanwuld the Swordbreaker –Slain in battle during the War of the Gallows.
595 - 601	Tam Jouvanwuld II –Ceased all campaigns against Ravenkort and declared an end to the War of the Gallows.
601 - 649	Kowor Ahdfulstone –Slain in battle with forces of Ravenkort.
649 - 683	Zynfurd Klophmire
683 - 721	Zynfurd Klophmire II
721 - 759	Zynfurd Klophmire III –Slain during the first of the Nomad Wars while aiding Orondyraq against Rhousthaq. This was the first joint effort at reconciliation between Kuhrzoth and Orondyraq since the murder of Sellene Nuuroc, wed to Arterium. She was the first daughter of King Aenedhan (Orondyraq).

759 - 809	Zynfurd Klophmire IV the Bald –Slain during the Nomad Wars while aiding Orondyraq.
809 - 832	Panfred Yorlech
832 - 861	Panfred Yorlech II –Slain during the Nomad Wars while aiding Orondyraq.
861 - 887	Aynral Ferdomurz the Nefarious –Beheaded for sedition and blasphemy under the auspices of consorting with the assassins guild.
887 - 902	Aynral Ferdomurz II
902 - 937	Aynral Ferdomurz III the Whirlwind –Slain during the Burning King War while aiding Orondyraq. This was the last of these invasions into Orondyraq by Rhousthaq.
937 - 954	Myk Moghdawan
954 - 986	Ilrith Dhoukinshield
986 - 1004	Ilrith Dhoukinshield II –Slain in battle. Began the Tenth Turning War with Ravenkort the first day of the year SA 1000.
1004 - 1038	Ilrith Dhoukinshield III
1038 - 1063	Blaqner Tavarain –Slain by bandits while on the way to Tourney.
1063 - 1090	Blaqner Tavarain II
1090 - 1107	Hynwid Oldevar the Bold –Felled by the Three-armed Ogre.
1107 - 1109	Elzur Oldevar the Daggerhand –Slain by the Red Wyrm.
1109 - 1120	Elzur Oldevar II –He and two sons slain in battle with forces from Oshghrul.
1120 - 1144	Deyemad Edulwin
1144 - 1162	Deyemad Edulwin II the Archer King –Slain along with nearly entire army while on campaign to assist Phanduzar against Rhousthaq during the Hundred Year War.
1162 - 1201	Deyemad Edulwin III –All three sons slain during the Hundred Year War by forces of the Krizna.
1201 - 1226	Thour Bonhammer the Fat –Choked to death on a turkey drumstick.

1226 - 1245	Thour Bonhammer II the Huge −Felled by a joutunn while hunting giant stag.
1245 - 1256	Thour Bonhammer III the Runt
1256 - 1298	Merod Hondagar
1298 - 1340	Merod Hondagar II −Slain in ambush during the Raider's Year. Several armed bands terrorized the outer regions of Kuhrzoth.
1340 - 1345	Udgar Sivercroft −Declared a cessation to all hostilities with Ravenkort. Mysteriously fell ill and died shortly afterwards.
1345 - 1378	Udgar Sivercroft II −Slain by the Bloodmaster Brothers.
1378 - 1407	Udgar Sivercroft III −Fell to his death from the highest perch in the Emerald Tower on the eve of announcing a reduction in the forces of the Emerald Order as well as an increase in shield tax and tariffs.
1407 - 1469	Nekas Sivercroft
1469 - 1478	Fhostro Sivercroft −Slain during an expedition into the Dulgannor to find new mining areas.
1478 - 1504	Rhunurick Sivercroft the Rumbold −Slain by the Witch Prophetess.
1504 - 1543	Rhunurick Sivercroft II the Shirker −Lost three of four sons and two daughters to a spree of wyrms that ravished the lands during the year 1525.
1543 - 1549	Eldrid Sivercroft the Feeble −Died from the Black Pox.
1549 - 1581	Golstan Sivercroft
1581 -	Baeynor Sivercroft the Amiable −Lost queen and all children to the Red Ache.

APPENDIX 2

AYLSH LINES

What the Aylsh call the First Days began around two thousand years before the current times. The Aylsh refer to the current times as *Meaghanon* (Following Days). The First Writings were dated back to before 2100 BA, claimed to have been scripted by none other than the Father of Aylsh, the True King, Thiliathain Lourendalthemee. It has been known that Thiliathain scripted the First Writings directly from the Olden within the Grypth (ancient halls below the Oadewoods in the Louren Ghuvruul). It was not specified as to which of the Olden these originated from, but always was assumed to be Lord Braxis.

The First Lines (those two lines that produced the noble lineage and all other lines):

Brinthwoulerieh   –The Eternal Mother's line. Completely eradicated by the Great Wyrm in the year SA 1525. About this same time, mysterious shades appeared throughout the Aylsh kingdom and outright killed all remaining and most pure descendants of the line.

Thiliathain Lourendalthemee of Enclave Noblynbindyn   –This Trone enclave being the first and purest.

Time Period	Reigning King	Notes
(In accordance with Thaldeian standards)		
2104 - 1876 BA	Thiliathain Lourendalthemee	–Brought forth the First Writings and is crowned as the True King and Father of Aylsh. The first of the Eternal Mother's line, Nephritaryah Brinthwoulerieh wed to Thiliathain the same year. Thiliathain is slain during the Lost Wars.
1876 - 1452 BA	Khelryl Lourendalthemee	–The first-born son of Thiliathain and Nephritaryah.

1452 - 1328 BA	Nalmurik Lourendalthemee –Slain during the Dark Rebellions.
1328 - 1191 BA	Endryn Lourendalthemee
1191 - 1038 BA	Saalghum Lourendalthemee –Slain by a poisoned arrow in an ambush during the battle of the Louren Ghuvruul.
1038 - 712 BA	Thilthan Lourendalthemee
712 - 541 BA	Berchmryl Lourendalthemee
541 - 465 BA	Chousendael Lourendalthemee –Slain during the First Tenargone War.
465 - 88 BA	Rhynaldiin Lourendalthemee
88 BA - SA 87	Launthor Lourendalthemee –Slain during the Yuanhad Wars.
SA 87 - 154	Khejroul Lourendalthemee –Slain during the Yuanhad Wars.
154 - 381	Ghalbrum Lourendalthemee –Slain during the Yuanhad Wars.
381 - 674	Xuulthebru Lourendalthemee –Slain during the Fourth Tenargone War.
674 - 947	Varilnaughryn Lourendalthemee
947 - 1061	Wendalurain Lourendalthemee –Slain during the thirty-third Tenargone War.
1061 - 1137	Zorosthelrii Lourendalthemee
1137 - 1525	Daumere Bari Lourendalthemee –Last of the true lines. Daumere and two sons slain by the Great Wyrm. The remaining son was slain in an ambush by yuanhad the same year.
1525 -	Aythelruum of Reft Xathughor, King Regent and head of the Aylsh High Court.

APPENDIX 3

THE KNOWN BLACK CLANS

The known Black Clans, or those of the Aylsh Ismaru, that have been recorded within Thaldeian standards at least (during the time of Arterium's incursion into Isnuuthghor).

Clan Thurpazkul   –Oldest of the Black Clans. Sparked the Order of the Dhourkuul.

Clan Omrasstefor
Clan Khajrynghul
Clan Tharasvrul
Clan Zhurkreej
Clan Dolnouraz
Clan Naathdurja
Clan Gourkhazal
Clan Lhowqarran
Clan Dhoulgharan
Clan Jashwour
Clan Uthraum
Clan Chlkarvrum
Clan Dhoskrol

APPENDIX 4

THE THALDEIAN KALENDA

The Thaldeian kalenda, used by all of middle northern Thaldeia, was at least recognized by most throughout the rest of Thaldeia. Its use originated in Kuhrzoth and has become the standard there, as well as Orondyraq, the Free Lands, Ravenkort, and Adan. The Aylsh also recognize it but have their own system (which begins with the blossoms of Stormswift). The Southern Kingdoms also maintain a similar one, although much of its population does not even know of the Thaldeian kalenda. The new year for the Southern Kingdoms begins in the sweltering heat of what the kalenda names as summertide.

The quarter-seasons of Thaldeia:

Mid-frost	–The first of Mid-frost marks the start of the new year. This was done in honor of King Arterium, who fell in battle with the Many Eyed One around the end of the year during the Revered Times. This marked the beginning of the current era, SA 1.
Coldwallow	–Coldwallow is known for its deep spells of freezing cold and heavy snow.
Stormswift	–Stormswift signals the end of winterfall. It is marked by the new growths of fresh greenery and sudden bouts of dark, stormy weather.
Tiller's Break	–Named for the period of the year when the planting of crops begins, it also marks the time when most folk begin preparations for the next winterfall.
Faire-set	–Faire-set brings in the first of the fair winds and seasonably nice weather. It starts the endless spree of markets and festivals across Thaldeia.

Greenglen	–The first day of Greenglen marks the start of summertide.
Tourney-mark	–The middle of summertide. This also holds the Tourney, a fortnight long festival of celebration and martial competition in the middle of Tourney-mark. Once held in a different kingdom each year, it was finally brought home to the Free Lands, in Longshadows. Too many long standing disputes and bloody battles broke out in its early days. Thus it was petitioned to be held every year in Longshadows as a more neutral ground since the year of our King 1040 (not that this brought the unruly violence to a halt).
High-suns	–High-suns signals the end of the golden weather but also shares the longest days.
Grandfest	–Grandfest brings in the start of harvestspell. In many smaller villages, it also spurs grand evening feasts that go well into the night.
Eavesmarch	–As the days grow shorter, Eavesmarch signals the final days for harvest.
Blustreve	–Blustreve is appropriately named for the wild and raging storms that plague the lands.
Snowset	–Snowset marks the start of winterfall.

www.ingramcontent.com/pod-product-compliance
Lightning Source LLC
Chambersburg PA
CBHW030236030726
47493CB00022B/17